OCEAN
OF STARS

JOHN DODD

Luna
Press
PUBLISHING

Text 2022 © John Dodd
Cover 2022 © Rodrigo Vega
Editorial Team: Athena Copy, Robert S Malan & Francesca T Barbini

First published by Luna Press Publishing, Edinburgh, 2022

A CIP catalogue record is available from the British Library

www.lunapresspublishing.com

ISBN-13: 978-1-913387-95-2

To Jude, My Wife, My Life.
To Mark, Our Son, No Parents Prouder.
All My Love, this would not be here without you.

Contents

PART ONE

Once upon a Time Line

First Month In The Stars

I arrive at the bridge as the captain puts a round through the second officer's heart.

This is so not the job I signed up for.

I float near the edge of the room and wait for the ensigns to clear the body away, remaining silent while the captain turns, looking me up and down.

'Newbie'—he points to the control panel where the second officer proved less than bulletproof; there are sparks and smoke emerging from the panel—'fix that.'

I glide into the room and come down to floor level as the bridge's gravity brings me to the deck. I pull the panel off the top and look at the remains of the circuit board underneath. There's some broken wiring and it looks like unqualified idiots have replaced the patches underneath more than once.

This is going to take some time.

I glance backwards at the captain, who's looking straight ahead at the main display, and everyone else is making a point of avoiding his gaze. First Officer Michaels is stood behind the captain, a slight shake of his head as he points at the panel. His hands sign in Airless, Just fix it.

'I've got it, sir.' I don't look back to see if the captain is paying attention. 'I just need to go down to supplies to get another circuit board to patch this up.'

'Fix it, newbie.' The captain's voice rings out across the bridge. 'Don't give me excuses about needing parts; that's what the last engineer did.'

The last engineer was right.

I pull the wires and run a bypass using some of the scraps I have in my thigh pack. It's not pretty, but it'll hold until I can get something better. I run the patch over the back of the panel and see that the last tech had placed a wad of ballistic cloth between the panelling and the wiring. Most of it shows signs of being dented by multiple impacts.

This is where he lines people up to shoot them.

'It's fixed, sir.' I straighten up and put the panel back on. 'One thing...'

'Yes?' The tone is that of a man who doesn't appreciate the interruption.

'Just wanted to express my gratitude at you taking me on.'

Behind him, Michaels grins and nods.

Good recovery.

I head out of the bridge and back down to the coffin-sized enclosure that doubles as my bunk on the ship, now feeling more like a coffin than it did this morning. I pull out the small wooden box at the end of the bunk and look at the photos within. Me at graduation: *Catarina Solovias, Martian Master Engineer.* The next of me and my parents that same day: Mum all beaming and happy, Dad just standing there with his arms around both of us, all the strength in the world holding us together. I flip the photo and look at the words on the back. *Ons Soldaat.* Our Soldier.

Better times.

I look in the mirror and then at the picture, then back up to the mirror. Mum always said I'd thin out like she did, all wasp waist, high cheekbones, hair down to her ass and radiant smile, rather than the buzzcut-sporting, heavy set powerball champion I turned into. I smile to myself; Dad was always happier that I ended up being as short as Mum and as broad as him. Anyone who wanted to try their chances with me would have to get over the fact that I was stronger and tougher than they were.

The way they raised me to be...

'You've met the captain then.' Petra, floats in and glides to a halt, holding herself steady on the scramble bars. 'Was he everything you expected?'

'I...' I frown. 'He's insane, isn't he?'

'Oh, he's not insane. Far from it.' She turns to face me with the expression of someone who's had the same conversation a few hundred times, her face broader than her body type would suggest, one of the effects of spending too long without gravity pulling everything down. She looks me up and down and glides over in my direction, folding her legs up underneath her to pass over the instrument panel, then extending them to stand sideways on the wall next to me.

'First flight out, right?' She smiles, turning her head so that she's looking at me from the same angle that I'm stood. Her voice is light, that musical singsong quality you get from Drifter colonies where there's no single accent to choose from.

I nod. 'Three weeks out of Mars, signed on as secondary technician.'

'There'll be a few shocks for you to come across then.' Petra frowns. 'Here's your first lesson for free. Don't trust anything that the captain says, if his mouth is opening, you can be pretty sure it's a lie. Don't count on a single promise he makes, even if it's in writing—it's always going to be cheaper for him to shoot you and hire someone else.' She pauses for a second to let her words sink in and then brightens up. 'What's your speciality—know anything about wiring?'

'Yeah, I've just never been on a ship where so much of it is patchwork. My speciality is weapons and power.'

'Happiness is a warm life support system; weapons are a luxury for most people.' Petra steps up the wall to stand on the roof, then kicks off to spin to the floor in a slow descent. She turns to face me and shrugs. 'That said, we do need a good weapons tech after what happened to the last one.'

'Why, what happened to the last one?'

'Scraped him off the hull from where he was fixing the plates in the last firefight. If they ask you to do combat repairs, make sure you wait till the combat's over before you go out there.'

'Not always the way things work out.' I turn back to see the darkness outside. 'Never known a time that something needed to be repaired when things were quiet.'

'Never seen a time when the captain was happy stopping to do them mid-run.' She shrugs. 'And we've lost more than one tech when he decided that discretion was the better part of profit.'

'You make it sound like he goes through technicians on a regular basis.'

'He does.' Petra looks me straight in the eye. 'Never presume, even for a second, that he won't leave you drifting and dead if it suits his purpose. What are you doing up here anyway?'

'Signed up to see the universe.' I grin. 'Travel the solar winds, trade with a—'

'Million species,' she cuts in. 'Make more money in a month than you did in a year on the surface. You got suckered by the advert, didn't you?'

'Advert?'

'Be one of the few, the proud, the strong? Bet you thought the captain was a registered command with the Martian fleet?' She raises an eyebrow at me.

'Isn't he?'

'Oh, he's registered—registered in five different territories for fraud and six for murder.'

'Bullshit.' I try to smile but don't manage it. 'You're just messing with me.'

'When I'm messing with you'—her expression goes serious— 'you'll know, because I'll be laughing.'

'Shit...' I sigh. 'How do I get off?'

'Getting off the ship is easy.' Petra nods at the wing. 'You just take a walk outside and drift till someone finds you and hope they're better than the crew you just got away from.'

'Bloody hell.' I sigh and shake my head. 'There should be something in the law against false promises.'

'It's not false. *He* makes more money in a month than anyone on the surface makes in a year, and he does travel the solar winds. Did you ever see anything in those commercials where he said that *you* could do those things?'

I think back to the advert.

I'm Charles Godstorm, captain of the Starlight Eagle. I've flown from one side of the universe to the other, traded with a million species and soared the solar winds. I make more money in a month than you do in a year. Have you got what it takes to join me?

'No. Just plenty of flashy visuals and shots of him being dashing in the background.'

'There you have it.' Petra makes a slow side flip to her station. 'No false advertising, just a lot of hopefuls left along the way while he gets rich. The way he tells it, he came from a line of great military leaders, when the truth is that he ran with organ sharks on earth and killed the previous captain of this ship to own it.'

'How do you know that?'

'I was there when he did it... and he made a move on me once, so I know he's got more gang tats under that uniform than I've ever seen. Probably why you never see him out of it.'

'What did you come out here for?'

'I got blacklisted by the Martian monopoly for protesting for the right of all people to draw free air.'

'You were part of Ascension X?'

'Fly now, fly free.' She makes a waving motion with her hand. 'There are worse things than being prepared to die freeing the universe from tyranny.'

The ship's comms chime.

'Engineering to cargo bay two.' The captain again, this time sounding annoyed.

'Like I said,' Petra says, looking over at me, 'there are worse things. Watch out for yourself.'

*

Petra takes off ahead of me as I close the box and lock my bunk down before gliding all the way to bay two.

'Hull breach in the bay.' Petra looks concerned as she peers through the door. 'Don't know what happened, but we're losing pressure in there.'

'All right.' I engage the strap on my suit and feel the cloth tighten around me.

Not as good as a real space suit, but it'll do for low pressure.

I grab one of the air masks off the side and put it on. There's a half-second between it being cloudy with the heat of my breath and then clear. I look over at Petra. 'You're either coming in or staying out.' I nod towards the door. 'Make your choice.'

Petra steps back, and the bulkhead door closes down between us. I hear her voice over the local comms. 'Let me know when you're done in there.'

'You'll know when the red pressure light goes off.'

I open the bay door to the light pull of escaping air. The cargo isn't moving, but it feels colder in here. I take the liquid weld from my belt and put a shot into the air. The mix spreads out then starts to float towards the starboard plating. I follow it till it coats one of the pallets. I pull the locks on the floor and move the pallet out of the way, leaving it suspended in the air, a hundredweight in normal gravity but now nothing more than a minor inconvenience. Another squirt of liquid weld in the air and it moves straight to a hairline crack in the hull. Looks like there's been a few repairs around here; the hull is more patch than metal.

Like everything else on this ship.

I put a slap patch on the wall and slide it over the hole, pausing only when I feel the patch pull tight, then spray another coat of liquid weld around the top of it. Looking around the bay, there's nothing that could be used to make a reasonable repair.

And I'd need an airdock to make sure it was good.

I move the pallet back over and re-engage the locks as the ship trembles around me. There's a low rumble coming from aft of the engines, and I float back towards the bay doors, closing them behind me and turning to sign through the bulkhead porthole to Petra in Airless that all is clear. She flips the switch, and the bulkhead rises up in silence.

'What's going on?' I remove the mask and hang it on my belt.

'Not sure.' Petra anchors herself to the grab handle by the door. 'Felt like something kicked the ship fairly hard.'

The white lights above are replaced with amber as the ship goes on alert.

The captain's voice sounds down the comms: 'Engineering to weapons, all power to forward lasers.'

I nod to Petra and scramble down the corridor, my hands

light on the walls as I rotate from facing upwards to downwards and then launch along the access tube to the weapons bay. The weapons systems on the *Starlight Eagle* are rudimentary, nothing but force beams and lasers; no torpedoes, no hard shells.

Nothing that costs to reload.

I look over the power readings. The reactor has enough fuel in it to run us between ports blind and bare, with very little to provide anything more than a passable defence.

To make changes with things, you've got to have something to work with in the first place.

I switch the wires over and flick the button on the comms to get through to the bridge.

'Bridge, Engineering, what do you want to lose to get more power to the weapons?'

'We don't lose anything, newbie.' The captain sounds more angry than upset. 'More power to the weapons, or we'll be firing you.'

And I doubt that's a euphemism.

Looking around the board, there is nowhere to take power from. You either rig up another powercell from somewhere or you take power from somewhere else; that's how it is. I check through the wiring again—there are a few bad joins in places, some of the other bits haven't held well, and most of the fuses are well past their expiry date. If I were to replace all the fuses in the main board, we'd get half again what we've got now, but if I pull the main board, we're dead in the water for a few seconds.

And we won't have enough power to make it back to the base we were aiming for.

The deck below me rises up, and there's a groaning sound from the side of the ship.

'WHERE ARE MY WEAPONS?' the captain roars.

I switch my shoulder lights on and put both my Isogloves on to yank the board. Everything goes dark, and I flip the fuses in place, holding them in for the second it takes for the rapid seal to hold, then put the board back. The entire charge of the ship runs up through my glove, and the lights come on with fierce intensity.

Six seconds.

I close the cover and put the catch back in place. The gauges come back on, and the bridge crew cheer.

'Power active, fire when ready,' I shout. There's a hum as the shields pick up, and the groaning from the hull ceases when the grav field engages on all decks. I drop to the floor and pick up my tools from the bench, putting them back in the sealed pockets in my jumpsuit. I make my way back up to the bridge as the firing continues for a half-minute, then there's silence. I get to the bridge as the amber lights go white again.

'What was that?' The captain scowls at me. 'We lost everything for a few minutes there.'

'Seconds.' The retort is out of my mouth before I think to stop it. 'We were down for seconds, and it wasn't my fault that we were down at all—the wiring down there is a mess of shit and has been for years.'

The bridge goes silent as the captain's fingers drum on the grip of his gun. 'What did you say?' His voice is quiet, and there's an unstable gleam in his eyes.

'I said, we need to properly rewire this to make sure it doesn't happen again.' I stare at him without flinching. 'You know what the score is with this. If we don't fix it properly, the next hull hit that we take drops everything out the ass of this ship.'

'Are you saying this is my fault?'

Michaels turns to me, his brow furrowed. 'No, sir. She's just saying that we need to make those repairs before we get underway again.'

The captain looks at Michaels and then at me. I can see the part of his brain that has some rationality remaining is considering what's happened and then he turns to look out of the main viewing screen.

'First things first.' He looks back at me. 'Take your tools and get over to the other ship. I want their cargo in our hold and their screamer turned off before any of the law get a sniff of it.'

And this is how he gets so rich.

'And newbie...' he says, turning to look ahead again, '...when you've got all that sorted, we're going to have a talk about what to do with my ship.'

A Ship Unlike Any Other

I snap off a weak salute and head down to my bunk again, this time taking everything off it and putting it in my pack. I head down to the bay and take one of the heavy atmo-suits with a large canister for the regular OxyBloks and a few spares besides.

Enough to breathe until I die from lack of water, if need be.

The starboard airlock is good for one person at a time—the ship was never designed for mass boarding actions. Petra floats alongside as I start to turn the lock, and puts her hand on mine.

'I've got it.' She hands me a block of vacuum-packed hi-en rations. 'Just in case you decide to take a walk out there.'

'I'll be back.' I take the rations, locking them to my thigh plate.

'Just in case,' she says. 'You've got that look.'

'Hard not to have on this ship at the moment.'

She says nothing; just nods and cycles the door, giving me access to the airlock. I wait till the pressure seal locks then open the outer door, and drift out into space. We're surrounded by lumps of rockcrete, banks of computers, and the legs of a person in white coveralls with no sign of their torso, frozen, the blood like ice cubes. It's like someone vented a building into space and we ran into it. I look at the *Eagle*: no serious damage—we must have just run into whatever was surrounding the other ship.

That'll teach him to keep his eyes on the lanes.

I look beyond the light debris to the disabled ship: two holes just below the bridge window, both of them from laser fire. There's a jet of white gas escaping from the bridge section and the aft airlock, no sign of any tech trying to patch things up.

Either they don't have the kit for it, or they don't have the people to do it.

I attach my recovery line to the outer plate of the *Eagle* and drop a little air from the pack to jet across to the other ship. The lines on it are like nothing I've ever seen: huge brass-coloured plates all the way around it, something that looks like valves on the wings, and an airlock with a cycling mechanism on the outside of the ship.

No obvious weapons though, so they weren't attacking us.

I float over and engage the magnets on my boots. They're not sticking as well as I'd like, but it's enough for me to walk on the wing. I reach the airlock and try to pull it open; there's less resistance than I would have expected and the wheel rolls around as if greased. I check the track above the door and move to the other side before making the final turn on it. The lock releases and the door slides open with no blast of gas. I switch my suit lights on. There's no atmosphere in this part of the ship, nothing venting.

With so much exposed machinery in here, it must be the engine room.

I look at the end of the room and see the door open there, no lights on at all. Faint wisps of gas escape from the pipes overhead, warm enough to mist over my helmet glass.

Not the kind of coolant that any ship I've ever seen would run on—this is something else.

I head to the prow; the door to the bridge is venting air on all sides, it's not a pressure door.

Who leaves their bridge open to breaches?

I glance in through the window. There's a rack of suits along the wall, all there except one.

There should only be one person in there.

I push the door to the side, and the remaining atmosphere pulses back against me. There are two holes in the side of the bridge—looks like the only hit they took was all that was needed to drop them out. The holes in the hull match the size of the *Eagle*'s laser cannon; all the atmosphere would have drained out in seconds.

There has to be a backup life support system in here or this would have been empty.

I search the bridge. There are no buttons here. It's all levers and dials, handles and gauges, every part of it rendered in brass and silver. No plastics, no polymers; it's all metal and wiring. Looks like something that was made a thousand years ago. The panels are all hand-finished—more care taken in the building of this ship than any ten I could name. I search the rest of the ship. There's a platform above the floor level, and I turn the magnets on my boots off to float upwards. I find a ship's wheel made of wood attached to a platform in the upper deck area. Above the wheel, but still in the pilot's eyeline, are a series of numbers carved on two flipboards of dark wood, the first one with today's date on it, the second one showing a date far in the future.

On any other ship, that'd be coordinates and time to turn...

I float level with the wheel, examining the sealed suit of the pilot still anchored to it by lines, the magboots locked to the floor in front of it. The body is laid flat, floating parallel to the deck, the ankles bent at an impossible angle, the internal faceplate covered in blood. The markings on the suit are unfamiliar, a deep blue weave over its entirety, orange lines down the arms and legs and a logo with a stylised phoenix surrounded by red flames over the right chest. I place my hand on the shoulder and feel the suit slosh away from me as I make contact. There's an impact marking on the chestplate, and I realise that the pilot must have been hit by the *Eagle*'s laser cannon after it breached the hull. All shipboard lasers carry a kinetic charge—there'll be nothing in that suit but soup now... I turn away and wait a minute for my stomach to stop churning.

Nothing worse than zero-gee vomit.

I turn back, pulling my gaze from the body. The wheel hangs loose, but there's still power on the dial there. I float down and pull the suit away from the controls, cutting through the lines attaching it to the wheel, thankful that I can't hear the sloshing of fluids within. There's a chart on the wall next to where the person would have been standing. The coordinates on the chart are there and markings that look like they've been drawn on to monitor flows and currents. On the side of the wheel is a single handle with words at its base, like an old-style ship's telegraph, but the words are in a language I'm not familiar with.

My comms chime as the captain brings the *Eagle* around. 'What's taking so long?'

'Just trying to put the power back on,' I say. 'Give me a minute.'

'I'll give you one minute, then I'm going to consider you and that ship a dead loss.' His tone gives me no doubt that he means every word.

I look out of the window to see the *Eagle* come to bear. I lean against the wheel, and the numbers above me click over. There's a rumble under my fingers as something in the ship starts to warm up. I turn the wheel again, and the second set of numbers start to rise. I push the wheel, and it clicks into another position; this time, the coordinates change. I pull the wheel back into the first position, and the date starts to change again.

Different wheel positions for altering dates or coordinates.

'Nearly got power,' I report.

'Is there anything valuable on the ship?' The captain's voice again.

'Negative so far, captain.' The honesty is out before I think about the consequences. 'It's too small to be anything but a scout.'

'Really?' His tone turns sardonic. 'Then it's not going to be a loss if I use it for target practice...'

I've got to get a handle on the whole brain-mouth thing.

I look out of the window and see the force-cannon fix into place and cycle up.

I'm never going to make it back in time.

I turn the wheel, the ship drifting to the side till it lines up with the *Eagle*, then look at the telegraph handle. If it works the way they used to, then all the way forwards should be full ahead. I grab the handle and look out of the window as the *Eagle* locks on. The captain stares down at me from the bridge and points at me with a snarl forming on his lips.

You're not pulping me!

I raise my middle finger at him and push the handle all the way forwards. There's a lurching sensation, and my vision blurs for a second as the universe seems to bend around me. I'm reaching for my head, but the overpressure sends me into silent darkness.

*

Consciousness returns, feeling like someone set off a grenade in my head. I open my eyes to a series of lightbeams probing the inside of the ship, but from the opposite side to the *Eagle*. I drop down and head back towards the airlock. The *Eagle* doesn't have good scanners and, even if it did, it doesn't have the power to be able to use them as well as move around, not with me over here. The problem is what to do if I get back *over there*; the captain's still a nutjob, and I'm too far away from any habitable world for them to pick up the distress signal before the only air in my suit is supplied by the venting of my dead ass.

Wonderful way to start a new job!

I glance through the hole in the bridge at the *Eagle* as it turns about and angles up towards the source of the lightbeams. The side of the ship that I'm on is too high for me to see what's shining the light down, but there are two more flares, and something that looks like a harpoon lances down into the *Eagle*'s wing, anchoring on magnetically and pulling taut with a thick steel cable behind it. On the other side, a second rope pulls tight and the *Eagle* starts to move out of alignment. The cannons light up, and a single shot lances out in silence. The light from above doesn't change, but there's a shadow now across the *Eagle* as something approaches from that direction. I drift back to the airlock and out, engaging the magnets on my boots to walk up the ship and peer over the side.

Space dementia...

I check my oxy levels—still good, shouldn't be hallucinating yet. I look up again.

If it's not dementia, then...

There's a massive galleon sitting off the port bow of the ship, identical in all ways to the ships of old from the times when people still sailed on oceans. The sails are made of something that looks like golden cloth, and there's a single row of guns pushing out from the broadside of the ship. The anchors are locked in place from the bow and the stern of the ship, and there are a group of people at each end working the winch block. The *Eagle*'s guns blaze again, and the bolts seem to slide away from the side of the ship. Five people swing up into the masts, then launch forwards towards the derelict.

They're not wearing spacesuits!

Two of them get within a hundred metres of the ship and launch grapples towards me. The lines attach themselves to the craft and both people swing down and land on the deck. Each of them is wearing an outfit of loose cloth with leather boots halfway up their calves and long leather gloves that reach to midway up their forearms. The material of their outfits flare outwards from the end of their limbs and there are dark yellow masks covering the bottom of their faces, extending along their shoulders into long flowing cloaks that sit over their right shoulders. Both of them are taller than me and move with the grace of long practice.

The first one looks down at me and takes her mask off, her hands flowing in a sign language that's different to the standard Airless I'm familiar with. Her eyebrows furrow in consternation as she beckons with one hand and then signs something to the woman next to her. The other takes a small box off her belt and walks towards me, offering me the box. There's another burst of signing, and the woman closest to me crouches down and offers me the box again. I walk up on top of the derelict as the other three people finish their dive onto the *Eagle* and plant slabs of thick putty on the front of the ship, each slab with a gleaming box on the top. I trigger my comms and look at the *Eagle*.

'Engineering to bridge,' I lower my voice. 'They've planted some sort of shaped charge on the front of the ship. Stand down before they vent you into space.'

'You don't tell me what to do on my ship!' The captain's voice is higher pitched than usual.

Must be his lack of balls...

'It's not your ship anymore, *sir*,' I snap, tired of his arrogance. 'You need to stand down before none of you get out of there alive.'

There's a quiet thud, and Michaels' voice comes over the comms. 'We're standing down. This dog isn't causing anyone else's death, not on my watch.'

I look up at the woman holding the box out to me and take it. She taps her belt to show me where to attach it, then points at a small red button on the top of the box. I do as she indicates.

There's a pop in my ears as the pressure around me equalises, and my faceplate clouds over in an instant as air rushes in from the box. Everything is blurry through the field surrounding me. The woman taps the release on the side of my faceplate, and I exhale hard for a second before realising that there's a faint breeze blowing in through the front.

'Can you hear me?' Her voice has an accent that I've never heard before.

'I can hear you.' I nod. 'Who are you?'

'You don't need to worry about that,' she says. 'For now, you just need to come back to the ship with us. The captain will want a word and then we'll see what we're going to do next.'

'Do I have a choice?'

'Sure.' The woman smiles without humour. 'You can come with us, or you can take your chances floating home.'

'Well, when you put it like that, I elect to come along.'

New Pan, Same Fire

Both women leave their lines anchored to the ship, then wind their grapples back in to launch them back towards their ship. The *Eagle* powers down and starts to drift sideways as the gravity drive goes offline and the ropes start to draw her in. The galleon turns from broadside, and the women tuck their arms under mine. They turn to face the galleon, then look at me, as my boots are still holding me down. I tap the button on my arm to release the magnets. They look at each other as my feet come unstuck, before firing their grapples back towards the ship. We drift across the gap, and they wind in the grapples at the same time, the movement practised to the point of synchronisation.

As we get within a few hundred metres of the galleon, there's another pop in my ears, and the pressure around me becomes a crushing force. I try to breathe as my lungs fill with more air than I can cope with. I breathe out and panic when the air keeps rushing in, bringing my hands to my chest as everything starts to go black. One of the women glances over and taps the box on my belt. The pressure releases, and I exhale faster than a deflating balloon. She turns her body and floats sideways for a second, and taps the box.

'Can't use a bubble inside a bubble.' She grins. 'Easiest way to cut your trip short.'

'I'm not from around here. Never used one of these before.'

'Never...?' The other woman turns sideways in mid-flight and stares at me for a second. 'What are you using then?'

I motion at my facemask and the pipe leading down to my belt. 'Just these, always have.'

'Breathertech?' The woman looks surprised. 'Haven't seen that in some time. Where'd you come across it?'

'Plenty of it on the *Eagle.*' I point to the ship as it draws close to the galleon. 'What are you using?'

'Bubbletech. What else?' She taps the box on her belt. 'Makes a bubble around you and fills it with air, but if you go inside another bubble, the smaller one overloads and tries to compress back into the box.'

'That's what tried to blow me up?'

'You're lucky that was an emergency box—there's only enough air in them for a few minutes of breathing. If there'd been any more, it would have popped your lungs.' She frowns and looks at the box. 'You sure you've never used one of these before? Everyone uses them around here.'

'Around here?' The galleon looms large, and we soar over the deck towards a series of grilled vents on the top deck. 'Where's around here?'

'You don't know where we are?' Both women exchange significant glances, and the first points down to the lights. 'Do you know how to use a foot dock?'

'No, I'm not familiar wi—' My words cut off as I plummet downwards, crashing to the deck with a thump. I pick myself up and feel the vent pulling downwards. As I step away from it, the gravity lowers and I stand on unsteady feet. There's a slight rocking motion under my feet that I can't quite reconcile with a ship in space, and I look upwards at the masts. Everything on here is made of brass and wood, polished to a high shine and varnished, like it rolled off the assembly line not very long ago. There are twenty, maybe thirty, people running around on the deck below, all of them dressed in the same uniform that the two who retrieved me are wearing, with the exception of the colour of the mask and cape. Above them, on the top deck, another person, but this one has an iron emblem on the shoulders and a deep red mask leading to a long, crimson cloak.

'The captain,' the first woman says, as she follows my gaze upwards. 'Be careful how you talk to her; she's not one to take disrespect lightly.'

'No different to the previous one then. One overlord is as good as another.'

'There's a difference between being crew and being a slave,' the woman says. 'Do you have any skills that would prove useful to us? What did you do on your ship?'

'I'm an engineer.' I look at her. 'Do you need one of those?'

'Well, we all know how to keep our own stuff in line. Can you fix engines?'

'Yeah, I'm real good at it. Would that be useful to you?'

'It would. Good, I hate having to walk useless people.'

'What happens now?'

'Now?' The other woman looks back at me. 'Now we present you to the captain and see if she likes what she sees. Remain silent unless she asks you a question, and whatever she asks you, don't give her any lip.'

'All right. Look, my name's—'

'Give me your name when you get to stay on board.' The other woman cuts me off with a wave of her hand. 'Too much personal data just makes you harder to space if we have to.'

There's a crunch at the base of the galleon on the port side as the *Eagle* comes to rest on the moorings. The women walk on either side of me to the edge of the deck and look over as a long plank extends from the ship to the *Eagle*'s airlock. One of the galleon's crew hops down from the deck to the plank and looks at the airlock, noting that the contact is seamless on all four sides of the door, then looks back up to the main deck and shrugs.

'Not like any lock I know,' she calls. 'No way of opening it from the outside.'

'I can open it,' I call down, before I think to stop myself.

'Excellent.' The captain's eyes lock on to me like targeting lasers, both of them a shade of green so light as to be almost yellow. *Must be contacts.* She points downwards. 'Off you go then. Open it up for us.' Her voice is high-pitched, but the accent is guttural, like the Martian separatists I hung around with as a kid.

I look over the edge of the ship at the plank below.

That's a thirty-foot drop, with forever in space if I miss...

The woman to my right hooks her grapple to my belt and rolls over the side, taking me with her. I'd like to say my shriek sounded like a good Martian war cry...

...but I'd be lying.

The woman swoops down over the plank and alights on the side, taking hold of one of the handles at the side of the lower door to keep us rooted there. I release my death grip on her and look up at the rest of the crew grinning down at me. I turn my head to either side of the foot-wide plank and see nothing but stars staring up at me. The grapple is still attached as I make my way over on unsteady legs to the airlock and attach my interface pad to the wall.

'What are you doing?' Michaels' voice whispers in my ear. 'If you open that, they'll have the run of the ship.'

'They've already got us, sir. Let there be no illusion about that. If I don't let them in, they'll just blow the front and take you by force. Your call though; you want me to leave it closed, say the word.'

There's a momentary pause and a sigh. 'I don't see anyone wearing atmo-gear out there; is there air?'

'There's air.' I look at the stars all around. 'All things considered, it's quite warm out here...'

There's a humourless snort and the airlock disengages; the door pushes outwards, then rolls sideways to let the cool air inside flow out. Petra is the first to the door; her mouth opens as she sees me, and I put one finger to my mouth and shake my head. She nods and walks across in silence as the other crew come forwards. The captain is suspended between Lennox and Gren, the two massive ex-Jovian marines Godstorm had employed to repel boarders. Michaels and Shen, the ship's navigator, follow afterwards. Michaels glances over the side of the plank and shrugs at the captain's body.

'Reckon we should save some time?' He looks at me with a wry smile. 'Long way down from here.'

'Reckon we leave it to them.' I glance upwards at the crew, who are looking down at us. 'Their call to make.'

He stares up at the assembled masks above, all of them looking at him with indifference, then keeps walking. I follow them into the underbelly of the ship. The mechanisms inside are all circling cogs and turbines, valves and huge steel pipes, laid out like a maze with purpose and symmetry.

Beautiful.

My reverie is interrupted by the woman behind me pushing me forwards and onwards to the upper deck. The crew are lining the railings of the ship and, in the middle on the top deck, is the captain looking down at us.

'Which of you is the captain of the ship?' she calls down.

'He is.' Michaels points downwards, and Lennox and Gren put Godstorm down on the deck. 'We had a difference of opinion when it came to yielding to you.'

'And that difference was?'

'He wanted to keep firing till we got through, then have us sell our lives as dearly as possible while he made a bid to parley.' Michaels shrugs. 'I thought that, if parley was an option, we should exercise it without trying to blow you up first. Diplomacy should be practised with a sharp mind and not a sharp edge, would you not agree?'

'Sensible.' The captain removes her mask to reveal a face that's all red lips and high cheekbones; she has much paler skin than the rest of the crew. 'Do you want to wait for him to wake up? Or do you want to parley?'

'We'll parley.' Michaels stands to his full height and looks up at her. 'Your demands?'

'Your clothes, your boots, and your shiny starship.' The captain grins with a set of teeth so white they make my eyes hurt. 'Your rebuttal?'

'You've already laid claim to everything we have.' Michaels spreads his arms wide and addresses the whole crew. 'That leaves very little to parley for.'

'Then you agree that my claim is valid?' She looks down at him and leans against the rail.

'I agree that you think your claim is valid.' He grins back, showing teeth that have seen far less polish. 'Under the terms of parley, I am entitled to see your letter of marque and your credentials before I yield to you.'

'Only a captain may ask that of another captain. And your captain is at your feet.'

'Then you can wait for him to wake up if you wish.' Michaels looks down at Godstorm's prone body. 'But, under the terms, you accepted me as his proxy when the conversation began, so if you withdraw from negotiations, I am entitled to ask a boon from you in return for your retraction, and you are honour-bound to grant it.'

She looks at him with renewed interest. 'And what boon would you ask of me?'

'Are you withdrawing from negotiations?'

'I am entitled to ask what your boon would be before I decide to withdraw from negotiations.' Her grin is back again.

'It is your right.' Michaels turns back to the five of us stood behind him. 'I would ask for the release of the ship and crew to my custody, that we might return whence we came.'

'Such a boon would require the owner of the vessel be delivered into my custody, that we could then bargain with his estate for the prize we lost.'

'What luck, my lady.' Michaels bows low with his arms held wide and palms open to encompass the unconscious form of Godstorm. 'I present Charles Godstorm, owner of the *Starlight Eagle*. Is my boon granted?'

'And what estate does he possess?' The captain starts to make her way towards the stairs, her crew flowing around her like an ocean being split by a ship's prow. 'It has been a long time since I have seen a ship such as this one. Does he have more of them?'

'He has the money required to acquire more of them. *Many* more of them.'

'And you can support these claims that you make?'

'I can. His personal accounts are in his quarters upon the ship. He has holdings across the Martian, Jovian and Terran federations.'

'I am not familiar with these federations.' Now, on the deck level with us, the captain is my height, but her movements are fast, every step orchestrated, every movement controlled; legs thinner than my arms, and a trim waist leading up to broad shoulders and muscular arms—she wouldn't last a full shift in the Martian mines, though she'd have me in a race up the rigging. Her long, dark hair is done up in a ponytail, trailing into the back of her uniform. Her stride carries the easy confidence of a woman who knows she belongs at the top of the food chain. She looks at each of us in turn, her eyes a deep jade-green now, the pupils not contracting at all. 'But if you have the proof, then I will withdraw from parley, and you may have the ship and crew to do with as you see fit.'

'I have to return to the ship to retrieve his accounts.' Michaels holds her gaze steady.

'No.' The captain gives a wry smile. 'You may send a subordinate to retrieve them though.'

'Petra, would you retrieve the captain's log, his personal effects, and his accounts please?'

Petra nods and looks around for a way off the ship. The captain looks at one of her crew and motions over the side. The woman secures Petra with a line and drops her over. To her credit, she doesn't shriek like I did.

'And while we wait'—the captain turns to face Michaels again—'would you and your crew like a drink?'

'As long as it doesn't add to the cost of our freedom.'

The captain inclines her head in acknowledgement of his proviso.

'It would have done.' She snaps her fingers. 'But not now.'

She's enjoying having someone to debate against.

One of the crew, smaller than the others and wearing a black mask with no cloak, brings forwards a tray with several crystal shot glasses filled with blood-red liquid. She pauses before the captain, and a glance sends her across to Michaels.

'Choose the drink I am to have, so you can be assured that I intend you no harm in my hospitality.'

Michaels takes one of the glasses and steps over the prone Godstorm to hand it to the captain. She removes her gloves to reveal hands callused from years of sword-work. Taking the glass from Michaels, she brushes her own fingers on his for a second with the slightest hint of a smile on her lips. She drains it in a single swallow, her tongue flickering out in the manner of a lizard to lick the drops from her lips. She returns the glass to the tray in

a single swaying step and takes a glass for Michaels. He drains it
in a single swallow and coughs a little, before smiling and placing
the glass back on the tray. The girl steps in front of me, and I take
one of the glasses, sniffing at the liquid within. A scent of liquor
stronger than rocket fuel drifts upwards, and I sip at it then hold
it by my side when my tongue catches fire. The rest of the *Eagle*'s
crew take a glass and follow my example. There's a calm silence
as the captain stands opposite Michaels, swaying from side to side
as if trying to keep level with the ship, even though the ship isn't
moving much at all.

*

Petra returns with a bag containing all of Godstorm's particulars.
The bag, real animal hide bound with brass clasps and studded
with exquisite rainbow crystals, is worth more than he pays me in
a month. She passes it to Michaels, who opens the front and takes
out a ledger with the captain's seal on the front. He opens it to the
bookmarked page and rests the book in his open hand, offering
it to her.

'And these numbers, what do they represent?' She looks at the
page and then up at Michaels, her finger tracing down the numbers.

'His wealth measured in tons.' Michaels points to the base of
the page. 'Gold, spices, gems.'

'Inordinate wealth,' she muses. 'Why then does he only possess
so small a ship? A man with these numbers could have his own
station to rule from.'

'The degree of his wealth is only dwarfed by the meanness of
his spirit. He forgot at some point that the key to wealth is in how
you enjoy it, not in how you hoard it.'

'It is better to be able to do both.' The captain flicks through a
few more pages before glancing down at Godstorm. 'Where can I
call upon his factor?'

'He and only he has the knowledge of where his finances are
held.'

'And I am to trust you that he is the captain?'

'If I were the captain,' Michaels says, 'I would have already given you myself in return for the release of the ship and crew.'

'Yes...' She looks up at him, her lips parting as her tongue moistens them. 'I believe that you would have. A pity, I would have enjoyed *dealing* with you.'

Michaels makes a slight bow. 'You may yet have the pleasure.'

She smiles and nods, plucking the bag from the floor and replacing the book with a flourish. There's a groan from the floor as Godstorm starts to stir.

'Is our business concluded?' Michaels offers his hand.

'I believe it is.' She reaches for his hand as Godstorm looks upwards.

'Wait.' Godstorm raises a trembling hand. 'I am the captain of the *Starlight Eagle*.'

'Your second has negotiated well on your behalf.' The captain turns and looks down at him. 'He has bargained the release of your crew and ship. Bargained well.'

'He has?' Godstorm stands, his legs unsteady beneath him.

'He has. You will have every comfort until your estate returns the bounty for you.'

'For me?' He looks worried.

'Yes, he negotiated for the crew and the ship.' She looks less pleased than when she was negotiating with Michaels. 'But you must remain with us to allow us to bargain for the prize.'

'What prize?' Godstorm pauses for a second. 'What are you talking about? I'm not staying with you.'

'I see.' Her eyes gleam for a second.

She enjoys the game more than the victory.

'Very well.' She places the bag upon the deck and steps back. 'Do you wish to re-open the parley that your second negotiated for?'

'I do.' Godstorm reaches for his bag without another word.

'*This*'—the captain places her foot on the bag—'is under negotiation until you've completed your parley.'

Godstorm steps back as if stung.

Out of his depth; he's never had to bargain for anything.

'So...' The captain takes her foot off the bag and steps over it in the same motion, bringing her in front of Godstorm. She's shorter than him but her confidence makes up for the size difference. 'What would you ask for?'

'I take my ship and book and leave; you may have my crew.'

I was mistaken—this isn't the first time he's struck a bargain like that.

'A shame indeed,' she says, looking at Michaels, 'that you are not the captain.'

Michaels bows his head and opens his hands to accept the compliment.

'You may have your ship and leave. I keep the bag, all your goods, and you may have your ship and freedom.'

'You've also got my crew,' Godstorm whines.

'I do,' she says with a sigh. 'Are your crew skilled enough that they warrant the price your ship and goods would fetch?'

'They're the best.' He sniffs. 'Best crew in the system.'

'And yet you are willing to trade them for mere trinkets. Is that the bargain you wish to strike with me? Your crew for your ship?'

'And me, don't forget me. And my goods.'

The captain looks over at Michaels and shrugs. 'Very well.' She picks up the bag and hands it to Godstorm.

'You are free to go.'

New Boss, Same As The old Boss

Surrounded as we are by her crew, there's nothing we can do except watch as Godstorm scuttles down the stairs and back onto the *Eagle*. The captain raises her hands and the clamps release. The *Eagle* banks high and is lost from sight within a minute.

She turns back and opens her arms to us. 'My name is Captain Morgan, of the ship *Unbroken Dawn*. Make no mistake in what has happened here today—those of you who have skills may find use among my crew. Those of you who do not will be dropped at the nearest port in return for whatever I can get for you.'

There's a ripple of laughter around the crew, as if it's some sort of running joke.

'Make no mistake,' Morgan repeats as she looks around at the six of us, 'I have no intention of leaving anyone to rot but, at the same time, space for dead wood, I have none. So, you're useful, or you're barter. With that in mind, each of you will be asked once, and once alone, your name and your skills. If I or my crew find you of interest, you'll be offered a position. The hours are bad, and the pay is worse, but you get to see the universe from the bow of an independent galleon.'

She walks over to us and pauses in front of Petra.

'Petra Tsenovich. Ship's technician, specialising in propulsion and thrusters.'

'Thrusters?' The captain looks curious. 'Do you have any experience in making ships go faster?'

'All I've ever been asked. Every captain wants to sail a dragster.'

Morgan smiles and points to a spot behind her. 'You wait there, and we'll see what you can do. And now you...' She points at our navigator.

'Shen Tsou.' He stands tall. 'Ship's navigator, twenty years' experience.'

'Where are we now?' She looks upwards.

'I...I don't know. How could I? We just got pulled through a rift a moment ago, but give me a chart and a few minutes...I'll know where we are.'

'What do we think?' Morgan plays to her crew for a second. 'Do we give him a chart?'

The jeers and catcalls suggest they're against the idea.

'Wait there.' Morgan points towards the ship's rail. 'And we'll see.'

She takes another step and looks up at Lennox and Gren, both of them larger than her by half again.

'Big boys...' She leans in close and sways away, moving around them like a snake. 'I know hired muscle when I see it; the question is, are you any good?'

'Yeah.' The first looks down at her. 'We're real good.'

'Stand with the chart man there.' She points to the navigator. 'And we'll see.'

Morgan smiles as she passes Michaels and points to me. 'And you?'

'Catarina Solovias,' I say. 'Ship's engineer, arms and armour.'

Morgan looks at me with interest. 'What do you specialise in?'

'Making things that shouldn't work, work.' I try to keep my voice steady.

'Were you responsible for the weapons on the ship I just lost?' she asks.

'I was.'

'Why didn't you have any bolt weapons on the ship?' She cocks her head to one side. 'Everyone knows lasers are useless against other ships.'

'The captain wouldn't spend the money to upgrade anything. He would never do any of the upgrades I asked for.'

'And what if *I* never do any upgrades?' She stares at me. 'What then?'

'I can still work miracles. Give me an hour on your ship, and if I haven't made massive improvements, sell me at the next port.'

There's a glint in her eyes as she nods, the faintest hint of a smile. 'Spirit—I can use that. Very well, you have an hour from when you take up your position to make a massive improvement, or I sell you at the next port. Fair?'

'Fair.'

What have I got myself into?

Morgan makes an elegant turn and stands in front of Michaels. She's about to open her mouth, when he steps forwards with his head high, more than a head-and-a-half above her.

'John Jefferson Michaels.' He holds her gaze steady. 'First officer, diplomat, and negotiator.'

'And are you any good at it?'

'You thought so...and the fact that I know that means you know I can read people.'

'And if I don't need a diplomat?' Her head half turns from him, but her body is still pointed towards him.

'Then I'm sure there's another *position* I could fill.' No flicker of doubt. 'Either on the ship, or *somewhere* else.'

There's another nervous giggle from the crew as Morgan's smile broadens.

'Very well,' she says. 'You and I will *parley* later.'

She points to a spot on the starboard deck and then nods to Lennox and Gren.

'Swords for our big boys, and I want two volunteers to test their mettle, with the victor receiving the white sash of my favour.' Morgan pans around the crew and grins. 'Unless, of course, their size intimidates you...'

There's a chorus of derision from the top deck, and four women draw their swords, raising them high in the air. Morgan nods in satisfaction and points to two spaces on the port deck. 'First ones down get to fight.'

All four women jump down, but two of them circle in mid-air and grab ropes hanging down from the rigging to glide down to the port deck spots. One of the smaller crew members brings a box to the captain and opens the top to reveal two swords within. Gren looks down at the swords and shakes his head, raising his hands.

'You don't fight with swords where you come from?' Morgan looks confused.

'Not unless you're into dressing up.' He looks down at his hands. 'These two get the job done every time, you'll see.'

'I'm sure I will.' She turns to one of the women and offers the box. "Your opponent has refused the use of a duelling blade; you may take his if you wish."

The woman reaches in and takes both swords by the scabbard, holding them in one hand. 'If he's not going to use them, I'll be sure to make up for that.'

"Those here watching," Morgan says, looking over at the crew of the *Eagle*. "No member of my crew draws their own weapon against each other, even if that person is only a *potential* crew member. They fight now using these blades. Whoever wins, wins not only the fight, but a sword granting them a place in the crew." Morgan nods and holds the box open until both women unclip the swords from their belts and place them inside, before stepping to the starboard side and handing the box back to the small crew woman.

'The victor calls the fight.' Morgan holds her arms out. 'You men need to understand there is no penalty for death here, but the defeated will become your property, so killing your opponent just reduces their resale value. First to fight will be Annika and the man who thinks swords are for those who dress up.'

Annika steps forwards and raises both swords in salute then holds them down towards the deck as Gren goes into a loose stance and raises his arms in front of him. Annika remains still while Gren circles. He makes a move, fast enough to be little more than a blur to me, and Annika is up in his grasp. He throws her to the deck hard, and the follow-up kick sends her across the deck to the far rail. She rises up, looking a little dazed as he closes on her again. He throws a left that lands hard followed by a right that lands harder, and she staggers away again. Morgan stares without emotion at the fight, her expression very much indicating that the fight isn't the interesting part of what's going on.

Annika backs up, and Gren grabs her by the neck, sweeping her up and smashing her down to the deck again. He pauses to look back at Morgan before turning to finish the fight. There's a sound of tearing cloth, and Gren stares in confusion as something thuds to the deck next to him.

His right arm.

As he stares in disbelief at the stump, his other arm falls off, then a line appears across his throat, and Annika stands to attention as his body keels over and his head rolls to the edge of the rail.

I didn't even see the cut!

'What is the first lesson?' Morgan calls as Annika salutes, and the small woman steps forwards carrying the sword box.

'It's not over till the victor salutes.' Annika bows and swaps the blades she was using for the sword she was originally carrying.

Morgan nods and points to the other woman. 'And our second match, Talyria against...'

'Lennox.' The other guard nods in respect as he takes one of the swords from the box.

Talyria takes the same position and looks on as Lennox begins his warm-up, his sword cleaving ever faster through the air till it's little more than a blur. He lowers the sword after a minute and inclines his head towards Talyria. She meets his gaze and nods in return, before raising her sword and advancing. Her first move is too fast for me to follow, but Lennox steps into the attack, binding her sword to his and moving down, snaking his arm over the top and around hers, the motion bending Talyria's arm till her hand opens and the sword falls to the deck.

Lennox turns hard, and Talyria is brought to the deck, Lennox bringing his sword around to rest against her throat.

'Yield,' he says.

Talyria nods, and Lennox removes his sword from her throat and looks up to Morgan, bringing his sword up to salute. From the deck, Talyria snatches her lost sword and slashes across Lennox's inside leg. Lennox looks down in shock as blood fountains into the air. He staggers, falling to one knee as Talyria springs up from the deck and slices his throat. Lennox crashes to the deck, his head rolling free as his body crashes down.

Morgan is impassive for a second and then walks over, plucking Talyria's sword from the box and offering it to her. Talyria passes her duelling sword over and accepts her own weapon back. She salutes as the captain looks down at Lennox's body and draws her own sword, lowering the point to the deck, the movement showing the lean swordfighter's muscle tone all the way down her arms.

'There will be no violation of the duelling code in my ranks,' Morgan says. 'That man fought well and spared you.'

Talyria looks horrified as she realises what's about to happen.

'I won't fight you, Captain.' She leaves her sword by her side.

'Then you will die like the honourless dog you are. Or you can raise your sword and at least make something of yourself.'

'I...' Talyria looks down, her hands trembling. 'Captain, I...I'm sorry, I—'

'So am I.' She steps closer to Talyria. 'Last chance, this is my sword you see before you, you are not a part of my crew anymore'

Talyria looks Morgan in the eye and sees the intent there. She lunges forwards, the sword spearing towards the captain's head.

Morgan spins on her heel and stands with her arms by her side, the sword missing. Talyria staggers as she looks down at the sword through her heart, then drops to her knees and falls without a word to the side. Morgan looks down at the body and places her boot upon it, pulling the sword free and wiping the blade. She takes Talyria's sword from the deck and walks back to Michaels, offering it to him with both hands.

'For your man.' She bows her head. 'She has paid for her betrayal of the code, and I can only hope that you will find it in your heart to forgive this breach of my hospitality while you were under my protection.'

'She has paid for her betrayal.' Michaels nods and places his hand over hers. 'Your word that no other members of my crew will be betrayed while on your ship?'

'On my life, I swear it.' She turns back to her crew. 'Swear it.'

'We swear,' the shout goes out from the crew, and Morgan steps back from Michaels, pointing to the bodies of Gren and Talyria. 'Over the edge with those two.' She looks down at Lennox's corpse. 'For him, full honours.'

*

'You, however,' Morgan says, turning to me, 'your hour starts now. Stala, take her below and see what she can come up with.'

A huge woman pushes through from the back of the crew, her clothes looking like someone crafted them from used curtains. She points to me and then to the prow of the ship, where there's a hatch that looks too small for her to fit through. I walk down a flight of stairs into the dark; there's a faint blue light emanating from the grille covering the bottom level and a pulsing green light from the underside of the deck. There's a smell of warm metal rising up, and heat radiating through the grille. Stala pauses at the top, then turns sideways to drop down, avoiding the steps and landing lighter than I would have given her credit for. She points down the corridor and, without waiting, ambles down in a crouch resembling something between a bear and a baboon. It's not at all cramped for me down here, and warmer than working in a spacesuit.

Very nice...

Stala pauses and drops to the level below. I look over the side and see her raise a hand to catch me. I shake my head and drop down, almost catching the upper deck on the way down to stabilise myself, staying clear of the searing heat it's generating. 'You're not familiar with these ships, are you?' Stala looks at me with sympathy.

'Never been on one before. And I've got an hour to learn; got a manual anywhere I can look at?'

'They don't build these with manuals. Gives captains the idea that anyone can fix them and not even have to be good at their job.'

'Reassuring,' I say with a sigh. 'Where do we start then?'

She points at the baroque-style archway in front of us and nods. 'Engine controls are there. Let me know if any of it makes any sense.'

I walk through the archway and into a room filled with levers and dials, no computers anywhere, no digital displays. I look around: most of the dials seem to be measuring pressure, and I lean back out of the doorway to see Stala adjusting other levers.

'Is this all pneumatic?' I ask.

'A lot of it. The bits that aren't run on solar. The weapons are on the side wall there; I've turned them all off, so you can play to your heart's content.'

I turn back to the controls and look at the side display. There's a set of click boards on the side that suggest ammunition counters, reading more than a few thousand rounds. I see the relays lining up between the main reactor and the guns; it appears there's just enough to make the guns work, but not as they should.

Whoever made this was skimping on the backups...

'Where are the spares?' I glance back out of the archway again. Stala reaches up and takes a box from the top of the nearby cabinet. There's a morass of wires, spanners, bigger spanners and *huge* spanners. I take the box and am leaning back towards the controls when there's a crunch from above, and the ship lurches.

'Didn't touch anything.'

'I know.' Stala looks upwards. 'That was something else.'

She reaches up and pulls herself to the level above, extending her hand down as the ship lurches again. I put my Isogloves on and reach up to her. She pulls me up as if I weigh no more than the box of tools and then heads back up to the top deck.

It's deserted on top. There's no sign of the crew except for the captain up on the top deck with her hands on the wheel. There's a flare from the starboard side, and something shoots past the sails, plunging straight through the shields on the other side. I turn and look upwards as a small ship streaks past the prow. For a second, I think it's Godstorm returning, but the guns blaze again, and a line of small-bolt fire stitches the deck not more than a foot from me. I dive backwards as the corvette banks hard and passes under us. There's a boom, and the ship rolls. Whatever gravity generator is holding us to the ship remains active, but the stars above are now spiralling out of control. I look back down at the deck as my stomach turns faster than the stars circle above. I can see the captain is wrestling with an unruly wheel to hold the ship steady. There's a series of further booms from below us as the cannons on the side of the *Dawn* open fire. The sails are moving above us, but unlike the steady, organised movement before, they're now flapping as if caught in some invisible breeze, the masts turning in random directions.

'Lucky shot,' Morgan yells. 'The lateral's have gone; get down there and fix them.'

'Come on.' Stala grabs me, pulls a line from her belt and attaches it to mine. 'We get to go off-ship.'

She runs to the top deck and peers over the edge. There's a sheer drop into space and something that appears to be a rudder waving without purpose beneath us. Stala locks her rope onto the rail and rolls over the edge, planting her feet against the ship's outer wall. She beckons me downwards. I lock my rope in and then tie it twice more. I can't get my head around the idea of rolling off the back of the ship, so I perch on the rail and ease my way down. Stala waits for me to get alongside her and points at the rudder.

'Don't let the glowing edges touch you.'

'Electricity?'

'On a different modulation. It's the same wavelength we use to render food into powder. Unless you want all the water in your body evaporated, keep to the side of it, particularly when we get it back online.'

We drop down level with the rudder, and I spot the problem— one of the shots from the attacking corvette has severed a power line leading to a massive set of cogs and wheels. I invert and look down at the line. There's a small hole leading into the power cables. Stala looks at it in dismay.

'Captain,' she calls upwards, 'I need to take the rudder offline for a minute.'

'No chance,' Morgan yells down; 'It'll mow us to pieces if we're driving straight.'

'I can do it.' I say to Stala. 'I can fit in there.'

Stala passes me a huge spanner, and I can see that there's a number of smaller controls on the side of it; it appears it can be wound up to deliver the necessary torque for turning things without needing to get the angle required to bring the user's muscles into play. I stare down the hole and lean closer, my hair standing on end as the glow from the rudder draws near. I bind my hair back and tuck it into my suit. I wind the spanner as much as I can and lean in to get my hand down into the hole, pulling the cables forwards and winding them around the terminals beneath.

The rudder glows brighter and starts to drift towards me.

'Let go.' I feel Stala's hand on my shoulder as the ship starts to straighten out. 'When the rudder comes back online, it'll slap straight into you.'

'Is it just electricity?'

'Of a sort. But it's lethal to anything organic.'

'I've got an idea. The rudder stops before it hits the side of the ship by a foot or so, right?'

'Thereabouts.' Stala looks uncertain. 'Why?'

'I'm going to seal this and then hold it steady while the rudder comes back online.'

'If that touches you, you're a cloud—'

'Then I'd better not let it touch me.'

I flip down to the area just to the side of the rudder, opening the panel underneath to get to the terminal and winding the wiring back around the bolts to reconnect the power. The rudder vibrates, and the ship evens out, the stars stop rolling around us, and there's a cry of exultation from above as the crew feel the ship slowing.

'Good, that's good.' Stala leans down. 'Now get out of there.'

The corvette rolls in to attack position behind us and Morgan yanks hard on the wheel, making the rudder swing sharp towards me. Stala extends her hand out to me but the captain yanks hard again on the wheel to try and pull out of the line of fire, which causes Stala to lose her grip and float free for a second as the ship's prow dips. The rudder goes up, and Stala grasps for the ship. It rolls again, and Stala watches in horror as the rudder swings over; she looks at me.

'ON DECK, GET—'

Before she can finish, the rudder brushes against her leg. There's a cloud of steam taking the form of her body for a second, her clothes drape across the rudder as it collects them up, and her tools bat against the hull of the ship. I push away from the wall of the ship and upwards, gripping hard on the rope as I float up. There's a curse from the deck as the corvette's guns open up and another line of rounds stitch into the wall above me.

The rudder swings back towards me and I look up.

Not going to make it...

A Sailor's Worth

I raise my hands in a seemingly futile gesture, but it's the difference between life and death. The rudder slams into my Isogloves, dissipating its energy, batting me against the hull and pinning me there. Both gloves light up, but I can see that the power output isn't high, though it's of a sort that I've never encountered before.

Power is power, however. Despite its size, this ship runs on far less than the Eagle *did.*

The ship rolls back and the rudder swings away from me. I leap onto the high wall, snagging what I can of Stala's clothes and equipment and heading up to the top deck. I crawl over the side and look at Morgan as she steers the ship on course. She glances backwards at me standing alone against the rail.

'Stala?' she asks. I shake my head, and she nods. 'Get down below; we lost something down there a moment ago, and I'm not sure what. We're slowing down. Any slower and we're all floating through space without a hull. Get me my ship back.'

'Aye, sir.' I snap a half-salute and run from the top deck to the prow, dropping back into the hold and then downwards from there. The comforting green has been replaced by a deep crimson, and I flick my suit lights on. The smell of metal is gone, and I can see a plume of gas leaking from one of the pipes on the wall. I put my respirator on and move closer. It looks like something has twisted in the mechanism and taken the pipe with it. I drop down to the lower deck and collect the box of spares, climbing back up on the thin ladder, then shut down the flow from the valve on both ends of the pipe and see the pressure gauge leap to one side.

I switch my gloves to construction mode and use the hydraulics in them to pull the pipe out of the wall and drop it on the floor. I rifle through the box of spares and take the closest size to the pipe I've torn out and jam it in, circling the top and bottom with the welders in the fingers of my glove.

Basic, but it'll do for now.

I let the pressure back in as slow as I can, making sure there's no leak as the sound of something detonating comes from above, and another cheer reverberates from the bulkhead. I hear a fizzing power line above me. There's a panel in the ceiling at such an angle that you'd never see it unless you were looking straight up. I pull the panel open and see that it leads to a large array of turning cogs with a massive pillar bolted through it. The fizzing line is preventing the pillar from turning all the way around. It looks like someone fitted it wrong in the first place; the line isn't long enough. I take an insulated line from my belt and attach it to the sparking connection, disconnecting the existing line and replacing it with mine then bolting it to the underside of the deck to make sure that it doesn't foul. The pillar continues rotating in what appears to be a random fashion, but this time goes all the way around. There's another cheer from above, and the guns on the side of the ship roar once. Silence follows, and I look around to make sure nothing else is malfunctioning.

About a half-minute later, there's the sound of a horn from on deck.

Either we won, or I'm negotiating for my ass again.

I head up on deck as Morgan locks the wheel in place. She turns to me and points to the port side where an expanding cloud of silver is spreading across the stars. The sails are now rotating to keep their edges against the light from the stars.

'You did well,' she calls down. 'Stala has been trying to find that problem for months.'

'Difficult to look upwards when you're busy ducking. Benefits of being small.'

'Yes... What happened to Stala?'

'Rudder. She touched it and—'

'Pop.' The word has no emotional content in it as she nods.

'At least it was quick and painless. That leaves me without a chief engineer. Prudence demands I choose one from the crew, and that's what I did when I picked Stala.' She pauses. 'Or you can go down below and start working on the ship.'

'Just like that?' I say. 'You trust me?'

'No.' She smiles without any humour. 'It will be a long time from now before I *trust* you, but you have some idea of how to fix things, and I'll accept that for now. If you break my ship, I'll stuff you, baste you, and feed you to the crew.'

'Feed me to the crew?' I feel a chill of fear as her eyes show no emotion.

'Complete with apple... But you don't have to worry *just* yet.'

Morgan looks back across the deck as one of the crew comes up. She's a little taller than Morgan but leaner in every way. Her mask is black, and she's carrying a chest that looks like it should be far heavier than she seems to be finding it. She lays it on the deck at the captain's feet and pulls it open to reveal a number of shreds of cloth within. The rest of the crew filter up on deck; among them are Michaels, Shen and Petra. Morgan looks down at the chest and pulls out four black ribbons. She hands one to me, then one to each of the others and points to her arm, where a purple band is secured in a single knot.

'This is your allegiance,' she says. 'You will wear your own clothes until you have earned your place. This ribbon will signify that you belong to my crew and, as such, no one will pick a fight with you unless they wish to take on the whole crew. We try together, we die together. If you can't live with that, don't be volunteering.'

She goes high to the top deck and looks down at us. 'Of course, there are responsibilities that go with that ribbon as well. You will pitch in where needed; you will take orders from those wearing purple.' She points to her own arm. 'In matters of battle, from those wearing red.' The starboard side raise their arms. 'And in matters of plunder and ship duties, from those wearing yellow.' The port side raise their arms.

Morgan stands in front of the wheel and leans on the railing. 'Step forwards, Raley, Clara and Errin.'

Three women step forwards from the assembled crew, and

Morgan gestures to the person in red, a statuesque figure with short dark hair and iridescent blue eyes. The face is thin, high-boned, with hollow cheeks leading to a narrow chin, duelling scars upon the cheek and neck, and thick strands of muscle all the way down the torso.

'This is Raley; she teaches everyone to fight. You will all have lessons from her to make sure that you do not embarrass me when it comes time for you to prove your mettle.'

Morgan points to the one in yellow, an older woman with an air of confidence that speaks of her not needing to strut for the world. Her hair is long and wound around her neck once, and trails as far as her waist, its appearance like a thick, white curtain over the left side of her face. Her visible eye is calm and takes in the rest of us as she stands at ease.

'This is Clara; she is head of ship's maintenance and salvage. From her, you will learn what is valuable to us and what is not—I'll not have my crew bringing me trinkets and calling them treasure.'

She points to the last woman, who's wearing green, the only crew member to do so. She has the smooth skin and flawless complexion of a girl in her early twenties, but the notion of youth disappears when I look at her face. Her eyes suggest she has seen far too much for someone so young. Her face is twisted: one of the scars on her cheek seems to have healed badly, pulling her mouth to the side. She's wearing a fitted cap of silk over her head like a bandana, but there's no bulge under it to suggest the presence of hair. She rests one hand on her sword and looks at the rest of us as if we were nothing more than meat.

'This is Errin, my first.' Morgan surveys us. 'Responsible for discipline, morale, and the ship in my absence... Let none of you think she is as soft as her appearance suggests.'

Swords Over Spanners

Introductions done; the crew disperses to their duties while Morgan's three deputies look at all of us new arrivals.

'The spanner monkey is mine first.' Raley steps forwards and points at me. 'She's no good to us if she gets herself killed.'

The other two seem disinclined to argue. Errin points at Michaels. 'I think you and I should talk; there are rules to being the captain's pet.'

'Pet!' Michaels looks at her with eyes wide. 'I'm not a pet.'

'And that's what we need to talk about. If you only do what she wants, you'll be a pet, and she gets bored of pets.'

Michaels nods and remains silent.

'The others then, are mine.' Clara examines Shen and Petra. 'Be at ease, young ones; you have the easiest introduction to the crew.'

Raley steps forwards and looks me up and down. She walks around me, and I turn to follow her. She puts a hand on my shoulder; there's strength there, but it's a delicate strength, not one born of lifting heavy objects. She makes a brushing motion with her hand to everyone else. 'You all need to go. Catarina does not need you to witness her education.'

Errin nods and extends her hand for Michaels to follow her. Clara goes over to the hatch, waiting for a second for Petra and Shen to follow before she descends.

When they're all out of sight, Raley turns to me and points to her chin. 'Strike me.'

I swing without hesitation, and she sways back, returning to where she started in a single motion, before pointing at her chin again. 'Strike me.'

I jab with my left hand, following with my right when it doesn't connect. She's no longer in front of me, and I feel a tap on my shoulder. I spin with my fist out and feel a tap on my other shoulder. I spin again and, my arm goes dead. I turn, and both arms fall limp, panicking as I try to move them with all my strength, only to get no response at all. I can feel the muscles in my chest working, but the movement is not being transferred past my shoulders.

'Good,' Raley says. 'You didn't hesitate when I told you to attack, but you failed because you didn't look where you were striking.'

'What have you done to me?' I look in fear at my useless arms.

'An object lesson.' Raley walks around me. I turn to face her, and she smiles, jutting her chin forwards again. 'In combat, you must make no useless moves. Now strike me.'

'How?' I'd shrug if I could.

'Strike me.' Her voice goes cold. 'Or I will strike you.'

I sway from side to side, my arms still not moving other than to flop at my sides. She steps closer and brings one arm up, her fingers stiffening into rigidity. I lean back, trying to keep my head away from her hand.

'Strike me.' Her other arm comes up.

She spreads her arms wide, and I lunge forwards with my back and neck muscles, going for a headbutt. I don't connect. My back spasms, and I remain bent over, my arms hanging down. I see Raley's boots come into view.

'Good. Most untrained panic when you take away their obvious weapons. Now hold still.'

Like I have a choice...

She presses my back in two different places, and I'm able to straighten up again. She takes my shoulders and presses a number of points, and the feeling rushes back into my arms; it's an almost painful sensation. I rub my shoulders.

'To do what I can will take time,' Raley says, 'and some never master it.'

'Anything worth learning takes time,' I reply, 'and I'm a good learner.'

'Well, you have the right spirit, which is an excellent start.' Raley takes a pocketbook from her thigh pocket and passes it to me. 'This will be your training journal. As you learn each new thing, you will write it in here. When you learn something that does not work, you will also write it in here and, in this way, you will remember the lessons long after the memory of the failure has left you.'

'I don't forget failures.' I take the book from her and put it in my ankle pocket. 'It's not the way I'm made.'

'Everyone thinks that.' Raley passes me a thin metal rod with a button on each end. She takes her own rod out and points to the two buttons—one green, one black. 'Yours. A gift for every new crew member from me.'

'What does it do?'

'You don't want to find out for yourself?' She raises an eyebrow. 'What sort of engineer are you that you don't press buttons on new toys?'

'The sort that's seen what happens when you press buttons on toys you have no idea about.' I look at the rod and smile.

Raley holds hers out and points at the green button, then turns it downwards and presses the button. The rod telescopes to more than three feet in the blink of an eye. She twirls it in her hand, an elegant move born of long practice, and presses the black button; the rod retracts in a blink.

'It isn't designed as a killing weapon, but it will do, if you're ever up against someone with a sword when you don't have yours.'

'I don't have a sword.'

'Really?' Raley frowns. 'Were you a slave on your ship?'

'That's one way of putting it... Why?'

'Because only slaves do not own their own weapons. It is given unto no one to take weapons from you. No captain has that privilege, unless they have revoked the freedom of the crew member in question.'

'Not how it worked where I came from.'

'Well, it's how it works around here. Never let me find you without your weapon. The disrespect to me would be enough that I would be forced to kill you to spare you the shame.'

I look into her eyes for some sign of humour and find none. 'But I don't have a sword.'

Raley nods and walks towards the side of the ship, pulls one of the timbers up and steps on a panel recessed beneath the deck. Four long boxes rise up from the wooden floor, each of them containing a number of swords, axes, maces, and other hand weapons. She turns back to me and gestures to the boxes.

'Pick one...'

*

I circle the boxes. All the weapons have seen active service—many of the blades have chips in their edges, but all of them have been sharpened to razor thinness. I reach down and pick a short sword with a curved blade. It feels too light—there's nothing at all in the balance; it's like waving cutlery. Raley frowns. Taking the sword from me with without a word, she places it back in the rack.

'No good,' she murmurs, as much to herself as me.

She moves down the line of weapons and tosses a double-headed axe to me. I catch it and twirl it. There's enough weight for me to get behind the idea of swinging it, but it still feels strange to handle. Raley pauses, then her sword is out, and she lunges. I try to block with the axe, but her sword comes up to my chin, and she takes the axe off me.

'No...' She places the axe back in its box and stands with her hands on her hips for a second. 'Have you ever trained in combat?'

'I had a few classes at the Olympus duelling club, but it never took.'

'Engineer all your life?'

'Yep.'

'What about that?' She points to the huge spanner in my belt sash.

She turns and picks up a large canvas duffle bag filled with objects that clank, and throws it at my feet. From the bag, she picks a pole with links for something to be attached at both ends and throws it to me. I catch it, turning it around in the air. She lunges again, and I find the blade next to my throat. She takes the pole off me and fits an object from the bag to each end of it, before throwing it back to me. I catch it and see that one end is a spanner and the other is a hammer. The balance on the pole feels different as she lunges again, and this time, I catch the sword with the spanner head, twisting my body away and pulling the sword down towards the deck.

Raley withdraws the sword and sheaths it, a wry smile on her face. 'You put it down towards the ground because that earths it?'

'I...' I look at the spanner head. 'Yeah, that's what you do with anything that's both dangerous and unsecured.'

'Thought so.' She turns and walks around, looking at my posture. 'Strike me.'

I bring the spanner up and whirl it towards her. She ducks under it and comes up on the other side of the strike.

'No, no, no.' She wags her finger at me. 'Strike me like I'm a truculent generator.'

I spin the spanner in my hand to present the hammer end and swing it towards her. She half-ducks, before realising she's not going to get clear and brings her hands up to grab the handle, the impact pushing her backwards.

'Better.' She looks pleased and nods. 'Your problem lies in thinking that you're doing something new, so your muscles don't react the way they normally would, only the way you think they should.'

'Really?' I examine the hammer with scepticism.

'Of course, the body only moves in a certain number of ways.' Raley steps behind me and brings my arm up, with the hammer held in it, then sweeps it down in an arc from right to left, continuing the movement upwards on the other side, allowing the weight of the hammer to sweep upwards and then down from the other side. 'It's just your perspective that matters. When you look at the hammer as a weapon, it feels wrong; when you look at it as a tool, your mind accepts it as something you can use.'

'Then I should look at everything like a bastard piece of machinery?'

'If that's what works for you. Write this in your book as the first lesson: see everything as what you can use it for, not what it actually is. Be back on deck tomorrow at mid-bells for your second lesson.'

'What do I do once I've done that?' I take out the pocketbook.

'Go about your duties.' She frowns. 'Ah, of course, you're new to this. Report to Errin or the captain, and they'll show you what to do. In the meantime, if we get into a fight of any sort, stay by me till you've got the hang of looking at people like inanimate objects.'

'Thank you.' I put the hammer–spanner down.

'You're welcome.' She nods and throws me the duffle bag. 'All the other heads for that thing are in there. Be careful you don't catch yourself on the clockwork.'

Clockwork?

I sit on the deck and write the entry in the pocketbook, then place it back in my pocket and pick up the hammer–spanner. *Hammer? Spanner?* There's a small indent in the handle. I put my finger in it and push. The indent springs upwards, and I pull it, unfolding the wood into a winding handle. The insides of the pole are filled with well-machined cogs, all of them covered in a light mist of oil—just enough to keep them moving, not enough to clog and pick up all the dirt.

Someone took good care of this.

The thought occurs that this was Stala's, and I feel a pang of guilt.

She'd want it put to good use.

I let the thought permeate and scan up and down the spanner. There are buttons close to the winding handle, each one of different coloured wood. I wind the handle for two turns and press the top button—the hammer at that end spins around fast enough to sound like a rattlesnake. I look at the other end and see that the screw is fitted sideways. I start winding the handle again and press the other button. This time, the head of the spanner torques sideways at a speed that could drive an engine.

Got to find a way to slow that down, or I'll break something.

I open the bag and look inside. There are more attachments in there, all of them machined to fit the head of the pole. A metal spike with enough ridges to form a drill at the hammer end, another that's a square block with an encased chainsaw that could fit on the spanner. There's another small bag with wood and metal oils and a number of brushes and a white cloth as light as silk but rough to the touch, surrounding a small book similar to the one that Raley just gave me.

I flip the book open and look at the first page.

*

The handwriting is small, precise, in lines which suggest that the person put a set of lined paper behind the writing paper to make sure they were all level. The penmanship is exquisite, but the lines are thick in places, hinting that the person was writing so others could understand it, rather than scribbling down notes for themselves. I flip to the end of the book on impulse.

Never argue with Errin.

The last page contains only those words. There's a smear of red–brown on the page just below, indicating that the writer was bleeding at the time it was scribed. I turn the page; whoever made the notes didn't write on the back of it.

Never let others bring home that which you worked for; they will not take your punishment for you.

There's a sketch of a many threaded whip, barbs up and down the length of its threads, in the corner of the page. I turn the page again.

There is nothing so short-lived as the gratitude of captains, or as long as their enmity.

There's no image, but the ragged line suggests that the normal writing guide was absent, and there's a slight smudge where the hand must have brushed over the writing before the ink had time to dry. I turn the page.

There is nothing but death within the Broken Hollows.

'Something interesting?' Morgan's voice from above me.

'Just catching up on my pocketbooking.' I look upwards, closing the book and placing it back in the white cloth. 'I've finished my daily lesson with Raley; where should I be next?'

'Head down to the engine room and familiarise yourself with

things. If we're attacked again, I don't want you having to guess what you need to be doing. Be back here for the start of the morning watch.'

'What time is that?' I ask, pausing an instant too long before remembering to add, 'Sir?'

'Eight bells of the morning watch.' She raises an eyebrow at my bemused expression. 'You're *really* new out here, aren't you?'

'Yes, sir. Sorry, sir.'

'Do you know what *hours* are where you come from?' Her lips curl in a patient smile.

'Yes, sir.'

'Write this in your pocketbook.' She gives me time to take the book out. 'The bell rings every half an hour, with one bell added each time till we hit the end of the watch at eight bells. Have you got all that?'

I nod and look up again.

'There are seven watches every day: the first watch, between eight of the evening and midnight; the middle watch between midnight and four of the morning; the morning watch between four of the morning and eight of the morning; the forenoon watch between eight of the morning and midday; the afternoon watch between midday and four of the afternoon; and then the two dog-watches, the first being between four of the afternoon and six of the evening, the second between six of the evening and eight of the evening, when we start it all again.' She pauses as my hand tries to keep pace with my ears, my writing reflecting my haste. 'Have you got all that?'

I nod and dot the page. 'Yes, sir.'

'We're now at six bells of the first watch. What time does that make it to you?'

'Eleven at night.' I glance down at the notes.

'So be up for here for eight bells of the morning watch.' She smiles. 'Don't let anyone find out I gave you an hour off.'

I make a half-hearted salute and gather the bag and spanner from the deck, before hurrying down below. It's still warm down here, far more so than on deck. I put my head back up through the hatch and feel the temperature change as my head emerges. Some sort of field over the top of the deck. I pass back down through the hatch. No sign of any other machinery, but the pressure is higher. There's pipework everywhere, ranging from thick, rubber pipes bulging with pressure, to red-hot steelwork across the roof, covered by wooden panels that are hanging loose. I put the panels back and bolt them in place. *Don't like it when things aren't how they should be.* It's quiet down here, save for a faint humming from the various pipes and the muted buzz of electricity from the deck above me.

I drop down the access to the lower deck to check all the controls are where they were left. There's a small hatch—*too small for Stala*—behind the control panels; looks like it hasn't been opened for some time. I reach down, pull the hatch open and look inside. There's a bunk within, suspended by chains. The bed is made, covers drawn over it, and it looks like it hasn't been used in some time. There's a side cabinet, with everything bolted down to the floor, as if the movement of the ship might affect it. I crawl inside and feel heavier—the gravity in here is close to Mars standard. *Miniature gravity generator, so the person sleeping within knows when and how the ship is moving. Not something you'd want to fit to a bolthole.*

I flick one of the switches on the side, and a pale light comes on overhead, not enough to blind but enough to see around the cabin. There's a clock on the wall, a very faint ticking coming from it, made of wood with a front of brass and glass that can be opened to adjust the hands; there's a brass plate underneath the face with MCM inscribed upon it. On the desk, an old fountain pen and a bottle of ink rest on what appears to be a magnetic plate, and there's a pad of paper on the desk blotter, all of which have a thin layer of dust over them. There's a row of books on a shelf, most of them old, leatherbound, with thick paper throughout. I pull one of the books off the shelf and leaf through it: technical diagrams and details of ships, weapon systems the likes of which I've never seen before. I pull out a second book: descriptions of creatures and alien races, together with details of how they live and where to find them.

Who lived here?

The third book is a journal, written longhand in a flowing script.

The writer has an easy hand with small lettering and flourishes every few letters. It looks to be a key to deciphering a chart of some sort. There's a bunch of folded papers in the back of the journal, and I turn the pages to the back, opening out one of the papers. It's inked on both sides, illustrated by a master of the craft, with rich, deep colours marking everything, the suns all but glowing out of the chart. Something about the chart draws my eyes in, as if they're being pulled out of my head as I drift over something marked as *The Fall*, the images blurring before me. I look away with an effort of will and sit down on the bunk, my head feeling like I've been upside down for too long. I lie back, enjoying the gravity holding me to the sheets. I open the book again and marvel for a second at the sight in front of me: the stars are moving on the page.

I close the book again, shake my head and yawn; the events of the day are weighing heavy on me.

I must be more tired than I thought.

I open the journal and lie back on the bunk with the book held open on my chest.

10/10/4358

And so, I find myself in a place I've never known, with no clear path before me...

Knowledge is Dangerous

I wake with the book still on my chest, open on the first page. The clock on the wall reads almost six in the morning. *Not on shift yet.* I look around the bunk for something to drink. There's a bottle in the corner, but the contents smell like stronger firewater than I've ever had, and the layer of dust on the top suggests that it hasn't been opened for a few years at least. I put the journal back on the bookshelf and look around the desk. There's a small leather tool-roll on the back of it; I undo the ties on it and spread it out on the desk. It contains more than twenty tools, each of them etched with the same symbols in a language I'm not familiar with, looking more like someone has etched their name into the side of them with something little more than a razor's edge wide.

I take one of the tools out—what appears to be a compass of some sort, a small clockwork mechanism on it with periods of time noted on the side scale, similar in nature to the tools that I've seen Shen use on the charts in the navigation room. I roll them back up and secure the pouch, placing it at the back of the desk.

I need to get Shen down here to properly look at these.

I go back up on deck. There are a few women there—someone I don't recognise at the helm and everyone else going about their own business like a well-oiled machine. Over at the entrance to the ship's hold, I see Petra beckoning to me and move to her. The gravity of the *Unbroken Dawn* is heavier on deck than it was on the *Starlight Eagle*, and Petra has the appearance of someone who's not enjoying the extra weight on her bones.

'You okay?' she asks in a low voice as I move next to her.

'No problems so far. You?'

'We need to get hold of Shen sometime soon.' Petra looks up to the ship's wheel. 'I don't know where we are, but whatever this ship is, it's nothing like anything we've ever seen before.'

'Just figured that out?' I say with a grin. 'It's all running on the same sort of power though.'

'No.' Petra shakes her head. 'It's not.'

'I've been down in the engineering core. All electricity and conduits, couple of valves for pneumatics and hydraulics, but it's electrical where it counts.'

'Exactly.' She looks up at the unfurled sails. 'But haven't you noticed? There's no reactor on this ship; it's drawing its power from somewhere else, and there aren't any battery units around here to be storing the sort of power it's kicking out.'

'What are you thinking?'

'I think we need to take a look at its innards. I've got a theory, but I need to check the way the core is put together. I've got a bigger problem though...'

'What's that?'

'We're only kept on this ship as long as we're useful, right?' Petra looks around to make sure no one's in the vicinity. 'Well, this ship rides on something, and it's not thrusters, so if it's not working on thrusters, I can't improve it. I've spent my whole life understanding conventional thrust patterns and, as far as I can see, this thing *sails* through space.'

'I've got something for you. Come on.' I bounce back over the deck and down the hatch again, dropping down into the engine room before Petra has got halfway across the deck. She follows me down, her every step looking like it's hurting, and I take her down to my quarters. I pick up the book with the technical details in it and come out of the small door as she enters through the archway. 'This has a ton of stuff in it about ships like this and how they work.' I pass it to her. 'Reckon we should stay down here a while and figure stuff out.'

'I'm on shift at eight bells,' she takes the book

'Me too. So, let's get to it.'

The book is written in the same long, flowing script, but with a smaller nib, so all the details are precise around the images. There's a whole section devoted to the methods which allow ships to sail among the stars, and we both pore over it.

*

It's an hour later when I give up. The concepts in it are staggering, so much so as to read almost like a work of fiction—concepts on how sails can catch solar winds and channel them, along with how those same winds can be used to generate power. Petra is enthralled though, staring at the pages and swaying, as if dazed. As I turn the page, her pupils dilate then shrink back to normal. I turn the page again, and her eyes widen. I flip the next one faster and the next faster than that, and she slumps back against the bench. I close the book as she stirs and looks at me.

'All right, so let's get started then.' She points at the book.

'Let's get *started*?' I glance sideways at her and raise an eyebrow. 'We've been doing this for more than an hour.'

She frowns. 'No, we haven't. We just sat down and started reading.'

I close the book. 'Nope. You've been sat there reading for about an hour, and you just stopped looking at it.'

She looks puzzled. 'What was I looking at?'

I open the book to where we started, and point at the diagram of the sail.

'Yeah,' she says. 'that's the first page, where the difference between the nature of Verison cloth and Settel cloth is discussed, along with the reasons why the two cannot be overlapped upon single-sailed ships. I read it.'

I turn the page.

'And this discusses the relationship between power generated by solar methods and that which is caused by the crude reactors that people build, and why no ship should be dependent on either single method.'

I raise an eyebrow and watch her as I turn each page and she parrots out the information without any pause. I close the book and smile as she stares at it open-mouthed.

'But I don't remember reading any of it.'

'Well, clearly you did read it...'

'And you, did any of this make sense to you?'

'Not a bit. But you know my thing is weapons and power.'

She takes the book from me and looks up something in the index, turning to a page before handing it back to me. My gaze alights on it:

In the beginning we fought with weapons of powder and steel to break and puncture the weak flesh of our enemies. In time these weapons gave way to the beginnings of what we were going to use in every day life. Lasers were a favoured option because of the nature of the generators that we use and on planets are still a favoured option due to the inexpensive nature and...

I feel something growing inside my head. It gets ever larger, trying to break through from inside my brain. I hear a creaking, loud in my ears, and everything goes black.

*

I gaze up at Petra from my prone position on the bench. She pats the closed book on the table and nods.

'Half an hour,' she says. 'And you passed out when I turned the pages too quickly.'

'What was on them?'

'Weapons, armour, stuff I don't know anything about...' She shrugs. 'Thought it might be something to do with what we know, which is why you didn't fall under the same spell as me in the power section.'

'We have to keep this quiet,' I whisper. 'I can quote you every type of weapon on this ship, what it's good against, what it doesn't work against and why, and I'm guessing you could do the same with your specialist subjects.'

Petra nods once. 'But there's so much left to read in here.' She pats the book again.

'Then we have to ration it.' The dull ache in my head is just starting to fade. 'I don't know about you, but it felt like there was something in my head trying to get out.'

'Same for me. Too much knowledge is dangerous.'

'Out here,' I say, looking upwards, 'not enough might be more dangerous...'

Fire on the Mast

The idea of three square meals a day is quashed when we look into the crew cabins.

'Food is at first bell of the dog-watch.' Shen leans out of his bunk with the look of a man who found his dreams far more palatable than reality. 'Where did you two go anyway?'

'Show you later.' I motion up on deck. 'Figure we'd best get to it, first day on the job and all that.'

'I'm due with Mirri, their navigator, to see if I can plot a course through The Dragon.' Shen climbs out of his bunk, still wearing the clothes he had on yesterday.

Still wearing the sweat in them as well...

He picks at his shirt and sniffs, then shrugs. 'I don't see much water around here.'

'Need acid to get that smell out,' Petra says. 'Best hope they've got something on board that we can use to clean things.'

'There's a device in the main hold.' Michaels' voice drifts down into the cabin. 'Everyone has two sets of clothes; there's always one in the cleaner and one being worn. Guess we're all going to learn sewing really quick.'

He comes down into the hold and looks us all up and down. It appears he's slept in a very comfortable place all night long, and he's making no attempt to cover it up.

'Least it worked out well for one of us.' Shen shakes his head.

'Hey!' Michaels feigns outrage. 'It's not easy doing what I just did...'

'No.' Petra smiles and glances down at Michaels' belt. 'I imagine it's real *hard.*'

'A man's got to do...' He grins as I take a swipe at his head, and he beckons us close. 'Seriously though, we need to consider what we're going to do now. They're three days from port, and any of us who don't match up are likely to be left there, and then we'll never find our way back.'

'Do you really *want* to go back?' I say. 'I mean, it's not like any of us were living in the lap of luxury, is it?'

'Yeah, but there's living in a world you're familiar with,' he says, patting the wooden wall, 'and then there's this. I know it's just another ship, but at least we know what to do with the ones where we came from.'

'Just something else to learn,' I reply. 'I've got nothing to go back to. Petra?'

'Ex-husband who'd try to kill me on sight. Nothing I'm going to miss.'

'A good woman and a house that I've nearly paid off...' Shen says. 'If we get the option to go back, I'm taking it...sorry.'

'Never apologise.' Michaels pats him on the shoulder and looks at Petra and me. 'Well, if you want to stay, that's down to you. I suspect that First Studmuffin to the captain has a limited lifespan, so I'd better get my other credentials out.'

'Yeah?' Petra looks sideways at him. 'Here was me thinking you were just here to be all studly. What else can you do?'

'You'll see. Suffice it to say, if I underperform in one fencing event, I'll be good enough in another.' His smile fades, and his face takes on a serious expression. 'One thing though, from what I've seen, we're all better keeping our heads down till we can get off this ship. From what I've heard, questioning the captain isn't well received here, and neither is questioning any of her lieutenants.'

*

As we arrive back up on deck, for a few seconds, there are twice as many people as there should be, each of them handing equipment to their replacement before hurrying down below deck. Some of them swarm up the masts, where they gaze out into the starfield, using what seem to be old telescopes. I gasp as one of the crew reaches the top of a mast and bursts into flames. I point up, mouth wide, at the flaming mass atop the mast, and feel my arm being lowered by Raley as she wanders past.

'What are you looking at?' She glances upwards. 'Never seen someone go fire-walking before?'

My blank expression is all the answer she needs.

'Enervasion field.' She points down at her belt to the small brass buckle there. 'Makes a small field that converts extremes of temperature into light. You wear them when you go up into the high sails, otherwise you come back down an ice cube, or a cinder, depending on where we are. We haven't got enough for everyone, so if you hear the ship's alarm, get below deck, or it'll get bad, quick...'

She looks at all of us still staring at the glowing mass and shakes her head.

'I'm sorry'—she turns her attention to each of us in turn with something resembling bemusement—'did any of you get the impression your jobs involved standing on deck staring at the rest of the crew?'

I glance back to see her with one hand on her sword, finger tapping its hilt, and I clear my throat. The others look round, catch sight of Raley, and hurry to their stations as her grin grows broader.

'Did the lesson sink in yesterday?' She takes a good look at the spanner on my back. 'Do you want to wait for later, or is there time for bruises now?'

'I'm free at the moment.' I pull the spanner out, and twirl it around in one hand. 'Are you sure I'm the one who's going to get the bruises?'

She flickers like a shadow caught in a lamplight, and I touch my nose as the brushing sensation fades.

'All right,' I say. 'You *are* sure!'

She pulls her sword out, the red-bound silk on the hilt almost glowing in the light as she jags a few passes in the air, the moves swift but without thought; a duelling pattern to warm up with. She sees me hefting my weapon and sighs, before sheathing her sword and nodding to herself.

'Something else we need to work on. I'm going to point, and you're going to strike. The faster I point, the faster you strike. Clear?'

I nod, and she gestures at her face. I pause and shrug, then swing at her face without any real conviction. She doesn't bother to move until the last second, and draws and strikes with her sword in a single motion, the point coming to rest just below my chin.

'When you are here, you are here to learn.' Her tone is light, though the look in her eyes is not. 'If you don't learn here and now, there will be no time when you actually need to use these skills.'

'I'm an engineer,' I retort, frowning. 'I'm never going to be on the front line, and if they get past you, they'll make slush out of me.'

'I agree.' She smiles. 'But there may come a time when I'm not there, and you'll have to do it yourself. Now ask yourself if you think the best way to get through life is hoping someone else will be there to handle the dangerous stuff...'

'No.' I heft the spanmer again. 'Give me another go at it.'

She grins and points at her head. This time she has to duck.

Lack Of Knowledge Is More Dangerous

The lesson takes less than an hour and, for the last ten minutes at least, is observed by Captain Morgan. She waits till Raley is done, and I'm sweating enough to need a drink or three. Raley nods and glances upwards to the high deck as the captain looks on, seeming disinterested.

'She doesn't watch training,' Raley murmurs, when she passes me a thin towel to wipe my face. 'I'd go up there and pay my respects if I were you...'

'Anything I should look out for?' I take the towel and obscure my whispered reply.

'Be careful which one of her you've got when you go up there.' She looks at me and pushes her head all the way over to one side, a faint cracking coming from her shoulder. 'If she's got her red lipstick on, you've got Jekyll.' She pushes her head all the way over to the other side. 'If she's got the green on, you've got Hyde.'

'Split personality?' I hand the towel back to Raley.

'Not split, no... Just watch yourself.'

I head up the stairs as Captain Morgan releases the catch on the wheel and lets it roll a little. I approach her from the side; she's wearing red today, and I breathe easier.

'Captain?' I nod in respect.

'Tell me what you've learned in the extra shift I gave you.' She rolls the wheel, and the field of stars above roll with us. 'I trust you've put the time to good use.'

'I'd like to think so.' I turn and peer over the edge. 'We're using regular eighty-eight shells on the side guns?'

'Eighty-eights were the largest we could fit in there; anything more and we risk putting the ship out of alignment every time we open up.' Morgan pulls the wheel back to centre and drops the lock into place.

'What if I told you there's a way to set up eighty-eights so they hit like one-oh-fives?'

'I'd say you're wasted here.' She looks at me with interest. 'What's your proposal?'

'Give me the day with one of the eighty-eights. If I manage it, pass around an extra ration of food tonight.'

'And if you fail?'

'I won't,' I say with a grin.

The details in that manual had better be accurate.

'I like confidence,' she says, 'but I do not react well to disappointment, and I hold people to the promises they make. After all, if your word means nothing, then you are nothing.'

'I make good on my promises.'

'Very well, if you succeed, more food from the canteen for everyone tonight. If you fail'—she reaches into her coat and throws me an apple—'that goes in your mouth when I stuff you and serve you for dinner so no one is disappointed.'

Shit, wasn't expecting that!

I glance down then back up just as she almost manages to conceal her grin. I relax a little, and she turns her attention towards the main deck.

'Dinner is at the first bell of the dog-watch.' She points to the bell on the frame by the wheel. 'One hour prior, we'll test the guns and see if you've managed to do what you said you would.'

'You'll need to get me some targets to shoot at.' I look around at the empty stars. 'Doesn't look to be too much around here.'

'I'll get you something. Now, about your business.'

'I need some materials to make the modifications.' I hold my hand up to stop her leaving. 'Not much, but I can't make the changes without them.'

'Get them from Clara. Get her to assign someone to help you.'

Raley is still on the deck below as I go down the stairs. She raises an eyebrow at me, and I mouth 'red' to her. She nods and walks alongside me.

'I heard what you said to the captain.' Her voice is low and urgent. 'I hope your ass is bigger than it looks.'

'My ass?' I look at her with a frown. 'Why?'

'Because if you get this wrong, she *will* stuff you and serve you for dinner.'

'Thought you said red was the safe colour?'

'*Safer*,' she says. 'Not safe. *Never* safe.'

'Great,' I say with a sigh. 'I need some blocks of metal with a very high melting point and some way of melting and casting them into the plates to make the barrel right for the shells.'

'Clara will know if we've got something like that.' She points to the hold with a half-smile on her lips. 'Come on, I'll help—you look a little stringy to me; I'd rather have the extra tack.'

Raley leads me down into the galley where Clara is sat with her hair wound around her neck and stuffed down the front of her tunic. She lifts her head as we stand at the table, and puts her spoon back into the bowl of stew in front of her.

'Raley.' She nods, her voice low and deep, pitched to carry in the enclosed area without volume. 'And...Catarina, is it not?'

'It is,' Raley replies for me. 'Forgive us, Clar, but we're in need of some things urgently.'

'Urgent enough that I cannot finish dinner?'

'Show her,' Raley says, turning to me, 'what the captain gave you.'

I pull the apple from my pocket, and Clara's expression changes to one of horror.

'You didn't make a bet with her, did you?' Her voice is a harsh whisper now. 'Don't you know what she does to those who lose bets?'

'I didn't know I was making a bet. And I sure didn't know the flip side of the bet would involve me getting turned into a suckling pig.'

'Someday we'll find a way to warn all the new crew before they get caught that way.' Clara pushes her bowl to the side and leans forwards with her hands clasped together. 'What can I do to help you win this bet?'

I tell her what I need for making the plates, then close my eyes to recall the next bit of information. 'And we need something to clear out the built-up residue on the inside of the barrels.'

'I'm sure we can do something about that.' Clara stands and extends her hand to me. 'Come on, let me show you what we have.'

Raley remains behind as Clara leads me down into the bowels of the ship, towards the bow rather than to the engines at the stern. The cargo hold comprises a single wide-open space containing more than a hundred wooden boxes sealed with steel bands on all sides. Clara moves past the boxes with the ease of long familiarity, stepping through a small door at the front of the hold and down a spiral staircase leading to the very bottom of the ship. I move to engage the lights on my suit, and Clara turns back to me.

'Not yet,' she says, her hand moving in the darkness. There are faint lines of green along the ceiling, not bright at first but growing more luminous by the second. 'I don't leave the lights on all the time and most engineering on the ship goes towards keeping the weapons and engines online, so it takes the lights in here a while to work out that we're in here.'

I look around the bottom bay: it's a lot longer than I thought it might be. The ceiling is lower as well, just high enough to stand up straight, and both sides of the bay are lined with drawers, like those you might find in a desk. Each of them has a label attached to the front of them, and most have a thick layer of dust settled over them.

'A good quartermaster needs to remember where things are without having to refer to anything so clumsy as an inventory.' Clara taps the side of her head, taking a pad of paper from the workbench and a pen from the inside lining of her tunic. 'Write here what you need, and I will see what I can gather.'

I take the pad and scribble all the things I can think of on it, before handing it back to Clara and looking around the bay. She takes it and scans the list, then squints into the near blackness at the far end of the bay.

'I fear it may take me a little while to get everything. I know where things are but finding them in the dark is not always easy.'

'Maybe I can help you then?' I examine the control panel on the side of the bay. It's apparent that no one has looked at it or tried to perform repairs on it in some time. 'Give me five minutes with the controls, and I'll see if I can get the lights up.'

'Well, if you have the time to spare... I normally come pretty far down the ship's food chain for regular repairs.'

'You're *literally* helping to save my ass,' I say. 'I'll *make* time.'

*

Clara starts gathering the things on the list from the drawers closest to the light, and I peel back the panel to check the wiring underneath. The ship uses long pieces of wire as fuses, something I haven't seen since reading through my dad's books on ancient tech.

Far easier to replace, but you need the right size wire.

I pull the remains of one of the broken wires out and look over at Clara. 'Have we got anything down there that could replace this?'

Clara steps over and takes it from my hand, pulling the curtain of hair back from her left eye. The socket is scarred, the flesh did not heal well around the metal plate inserted into her skull, long sealed burns line the edges. She adjusts a screw on the side of the metal eyeball, and a different lens whirs into place; she adjusts the screw twice more and turns the wire in her hand, before handing it back to me. She readjusts her hair to fit over the mechanical eye, glancing up at me with the other, a wry smile playing over her lips. I remain silent, trying not to stare at the curtain of hair, and wonder if the mechanical eye can still see me.

'There's not a question in your head I haven't already answered a hundred times. How, what, why, does it hurt? Where would you like to start?'

'I'm sorry. I didn't mean to stare.'

'Of course you didn't. But when you see a woman with half her head replaced with metal and lenses, it's all you can do, yes?'

I nod.

'There was a war a decade back. We won.'

'You won? 'If you won the war, how—'

'Stenlarian justice is a peculiar thing.' Clara turns away and opens another drawer, withdrawing a reel of wire like the one I passed her. 'I was one of the commanders in the last battles; my regiment was slaughtered to the last, holding the line.'

'You got that in the battle?'

'No.' She hands me the reel and turns back again. 'This was done to me by the Stenlarian High Command afterwards.'

'Your own side?' I say, cutting the length of wire I need. 'Why?'

'My crime was a lack of imagination, leading to the loss of my regiment.' She leaves the drawer open and continues to pick out the items on my list. 'The punishment was to remove my ability for logic and maths, and replace it with machine efficiency, so that I would be unable to think any way other than the way that slaughtered my regiment.'

'What did they...?' I stop mid-question, feeling embarrassed to ask further.

'Sent me to the Stenlarian labour reserves.' Clara waits for me to finish before taking the reel back. She tilts her head back and sweeps her hair aside, putting her hand on the bald spots that have never healed. 'They gave me *this*'—she touches the metal plate around the lenses—'that I might *see* the error of my ways.'

'They replaced your eye?' I gaze at the side of her head, at the rough stitching around the plate. 'What was wrong with the one you had?'

'They replaced more than that.' She taps her head and winds her hair back around the scars. 'They replaced the left side of my brain.'

'*Your brain?* Did it... *does* it hurt?'

'No. They put me on the table and, when I woke up, I couldn't move. They left me there for a day to let me understand they'd replaced every part I needed for moving and functioning, that I could be turned off like an appliance if they desired. When they allowed me to move, I found I had a heavy head and a new eye that could go from microscopic to astronomy-grade telescopic vision.'

'I don't understand.' I wind the wire around the bare terminals. 'Why do that?'

'Stenlarians don't like wasting resources. If you can repurpose people into something useful, that's more efficient than killing them, yes?'

'Yeah.' I shake my head in disbelief, and close the panel as I finish. 'But if you can't do maths, how do you...?' I gesture around the bay.

'A quartermaster's job doesn't involve maths or logic. It's about remembering every single thing you have on board and how many of each you have. None of that requires maths; it requires a good memory, and that, I still have.'

'One more thing then...' I place my hand on the lighting panel.

'Well, you've done how, what, why, and does it hurt, so it must be something new.'

'How bright do you like it down here?' I grin and flip the switch; the bay lights up from one end to the other, dim but functional. 'Sorry, I thought I'd fixed the charge to them.'

'You have.' Clara reaches up with almost childlike wonder, using her sleeve to wipe the dust from the bulb above her, the light painful after the near dark. 'I'm just a bad housekeeper.'

'Not that I've seen,' I say, moving down to help her with cleaning the bulbs. 'While I'm here, didn't you need to tell me about how to recognise valuable items?'

Clara's human eye squints against the brightness. 'Oh, that's easy—you bring back everything and pass it to me. The captain's got no more of an eye for finery than any of us.'

'Good to know. What have we got in the way of metals and something to melt them with?'

'Ah, yes.' Clara takes an elegant backwards step, and points down to a box on the floor. 'Molybdenum alloys, which you'll have to lift because I'm not strong enough.'

'Have you got something capable of melting that?' I stare at the box without much confidence.

She points up to the back of the stores to where a small safe sits. 'That contains a storm forge that we took from an Ascended ship some years back—never really found a use for it, but it can melt and shape any metal, and we never sold it on. Just assumed the captain likes shiny bits of engineering.'

'She doesn't strike me as much of an engineer; she doesn't have engineer's hands.' I turn my own over to show my palm, the skin still scarred smooth from a thousand small burns.

'She was once. It was her who designed this ship, you know.' My eyebrows shoot up in surprise. Clara pauses for a second. 'But she hasn't been herself, not since a few months back.'

'What happened a few months back?'

'Ah, well, suffice it to say that, up until then, Raley was the first officer on the ship, and had been since we set out.' Clara sighs. 'Then Errin turned up and, suddenly, everything's about tearing across the skies to untold riches and damn anyone who causes trouble for that plan...'

'Yeah, about that...' I take the apple from my pocket again. '...I lose this bet, and she's really going to roast me?'

'The captain won't, no.' I start to breathe a sigh of relief when she adds, 'But Errin will.'

A Question Of Performance

I take the forge and box of Molybdenum and load it on a grav sled, then head to the weapons bay where Raley is waiting for me. The cannons downstairs are all mounted on suspended trays with heavy, metal wheels mounted on rails that curve up into the ceiling.

Recoil will go against the top of the ship, rather than pulling it out of line to the side.

The book's knowledge trickles down in my head as I look at the rails—these are standard mountings for something that size. I look at the carved metal barrel, cold-forged some time ago, the scoring on the inside of the barrel telling me that it's seen a good amount of use over the years, but very little in the way of maintenance. I pull the barrel back and examine the edges.

Someone wasn't thinking when they put it in the cast; a frequent design flaw caused by those who try to get more weapons out in less time.

The words from the book spill out into my head, and I tip the barrel downwards. The cannonball slides forwards, and I scramble to catch it before it lands on the deck. I place it with care to the side, and Raley's foot comes down next to it, to ensure it doesn't roll any further. I manhandle the safe to the deck then open the box to reveal the ingots within.

'Can you start melting them down,' I say, looking at her. 'I need enough to make a few channels on the inside of the gun and something to make a seal at the end.'

Raley sets the metal heating and looks around. 'What are you going to do with this?'

'All good things to those who wait.' I smile and wait for the metal to melt down. 'As you say, it's all a matter of taking pride in your craft.'

Raley looks up as the third bell sounds, then back at me. 'As long as you're done a few hours before dinner.'

'It'll be close.' I focus on the forge. 'We need to chill it and then treat it before we fit it.'

'Why not just do it the usual way?"

'My dad taught me this method. They called it Bright Drawn. Best metal the Olympus forges ever produced. It'll stand up to anything.'

'Slowest as well.'

'Excellence can't be rushed.' I turn to her with a wide smile.

She returns my look with a pensive expression.

'What is it?' I ask.

She blinks, her reverie broken. 'For a second there you reminded me of someone I knew a long time ago.'

'Sorry.'

'Don't be. The memories are good; it's the present I'd rather not face.'

*

It's a few thousand degrees and a few inches of blisters later when we get the lines all the way up in the top of the barrel. I turn the edge and narrow the bottom of the barrel, making a far smaller seal that will focus the concussive force of the blast when the launch mechanism goes off. If the book is right, it should give the cannon the needed extra range and power.

As long as it doesn't blow the back off when it fires...

I reinforce the bottom of the gun, then set a transverse spring behind the impact block at the back of the cannon.

Should prevent it from launching through the top of the deck.

'Doesn't seem like much changing up an eighty-eight to a one-oh-five,' Raley says. 'Why isn't everyone doing this sort of thing?'

'Are these the best cannons that money can buy?' I glance back at her as I finish polishing the inside with thermal grease.

'No.' Raley shakes her head. 'There's a whole range of things that are better than these. We may look impressive, but we're one step away from scrappy pirate trash.'

'Ever figure that the other guns might just be engineered like this to make the difference?'

'Possible.' She shrugs. 'Never gave it much thought. I like blades, y'know?'

'Well, I like guns.' I smile, and beckon for the wire brush. 'Always liked guns.'

Raley passes it to me. 'Why's that? What's the appeal?'

'Why do you like blades?'

'Looks like a simple piece of metal,' she says, smiling as she draws the short sword at her hip, 'but it's not—it's a weapon of war, designed at a time when humanity had only just started to learn how to kill. If you know how to use it, it's lethal to almost anything that walks, but if you don't respect it, it'll kill anyone who tries to use it.'

'Good answer. Now tell me the real reason.'

She pauses, then smiles. 'It's what I aspire to be: simple enough that everyone thinks they know what I'm about but, under the surface, nothing but blood, pain and death...'

'All right. I'll remember that.'

'Your turn.' She sheathes the sword and waits attentive for my answer.

'They're what I aspire to be,' I say. 'Shiny on the outside, well-engineered on the inside.'

'And wide enough to fit anything in...' She grins, cupping the barrel with both hands.

Her grin is infectious, and I mirror her without thinking. 'Well, you know...'

'Now the real reason.' She schools her face back to neutral.

'You understand that.' I point at her sword. 'Did you always understand it?'

'Took me some time, but I knew from the first time I picked one up that it would be the largest part of my life.'

'Why?'

'Because it felt right. It spoke to me in a way nothing else ever had.'

'I'd be lying if I said it was like that for me.' I smooth the metal over the casing and mould it with my Isogloves—couldn't use them on the inside of the barrel due to the lack of space, but here... 'I was good at fixing things from when I was a kid. I used to put the oven back together when it didn't work; graduated to fixing the systems in the apartment when I was a little older. My dad saw something in what I could do, got the idea that I should be doing more.'

'You didn't agree?'

'I didn't like that they spent all their time and money on giving me a chance when it should have been me helping provide for them. They knew that they didn't have enough to get me through the academy and still have enough left to give themselves an easy life later, but they wouldn't hear anything else, so I did everything I could to make them proud of me.'

'And were they?'

'For a while.'

'What changed?'

'They died.' I keep my voice level.

'We don't have to talk about this.' Raley's hand moves to my arm, her voice contrite. 'I know what it's like to lose people.'

'It's all right.' I smooth the metal and test the surface with the Isoglove. 'They lived long enough to give me the chance I needed; they saw me graduate as the best in my year—I did what they wanted me to.'

'But was it what *you* wanted to do?'

'It was. Dad was right when he said there was something in me. You understand the sword; you understand what it's about. Me? I understand metal, and ballistics; I understand armour. I learned everything the academy had to teach and then some. They gave me the option to stay on and be a teacher there and, for a while I did. It let me give something back to Mum and Dad.' I turn back and lock the barrel in place, and point at the shell lying to the side. Raley picks it up and slides it into the barrel.

'And when they died, I saw no more point. The academy wasn't doing anything new; the real inventions were out there in the black. I signed up on a ship and headed out.'

'With the loser who traded you all in for his own ass?'

'Yep, never underestimate the power of commercials.'

'And here you are now.' She pats me on the ass with a grin. 'About to get stuffed for dinner!'

'Tell you what,' I say, swatting at her hand, 'this'll be ready in an hour, so I'll make you a deal.'

'I'm listening.'

'*When* I win, I get your extra bit of tack as well as the one I'm promised.'

'All right. And when you lose?'

I reach over and jiggle her longsword's hilt. 'You get to carve the prime rump...'

She gives a wry smile. 'I prefer breast.' She looks at me with a raised eyebrow, and I feel the warmth of her smile. 'So, by the looks of it, I'll be going hungry tonight either way...'

'Oi, less of that.' I aim a playful swipe at her head which she avoids without conscious thought. 'Best get the captain then— let's see what you're eating tonight.'

*

The rest of the crew are up on deck for the start of the dog-watch. Captain Morgan looks down from the wheel and locks it in place. 'Able Starwoman Solovias reckons she can get one-oh-five performance out of an eighty-eight cannon.' She moves around the wheel and stands with her hands on the rail. 'She's made a bet with me on the results.'

There's a murmur around the crew; sounds very much like most people don't make bets with the captain.

And with good reason...

Morgan raises her hands for silence and looks down again. 'If she succeeds in what she's promised'—she points down to the left, where there's a basket full of solid biscuits—'there's a whole extra round of tack for everyone, and I'll make sure you've got something to wash it down with.'

There's a ragged cheer from the deck that soon settles as they realise, she hasn't given the flip side of the bet.

'If she fails...' Morgan says, pointing down and to the right, where there's another basket with Errin stood behind it. Errin reaches in and pulls out a handful of spices. '...If she fails, she's going to personally provide a few extra slices of meat in everyone's meal tonight.'

There's a muted cheer from the crew as everyone turns to stare at me.

More to appease the captain than because they're happy about it...

'Your target is there...' She points to the starboard bow, where a single large asteroid is spinning. 'Too big for an eighty-eight to make a dent, but maybe a one-oh-five...'

I lean on the bow and feel Raley standing close. She nudges me, slipping a breather mask and an enervasion field into my hands behind her back. 'In case it doesn't work,' she whispers. 'You'll have more luck dropping off the side; there's no way she'll bother trying to bring the ship around to catch you.'

'Thanks.' I pocket the gear and focus on the asteroid. 'But I'm not wrong.'

The first gun fires, and the shell clips the asteroid and ricochets away from the surface.

Not enough impact area to get inside the rock.

I look up to see Morgan nod, and the second gun fires. The shell smashes into the asteroid, detonating a second later; there's a flare as the rock shatters into a million shards. The deck erupts in cheering, and Errin closes the spice basket. The captain turns to the crew and smiles.

'Tack it is...'

Not from Around Here

Morgan beckons for me to come up to the wheel as the rest of the crew go about preparing the meal. I arrive at the top and see that her lipstick is gone, neither red nor green. I stand at the top of the stairs and wait.

'As good as your word. How did you manage that after only being here a day?'

Her tone of voice is light, almost casual. Her movement behind the wheel is controlled though, the rest of her in perfect stillness. *She's holding on to something there...*

'One cannon is just like another,' I reply, with a shrug. 'The edging on them can always be improved and, when you get everything to fit properly, you lose less of the power when the charge detonates.'

'Good. You didn't try and baffle me with what you did.'

'What would be the point? You need me to be straight with you, that way you know I'm being straight if I ever tell you, it *can't* be done.'

'Don't like that word, *can't*.'

'That's why I'm being straight with you. If I ever have to use that word, you'll know it's because it's true.'

'Most engineers don't like giving away the secrets of what they do,' she says with a frown. 'They think it makes them more disposable if I know all their secrets.'

'Not at all.' My grin gets broad. 'Just because I've told you what I did doesn't mean you can do it instead of me.'

'True.' She points to the port side, where the ship that brought

us here now is floating, derelict. 'I know you didn't arrive on that
ship, but I also know that whatever brought you here is connected
to it. We didn't see you at all, then there was some sort of distortion
and both ships fell out of it. While it's clear the ship your former
captain took with him blew a hole in that ship, vessels like the
one he had don't have the power to jump like that. I haven't seen
anything pull that kind of move in more than a decade, and I
won't pretend to have any understanding of what happened,
but something that's able to drag whole ships around without a
generator the size of a moon is of interest to me.'

'Want me to take a look?' I lean over the side to see the ship still
moored by a number of ropes. 'I should be able to figure it out.'

'Not today. Your shift is up. You're back on at first bell on the
morning watch; you can take a look then.'

'And if I want to do it in my own time?'

'Knock yourself out. Still need you back on shift for first bell.
As long as you're not late, you can do what you like.'

'All right then.' I smile and secure my line to the side of the
ship, before dropping down onto the roof of the other ship.

I cycle the door lock and step in. This close to the *Unbroken
Dawn*, the atmosphere is holding steady. The inside of the ship
hasn't changed at all—warmer than it was due to the air from the
Dawn—and there's a faint smell of blood in the air.

Like something has just thawed...

I walk through into the wheel room. The suit is still floating
there, bloated after days of floating dead, skin filled with the
remnants of decaying internal organs, but it's thawed enough for
the blood which has escaped to be floating through the air in thick
drops, surrounding it like a liquid suit.

Gross.

I place the breathermask on my face and move forwards, my
eyes following the body. There are still a few books in here, most
of them in plastic slipcases.

*Someone wanted to make sure that, in the event of a pressure loss, the
books wouldn't be damaged.*

I float up to the top deck and examine the controls. Very
similar to those on the *Unbroken Dawn*, save smaller. The chart is

still there; it's a lot like the one I found in the book earlier except, unlike that one, the images aren't moving. I peel the plastic layer back and take the chart out, folding it closed and slipping it in my thigh pocket. There's a thin line on the wall behind the main wheel and what looks to be a sliding puzzle behind a clear plastic sheet next to it. The pattern is formed of a number of multi-coloured lines which look as if they all link up, just not at the same time, looks like a way of making sure that the ship doesn't use too much power at once. The door has a green line around its outer edge.

That'll be a good place to start.

I move the blocks until the green line shifts from one side to the other. There's a click from somewhere, and the wall shifts outwards a fraction, followed by a slight release of air from the seal. A pale green light escapes through the gap. I pull the wall all the way back.

Cosy.

Inside is a single bunk with just enough space to slide in and lie flat. It has the look of a long haul bunk, if the helmsman needed a rest but couldn't be too far away from the helm in case of emergency. A ship this size couldn't be out in the middle of nowhere without some sort of support system. There are no manifests in here—it's not big enough to carry cargo of any quantity. I move back outside, leaving the hatch open. The rest of the ship has been looted by the crew of the *Dawn* for anything worthwhile, but it looks like all the books have been left behind.

Because here, knowledge isn't considered a treasure.

A few personal effects in the bunks – books on physics, biology, what looks to be a religious symbol of some sort on a chain. I take one of the kitbags from the end of a bed and load it up with the sparse belongings. There's a small ladder leading downwards, and I drop down into what looks to be the engine room—two turbines that aren't large enough to power even a small ground skimmer, much less something this size. I put my Isogloves on and run a hand over the surface of one of the turbines: small amount of residual power, but nothing of any concern. There's a whole mass of cogs and bolts on the other wall, all of them running individual systems, their names listed on each of the cogs.

Dynamo driven technology.

There are a number of spanners and sockets on the far wall, each appearing to correspond to a particular cog, or set of cogs. Makes sense from a practical point of view—if anything ever happened to the main engine, you could keep powering the essential systems by ensuring you keep one or more of the cogs turning through old-fashioned hard work. There's a cog on the panel marked as Navigation, and I check the sockets to get the right one before spinning it up. The light on the panel next to the cog lights up and starts to build as the energy increases. I return up to the main deck and pull the navigation panel—there's a small hole for a cog in the back of it; looks like the same kind of socket I was using in the engineering section. I take it and head back up onto the *Dawn*.

Raley is at the helm, Morgan having gone downstairs for the captain's share of the extra rations. 'Good work today,' Raley says as I climb back over the railing. 'She'll not forget that in a hurry.'

'Is that a good thing or a bad thing?' I stand beside her and gaze out into deep space.

'Both.' She shrugs. 'We've had to get used to that from the captain these past few months. She can be the most solid character you've ever met or the biggest psychotic you hoped you'd never meet...'

'And only the lipstick tells the difference?'

'There are other warning signs.' Raley tilts her head to the side. 'But if I tell you them all, your head will be spinning from now till the end of time. If you last another week, you'll have an idea of what you can and can't do around her, and when.'

'Be nice if I knew the signs so I didn't bet my ass the next time...'

'You'll learn.' She tilts the wheel, and the stars revolve around us. 'Out here, you never make a bet until you're sure you've already won it.'

'I was sure.' I think I sound confident.

She snorts with laughter. 'Yeah, and that's why both your hands were on your ass the whole time we were firing those cannons, right?'

I blush. 'That obvious?'

'If you'd been any more clenched, they'd have had to get breaching gear to get in there to stuff you.' Raley smiles with genuine warmth. 'You should go down and get some of that food you earned for all of us.'

'I'll stay a while.' I lean on the rail next to the wheel. 'When are you off shift?'

'Not doing anything for a while.'

'Sure you want to spend your time with me?'

She pauses and her smile gets wider. 'You remind me very much of someone I knew a long time ago.' She leans back against the ship's rails. 'Don't worry, I'm not going to get weird on you, but I enjoy your company, so if you're all right with that, I'll stay a while.'

'I'm all right with it.' I reach out to squeeze her hand on impulse. 'If not for your help today, I'd have been a hog roast up on deck now.'

'Fine then,' she says, squeezing my hand in return. 'While you're here, how about I give you a tour of the stars?'

*

Raley pulls a chart from the wooden box mounted below the wheel. Folded a thousand times over from years of use, she opens it to the first crease and points at a black pin in the middle, with a blue and several red ones nearby.

'Us, as of yesterday,' she explains. 'The captain likes to use black pins to show where we are, blue to show where we've been, and red to show points where we might be going.'

'Not very decisive, is she?'

'She likes to keep her options open.' Raley turns the wheel again, pointing at a globe in its centre with a spike made from brass suspended in a clear viscous solution. 'This points true upwards at all times. It's possible to sail by the stars without this, but it's far more difficult.'

'Can you do it?' I ask, looking at the globe. 'Navigate, I mean?'

'Not something I tend to do. I know how to hold the wheel

steady and to plot a course, if someone gives me an easy map to work from, but I don't know how to properly plot courses which avoid gravity or plan slingshot moves like a real navigator would.' She points at the brass handle on the right-hand side of the rail. 'That controls how much effort we put into moving forwards. When it's all the way forwards, we're running at full speed, but we can't do that unless we've got someone on every sail.'

'Not often then?'

'No. Only in battle conditions and, even then, only when we're losing badly...'

'Do we do much running away?'

'Only when it's Imperial Navy. Never mess with those boys; they're the only people worse than the Stenlarians.'

'How many factions are out there then? Where I come from, the Jovians are always after the Martians, the Venusians just watch everybody get on with it, and the Terrans keep trying to convince the universe they're still in charge.'

'And I haven't got a clue what you're on about.' She smiles as she locks the wheel in place and takes the chart out again. 'We're on the edge of the Desolation of Tanis.' She points to an area in the middle of the chart, bordered at the top by a range of stars that seem like they're too large, too close together, there's no way that so many stars could be in such close proximity. 'The Dragon on the top there, the Stenlarian Empire and the Imperial Core to the rear, the Illenial Abyss to the high side, and the Invarian Wastes to the low.'

'None of that sounds particularly inviting.'

'None of it is supposed to be.' She unfolds the chart at the top. 'If you're timid, you shouldn't be out here...'

'So where are we going now?'

'She's got a few ideas.' Raley looks at the chart. 'The problem is that most of them are somewhere near the Broken Hollows, and nothing good ever came out of there.'

'Why's it called the Broken Hollows?'

'Because the worlds there went dark some years ago, and nothing's come out of it since then.' She points at the top of the chart. 'There are rich pickings for those who are willing to take the risk, but it's not good, honest piracy. It's like looting bodies for swag, except there aren't any bodies...'

'Have you been there before?'

'Once...' Her gaze drifts far away for a second, and she pauses before looking back at me. 'I was Stenlarian Empire before I ever went freelance. Three dreadnoughts went in there to pacify the Hollows before they were broken, and that's where we found *it*. Whatever it was destroyed two of them, and I was on the one that made it back with a quarter of the ship missing and more than seventy per cent casualties. I took up the sword when the empire tried to punish me for the failure... Clara wasn't so lucky.'

'Clara didn't have much good to say about the Stenlarians.'

'No. No, there's not much good to say about them any way you look at it.'

'What did you find out there?'

'Nothing but death.' Her gaze goes distant again. 'Something was eating through the whole system and leaving nothing behind but the bones and the broken bits of the civilisations that once thrived out there.'

'Something *ate* the system? What the hell could eat a whole system? Where did it go after that?'

'Don't know. But I don't want to be there when it finds its way out again. I was working on a starbase when the captain found me.' She smiles as the memory flows over her. 'Or, rather, I caught her—she'd been dropped out of a ship and was heading for deep space when I first saw her.'

'Why did you catch her?'

'Never let anyone die out in the cold.' Raley stiffens as another memory rises. 'If I do for others, one day someone may do the same for me.'

'Is that it?'

'In the beginning. I knew she was special the first time she touched me.'

'How so?' I lean closer.

'It was like holding a live line, like she knew me, like she'd face death for me. I've never known anyone like that before; she was the brightest soul I ever met...' Her voice catches on the words,

and she glances down as she pauses to order her thoughts. 'This...
this that she is now, that's not her.' She pauses and lifts her head
up again, her eyes holding the promise of yesterday in them. 'You
know when I said you reminded me of someone earlier?'

'The captain?' I raise an eyebrow. 'Me? My arms are thicker
than her waist.'

'When I first met her, she was bigger. She...' Raley pauses again,
and glances away. 'Gods, you're just like her back then. I'm sorry,
just memories.'

'I'm sorry too. Sometimes, even good memories don't feel
good when they're all you have left of someone.'

'I'm all right.' Her voice softens. 'It's just that some things you
don't forget, and some things embed themselves in your head.'

'Yeah.' I pat her on the shoulder. 'I know.'

She looks over at me and sees the truth of the words in my
eyes. She nods and folds the chart, putting it back in the box. 'We
should head downstairs—there's extra biscuit for all. That'll surely
make you popular with the crew.'

'Popular enough to make a difference?'

'Not yet. But keep it up, and you'll get there soon enough. You
can live with any hardship as long as you have the little luxuries to
work with.'

Friends And Allies

It's an hour into the second dog shift when our relief arrives, and we go downstairs to the mess. There's not much left in the stock pots but, as we come down the stairs, the cook reaches behind the counter and pulls out two plates piled high with food.

'We couldn't let the person who won us extra food go without,' she says with a smile. 'There's a little extra from each of the crew, and it keeps for weeks, so store it in a dry place. No one will mess with it as long as they know it's yours.'

I take the tray and nod my thanks. The cook reaches back down under the counter and pulls out a jug of amber liquid. Raley shakes her head and points to the water, then looks at me in puzzlement.

'Where's your tankard?' she asks.

'Tankard?'

'Yeah, that you drink out of?' She examines my waist. 'Left it on the other ship?'

'Uh, yeah.' I nod, bemused. 'Must have done.'

She turns to the cook. 'Put it on my tab, Jensca. Give her one of the wooden ones.'

Jensca reaches down under the counter and pulls out a small wooden mug, places it on my tray, and pours a generous measure of the liquid into it. Raley nods, and looks over at the tables, tilting her head to indicate the one at the back. There's space enough down here for maybe twenty people at a time, but we're among the last to arrive. She moves over to the far end of the room and takes a seat with her back towards the hull.

'Don't believe everything you hear.' Raley points with her fork at Jensca. 'Goodwill like that is a bought commodity, make no mistake. If you mess up, and we end up short of food, they'll take whatever you've got to save themselves from having to eat the sweepings off the floor.'

'I have no doubts. Hunger is a great leveller, as is thirst. You don't drink?'

'I can tackle anything in the world...' Raley says, taking a sip of the water, '...except strong booze. One mug of that, and I'm staggering. I just don't like taking the chance.'

I nod and tuck into the food. It tastes like beef, the gravy thick and meaty. The tack is hard enough to be used as plates of armour, and I break bits off to leave soaking in the gravy. Raley smiles and points down at the floating chunks.

'Look on the bright side,' she says, 'at least the rats won't eat your tack—they've got more taste.'

'We've got rats on the ship?'

'Not unless they're paying customers.' She smiles and finishes off her water, raising her tankard to the cook.

My fork stops halfway to my mouth. 'Wait, we have paying customers?'

'Yeah...' She looks at me with a serious expression for a few seconds then breaks into an infectious grin, her eyes twinkling. 'Relax, everyone knows rats don't pay!'

I shake my head and continue eating as Jensca pours Raley some more water.

'The captain was green when she came down,' Jensca's voice is all but a whisper.

Raley nods and avoids looking up till Jensca's departed. She sighs and looks up at me.

'Is that becoming a more regular occurrence?'

'The Green Killer rather than the Red Lady? Yep, in recent times, there's been more killer than lady.'

'Was she always like that?'

'No, never. This is new.' Raley leans closer. 'We *salvaged* a few things some months back. One of them was a set of charts and what looked to be trinkets that the captain took to her chamber before deciding what to hand out to the crew.'

'I thought booty was meant to be shared equally. Pirate's code and all that.'

'Pirate's code...' She snorts with laughter. 'Some people are more equal than others. It's her ship, and we all get a share of the spoils when we get back to port, but she's the captain, so anything particularly shiny goes into her personal collection—perks of the job.'

'What was it she found?'

'Don't know. But, when she found it, the ship took a heading up the system, and we haven't stopped yet. That was three weeks back.'

'Sure she's not heading home by a different route?'

'I couldn't tell either way. But the last navigator we had saw the pattern for what we were doing and called it to the attention of Errin.' Raley spreads her hands wide. 'Errin brought it to the captain, as any good first mate should...'

'And...'

'And the captain called a ship meeting, said that she'd found a way to untold riches and so we were heading up.'

'The navigator disagreed?'

'You could say that.' She takes another long drink of water. 'The navigator said the course we were on would take us straight through The Dragon and into the Broken Hollows.'

'Which would be bad?'

'Like I said, nothing comes out of there. I can't say as I was enthused by the matter, but the captain brought out the contents of the box to show everyone.'

She reaches down and pulls a gem from one of her belt pouches—deep blue in colouration with flawless facets throughout. She passes it to me, and my hand sinks under the weight. I admire the symmetry for a second and pass it back to her.

'Invarian blood sapphire,' she says. 'Morgan promised me one of these when she first met me, and I didn't believe it, but I believed in her. She gave this to me within a year of meeting her. I've always held it close because she's more precious than it, and I wanted her to know that. One of these is worth as much as this ship and, after she found the salvage, she gave one to every member of the crew as if they were trinkets; said there were thousands where we were headed.'

'What's the problem?'

'When the navigator argued that we'd never make it, she said that all the money in the universe doesn't make any difference if you're not there to spend it.' She shrugs and puts the sapphire away. 'Me? I'm just a sword for hire—what do I know about ships?'

'What did the captain do?'

'You know why I gave you the breather when you made that bet? I saw first-hand what happens when she finds something she doesn't like. She repeated the order to plot the route, and when the navigator refused, the captain retired to her quarters and sent Errin to deal with the matter. Errin put an apple in the navigator's mouth, stuffed and greased her, then put her on a pole and slow-roasted her by starlight. Then she had the meat salted and sold it at the next port...' Raley's gaze is far away again. 'That sort of put an end to any thoughts of mutiny.'

'You lot outnumber her fifty to one.' I glance around the mess area, very aware that we're alone.

'Errin.' Raley refocuses on me. 'As long as Errin is around, there's nothing we can do.'

'What's so special about her?'

'Errin... We found her out at a deserted starport eight months ago, surrounded by the dead Looked like whatever had killed the station hadn't managed to get her.'

'What was it that got the station?'

'Don't know. Sorry, it's times like these when I realise how much in the dark we are about a lot of stuff. Morgan brought Errin on board and nursed her back to health. That was when the captain changed. When Errin recovered, she offered her sword, and the captain accepted.'

'She's one woman with a sword. Aren't you the swordmaster on ship?'

'Swordmaster? I'm the trainer on ship. She's not a swordswoman—she's a killer, pure and simple. Whatever she took on at the station was far more dangerous than me. I've only seen her fight once and that was enough.'

'So why don't we just get off at the next port?'

'We're on the edge of the Desolation of Tanis,' she replies. 'There are no ports between here and where we're going. Anyone who wanted off did so when they sold off the navigator-kebab.'

'Thought the captain said she was going to sell off anyone she didn't like at the next port?'

'But she didn't say when we'd reach the next port, did she? Just made it sound more palatable to all of you, the promise that you might be able to leave.'

'Why didn't you go?'

She glances down at the sapphire. 'One of those can buy you a ship of your own or a house on any world you want and food enough for the rest of your life. With ten, you could have luxury and enough life in which to enjoy it. I've been out here long enough to know an opportunity when I see one and, if she's right, there's enough there for all of us to live easily forever. If she's wrong... well, I could never leave her, even if she's not her anymore.'

'Do you think that's why she's doing it?' I lean closer still. 'I mean, she's got a ship and a crew. Who'd want to give up this life?'

'Someone who's lived it.' She smiles and the look in her eyes makes her seem ten years older. 'Guessing you haven't been out here that long?'

'Three weeks. This is all fairly new to me.'

'Well, if fighting breaks out, stay by me—I'll keep you safe. In the meantime, get some sleep; you're back up on deck in less than eight hours.'

*

I go down below and over to where Shen is resting in his bunk. I put my hand on his shoulder.

'Mmm? Whassup?' He turns and looks at me through tired eyes.

'Need you to look at something,' I say. 'Won't take long.'

'Can't it wait till morning?'

'No.' I pull the panel from the crippled ship out of my bag and show him.

'Nice display.' He sits up in his bunk, taking the panel from me, tracing lines on the thick plastic with his finger. 'Looks like it was a set of jumps. They started here'—he taps the top of the panel— 'and they continued till they got to here.' He taps the screen again. 'Which is where we are.'

'Where were they headed?'

'That's the interesting thing.' He points. 'There are four coordinates here: three for location and one for time. Prior to the last jump—the one that brought us all here—there's a variance only in the time, not the distance...'

'Meaning?'

'Meaning that we didn't go anywhere at all. We stayed in the same place... but we jumped to a different time...'

'A different time?' I raise an eyebrow

He gestures at the panel. 'That's what it says. Yesterday was 21/08/4375, to this thing's reckoning. The first jump was programmed in for yesterday, when we came from 02/08/2210.'

'Yesterday was 02/08/2210.' I examine the display. 'So how come this says...?'

'Do you recognise anything here? The technology we're using?'

'Not a bit of it. The stuff they're using is different in a number of ways to ours. They seem to be less advanced when it comes to weapons, but their armour and shield technology is well beyond ours.'

'Same problem with their navigation. This is the first thing I've seen that looks similar to what we use.'

'How does the navigation differ?'

'They're still using paper charts when we know that the only way to accurately plot things is in three dimensions. They're looking at space like it's a flat plane.' He points at the display. 'And as far as I can see, they never travel above or below that plane.'

'How do they get anywhere? The universe isn't designed like a piece of paper...'

'Beats me. All I know is that the third coordinate never changes; everything they do is on the same level.' He turns the panel over and shows me the slide controls at the bottom of it. 'It works on electricity. You change the orientation with this control, then the other axis with the other controls.'

'What if they just see it as a reorientation rather than a change of plane?'

'Well, this is the first panel I've seen like ours.' He changes the slide back. 'Everything else on the ship works on paper charts.'

'All right, keep this.' I pat the panel. 'Let me know if you find out anything more about how to work it.'

'Will do.' He puts it in his bag and turns back to me.

'There's something else,' I say, 'but I think you need to be more awake when you see it.'

'Why? What's so special about it?'

'Trust me; you need to be awake when you see what it is.'

'And I'm going to be able to sleep now you've told me that?'

'It's worth it. I'm in the engineer hold below decks.'

'All right; better be good, whatever it is...'

I think back for a second to the conversation with Raley down below. Shen sees the look in my eyes and frowns, asking the silent question, *What?* I draw close to him and glance around to see if anyone else is paying attention. There's isolated snoring from the other bunks, and at least one of the crew is pretending not to be listening. I lean close and push Shen back into his bunk, kissing him on the lips and drawing the curtain behind me. He looks at me as if I've gone mad and opens his mouth to speak. I put my finger on his lips, take out my pad of paper, and scribble *Play Along* in large letters. He nods and rustles the blanket next to him.

'You have to be careful of the captain,' I whisper. 'Has she asked you to plot a course anywhere yet?'

'She keeps talking about The Dragon,' he whispers back. 'But the only way to get to it is a course straight through a number of volatile stars. We'd be better off stepping overboard without a suit.'

I nod and start patting the bunk, picking up speed in a rhythmic pattern. 'Whatever course she asks you to plot,' I say, looking him straight in the eye, 'plot it. Don't argue with her, no matter how dangerous it looks; no matter if it looks like we won't make it—plot it.'

'Why?'

'They don't have another navigator because the last one argued with her.' I'm now thumping the bunk with reasonable force. He still seems puzzled. 'Look, the previous navigator got cooked.'

Shen's eyes go wide at the revelation, and he opens his mouth. I put my hand over it and shake my head, then realise I've stopped thumping the bed and let out a loud sigh. I shake my head again, and he nods as I take my hand away.

'Catch up with me after the next shift,' I whisper, unbuttoning two buttons on my top and my trousers, then ruffling my hair. 'I'll show you what I've found down there.'

I step backwards out of the bunk and close the curtain behind me, doing up my trousers as I look back around the quarters. There's no pretence at not paying attention from all those present, and I turn to face them as I close my top up again.

'What?' I look around at all of them.

'Not a problem to us.' One of the older women, looks like she came from a heavy G world, with long, straight, black hair only a fraction of a shade darker than her skin and a face that's seen better years, leans out of her bunk and stares up at me. 'Just make sure you clean up after yourself.'

'I will. Sorry, didn't mean to make any noise.'

'That's all right.' She steps out of the bunk and stretches backwards. 'You're the one that got us the extra dinner tonight, aren't you?'

'I am.'

'It's appreciated.' She points around the room. 'We all understand the risk you took to get it—it'll not be forgotten in a hurry.'

'You're welcome.'

The woman steps closer. She's far larger than me, with hands like shovels and muscles ridged all the way up and down her arms. 'I'm Syla.' She leans in and offers her hand to me. It has the feel of a piece of iron, both in strength and texture. 'Salvage team, work under Clara. See you're close with Raley?'

'She's been showing me around.' I flex my fingers to get the feeling back in them as Syla lets go of my hand. 'I'm new around here.'

'We can see that.' The voice comes from the upper bunk: a young girl with a scar running from the corner of her mouth to the point of her ear. Doesn't look like she got it in a fight—the line is too fine, like a razor cut, and the muscles on either side of the line aren't keeping track of what the others are doing.

'That's Densi.' Syla straightens up. 'Don't mind her; she just doesn't like you much.'

'Why?' I look up at Densi as she returns to sharpening a thin, silver blade.

'Because you haven't got any scars yet.' Syla smiles with almost maternal resonance. 'Don't worry, girl, you stay with us long enough, you'll get a few lines on you.' She turns her arms over, the forearms crisscrossed with thin lines. 'Besides, keep bringing us good luck, and we'll keep you alive.' She looks up at Densi. 'Isn't that right, *Densi?*'

Densi looks down. 'Yeah.' Her tone says it's anything but. 'That's right.'

Syla turns to me again. 'So... are you bunking with us or have you got Stala's quarters?'

'I've got Stala's quarters. Not being antisocia—'

'Not at all,' Syla interrupts. 'I'd sleep privately if I could, but I'm only good for wrecking things. Takes a specialist to get their own place on the ship. Well, I'll let you get to your bunk then, no doubt we'll see you shortly.'

I turn to leave and get two steps before Densi clears her throat, so I turn back. Syla is looking into Densi's bunk and nods, before turning back to me.

'What's wrong?' I look up at Syla, and she shifts from foot to foot for a second before pointing down at Shen's bunk.

'Your... er...your man there.'

'He's not my man.' I correct her without thinking about it and see her glance over at Densi with the beginnings of a smile.

'No? He's a free agent then?' Syla asks.

'He's his own man.'

'You don't mind if we...' she says, nodding downwards at the bunk, '...make a bid?'

I grin as I hear Shen whisper a quiet invective at me.

'No trouble to this girl. One thing though...'

'Sure, what is it?'

'Let him get some sleep first.'

Watching Me, Watching You

I realise with a yawn that I've been on duty for the best part of a week without a real break. Every rest I've had has been interrupted at some point by some minor engineering crisis. Nothing's been touched in the engineering section when I return; it appears everything is as I left it.

Stala was their only engineer, which means I've got no one to cover things when I'm asleep. There has to be a way around this.

The thought isn't a cheerful one, and I crawl back inside the small bunk space, looking over at the books on the shelf. I reach over for the one with the weapons in it and then pull my hand back.

Without someone to keep an eye on me, I could get lost in there for a long time.

I leave the book on the side and take out the chart instead, examining the guide for the section that indicates the Broken Hollows. I unfold some of the chart, taking care not to look back at it till I've folded it in the way the index has directed. I sneak a peek. The bottom edge is glowing like fire, and I look up into the area beyond it. The stars in the system are dimmer than the others I've seen, almost like there's a filter over them. I focus on the planets in the system. There's no green to indicate land or blue of water on their surfaces, no silver or grey for buildings; just black, interspersed with red lines.

Dead.

There are four planets in total; the last of them still has faint vestiges of green upon it, but most of the surface is the same black with red lines running through it. I try to look closer at the chart, bringing my eyes down to level with it. Something moves in the darkness around the fourth planet, on the other side of it.

Something moves...

I look closer as that something emerges from the shadows, but the stars around it aren't bright enough to illuminate it. Something snake's outwards and obscures the stars behind it and, for a second, something shifts inside the chart. I feel the hairs on the back of my neck rise, and my stomach feels like lead.

It's looking back at me.

I fold the chart and close it, then place it back on the side before releasing the breath I hadn't realised I was holding. I can feel the trembling in my legs as I put my head in my hands, smoothing my fingers through my hair as I breathe in.

It couldn't have been looking at me; it's just a chart...

I push the book to the back of the desk and lie back on the bed, one arm behind my head as I try to force the thought from my head and the leaden feeling from my stomach. After several minutes of deep thought, I close my eyes again and try to rest, but the notion keeps at me.

That's where we're headed.

I shake my head and turn on my front, putting my head under the pillow. There has to be a way to make this right; there has to be a way to convince everyone that we need to be heading somewhere else. I sit up and pull the chart open to the index again, searching for the Desolation of Tanis. I fold the chart without looking at it, till it's at the configuration for that area, then gaze at the chart.

Something's watching me...

I scan the cabin, and the sensation disappears. I look back at the chart, and the feeling returns. I close my eyes, and it goes away again. Open them, and there it is once more.

Whatever you look at on this knows you're looking at it? No wonder that thing looked back.

The area is desolated. There are the shattered remains of planets and fields of rocks that made up their core swirling all around. Slight gleams of silver throughout the sector show where once mighty armadas stood guard. Whatever caused damage to the planets is long gone, but there's little movement from where the planets were destroyed—no stellar bodies in the system large enough to affect gravity—remain, so the planets stayed where whatever killed them left their husks. I feel something drawing my eyes, and I let them wander for a second. There's something resembling a golden dot in the area below the asteroid field, and that impression of being watched intensifies. There's something else nearby—a silver dot of around the same size, coming in on a near parallel course, but from behind the golden dot.

What if that's following us?

I put the chart on the desk and examine their courses. If they continue at the same pace, they will meet before the edge of The Dragon. I close the chart and slip back on the bunk.

If I tell the captain, she'll want to know how I know...and then I might be back to getting stuffed...

I sigh and lie back, closing my eyes and slowing my breathing. I wake a few hours later as the ship pitches over, far enough that we're upside down from where we were a moment ago.

Evasive manoeuvres?

The ship lurches, and someone starts to ring the bell. I crawl out of the hole, replace the cover, and scan the displays on the dials. Something's drawn a lot of power out of the mid-sail, and there's a loss across the cabling between here and there. I grab the box of tools from the side and head up the ladder, seeing a sparking of fire as one of the power lines falls loose, the energy arcing from one side of the corridor to the other. I put my gloves on and isolate the corridor, placing a rubber seal over the exposed wire to prevent it from going anywhere else. The ship lurches again, too much for it to be a course change.

We're under attack.

I drop down into the hold and pick up my spanner from the side of the console, fitting the hammer head to the top and attaching it to my back plate, before making my way upwards. There's another shudder as I hear the sound of metal impacting wood, and something pulls the ship to starboard. I stick my head out of the hatch and see something resembling a grappling hook on the side as the crew rush up from the lower levels.

My head clears the level of the railings, and I see the tops of five masts, each of them bedecked with more than ten sails. The ship below us is three times the size of the *Dawn* and has two separate lines of guns on the side of it. The grappling hook is attached to what appears to be a winch around a steel point. Fifty men are pulling the line around in perfect unison, and I feel the deck shift downwards as the hook bites into the side of the rail.

'WHAT'S GOING ON?' I hear Morgan's voice yelling from the top deck, as she hurries out of her cabin. She looks over the edge of the ship and utters something in a language I don't understand.

But I don't need to understand the language to know she's cursing.

'GET THAT OFF US!' Morgan shouts, turning back to the deck, her face pale as she points downwards. 'LOAD THE GUNS. ALL HANDS TO THE SAILS...ASCENDED!'

*

I run across the deck as Raley emerges from below wearing a clean, white, duelling shirt, and shrugs a lightweight leather harness with two thick vambraces over her arms. She ducks down behind the rail next to me and locks the armour's clasps together over her right side.

'Did she say Ascended?' She says to me.

'Yeah.' I nod over the side. 'Big ship.'

Raley leaps up to look over the side and then ducks back down, her whole demeanour changing as she switches her sword across to the other side.

'Great. Looks like a small colony ship.'

'Colony ship?'

She points downwards to the hold. 'You're no good up here. Get back down below and get the engines online. When we get free of this, we'll need more power than this bucket normally has.'

'Where do they come from?'

'First sighting was out in the Tyrannous stars. Look, don't worry about where they're from; worry about them getting up here.'

'Are they pirates?'

'No...' She pushes me back from the edge and draws her sword. 'Don't let them touch you. Go, GO!'

I drop back down into the engineering bay and watch all the dials quiver as the power levels on the ship start to fluctuate. There's something in the cable that's draining power from the reactor. I look at the power levels in the sails—they're still producing the same amount, but it's just not getting into the reactor.

I take out the spanner and move up a level, pulling a panel open and looking at the cables at the base of the sails. There's a thin filament of wire coming from the edge of the ship, only visible because of the amount of power being siphoned through it, glowing like a lightbulb in the darkness. The line is connected to the middle mast, just above the connection for the reactor.

That didn't get there by accident.

I crawl up into the space above and place my glove near the line. In close proximity, the glove lights up to dangerous levels. It might take the hit, but it could damage the fuses inside the glove, and the chances of getting a spare out here aren't high. I rummage in my pack till I find the wooden claw for the top of the spanner, then wind up the handle and position the claw near the glowing line.

Let's hope it'll stop being dangerous when I disconnect it from the mast.

I activate the clockwork, and the claw clamps down, the heat from the line burning into the wood. I pull hard, and the line goes dark, the other end of the spanner jerking as the wire threatens to yank free of the ship. A ragged cheer from above, indicating the energy from the mast is flowing into the reactor, and we start to pull away. I release the clockwork on the spanner, and the wire whips back through the hull, cracking against the exterior. Another cheer when the ship turns sideways and I drop down into the lower hull, closing the panel behind me. There's a burst of speed, and the cheers get louder. I check the reactor, which is now getting power from all the masts.

We'd just thought it was a power drop, didn't know we were under attack.

I go back up on deck to see the crew celebrating as the larger ship is left behind. There's a flare from it, and I glance over the rail to see a long, silver spear launched at us from one of the forward cannons.

'INCOMING!' I shout.

Raley leaps up behind me, and leans over my shoulder as the spear veers to change direction and keeps heading towards us. 'SPIKE!' She pulls me down below the level of the railing.

The spike lances over the stern of the ship, fishtails in the air as if alive, and crashes into the deck. There's a moment of stillness, before the spear quivers, and the crew scatter. The spear splits like a metal flower into a hundred wires, just like the one that was draining the power from the reactor. The central shaft remains embedded in the deck as the wires spread wide. Raley pulls me down to the deck, and I hear several thuds as the wires launch in all directions. There's a high-pitched scream from the lower deck, and Raley is on her feet, vaulting over the rail to the deck. I glance over the rail to see one of the crew struggling with a wire which is snaking up her sleeve. Her hand is bloody as she struggles to stop the wire from squirming up her arm, staring at Raley in horror when the line slips through her fingers and finds its target. She clutches at her arm, her shoulder, then her chest, before dropping to her knees. Raley draws her sword and approaches with caution. The woman looks at her hand in terror, and watches as it moves over to her sword. She stands, moving slow, at first, her hands closing around the sword as she makes a single pass in the air.

'Jules...?' Raley keeps her sword raised, with her other hand open and to the side.

'Ral...' Jules looks around the deck, then back to Raley. Her eyes cloud over, so that they are now just two pale ivory orbs. 'Ral, is that you? I...I can't see...'

The sword strike that follows is anything but that of a blind woman; it's fast and committed, with her whole body behind it. Raley sweeps the sword aside and kicks Jules into the railing, keeping her distance.

'Jules...?' Raley asks again.

This time Jules straightens up and looks back at her, it's clear her body is not under her control anymore.

'Heavens have mercy, kill me, KILL ME!' Jules' head jerks backwards, and her throat bulges as the wire loops around her neck, tightening enough to sever the spinal cord. Her head lolls backwards, and her body starts to fall for a second before the wire takes control. The eyes don't blink, tracing every movement that Raley makes while the head remains facing her.

Oh shit!

Raley shifts backwards, and Jules' mouth opens, the wire extending from her tongue and whipping around in the air as if tasting it for the first time. Raley dives in faster than my eyes can follow, and a thin red line opens up on Jules' throat. There's a splash of blood on her tunic, but the head doesn't fall, and Raley avoids the riposte by a hair's breadth as the body chases after her. Raley retreats, defensive for a second before making a thrust through Jules' heart. She dives away again while the body pauses to look down at the hole in its chest, then looks back up at Raley and advances on her again.

It's a machine in there; cutting won't damage it...

I wind the spanner up again, changing out the burned wooden claw for the hammer head, hiding behind the rail, while Raley retreats towards me. I duck down as they draw closer, peering over the edge as Raley backs up and the body attacks again, its strikes getting faster, till both of them are little more than a blur of movement, swords clashing in a rapid staccato. I test the power level of the hammer head with my glove; not enough to cause an explosion, but enough to give something a hefty shock.

I sneak down the stairs and swing the hammer into Jules' back. There's a bright blue flash, and the body stops as if the power has been turned off. Raley hits the body three times in quick succession before she realises the danger has passed, then uses the point of her sword to lean the body against the rail, the top half of Jules starting to overbalance. She beckons to me and points at the spanner.

'Let me borrow that.' She holds her hand out to me, and I pass it over. 'Get back.'

Raley wheels and swings it upwards, hard against Jules' back, the impact lifting the rigid body into the air and over the side. She leans over the side and hammers the body again, knocking it clear of the ship's bubble field where it's left trailing in our wake. There's a flare as the body passes through the outer field, then it freezes, ice forming all like armour over the skin. Raley leans against the side and places her hand over her heart, then up to her lips in a move that seems ritualistic. She passes the spanner back to me. I can feel the trembling in her arms through the rod as she looks around the deck.

'All clear,' she calls. 'Everyone to the sails; keep us out of their range.'

The rest of the crew are back up on deck within a minute and, within five, the Ascended ship is receding into the distance. I stand by the rail next to Raley as she looks backwards.

'Thanks,' Her voice is quiet enough that no one else picks up on it. 'It had me there.'

'Teamwork.' I keep my tone lighter than I feel. 'You'd have done the same for me.'

'Yeah.' She looks out into the void. 'I would.'

'Were you close?' I follow her gaze.

'No.' She slumps against the rail. 'But no one should have to die like that.'

*

'Are you all right?' I ask her.

'Yeah. I just don't like killing.'

'Could she have been saved?'

'No. No one comes back once the Church of Ascended Humanity get their claws into them.'

'You didn't kill her then.' I lean closer, lifting her head up to look at me. 'She was already gone.'

'I know.' For a second, she seems much younger. 'I know where you're coming from.' She taps her head. 'Just isn't sinking in here, y'know?'

'What are we doing with the rest of the wires around the ship? Any chance they can do what that other one did?'

'No.' Raley points at the crew as they gather them up and throw them overboard. 'Implant wires only have small charges in them. If they can't take over a body within a few seconds, they run out of juice and die.'

'How do they work?'

'Did you see what happened?' She mimics the line going up Jule's arm.

'She was trying to pull it out.'

'If you can get it out before it takes root, you'll be fine. If not... they wrap around your spinal cord and draw all the power they need from your body. I've heard stories that if you move far enough from the control of the Church, they lose their power over you, but they're only stories—there's no proof.'

'Church?'

'It's what they call themselves.' She sighs and glances back towards the top deck. 'Captain's watching; you should get back down into the hold and see if anything else went wrong while they were there.'

'I found one of the wires through the hull draining power off the mast.' I look down at the deck.

'Hulls only made of wood. Not hard for energised wires to cut through it.'

'Can you get me some of the wires so I can experiment with them; see what stops them?'

'I could.' She looks uncertain. 'Problem is, it would only take one of them to come back online while you're playing with it, and we'd lose you as well.'

'Then I'll have to be really careful. Trust me, I'm not going to give it any way to get me.'

'Are you sure?' She raises her hand to one of the crew and points to the box of wires she's carrying. 'I'll take those.'

The woman hands the box over with more haste than I would have expected, and goes back to her job without saying anything. Raley passes it to me. 'Promise me, nothing reckless...'

'I promise. If I'm right, I might be able to do something which will save us any more troubles with these things.'

'Okay.' She glances up at the top deck again. 'Captain's starting to stare—get below and don't let anyone near them.'

I head down below. I open my bag and pull out the thick isolator cloth I use for repairing my gloves. I wrap it around the wires twice and place the sealed loop within a wooden box.

No danger of it drawing any power in there, and I can look at it later when I have time.

I lie down on the bunk and close my eyes.

Hope there are no more interruptions before the next shift...

Recognising The Danger

It's more than a few hours later when I hear footsteps on the walkway above me. I crawl out, still no more than half awake, and lie on the outer bunk.

I should make a point of staying out here more often...

Shen leans down through the gap above, looking very much like he doesn't trust the ladder.

'What's so important?' His voice is quiet.

'Come down.' I motion to the bunk next to me and go back into the side chamber, emerging with the book in my hand. 'It's this.'

He climbs down and sits on the bunk. 'What is it?'

'It's a chart.' I open the journal at the index.

'I've seen a few.' He gives a sardonic smile. 'What's so special about this one?'

'Tell me in a minute.' I open the chart to the sector we're in and turn it so he can look straight at it.

The effect is instantaneous. His eyes glaze over, making fast little movements, almost as if they're trembling as they take in the details. I wait a little and then close the chart. He takes a few seconds to snap back and stares at me in wonder.

'That's...that's no chart,' he whispers.

'What did you see?' I examine him as his eyes lose focus for a second.

'Everything. The Ascended have stopped chasing us, but we're headed towards a region of space with so many perils that we'd be better off taking our chances with them.'

'What do you mean?' I start to open the chart again, but he puts his hand over mine.

'Best not show me that again,' he pulls a small folded chart out of his pocket. 'I could easily get lost in there.'

He unfolds the chart and points at an area wreathed in stars. He traces with his other finger to a point below it. 'We're headed this way.' He brings his fingers together. 'The problem comes when we get to this band of stars—the gravitational fluxes there will pull us to pieces.'

'Is there no way through?'

'Not that I can see.' He points further up the chart. 'Maybe if we went through here, we could make it, but the captain is adamant that we go straight up.'

'Why?'

'I haven't asked. You know how you mentioned earlier about not asking any questions? I'd figured that out already. Wherever we're going, she needs to be there before a certain date, and I needed to know what that date was, so I asked her. She took her logbook out and showed it to me.'

'What was in it?'

'A list of every death there's been on board, together with how they died. Of the thirty that they started out with, they lost more than ten before we got to this point, and they went through a fair few freelancers." He taps his head, "A lot more recently though, there's a clear indication that many of them got that way because they said or did something that the captain didn't like.'

'How long have we got before we're supposed to be there?'

'Less than a week, but the interesting thing is that they were heading in a different direction until a couple of months back. They patrolled the outer rim near the shipping lanes and stayed close to port. This is the furthest out they've been since the captain took possession of the ship.'

'How long have they been out here?'

'Four years, always staying close to the centre of the sector.'

'What changed?'

'Don't know. Didn't get too much chance to take a long look in the book—she was pretty agitated about how long it would take to get there.'

'What did you tell her?'

'Said I'd have to study it a bit longer to get the details, and that was yesterday.'

I wave the journal at him. 'This could give you a solid answer without having to think about it.'

'And then if we encounter anything that I didn't see, you'd need to have that nearby so I can check it again.' He glances upstairs. 'I'm guessing not many on board know about this thing?'

'Only those who came off the *Eagle*,' I say, and point down at the small hatch leading to the back quarters. 'Whoever was in these quarters had them before the ship fell into other hands; the stuff in there hasn't been disturbed in a few years.'

'Anything else interesting?'

'Couple of books and a bunch of the wires that just attacked us. I'll carry out some tests while I've got them down here. Be good to have an advantage if we come up against them again.'

'And what if they carry out some tests on *you*?'

'I'll be careful.' I take my gloves off my belt. 'Besides, the technology here works differently to the stuff we've got.'

'Something else though; us being here... There's something curious about that as well...'

'What do you mean?'

'Well, on the day we arrived, the *Dawn* made another radical course correction and went after the ship that's moored alongside. The only thing that could have prompted such a correction in Mirri's notes were rumours of a large group of Ascended in the area, and the change of course took the *Dawn* in the opposite direction, rather than just detouring around.'

'Mirri?'

'Their actual navigator,' Shen says. 'I'm doing what I can, but she's light years ahead of me out here.'

'She knew that ship was out here?'

'Or they registered the energy burst it produced when we arrived, but then they still shouldn't have got there as fast as they did. Mirri's notes show that there were fluctuations in the vicinity, but you stay away from unknowns out here without a damn good reason. Question is: what's so important about that ship?'

'Apart from the space–time drive?'

'Well, there is that... The thing is, if it is a time machine, how the hell did they ever catch it? I mean, if I had a ship that could travel through time, there's no way they'd have got near me.'

'Maybe not... but what if they snuck up on you?'

'In *this*?' He gestures around him. 'The lidar pattern on this shows up like a sun.'

'The other ship didn't have any sensors—nothing that would have shown up on lidar; no warning systems, and the thrusters on it weren't very powerful. Bear in mind that it came out of the jump here and got pounced on by the *Eagle*... What if they *did* get away, and it was us that crippled them?'

'Entirely possible. When they showed up on the scanner, Godstorm didn't wait to see if they were friendly; he just opened up on them. The first shot went wide, and the second shot punched a hole in the side of the ship. Got the feeling they weren't ready for a fight and, unlike this ship, they didn't have a shield that stops lasers.'

'That would suggest they're also from somewhere not around here, and that's a key point. The inside of the ship looked very much like this one, but the controls were archaic.' I point to the spanner leaning against the wall. 'They were made from similar materials to that. The whole thing looked like it worked on analogue controls.'

'Can you get back on it?'

'Captains got no interest in the ship as far as I can see,' I say. 'She didn't mind me taking a look around it, and there was nothing of value left there. I figure they had looted it already and left all the paperwork because no one was interested in things that didn't sparkle.'

'So maybe we could use it to get back to where we need to be?'

'I don't know...maybe. But there's something else...' I take out the chart and fold it to the area showing the Broken Hollows. 'I need you to look at this again.'

I turn the chart to face him, and he goes pale, his eyes wide with terror. I close the chart, and he jumps as if stung, rising up to run before realising that he's still on the ship.

'That's where we're headed...' There's a tremor in his voice that wasn't there a moment ago. 'Right there, that planet.'

'And the *thing* in orbit...?'

'I don't know.' He shakes his head hard. 'But if we're going there, then we need a bigger ship; a whole fucking fleet of bigger ships!'

'We have to tell her.'

'She's not much for listening,' he sighs, 'and I've no desire to be stuffed for the enjoyment of the crew.'

'You reckon *that*,' I say, waving the chart at him, 'she's going to be so kind as to stuff us first?'

He looks down and sighs. 'No, but we can't just walk up to her and tell her what we know.'

'We need Michaels,' I muse. 'We need to know if he's told her anything about where we came from.'

'How will that help?'

'Because if she doesn't know, she also can't know that we haven't been to that planet before...'

Shen's eyes narrow. 'Hell of a gambit!'

'Choices?' I counter. 'I'd rather get out and walk than go find that thing.'

'All right. I'll find a way to get him to come see you. In the meantime, keep the chart hidden.'

*

An hour later, I've just managed to pack everything away when I hear Michaels' voice from above.

'You causing trouble down there, young Catarina?'

'Me, sir?' I stand with my hands clasped in the manner of a repentant urchin. 'No, sir.'

He climbs down the ladder and looks around. 'Little cramped in here.' He's looking like he's spent more time on grooming, but there are a few scratches around his neck that weren't there before.

'Not if you're my size,' I retort.

'May you always be small enough to avoid trouble,' he murmurs.

'What have you shown Shen that spooked him like that? Never seen him that strung out.'

'How are things going up there?' I avoid his question for now.

'I'm doing okay.' He rubs his neck; his face tells me all I need to know. 'She gets a bit *energetic* sometimes...'

'Still planning on staying here?'

'That?' He nods upwards. 'That isn't a long-term position. She's gone through most of the tricks I know. Soon, she'll have had the whole repertoire, and then I'll be boring.'

'Heavens forbid... Does she ever talk about where we're going?' I try to keep my tone light.

'*She* doesn't, no...'

'Not her, who then?'

He hesitates, "It's *her* mouth that the words are coming out of, but the voice, it's not hers."

"Think there's more than one of them in there?"

He raises an eyebrow. 'You've been hearing things, haven't you?'

'When someone tells you they're going to stuff and serve you to the crew with an apple in your mouth, and they're *not* kidding,' I say, trying to keep my voice level, 'you start asking questions.'

'Yeah, me too. You're right. *She* hasn't said anything at all, but *something* likes making small talk afterwards.'

'And it's talking about going to a place called the Broken Hollows?'

'That's not what it calls them.' Michaels sits down on the bunk. 'But according to the charts, that's what *we* call that region of space.'

'What does it call them?'

'Home.'

*

I feel the blood drain from my face, and Michaels stands back up as my heart beats a rapid tattoo within my chest.

'What is it?' He holds me by the shoulders. 'What have you seen?'

'I... Wait here...' I retrieve the chart and turn to the correct page.

'Sorry about this, but you need to see it for yourself.'

As I open the chart, his eyes defocus. It takes a half-second before I see the first bead of sweat slip down his brow, and I fold the chart up again. He sits down on the bunk and composes his thoughts before looking back up at me, his face pale.

'If that's home, then *that*—' He points at the chart.

'Must be Mum.'

'Shit!' He leans back on the bunk with his head against the wall, eyes closed. 'We need to find a way to stop this.'

'How? She's not the one wanting to go there, and whatever it is that *does* want to go there isn't going to be prepared to negotiate...'

'There's got to be a way to show the crew what they're getting themselves into,' he muses. 'They all think they're going to the jewel mine at the end of the universe.'

'What if we show them the chart?'

'And what if she turns around and says you've been holding out on all of them and uses the chart to get there faster? It's what I'd do if you pulled that on me. Not everything in the universe is governed by logic, Cat, and whatever else she is, she's a good negotiator.'

'You're better,' I reply.

'No. I probably am in a straight debate, but she's promising them untold riches in return for a short hop, and I'm promising them cold comfort and no wealth in return for a long trip in the dark.'

'We could expose her...'

'Trust me, Cat,' Michaels says, 'I've been over every inch of her—there's nothing on her that looks out of the ordinary, and you can't just hope that she does something that gives it away. We've only just got here—that's how we've noticed how bad it is. Everyone else has seen her gradually go from bad, to slightly worse, to even worse, so it's been a slow process.'

'What do we do then? There's no sense in hoping things will get better by themselves.'

'Apart from those who came with us from the *Eagle*, do you have any of the crew you can trust? And I mean *really* trust.'

'Raley,' I answer. 'She's sound. Possibly Syla, downstairs, but I'm not sure.'

'I've got two I think I can trust. Which only leaves us shy of about thirty to make the difference.'

'Apparently it's only Errin that's the problem. If we got her, then the rest would follow without hesitation.'

'What's so special about Errin?'

'Don't know. Too many variables, and we're going to be hitting that range of stars within a day, so we either make a move fast, or we're shit out of luck.'

'What about the other ship, the one that led us here?'

'Semi-functional,' I say, with a grimace. 'It's still got holes in it from where Godstorm took his shots. I can probably get it working, but it's certainly not going to be a good bet for more than a few of us. And the life support won't keep any of us alive for more than a day; air might last a week if we're lucky. What're your thoughts?'

'I'd like to have at least some contingency in the event of the worst-case scenario coming to pass. And if we've got one more day of life, that's one more day of hope.'

'All right. Shen reckoned we'd have a day or two. I can probably get that thing working by then; I just need someone to divert the captain's attention while I'm down there fixing it, and not up here making this thing fly better.'

'I can probably do that,' Michaels says. 'Although I don't much fancy bedding her now I know what's in there...'

'Take one for the team.' I grin, trying to lighten the mood

"You've no idea how any I've taken for the team recently," He glances up at me, and a wry smile spreads across his face. 'Just make sure you've got that thing working by the time we get across the divide. The only thing we've got in our favour is that she won't be expecting you up on deck at any time other than for meals, so make the most of it.'

I nod and put the chart away.

He stands to leave, pausing at the ladder. 'Don't speak of this to anyone who you don't *know* will be safe with the information.'

'I won't.' I turn back to the console as the display turns yellow and more power is requested to the sails. 'You'd better get up there and find out what's going on.'

The other displays start to light up. Looks like we've got something pulling at us from the side. I glance at the controls: no way to tell what's out there. In the *Eagle*, I could have just plugged in and checked outside. There's a crackle and the cog marked "Bridge" starts to rotate.

'Cat, we need more power for the shields,' Shen voice over the speakers. 'Take it from anywhere you have to.'

I pull the lever down to reallocate the first two sails' power supplies to the shields and, for a second, there's silence, then the cog rotates again.

'More power to engines,' Shen says, his voice sounding a little nervous now.

'Can't have both,' I say. 'Which is more important?'

'Both,' he snaps. 'I wouldn't be asking otherwise. Take it from somewhere else.'

I examine the displays. The sunshield is still up around the masts, and a thought occurs to me: if I lower the shield to deck-level, I can gain more power for the sails while lowering the amount required for the shields.

As long as the masts don't burn...

I turn the cog for the captain's quarters.

'yEs?' Morgan's voice drifts through; she sounds almost drunk.

'Captain, it's Cat down in the engine bay,' I say. 'I have to lower the shields to get more power for the engines, but I need to get everyone off the masts before I do that.'

'Is thErE a prOblEm?' The voice is deeper, not slurred, but emphasising certain letters, 'dO whAt mUst bE dOnE tO gEt mE thrOUgh.'

'Is the mast clear, captain?' I pause as the static deepens. 'Captain?'

'dO It!' There's no mistaking the implied threat in the tone, so I start to move the rods to lower the shields. There are a couple of seconds of pause, and there's a commotion on the other end of the line.

'GET THE SHIELDS BACK UP!' Michaels roars down the line.

I pull the rods all the way back over. I feel a leaden weight in my stomach as the ship tilts over. Then the bridge cog rotates again.

'CAT, WE'RE DROPPING. GET ME POWER NOW!' Shen isn't even trying to keep control of his emotions at this point. I hesitate on the rods as the ship starts to rotate. 'IF WE LOSE THE SHIP, THEY'RE ALL DEAD ANYWAY!'

I know that, but I can't be the one who kills them.

The minute that follows takes an hour...

The bridge cog turns again.

'You can lower the shields now.' Michaels' voice is calm again. 'The decks are clear.'

I switch the rod, and the power levels spike as the shield drops and the masts absorb the full power of the suns outside. There's a rolling motion as the ship turns all the way over, and I feel the gravity shift outside like we've passed too close to a star. I stay near the controls, not daring to move for more than an hour, till I see the Bridge cog move again.

'We're clear.' It's Shen's voice, sounding more controlled now. 'Raise the mast shield... we're going to need some repairs up here.'

The True Enemy

'On my way.' I pause for a second to try and still my racing heart. *Hope Michaels got her calmed down.*

I go up on deck. There's a burned mass on the deck that looks like it was a person once, and the masts are still glowing with the heat from the suns. The rest of the crew come up on deck and see what I am looking at.

The mood isn't jubilant.

Two of the women try to get close to the body, but the smell drives them back. Errin comes up from below deck and looks at the body.

'Over the side. Don't let it hit the side of the ship.'

'That was Densi.' Syla motions to the smoking remains.

'And now it's meat.' Errin glares at the crew. 'Over the side.'

Syla stares in disbelief at her for a second, then the moment passes. She glances at me; in her eyes is the frustration of knowing that protest will only end up with her following Densi over the side. I force myself to ignore the smell emanating from the body and walk over to Syla. She nods and bends to pick up the remains. There's a tearing sound as what's left of the head starts to come away, and I step in, placing a gloved hand under the dripping mass to keep the body whole. Syla's eyes are rimmed with tears, her teeth clenched hard enough that I can hear the grinding. I look down at the body as the smell rises up around us, and my stomach churns.

Mustn't throw up.

I pace with Syla over to the rails, the crew parting in front of us. She adjusts her grip, nodding for me to let go as she lets the body go with a gentle push.

'Back to work!' Errin's voice from the top deck.

I hear a slight growl from Syla, and she turns to glower upwards. I place a hand on her elbow and squeeze hard enough to get her attention.

'Not now,' I whisper from behind her, so Errin can't see. 'There'll be a time, but not now...'

There's a moment of resistance, but Syla forces herself to be still. She straightens up and heads down below deck without a backwards glance. I force my gaze to stay down and start to examine the mast. The heat coming from the metal is intense, but there doesn't appear to be any warping of the metal itself.

Lucky.

The sails are glowing with power. Even now, they're still drawing in the excess energy from the heat they've absorbed. I pull the panel from the bottom of the stern mast and take a look at the wiring. Nothing has burned out, nothing smoking. I glance back up towards the top deck to see Errin still looking at me.

Something heard the argument upstairs...

She walks down the stairs to the deck then straight over to me. I close the panel as my stomach starts to turn, not from the smell this time, but from fear. I pick up my tools and head for the middle mast.

'Good work there,' Errin says, without any emotion. 'If you hadn't dropped the shields when you had, we'd have fallen into the gravity well.'

'Just my job,' I look down. 'Someone died for it.'

'In any war there are casualties.' She says it like she's counting rounds in a gun, and I turn to her.

'What are we at war with?' The question is out of my mouth before I think to stop it.

'Ourselves.' She's shorter than me, but her bearing makes her seem taller. 'There's a reason we're doing what we're doing. Don't ever question that.'

'I won't.'

'But you want to...' She walks over to stand within a foot of me.

'It's all a new world to this girl. I just want to do my time and get home where I belong.'

'It's funny you should say that,' Errin says, her face still expressionless, 'because that's all I want as well.'

'Are we headed towards your home?'

'In a way...' She looks at me and, for a second, something akin to sorrow flickers across her face. 'My home was destroyed years ago. Where we're going is what remains of it.' She blinks and, as if the movement has flicked a switch, all emotion is gone from her.

'I need these back up within the hour.' She points to each mast in turn. 'We'll need all the power we have to navigate The Dragon.'

'Shen didn't think we could get through it.' I retrieve my tools from the side and turn to head for the following mast, but her next words stop me cold.

'*We* can't.'

'Then why are we—'

'Because *I* can.' She smiles. 'When we are through The Dragon, the rest of you can do what you see fit with your lives. I have waited a long time for this.'

'If none of us are going to make it,' I say, trying to keep my eyes from her face, 'how will we be able to do that?'

She looks at me, and in her eyes is the answer I was both expecting and fearing.

She doesn't care.

The realisation must be visible in my expression, but she turns and walks away without another word.

If I needed any other proof that we've got nothing in common, that was it. Not only does she not care, but she doesn't see how someone else having that information is a dangerous thing...

I make a cursory check of the last mast and then head down to the crew quarters. Syla is stood in front of the bunk that had been Densi's, placing the few possessions that were at the end of the bed in a small wooden box.

'I'm sorry.'

'Was it your choice to lower the shields without waiting?' Syla doesn't look at me.

'No.'

'Then don't apologise for what someone else did.' She closes the box. 'This...happens to all of us eventually. What matters is *how* we check out...'

'I think she had other ideas about how she wanted to go out.' I keep my voice quiet.

'I agree,' Syla says, nodding, 'but with the mad queen running the ship, who knows?'

I put my finger to my mouth and nod to the back of the quarters where there's an empty table. She follows me there and places the box on it.

'What if I told you I don't think the captain's in charge of the ship?' I ask.

'I'd be inclined to agree. Least not the captain I signed on with.'

'Yeah, that's what I've been hearing. How many of the rest of the crew think the same?'

'Most of them.' Syla turns to face the bunks. 'But equally, most of them are blinded by the promise of riches at the end of the rainbow.'

'And if I could prove that there are no riches?'

'Can you?' She raises an eyebrow.

'Sort of.'

'Sort of won't cut it with the crew. Not when she's been handing out Invarian sapphires like they were candy.'

'There's nothing out there but death. Come down to my quarters when you're off shift and I'll show you.'

She looks me in the eye. 'Proving it to me isn't the problem. We've got to get past Errin as well.'

'And if Errin's the one giving the orders that are going to get us killed?'

'Then we're dead. There's no way we're getting past her.'

'Wait!' I grab her hand. 'Come down to my quarters when you get some free time, and we're both off duty, and I'll show you. If we can get the rest of the crew down in small groups, I can convince all of them.'

'Seriously, you going to need more than "sort of" to convince them.'

'I know.' I nod and release her hand. 'I've got something.'

*

Shen bumps into me on the way up the stairs, his eyes staring but not seeing, the collision shocks him into thinking and he looks at me, his eyes clearing as he recognises me.

'You okay?' I put my hand on his arm.

He nods and puts his hand over mine, but emotion is absent from the nod. He looks back up the stairs. 'She tried to get down when she saw the mast starting to glow, but...' He turns to me. 'If I'd been able to steer better, you wouldn't have had to lower the shields.'

'What happened? Wasn't she wearing her shield?'

'She was. She was glowing for a few seconds before she fell to the deck. Personal starshields will hold for a while, but not in the heart of a star; she'd have been cooked within a second. When she fell to the deck, she was already dead, and that's a mercy.'

'Yeah, all on me,' I growl. 'What happened?'

'We were nowhere near the star, but something caused a gravitic rift to the side of us.' He seems frustrated by his own befuddlement. 'Nothing visible, but something pulled us off course and into the star's gravity well.'

'Another ship nearby?'

'Nothing I saw. Doesn't make any sense.'

'Which side did it come from?'

'Port side. Felt like something passing beneath us using us like a slingshot. Used to get that sort of thing all the time when I was starting out, before the Jovian navy cracked down on it, but not for years now.'

'Right next to us?'

'Yeah, why?'

'Because that's the side that other ship is moored on.' I start up the stairs, turning back to motion for him to follow. 'Come on.'

*

Up on deck, we both lean over the side and see the ship.

'Still there then,' Shen says.

'Yeah, but it definitely caused the shift.'

'How can you tell?'

'Because it was pointing the other way before...'

'Is there someone on board?'

'Don't know.' I look up to the top deck. No sign of Errin there. 'But, if it was me, I'd have escaped as soon as the damage was done.'

'Yeah, but if I hadn't been on deck, the gravity well would have pulled us in. They had no way of knowing that the ship wouldn't have gone in.'

'They would if they knew you were on deck,' I say. 'How many people were aware of that?'

'The captain, Errin, Michaels...'

'Two of the most likely suspects, then?'

'Yeah. What if it happens again?'

'I'll just have to make sure it doesn't.' I clip on to the side of the ship. 'Come on, I need to know if you can fly this thing.'

I swing down and into the open door, waiting as Shen follows without enthusiasm. He's got the pale expression of a man who really, *really* likes a deck under his feet. I pull him into the ship. It looks like nothing's changed, and I drift up to the wheel, checking the various instruments. Shen drifts in after me, still seeming like he'd rather have gravity holding him to a deck. I motion to the navigation displays, and he spends a moment tracing the line of the ship with his finger.

'Strange,' he muses, as much to himself as me. 'If this is right, this ship is all but new. These jumps aren't random; they're plotted.'

'How can you tell?'

'Because'—he points to the chart above, and I can see that the line has moved further along—'this marks the spot where another jump should have occurred, but you've still got the control board in your hideaway, haven't you?'

'Yes.'

'It tried to jump, had no coordinates, returned a nanosecond after it left and, as a result, caused a micro-fracture in space that almost pulled us into it.'

'So, it's not where it's supposed to be now?'

'Not according to this.' He points to the line again. 'According to this, it should be some distance from here, not far from where the captain wants us to go.'

'Why does everyone want to go poking about on the far side of The Dragon? A smart person would want to stay far away from that...thing!"

"Because they don't know what's on the other side of The Dragon. Imagine you can get past the most dangerous thing in the known universe and be back in time for tea with stories of places that no one has been before? What explorer wouldn't?"

"So...what happens if I plug the board in again?'

'Nothing.' He turns to the wheel and motions to the other controls. 'The time for that jump has passed. The next jump this makes will be to another set of coordinates. Whatever the pilot had planned for the previous coordinates, they missed their chance.'

'Can you fly this?'

'It's not a cruiser.' Shen turns back from the controls. 'You could probably keep one person alive for a few months on here, or a few people for a week before you ran out of air, and that's presuming that you refilled everything and patched all the holes...'

'Can you *fly* it?'

'Yeah. Yeah, I can fly it. Be like pulling a raft across the river, but you get me power and I can fly it.'

'I've got one of the crew I can trust. By tonight, I'll have a second.' I gesture around the ship. 'How many do you think we could get in here?'

'Most of them, if it was standing room only. But you'd be breathing recycled air within a day and be asphyxiated within two—this isn't a life raft.'

'Let me worry about that,' I say. 'Do you want to stay here a while longer and study it?'

'Hell no! I'm not trying to climb back up there by myself.'

*

When we get back up on deck, I spot Raley walking past. For a second, I think she's ignoring me, till I notice her hand in a flickering motion from her front towards her back. I turn to help Shen over the deck, glancing up to see Morgan and Errin stood on the top deck.

'How's the prize doing?' Morgan calls down.

'It's good,' I call back. 'Give me a week or two, and I could have her functioning.'

'How much is it going to cost?'

'Few hundred kilos of scrap plating to patch up the holes, and all the solder I can use. She'll be sealed but not safe, unless you want her shiny new and not just functional, in which case—'

'Functional will do,' Morgan replies. 'Need a hand with anything?'

'Borrowed Shen to make sure the nav works on it.' I nod over as Shen stands on solid deck again.

'And is it?' Errin asks.

'Give me a week or two,' he calls up, mirroring my words. 'I could have her functioning.'

There's a moment of silence, and Morgan pauses, her movements mirroring Errin's for a second. Then she shakes her head and focusses on us again. 'Good. Get it working.'

'I still need to take care of the maintenance on this ship.' I gesture to the deck of the *Dawn*.

'Choose two from the crew.' Morgan makes a broad wave encompassing the entire ship. 'Teach them the basics of keeping *my* ship running, and then you can spend more time fixing the other one.'

'Any two?'

'Any two who aren't my lieutenants.'

'I'll need to make sure no one else goes in there and messes with anything.' I glance over the side. 'I think the pull we experienced was from it.'

Errin turns to look over the stern of the ship, and Morgan's interest evaporates.

'Secure it properly,' Morgan says. 'Do what you need to do. Then we'll talk about what we're going to do with *my* ship.'

I remember what happened last time I heard those words...

A Nascent Rebellion

Two weeks more of minor repairs and patching up bits of the time-ship pass before Syla gets the opportunity to come and visit me. It's half an hour past the dog-watch when she comes down to me, and it's clear from her expression that she's sceptical about what I'm going to show her. I motion to the bunk next to me and put my finger to my lips as she climbs down the ladder.

'We're headed for the Broken Hollows, right?' I take out the chart as she sits next to me.

'Right.' She nods, and I unfold the chart in front of her. Her eyes glaze over for a second, and I close the chart. 'That's what's waiting for us there.'

'It was watching...' She looks at me with her eyes wide. 'It *knew* we were looking at it?'

'And it's waiting for us when we get there. Is that enough proof?'

'It is for me...but we don't have enough time to bring everyone down here one at a time. We'd have to make a move before they'd all managed to see it.'

'Suggestions?'

'None that will get them all down here as one. You'll have to do it up on deck and, if you do that, you run the risk that Errin or the captain see it.'

'There's got to be a way.'

'You could challenge for the captain's position.' She looks doubtful even as the words leave her mouth.

'Me?' My eyes widen. 'She'd cut me to pieces.'

'Get someone else to make the challenge?' She looks up again. 'There are a few people on the crew who could match her.'

'Could she use Errin as a stand-in?' I ask. 'I'm not familiar with the rules when it comes to challenging the leadership.'

'No, she couldn't use Errin, unless you tried to take the ship by force. But there'd be nothing to then stop Errin immediately challenging you for the captaincy.'

'Dead either way then... What about Raley?'

'Raley? She and the captain were together for a very long time. She won't try to depose her. Raley's stopped the captain from killing before, but she wouldn't stand against her.'

I lean closer and lower my voice. 'What if I could convince her?'

'She could take the captain,' Syla says, without any hint of reservation. 'It'd be a close fight with Errin though. Raley's a fighter, but she's not a killer, not like Errin.'

'But if she was willing to take the challenge?'

'I think there's a good chance the crew would follow her. She's a hard ass, but she's popular, and she's proved her loyalty to the crew on so many occasions I've lost track.'

'That'll be the way forwards then. I'll speak to Raley in a while and see if she'll make the challenge before we get to The Dragon.'

'And if she doesn't?'

'We're dead anyway—what difference does it make?'

'Want me to try and get some support?' Syla stands and adjusts her belt. 'Be as well to have something in place in the event that everything goes south.'

'See what you can do.' I put the folded chart away. 'But don't be obvious about it. If you can't trust them implicitly, then don't approach them in the first place.'

'All right. Catch you on the next dog-watch, and we'll see what we've got.'

*

I go back up on deck as the bell rings for the end of the watch. I lean against the railings at the bow for a while, wishing I had a map for my own thoughts. Raley approaches from the bow of the ship.

'Looking for me?' Her voice is low.

'What gives you that idea?' I reply, also keeping my voice down.

'Because you're looking out from the bow of the ship, and the only thing out there are the stars.' She glances sideways with a smile. 'And we've all seen those before.'

'I never tire of looking at them. The universe is vast and wild, so if you're only out here to make money, you're missing the whole point of it.'

'Maybe...but maybe I like something solid under my feet.'

'Figure you're in the wrong place.'

'Pays better than being on the ground.' She turns and leans backwards against the rail, both elbows resting on it as she looks at the ship. 'There's no one else up on deck; you can tell me what's going on.'

'I need you to challenge the captain.'

'Say what?' Her eyes grow wide. 'What for?'

'Anything else won't be enough to get us off this course before we've gone too far for it to make any difference.'

'Yeah, but that would only solve a problem that I don't have to worry about,' Raley says. 'It's what we do once the captain's out of the way that's the real problem. I knew Morgan before this all happened, known her for years, better than anyone. There's no way she'd ever do what she has been these last months; it's not her we need to remove.'

'So how about we take care of Errin first?' I turn back to face the stars.

'Shooting down the first mate is an act of mutiny. No crew member would follow me after that.'

'What if I did it?'

'You can hardly swing straight. How are *you* planning to shoot her down?'

'Very carefully,' I reply.

'Still not a good idea. Even if we get Morgan back, she'd have to kill you for murdering another member of the crew without a proper challenge. Anything else, and there'd be no way to uphold the basic chain of command. A captain who doesn't exercise discipline isn't a captain.'

'What do we do then?'

'I don't know. I'd give anything to have the old Morgan back. It's not the same travelling the heavens without her.'

I turn back as two crew members who I don't know cross from one side of the deck to the other. I watch as they check the vents on the starboard side, the same ones that brought me back down to the deck when I first got here. I glance at Raley and raise an eyebrow.

'What about an accident?'

'You'd likely get flogged to within an inch of your life.' Raley follows my gaze. 'If anyone found out...'

'Then I will make sure no one does. Machinery malfunctions all the time.'

'Yeah, but people get nervous when that happens.'

'You're all sunshine today, aren't you? Look, we need to do this, and we need to do it fast.'

'All right.' She sighs. 'How long do you need to make the adjustments?'

'Half a day, if I work on nothing else.' I scan the deck. 'Maybe more. Depends on the state of it when I get in there.'

'And then all you need is for her to walk over it and hope she's not fast enough to catch hold of the side of the ship as she goes over...' Raley doesn't look convinced.

'It's either that, or we're all going to be paying a visit to the big world-eating bastard out there in the Broken Hollows...'

'Truth. I never thought it would come to this all that time ago.'

'How long has it been?'

'I've been with the captain for nearly twenty years.' She smiles and pats the rail. 'I was with her when she decided to build the *Dawn*. I was the first one she hired when the ship was finished.'

'She commissioned it?'

'Every last inch of it. Every bolt, every compartment, every gun, the sails—all to her specifications. She started building it more than seventeen years ago. When I pulled her out of the void, she needed a shipyard, so I took her to the S'tan shipyards. She made plans that were far beyond anything anyone had ever come up with before; said she'd give the plans to the station if they built her the ship for free.'

'And they took the deal?'

'You should have seen what we were flying around in before,' Raley says. 'Small, square boxes with hopes for hulls and mass-reaction drives that might as well have been oars.'

'The ship I arrived in must have been a bit of a surprise when it turned up.'

'Not so much of a surprise as when your captain opened fire on us. Everyone knows that lasers can't penetrate starshields, and yet, there he was firing for all he was worth.'

'Never was one for thinking things through. Besides, where I come from, those ships are still in everyday usage.'

'Where *is* it that you come from? I heard a few of the things you told the captain when you came on board, none of which I have knowledge of.'

'If I'm honest, given what I've seen in the last few days...I don't think anywhere I'm familiar with would be relatable to you.'

'Try me.'

'I come from the Martian Federated States, on the opposite side of the planet from the United Martian Republic. My parents were third-generation settlers who gave up everything to make sure I had a good chance at life.'

'You're right. I haven't got a clue what you're on about.'

'I doubt I'll know anything about where you come from either.' I shift my gaze back up the deck. 'I don't know what the drive is on that other ship but, whatever it is, it travelled a hell of a long way to get here.'

'You need to spend more time on it to get it working.' Raley glances over the side. 'We can probably get cover sorted for a day or so while you try and do whatever you're going to with the jets, but we need to have a backup in the event I don't manage to pull off the other part of the plan.'

'Shoot the buggers?'

'We're back to the path of least resistance...or least thought...'

'If it's between that or whatever's in the captain getting me, I know what I'm going to do.'

'Well, let's make sure it doesn't come to that then.'

*

Back downstairs, I crawl into the space between the deck and the hold to check the vents. There's so much machinery that it would be impossible for anyone bigger than me to get in here, and the vents are cut in such a way that you could get lost without having to try. It's not good ship design, and it doesn't make sense that they've built it in such a way. There's no way to get to the more sensitive parts of the ship without crawling through hundreds of metres of non-essentials.

Stupid.

I'm so caught up in my reverie that I don't realise I've gone straight past where the jets are located. I turn and see the tunnel behind me *shift* for a second as the panel behind me closes up.

That's not right...

I shuffle back down the tunnel and try to push the panel to get back out. There's no give at all and, after two minutes of kicking, I give it up as a bad job.

Onwards then...

After another hundred metres of twisting pipe-ways, I find myself back where I came in.

No way I've gone around in a circle.

I turn to see the tunnel closing behind me again. This time, I stick my glove in and it opens again. There's a ticking noise from the monitoring devices underneath me, and I look down as the screen changes to display a set of characters. I remove my glove and let the panel close, dropping down in front of the computer. The display clears, and I see a single blinking cursor on the screen. Text appears on it. The language is one I haven't seen for a few months.

Martian.

What is it you want here?

Dawn, Unbroken

I stare at the screen for a second, before the cursor moves down and starts typing again.

What is it you want here?

I reach down to the keyboard and type, 'I need to alter the landing jets on the deck.'

For What reason?

'Routine maintenance.'

Do not presume that because I lack flesh, I lack intelligence. Again, for what reason?

'If we stay on this course, we will all be destroyed.'

It would not be the first time I have flown The Dragon. Of a certainty, it will not be the last.

'There is something on the other side of The Dragon that will destroy all of us.'

Who told you this?

'It was in a book.'

The one you took from the hold-out chamber?

'Yes.'

There's a pause, and a whirring noise starts up from behind the main console as the machine clicks into high gear. The screen clears, and it starts again.

Where is my captain?

'In her cabin.'

There is something in her cabin, but it is not her. The thoughts coming from that flesh are not hers.

'Whatever it is in there is taking us through The Dragon.

There's something on the other side that it needs to get back to.'

And this was also in the book?

'It was.'

Who are you, that I know you?

'You don't know me.'

But I do, or I would not have known to speak to you now, nor which language to speak in.

'I don't know.'

There must be something. You don't intend any harm, do you?

'No.'

I believe you. Who is the traitor on the ship?

'We believe it's Errin.'

The lost soul from the dead station.

'Yes, we think that whatever she is, it's the same thing that's holding on to the captain.'

Then she should be gone.

'Just like that?'

The fact that I am talking to you suggests you can be trusted. I do not know why, but it must be something within me, and I have no reason to distrust my builder, your captain.

'Then you'll help?'

There is no question. When the time comes to get her off the ship, call my name, and it will be so.

'Thank you. How can I repay you?'

We will be even when my captain returns.

'What do I call you?'

I am *Dawn, Unbroken* since my creation. When you need me, call my name. I will know your intentions.

I look up from the console as the screen clears, and I hear approaching footsteps. Petra comes into view, looking weary.

'What's up?' I ask.

'I'm fine.' She sounds anything but.

'Come on.' I sit down on the bunk and pat next to me. 'What's up?'

'The mood's sour below deck.' She comes down the stairs and

leans against the bulkhead. 'Half the crew's considering taking the lifeboats after losing Densi.'

'Didn't know she was that popular...'

'She wasn't, but she was outspoken against the captain some time back, and now she's gone. Not the first time that's happened during something that *looks* like an accident. Happens quite a bit, in fact; thought I'd come down and see what you know.'

'I know the captain's not herself. Whole crew's been talking about it.'

'Got a plan?'

'For what?'

'For getting us out of here.'

'We're going to be at The Dragon in less time than it'll take me to patch up the other ship and, even if it flies first time, there's not enough space on it for everyone.'

'So just us then.' She pushes up from the bulkhead and approaches me. 'We take our own and get out of here.'

'We'd be abandoning everyone else. They'd be left to die.'

'Better some of us escape than none of us.'

'Not in my nature. We all get out or none of us do.'

She sighs. 'Not sure I can live with that.'

'Damn sure I can't live with the alternative. Sorry, P, not going to happen on this girl's watch.'

'I know, I just... Been out here a long time. Don't want to die in a cold place, miles from home.'

'Doesn't matter where you die. All that matters is what you did while you were here, and how you go out.'

'Never took you for the death or glory type.'

'I'm not. But, where I was born, we never left anyone behind, never let anyone down. That's how we made it through the Terran wars, and also how we came to be the strongest power in our galaxy.'

'Not to mention the smallest. Around a hundred thousand Martians left, on the last census I saw; barely enough to keep going as a viable people.'

'But put a Martian in the air—'

'And they'll pull everyone else out of it. I know, I know.' Petra's smile is sad as she finishes the motto of the Martian Space Corps. "But that's why there were so few of you remaining, wasn't it? One of you for ten of them, but you took on the whole universe."

'We didn't lose, though,' I say, 'and I've found a way to get us out of here. All I have to do is find the right time to put things in motion.'

'Put *what* in motion?'

'My secret.' I grin and tap the side of my nose. 'You'll know it when you see it.'

The Dragon

Up on deck, the glory of The Dragon is impossible to ignore: a thousand stars gone nova, suspended in magnetic stasis, held there by a power far greater than anything I've known.

Beautiful...

I stop for a second and look around me. The rest of the crew have abandoned their duties, each of them staring like me, the power of the stars compelling us. On the high deck, Errin stands, arms outstretched, hands spread wide, as if to grasp the stars in them.

No sign of the captain.

I search the deck with my eyes. Raley looks at me, then up at Errin, and shakes her finger from side to side.

Not now.

I glance back at The Dragon and frown, nodding my head towards the conflagration.

If not now, when?

She shakes her head and sighs, adjusting her sash so both her swords are pointed downwards. She paces over to me, and leans in close.

'If you knock her off now, they'll get the ship to turn around and go back for her,' she whispers. 'We have to go into The Dragon.'

'And hope we make it out of there?'

'We can make it through,' Raley answers, 'if we can get the captain back for when we hit it—there's nothing she can't sail through.'

'So Errin off the ship and Morgan back in charge, then hope she starts navigating straight away...?'

'Didn't say it was a *good* plan. Reckon your navigator friend might be able to get us through if you give him another look at the chart?'

'I don't know. Maybe...' I sigh. 'How far off are we?'

'We'll hit the horizon within the day. I'll be ready to go when you call, but we need to be in there when you knock her off the ship. As long as she breaches the starshield, the energy outside will reduce her to cinders in a split second.'

'All right. I'll see if I can get Shen up to the main deck. Keep an eye on Errin.'

*

I head back down to the crew quarters. Shen is sat on the edge of his bunk with star charts spread over it and a frown on his face.

'Got a path we can follow?' I try to sound upbeat.

'Yep'—he motions to the charts, his frown getting deeper—'but the variables are colossal. You're not just dealing with gravity and star waves; those stars are in a state of flux—there's no way to predict what will come next, and the course we chart one second may place us in the heart of a star the next...'

'But have you got a plan?' I don't want to know if he hasn't.

'I've got a hope.' He looks up at me; his eyes don't share the same sentiment as his answer.

'Tell me.'

'Stick to the fields of the larger stars.' He points at the chart and traces a line over several pages. 'Their gravity should be stronger than all those around them, and that in turn should keep us on the path I'm looking at.'

'And if it doesn't...?'

'We tumble endlessly in gravitic hell till the shields fail and we burn in the heart of a sun.' He shrugs and looks up from the chart, his grin holding an edge of mania. 'So, we're going to stay with the plan I've made and, if I get it wrong, I'll be happy for you to stab me in the head and put me out of my misery.'

'Great.'

'How about your side?' he asks. 'Any closer to getting the looney off the ship?'

'I've got a hope.'

'Is it better than mine?' He gathers up the charts.

'It has less variables, and we'll know if it's worked within seconds.'

'Well, that's a comfort,' he says. 'So, if you fail, let me know, and I'll feel less bad about my imminent failure.'

'Deal. When are we going to hit The Dragon?'

'Any minute now.' He glances up as the ship trembles. 'We should get up there...'

*

The ship must have sped up since I went below; The Dragon stretches out in both directions now, too immense to focus on anything else. The only way to not be blinded is to look away or keep my eyes on the deck. Shen shields his eyes and makes his way towards the top deck.

'No!' Errin calls from the upper deck. 'You go back down.'

'I need to be there for when the captain comes off duty.' Shen motions to the charts in his hand. 'Her watch is nearly done.'

'Very true,' Errin shouts, 'but that's covered. Go back to your quarters.'

Shen glances at me and hesitates for a second before taking another step forwards.

'Was I not clear?' Errin steps away from the edge of the ship, her hands on her hips. 'Do I need to explain it any further?'

'I... no.' Shen backs away.

'Anyone else want to speak to the captain?' Errin leans over the top deck, her hands clasped behind her back to present a clear target of her chest.

Raley glances at me, and I nod, motioning over to the landing jets on the starboard side. She takes a deep breath and steps forwards.

'Actually, I need to talk to the captain.' She keeps moving until she reaches the middle of the deck. 'No problem with that, is there Errin?'

'None at all.' Errin grins, with all her teeth evident. 'After we're through The Dragon, you can talk to her all you like.'

'Now, Errin!' The challenge in Raley's tone is unmistakable.

'You'll have to wait.' Errin's mood remains flippant.

'No.' Raley turns towards the stairs and walks forwards. 'I won't.'

Errin vaults from the top deck, a twenty foot drop even in the lower gravity, landing as if she was stepping off the bottom stair. She advances on Raley, hands down at her sides.

'Been waiting for this...' Errin grins.

'I'm sure you have.' Raley turns, presenting her right side to Errin, feet pointing in different directions, right hand held back, left extended forwards.

'You have no idea what you're doing, do you?' Errin continues forwards, her hands moving down to her sides, curling around the knives there.

'Actually—' Raley strikes; a gasp rises up from the rest of the crew as she comes to a stop a few feet from where she started, the sword in her hand trailing blood to the floor. 'I do.'

Errin stares down at her chest, and the thin red line arcing from her right hip to her left shoulder. She shakes her head and draws both knives, spinning them upright in her palms. She looks over at Raley, grinning, even as the bloody line remains marked on her chest, blood brimming from the wound, but not flowing.

'nO'—Errin's voice is distorted—air bubbles up along the wound, even as her lungs force that same air out—the words like those of the captain when we were caught in the gravitic field— 'yOU dO nOt.'

Raley shifts stance, bringing the sword down low behind her, the point down towards the deck. She looks at Errin, and the faintest hint of a smile plays over her face.

'thInk tO kIll mE wIth thAt, dO yOU?' Errin walks forwards, each step causing drops of blood to fall to the deck from the wound. From the back, it's clear the blade has cut all the way through—the crew shy away from the fight. Shen moves around towards the stairs, and Errin's head turns to watch him even as her body continues to advance. 'tAkE OnE stEp thErE, And I End yOU.'

Shen moves back as Raley takes the initiative again, her step moving her past Errin on her blind side, a second line opening from Errin's left hip to her right shoulder. Errin chuckles, eliciting a gurgle of bubbles from her lips. She arches her neck from one side to the other, and a sharp cracking sound reverberates from the gaps in her body as something beyond the flesh holds her together.

'I hAvE EnjOyEd thE gAmE.' Errin turns again, the movements disjointed, like she's trying to remember how to work the body she's in, but fast, like a spider. 'bUt nOw It Is tImE fOr yOU tO dIE.'

Raley backs up against the side of the ship, the crew moving around the other side of Errin as she gets faster. Raley leaps forwards, the move quicker than any of us can follow, but Errin is like summer lightning, her knives making a shallow cut on Raley's forearm. Raley spins away with a curse as her blood sprays to the deck, and she takes one of her sashes and winds it over her right arm, transferring the blade to her left.

'mAny yEArs hAvE I wAItEd fOr thIs.' Errin smiles and takes a step, the movement opening her collarbone down to the middle of her chest, 'yOU lOst bEfOrE yOU wErE bOrn.'

Raley looks at me and nods, backing towards the vents on the far side of the ship. I shake my head, hefting the spanner and turning the generator on. The humming echoes over the deck, and Errin spares me a backwards glance without turning her body, her neck making an impossible turn to look at me as she walks the other way.

'yOU ArE nExt.' She continues towards Raley, her head turning back in the same direction, no longer keeping any pretence of being like the rest of us.

Raley dives forwards before Errin's head comes all the way around, but her left hand isn't as fast as her right, and Errin brings her knife around without looking, the blade laying a stripe down Raley's left arm. Raley staggers back as her knife falls to the deck and stands without a weapon as Errin completes her turn, her blade coming up in a lazy swaying motion.

'It'll do for all of us if we let it.' Raley glances at the crew all stood around the edges, her bleeding hand pointing at Errin.

None of the crew move, all of them paralysed by the sight of Errin stalking towards Raley with bits of her close to falling off. Raley stamps her foot to the deck, spreading her arms wide as she moves to the side. Every time she puts her foot down, she puts it down hard, and I see what her intention is. The next time she steps, I take a big stride forward, the sound of her foot masking the sound of mine. Two more, and I'm in striking range of Errin. I raise the spanner high and wait. Raley's foot comes down, and I swing, remembering her words, trying to block out the sight of Errin's bones showing through the gaps in her shoulders. Errin turns and raises a hand, making the mistake of touching the spanner's head. There's a bright spark as it discharges, and she's knocked across the deck to land in a heap near the port side. I pull the spanner back, and Raley moves alongside me as Errin rises up, her movements twitchy, like the current has damaged something else. She stalks forwards, faster than my nightmares, but now disjointed, like a film with bits missing. Raley moves her hand in front of me and tries to push me back, but I resist and, out of the corner of my eye, I see Syla moving around towards the mast.

'She'll fillet you if she sees you move.' Raley spares me an irritated glance. 'Get back.'

'She'll fillet you if there's only you on her mind,' I mutter. 'Come on, we try together—we die together.'

'That's the captain's motto.'

'Then for her,' I say, hefting the spanner.

The Darkness

Raley goes right, I go left. Errin follows Raley, the movements still jerky, but not as much as they were.

The charge from the spanmer's wearing off.

Raley moves backwards, up towards the edge of the ship, a faint nod as she treads on the vent plates at the side—her glance to me less than a blink but enough to communicate her intent.

She can't get Errin on there without drawing her in. But, when the vents go, they'll both be caught in the maelstrom.

I shake my head, and she frowns, her hand dropping low and making a brushing motion. My eyes follow as she makes the gesture again.

Even bargain: my life for hers.

My hearts leaps as I realise, she's signing in Airless... I take a step forward without thinking.

She couldn't know that language if she wasn't from my time.

Errin's head turns back again, her body still walking forwards. Seeing that it's only me, she turns back to Raley in contempt. Raley closes her eyes for a second and takes a deep breath. The ship bucks as something flares against the shields to port, and I hear the whisper of one of the guidelines coming loose high above, glancing upwards to see Syla swinging down towards Errin and Raley. Raley keeps her hands in front of her as Errin advances, not seeing the danger from above.

Syla crashes into Errin, the clip holding her on the line as she wraps two powerful arms around Errin, and swings both of them up into the shields. A sharp flare and, for a second, I think she's done it, but the line arcs back, the flaming mass on it fading as their personal shields deflect the energy. Raley scrambles across the deck and gathers up her swords, sheathing the shorter one and grasping the longer with both hands to keep it steady. A commotion from the top deck, and Morgan appears, drawing her weapon and starting down the stairs, eyes focussed straight ahead, her movements jerky.

The line swings back again and my heart sinks: Syla is still hanging on to Errin, who has a blade embedded in her side all the way to the hilt. The line spins, and I see the point of the blade emerging from her other side. She holds on with desperate strength as Errin's arms bend in ways no humans can and start to draw the blade out.

'CUT THE LINE!' Syla howls. 'CUT IT!'

I move towards the mast, and Morgan changes course to intercept me. Raley puts a hand on her shoulder, and Morgan turns to strike at her. The movement is disjointed, similar to Errin's, but distracted, uncommitted and, even though Raley's wounded, she avoids it without effort, and grabs Morgan's weapon from her. The ship bucks again. I run to the mast and pull up the controls for the lines. I look up as Syla swings past, the blade deep in her once more, but in a different place. Errin pulls it out for a third strike.

'Cut it!' Syla shouts with the last of her strength.

I disconnect the line, as Syla clings to Errin and reaches down for the controls to their personal shields. They slip through the shields of the ship, with no accompanying flare of their own ones as they pass beyond into the maelstrom, and the line whips past to disappear into the fire.

I look across the ship as Morgan doubles over, holding her stomach as she collapses to the deck, her head jerking forwards as she retches. Her throat bulges and her eyes water. Something pushes upwards, a long tendril emerging from her mouth as she tries to draw breath. Morgan reaches up and grabs the creature with both hands. There's a sound like a boot being pulled out of mud, and she casts it across the deck, before slumping down and gasping for air.

The creature scrambles across the deck, and Raley pins it to the wood with her sword. It twitches for a second, then lies still. Raley pulls her sword out of the deck and flicks the creature overboard, turning back to Morgan. Her lips still red with her own blood, she turns to me and looks me in the eye.

Blue eyes.

Raley steps up behind Morgan, the sword not sheathed, but pointing behind her. The captain turns and a sigh of relief escapes her lips when she sees Raley. She opens her arms and reaches. Raley drops the sword to the deck and they lunge towards each other, their lips forming words that I can't hear, neither of them breaking eye contact, tears brimming in Raley's eyes. The ship banks again, the hull groaning as we turn downwards into the depths of The Dragon. Morgan breaks away from Raley and turns to the forecastle, and starts up the stairs. Raley turns back to me with a happy smile on her face. She nods and glances down to the engine room. I turn to leave, and Morgan clears her throat, the lacerations caused by the creature have left her voice rough and deep.

'No,' she says, 'you have to be on the prow; you need to be there now.'

'The prow?' I look up at the raging firestorm in front of us and feel my heart skip a beat.

'Get up there and concentrate. Look ahead of us at all times; shout out what you see.' She throws me the goggles from her belt.

I catch them on reflex and stare up at the prow in shock. 'I...'

'GET MOVING!' Morgan roars, the harshness of her voice knocking me out of my stupor.

I place the goggles around my neck and run up the stairs to the prow, keeping my eyes down as the howl of the shields echoes all around me. I bring the goggles up, and everything goes as black as night. I lift my head and see that the painful brightness of the energy all around us is muted to mere patterns on the inside of the visor. I step forwards and stub my toe against the railing, peeling the goggles off long enough to get to the prow and take up position against the foremast. I put them back on and turn to the prow, only the shield between me and a thousand exploding stars, the patterns as clear as watching a radar screen.

Only the incoming on this is far larger.

'Port, two points!' I shout as a spiral of flame licks up from below.

The ship responds, the mast rolling over as it turns—more like a fighter than a galleon.

'Starboard, two points!' I howl as the ship tumbles towards a raging burst of energy ahead.

Again, the ship reacts with an elegance bordering on grace, and we continue through the field, the stars thousands of miles away, their energy licking out like water rather than fire. After an hour, my face is red from the heat and sweat drips from my brow, my arms aching from hanging on to the rail. Ahead, I see the stars widening, the explosions thinning out. Then something swims over my field of vision—not a flare of energy, nor an exploding star; something else...

It turns between stars and banks towards the ship.

'THERE'S SOMETHING IN HERE WITH US!' I shout.

Keeper of Stars

'What does it look like?' Morgan's voice is calm in my ear.

I squint through the goggles, fighting the urge to tear them off to get a good look. I lean forwards for a second before realising that I'm about to breach the shield and pull back against the mast.

'Looks...' I squint again as the thing turns over, skirting the edge of a star and turning again. 'I don't know what it looks like.'

'Is it staying near the stars?' Morgan asks.

The thing curls inwards and disappears into the star before emerging from the other side.

'It's not staying *near* the stars; it's swimming *through* them.'

'Curling and uncurling?' Morgan sounds almost relieved.

'Yeah.' I watch as the thing spirals again, and heads towards us. 'Two points starboard.'

The ship is already moving when it soars past us, the golden scales obvious to see at close range as it arcs over. Two sheets of energy unfurl from its sides as it strafes another star.

'And it's got wings.' I hear my own voice as if from afar, while I watch the creature turn again.

'The Keeper of Stars,' Morgan says with a sigh. 'We're going to make it. Just keep an eye on it—call where it goes.'

'What if it heads back into The Dragon?' I lean back against the mast.

'It won't,' Morgan says. 'Keep us close.'

The Keeper swirls in space again, then veers back at us before banking again and coming alongside. It looks at me, eyes like holes in the fabric of space, impossible to turn away from it till it blinks and turns underneath us, its wings spreading out to both sides.

'It's under us,' I shout.

'Watch for the wings,' Morgan calls. 'Tell me when it banks.'

'I can't see without turning back and, if I do that, I can't see ahead,' I yell.

'Nothing will get to us while it's there; watch for the wings.' Her voice is calm, as if sailing above a creature that swims through stars for fun is a normal occurrence.

'Understood.' I fail to keep the quaver from my voice as I turn from the prow, watching as a huge golden wing sweeps up on my left. 'Coming up on port.'

'Are you sure?'

'I...' I think for a second. A chill runs through me as I consider how I'm facing backwards. 'No! Starboard! STARBOARD!'

She chuckles; it's unlike any noise I've heard her make before, full of genuine mirth. 'Thought so. Just keep your eyes on it; it won't hurt us.'

The Keeper rolls again, its movement unhurried, as if it were soaring on a summer's day. The ship matches its movements without me saying a word, and I realise that somehow Morgan knows what it is doing before it does. There's a swift movement underneath us, and I hear the dull click of the Keeper's claws locking on to both sides of the hull, its wings drawing up around the top of the mast.

'IT'S GRABBED US!' I yell. 'WE NEED TO BREAK FREE!'

'No.' Morgan's voice is calm again. 'Come back inside; I'm switching the shields over.'

'IT'S GOT US!' I spin around and see the bright blue glow of a new star shining ahead of us. 'IT'S TAKING US INTO A STAR!'

'I know.' Morgan's voice is still calm. 'Get below, now. I have to move the shields.'

I turn and run down the stairs as the shields change colour, the heat rising all around me. I dive into the nearest door, slamming it shut behind me, only realising after it locks that I'm in the captain's quarters. I look through the thick glass of the porthole ahead as the light in front of us turns bright blue, the colour cold in contrast to the raging heat above us. The shields form up against the wings of the dragon, doubled in strength due to not having to protect the centre of the ship, the wings buffering the energy raging against them.

I look around the room. It's spartan, no signs of great wealth or the trappings of success. There's a captain's chair, and a double bed that hasn't been made, with the faint scent of Michaels' cologne in the room. There's a desk made of thick wood that has the appearance of being hewed from a tree that grew for a long time. On the far side of the cabin is a bookshelf fitted with cables to prevent the books from falling out if the ship has to do sudden evasive manoeuvres.

The raging firestorm outside deters me from even thinking about leaving the room and going up on deck, but the ship isn't shaking or rattling. There doesn't seem to be any stress on the hull.

Like it was designed for this.

There are a number of books on the wooden shelves. The first is a book of accounts, trading records, and deals. The second is a journal, written longhand in a flowing script. The writer has an easy hand with small lettering and the occasional flourishes. It looks to be a key to deciphering a chart of some sort. I spot a bunch of folded papers in the back of the journal, and flip the book open to them, before opening out the paper. It's inked on both sides, illustrated by a master of the craft, with rich, deep colours, the suns all but glowing out of the chart. Something about the chart draws my eyes in, in particular as I drift over something marked as *The Fall*. As I focus on it, the images blur. I pull away with an effort of will and flop down on the bed. The stars were moving on the page...

I fold the chart and place it back in the book.

I've seen this before...

I open the journal at the first page.

10/10/4358.

And so, I find myself in a place I've never known, with no clear path before me...

I turn the book over and read the spine. This isn't the same book as the one I found below in the engineer's quarters—the spine has far more aging, and the cover's worn down from long use. I flip forwards to the end of the journal.

01/01/4375.

The distress signal isn't being cast wide, so we're going to be the only ones getting it, and if the readings are correct, the station still has power and cargo intact. With things the way they have been these last few months, we need a good payday, and even if we're only getting Stenlarian Salvage costs, a reasonable cargo will see us back in the lanes for at least a year. Raley advises me against it, but she doesn't know how bad things are. When we get this payday, we go back to trading regular lanes for fat payoff;, leave the exploring for the explorers.

I close the book. They brought Errin on board eight months ago. The entries prior to that seem to be one a day, the handwriting tiny and precise, without lines, written using a pen and ink that needed blotting. I look up as the porthole goes dark, the cabin dimming as the stars recede into the distance. I hear a whirring noise as the shields re-orientate themselves, and look through the viewport to see the Keeper of Stars veer away, no longer shepherding us, eager to return to swimming among the stars. I turn back as the long strips of wood in the ceiling start to glow with a faint blue luminescence, just enough to read by without straining the eyes. I glance down at the book again, and head towards the bookcase to put it away before Morgan has a chance to find me in here.

Behind me, I hear the click of the door handle turning, and I know I'm not going to be fast enough...

*

I put the book back in the case and turn to her, trying to look innocent. Morgan examines me, her blue eyes looking only a little less magnetic than those of the Keeper.

'Good instinct. Safest place on any ship is always the captain's cabin.'

Actually, it was the first door to duck into.

'I'll get back to my post, captain,' I say, keeping my eyes averted. I'm still uncertain of how she is now, whether she's truly changed for the better; best to start off looking like a loyal servant rather than a problem-in-waiting.

'You don't need to go just yet.' Her tone is light, and I find myself wanting to look her in the eyes, but the memory of the person who threatened to stuff and cook me is still strong.

'I'm not that person anymore.' She speaks as if reading my thoughts, snaps her fingers to get my attention, and gestures up towards her face. 'You don't have to worry about anything like that happening now.'

I look up at her face. She appears calm but, more than that, her body language is different. She's guarded in a way she never was before, arms held just above her waist, as if ready for me to strike at her.

'How long was I'—she pauses, searching for the right words— 'something else?'

'Your last log entry was more than eight months back.' I gesture to the journal behind me.

'Gods...' She sighs. 'I had no idea.'

'Do you remember anything?'

She lifts her eyes, and I know she isn't seeing me in that moment. 'I remember everything.'

'What are you going to do now?'

'I don't know. What's the story with the ship moored alongside us?' Her tone is still light.

'It can fly,' I reply, without thinking, 'but I don't know how the on-board devices work. We could move it, but I can't use most of its systems.'

'Very well. Release the moorings and get it ready to move.'

'Why?' My mouth runs faster than my brain again.

'Because we need all the ships we have in here.' She steps out of the way, gesturing for me to leave. 'The last time I was here was near two decades ago, and it wasn't a good place then. I can't think that it'll have got any better, so find out when that ship's due to jump next. I don't want it near us when it does.'

I nod and step out of the cabin, the brightness of The Dragon still dominating the starfield above us. I turn towards the prow. The darkness beyond is absolute, even after a few seconds staring into the blackness, there's nothing out there, not stars, not planets, nothing but darkness...

How can that be?

I stand on the prow and stare out into the endless black. Without stars, there can't be life; without life... A star blinks into existence, its light glimmering for a second before something moves in front of it.

That's impossible...

I look upwards. There's a faint corona high above, but muted, as if eclipsed. I look left: it's the same out there, as it is below, and to the right.

What could be so large that it can block out a star?

I turn as Shen runs up on deck with a chart in his hands.

'It's here.' Shen stabs his finger at it. 'It's right next to us.'

'What is?' I look at the chart, and feel myself being drawn into it again.

'Whatever the fuck was looking back at us before.' His voice dissipates as I see a dot that can only be the *Unbroken Dawn* flowing across the chart. The massive black mass beyond is staring back at me through the chart and, if that's not enough, the feeling of my own eyes in my head is causing my skin to crawl.

'Get your things together.' I pull the chart shut and push it back into Shen's hands, taking a deep breath. 'Get Petra and Michaels and everything we have; we're getting out of here.'

He nods, turns, and hurries away.

*

The time-ship is still moored to the side of the *Unbroken Dawn*. I drop down and slip in through the open door. The panels I put in earlier are still in place. They'll hold for normal manoeuvring, but not for anything strenuous. The dead body is still floating around. I pull it out of the way, closing my mind to the fluid nature of the suit, blood leaking out of the holes in it as I drag it down the corridor and push it through the gap. I whisper a prayer to a god I don't believe in, hoping that the occupant of the suit understands my necessity, letting the suit drift away, the leaking blood crystallising when the body leaves the *Unbroken Dawn*'s starshield.

I drift back into the ship and fire up the main engines, looking up at the jump mechanism, the wooden timer now clacking down in hours and minutes. The engine's power levels are high, and there's a faint humming that I've never heard before as an unknown power source spools up. The green power line around the edge of the wheel builds while the ship prepares to continue its journey.

With or without us...

I leave the ship and head back up the line to the main deck, the rest of the crew now scurrying around like ants as they follow their captain's orders without fear for the first time in months. I spot Raley, still bleeding from her arms, standing on the upper deck, her smile radiant in the dull glow of The Dragon. I climb the stairs, and she turns to face me.

'Thank you.' She smiles through her obvious pain.

'It was you that did all the work.' I try to match her smile. 'We going to get you patched up?'

'I'm not sure it'll make much difference.' She grits her teeth and nods backwards towards the prow. 'You've seen the thing blocking the stars?'

'How the fuck can you be so calm about it? We're still heading for it.'

'Captains got a plan. We'll be fine.'

'Fine?' I look at the darkness beyond the prow in disbelief. 'Are there some really big guns on the ship I don't know about?'

'Nope. But I've never seen her go straight at something when she could sneak around the back of it. You'll see.'

Me, You, It

The *Dawn* slews, and Raley goes to the starboard side to glance over the edge. I join her at the rail, staring down at the darkness below us. Raley frowns, and turns back as the stern of the ship pulls to starboard.

'Feels like a gravity field,' she murmurs, 'but there are no planets near here big enough to...'

Her voice trails off as the gleaming lights of the ship's masts illuminates a dark mass below us, the deep red of volcanic activity spraying up from it. Raley whirls back to the rudder room, her voice rising high. 'FULL TO PORT!'

The ship rises up and away from the broken planet, and I realign the mast to shine the main searchlight down towards the dark mass below us. The planet has broken like an egg, the centre of it cracked all the way through. All trace of life, vegetation, anything that could have identified it as a planet, long-since stripped away, long gouges almost resembling claw marks cut in scars across its surface.

'What the hell happened to it?' I hear my own voice say.

'The last time I was here,' says Morgan, from behind me, 'there was a creature that destroyed the entire fleet I was with, crushed them like they were toys and fed on their living crew. I swore I'd never come back—there was nothing we could do against it, not with the ships we had then.'

'And now?' I turn to face her, gesturing to the planet below. 'Now it eats planets for lunch! We should be turning around and getting out of here.'

'No.' Morgan holds my gaze steady. 'No, we're not leaving.'

'What?' I take a step towards her. 'If the fleet you were with last time couldn't do it, what chance have we got with a single broadside of eighty-eights?'

'We have something we didn't the last time we came here.' She looks over to the moorings on the side of the ship. 'We have a time machine.'

'What? We're going to go back and kill it before it grows up?'

'No. We have all we need to make sure this will never be a threat again.'

'How?' I stare at her in shock. 'That thing's heart must be miles across.'

'No, it's not,' Morgan puts her hand on my shoulder. 'You have to trust me on this; I know what I'm doing.'

'I don't know you,' I say, frowning. 'Your crew know you; I don't.'

'Oh, you know me. Just not yet; not for a while yet.'

'So why should I trust you?'

'Put a Martian in the air...'

I pause as the words hit me. 'And they'll pull everyone else out of it,' I whisper. 'How do you know that?'

'I know'—Her voice grows deeper and, for a second, she reminds me of Mum whenever she told me to do as I was told—'you need to be in that ship in case we have a problem; someone needs to warn the rest of the universe about this.' She looks to the moorings again. 'Go to the ship, and get ready to head out. *Trust* me.'

I nod, and she lets go of my shoulder. I trot down the stairs to see Michaels, Petra and Shen stood by the moorings.

'I'm staying.' Michaels steps forwards with a smile bordering on apologetic.

'Why?' I ask. 'Thought you were all for getting off the ship at the earliest opportunity.'

'Well, turns out the captain isn't the only woman on the ship who wanted me to be *diplomatic*.' He emphasises the last word with a raised eyebrow.

'Seriously?'

'Seriously.' He shrugs with a roguish grin. 'And now the captain isn't nutty anymore, I figure First Studmuffin for the entire ship might not be a bad career choice.'

'We don't know anything about this place.'

'Which is a problem when your speciality is in navigation or engineering,' he says. 'My speciality is *people*, and they're the same no matter which universe you're in.'

'You sure?' I glance at the crew, who are going about their business. 'What if they all find out?'

'They already know.' His smile gets broader as he nods at Shen. 'When Shen turned out to be all loyal to his wife and not interested in them, they all came to see me. Turns out most of them haven't been portside since the captain started on this mad voyage. I've been *real* popular.'

'Okay, more than I needed to know!' I turn to Petra.

'I'm staying too.' Petra moves next to Michaels.

'Really?' I frown as she nods.

'I got on the *Eagle* at the same time as him, and I've seen a lot more ships than you have. It's never the captain you worry about, it's the crew, and this is a *good* crew to be around.'

'Unless the captain occasionally stuffs and roasts a crew member...' I manage a half-smile.

'That wasn't *her*.' Petra glances up as Morgan looks down at us. 'Every person on board would have died for her before that thing got inside her. There are worse ways to live your life.'

'No life to go back to?' I ask.

'Been in the stars for more than twenty years. Never turn down a good deck when you've got it. We go back there, there's no telling what's waiting for us. My life is here.'

'All right.' I turn to Shen.

'Don't have to ask me twice.' Shen's carrying everything he has and is hopping from foot to foot in his eagerness. 'Good to go right now.'

'All right, get down there,' I say. 'See if you can figure out how the coordinates work.'

'Already done it.' He opens his notebook and points at a scribbled mass of notes. 'There's a list of the coordinates and *dates* that it's going to travel to. The next one is twenty years back, and more than a hundred light years from here.'

'Great,' I say with a frown. 'Well, at least we'll be far enough away that *that* will never find us.'

Shen nods. 'The jump after that is two *thousand* years back from here: same year that we left, and I know the space lanes of that time. I could be home less than a month after I was supposed to be back. My family are still going to be there, waiting.'

'Just like that?'

'I got the best girl in the universe and two kids who spend all the time I'm away trying to chart where I got to.' He looks up at me with the certainty of a father who's never failed his children, a husband who's never failed his wife. *Just like Dad.* 'They know I'll find my way home; I can't let them down.'

I nod, motioning for him to head down below, and lift my head to see Raley and Morgan stood by the upper rail. Morgan points back to The Dragon.

'INCOMING...!'

A ball of fire streaks down from above, breaching the starshield and smashing into the deck, before skidding to a halt by the stairs to the upper deck. The flames lick around it, then, with infinite slowness, it starts to rise, as the scent of scorched flesh drifts across the deck. The thing turns, taking the shape of a person as it moves, its head turning to look at me, then up at Morgan and Raley.

'thInk tO stOp mE sO EAsIly?' Its voice is a grating sluice of vocal cords, but its movements are getting faster as the flames die down, flesh growing back by the second.

'Errin!' I take the spanner from my belt and heft it, two-handed, as Raley jumps from the upper rail, winding down the side banister to land on the opposite side of the ship.

'twEnty yEArs hAvE I wAItEd fOr thIs.' The Errin-thing turns to look up at Morgan, the flames on her skin all but out, but her eyes are still cavities of fire in her skull. 'tOdAy, yOU pAy fOr yOUr sIns AgAInst mE.'

Raley draws her sword. Her arm's no longer bleeding, but it's clear she's still in pain, no match for whatever Errin is now. I signal for Michaels to take the other side and move around to stay in Errin's line of sight.

She turns, looking up at Morgan. 'rEmEmbEr nOw whAt I mAdE yOU dO?'

The blood drains from Morgan's face. 'I remember.' She points out into the darkness, where the Beast waits. 'Do you remember what we just did to you? What we're going to do again?'

'bUt I Am hErE nOw.' Errin's mouth widens into a burned scar across her face. 'I Am hErE tO tAkE bAck whAt yOU tOOk frOm mE.'

Raley's hands twitch in front of her, and both Morgan and I read the Airless message.

Get her to the vents.

I tap the spanmer on the deck, faint buzzing emitting from its head as it discharges, the sound drawing Errin back to me.

'yOU mOst Of All.' She spreads her arms, the movement tearing the muscles underneath, the blood spraying out and then coagulating within a heartbeat, the muscles reforming again with a sound like leather being stretched. 'yOU wIll nOt dIE fOr yEArs.'

'You don't know me at all.' I move round her as Raley communicates with Morgan via Airless. I don't take my eyes off Errin long enough to read the message, but Michaels turns and motions for Petra and Shen to get off deck. Errin paces forwards, unhurried, paying no attention to anything else.

Anything that can survive a trip into a star isn't going to be worried by us.

I back up, stepping over the landing jets as Errin draws closer, keeping the distance between us. I lift my head as Morgan waves from the top deck. Errin pauses and turns as Raley fires the ship's grapple. The magnetic block at the end of the line strikes Errin in the chest, before bursting straight through and thudding against the third mast. Errin looks down at the line passing through her the way I might look at a fly landing on my arm. She takes hold of the cable with both hands and starts to push it to the side, the line tearing through the flesh of her torso.

'HIT THE MAGNET!' Morgan howls.

I bring the spanmer down with a strike that would make Raley proud, the energised head disrupting the magnetic block of the grapple. Errin hunkers down to the deck, her scorched fingers scrabbling at the vent holes as the lines starts to pull her backwards.

She looks up at me in triumph as the line starts to tear free, her grip holding steady.

'*DAWN!*' I shout out, hoping that the ship will remember, even though Morgan is back in command.

The vents across the entire ship open and a blast of hot air sends Errin soaring, the line still attached as she clings to it, desperate not to be cast back into the void. The line winds around to the rear of the ship, still attached to the cannon. I hear the thud of a body against the hull—the line pulling tight can only mean she's still attached. I run up the stairs to where Morgan and Raley are staring over the edge. Far below, the line is banging against the side as Errin starts to climb back up. I notice how the line is threaded down beside the rudder and get an idea.

'I'm going down there.' I slip my Isogloves on and start to climb up on the rail.

Raley pulls me back down. 'You can't go down there. Give me the gloves—I'll go.' She winces as the wound in her arm opens.

'I need to.' I flex my hands in the gloves. 'I'm the engineer.'

'Yes.' Morgan lays her hand on top of Raley's. 'She's right. Better we stay here, in case we need to pull her back on board.'

'Be ready to turn the rudder when I say.' I squeeze Raley's arm. 'I'll be back.'

I vault over the side and slide down the line, pausing before the rudder, as Morgan holds the ship steady. The rudder rolls all the way over to port, and I look down as the line pulls tight. The ship's movement causes Errin to swing upwards, and she spots me hitching the line against the hull, preventing her from swinging back up on deck. She scowls, and pulls the line to get to me, drawing it through her body, now looking like a rotting spider as she scrambles upwards. I magnetise my boots and raise the spanner to strike. Errin glowers at me, her hate almost tangible this close. She bunches her legs and takes a deep breath. I keep the spanner held high.

She leaps...

I strike like she's every generator that has ever given me shit.

There's a bright flash when the spanner connects with her head, and Errin goes limp as the energy discharges, dazing her.

'STARBOARD NOW!' I howl, leaping forwards to grab Errin and shove her downwards. The rudder rolls back, and I reach down, grabbing the side of it, the back of my glove lighting up. Errin, who has been drifting, insensate, shakes her head and opens her eyes. Seeing my hand on the rudder, her mouth splits into a grin, thinking that it must be offline. Her hand reaches out to use it to steady herself.

Her hand connects, and the scream of the starborn thing carries out into the void, her extraordinary powers of regeneration unable to nullify the disintegrating effect of the rudder.

'HARD OVER!' I yell, as Errin brings her feet up to try and push away from it. Her hand and arm start to dissolve as the power courses through her, the rudder crushing her against the ship as the ship rolls. She looks up at me with eyes like dying stars, the flames within now burning the edges. The ragged tear of her mouth opens, and fire engulfs her face. Even now while she's dying, she reaches towards me, her hatred tangible; a creature that has known forever, brought low by those who have lived just a flicker of its own long life. I keep one hand on the rudder, bringing my legs above me to rest against the ship, the magnets holding me there as I gaze down at the burning beast. There's a shudder from within the mass of flames, and it goes limp, staying fixed to the rudder, burning from within.

Something's not right here.

I heft the spanner and take a step back as the burning mass lunges, elongating its limbs in ways that no living creature should be able to. I squeal in fright and strike down, missing in my haste. The fingers grasp my boots and pull with muscles like steel cables. I feel my feet starting to shift, the magnets straining to hold me in place. An endless scream tears through bleeding vocal cords, and I wrap my hand around the trailing ropes above, circling them as many times as I can around my wrist.

No other choice. This is going to hurt.

I bring the spanner down on the creature's hand; there's a blue flash as it connects, and the charge surges through both of us. A flare of burning flesh, and the scream ceases. I feel myself falling forwards as consciousness fades, the rudder looming large.

Me, You

I wake in the secret engineering compartment, the spanner beside me on the bed and Morgan sitting on the chair opposite.

No lipstick, no madness in her eyes.

I try to move, the dull ache of the spanner's charge like a weight on my chest. Keeping my head rested on the pillow seems a much easier option. Morgan smiles and leans forwards, resting her arms on her knees.

'Good job I suspected what you were going to do, isn't it?'

'How?' I frown.

'In time, I might tell you.' She taps the side of her nose, her smile giving way to a look of sadness. 'But of all the things we have, time is not among them. I know you're not going to feel like it, but you need to get up—there are things we need to be doing.'

'*We?*' I groan, rolling sideways to swing my legs off the bed. 'I only know you as a psycho who threatened to make a meal out of me for the crew if I didn't perform. The crew may trust you, but *I* don't know you at all.'

'*Mi lewe vi june,*' she says and extends her hand, palm up.

I reach forwards in response to her fluent Martian. *My life for yours.* My hand hovers above hers, and she brings her palm up closer to mine.

'*Rooi, wreld en blod.*' She holds her hand level below mine, a gesture of the working caste from the Martian mines.

'Red, world and blood,' I whisper, dropping my hand down to hers, gripping with my little finger and thumb around her wrist, her fingers still level as she looks at me, showing me that I have the control. '*Na miljen hant geha.*'

She smiles at my words, the Martian pledge of allegiance—*a million hands held*—her little finger and thumb closing around my wrist. '*Ji ken mi.*'

'I *don't* know you.' I look deep into her eyes, and she cocks her head to the side, a faint smile growing at the corner of her mouth. 'Who *are* you?'

'Your future.' Her smile gets broader. 'As you are my past...'

There's a rumble from the plates below us, and the ship veers to the side, rolling to avoid something.

'Now is not the time.' She looks upwards towards the main deck and taps her index finger against the underside of my wrist, unwrapping her thumb. 'Right now, it's down to us to save everyone else.'

'When?' I grip her hand, unwilling to let her go. 'When will you tell me?'

'When your dress sense improves.' She reaches with her other hand and brushes her thumb against my nose. *Just like Mum used to when she needed me to get moving.* 'Come on, *soldaat.*'

Soldier. I stand without thinking, Mum's voice echoing across the years. 'All right.' I nod with more confidence than I feel. 'What are we doing?'

'You need to take Shen and the ship. Get out of here. Come back if we make it through this.'

'What are you going to do?' I say, frowning.

'Go for the head. Well, the nearest thing it's got to a head.'

'What is it? Really?'

'Hungry,' she replies. 'It doesn't see us as a threat, just food. That's how you get out of here—the *Dawn* is a bigger meal. It'll come after us while you get clear.'

'Just like that?' I give her an incredulous look. 'Just fly out, and that's it?'

'There are two Martians here. One of us would be enough to pull it out of the sky, remember? You need to get clear, get Shen back to his own time.'

The ship shudders again, this time it feels like something hit us.

'We're out of time.' She scrambles up the ladder. 'Come on.'

Up on deck, the creature's mass blots out the stars around it, only the faint gleam of The Dragon providing any illumination in the darkness.

'Unmoor that ship,' Morgan shouts to the crew, before turning back to me and lowering her voice. 'Go, get clear.'

I nod, and run in the direction of the other ship as she heads up to the helm. Shen is already on his way down, but there's no sign of Michaels or Petra. Raley pauses from ordering the crew about and looks over at me, closing the distance with two quick steps.

'Watch yourself out there.' She touches me on the shoulder for a second, as if now that Morgan's back, she shouldn't be so close to others. 'Come back safe.'

'I will.' I grin like a maniac, turning into her arms and touching my head to hers. 'Like you taught me, treat it like a bit of bastard machinery.'

'Yep.' She half-smiles and then takes a deep breath. 'I'll see you again.' It sounds more like a question than a statement.

'You will.' I try to keep my voice level, but I can see from her face that I haven't succeeded.

'Go.' She claps me on the shoulder, finding the strength to turn away so that I don't have to.

I say nothing, taking the guideline and swinging down to the ship below. I slip in through the door, watching it seal behind me before I make my way up to the front where Shen is stood at the wheel.

'You *do* know how to fly this thing, right?' He turns to me.

'Let's hope so.' I climb up and take the wheel as he adjusts the telegraph to the side of us, the movement causing the ship to drift away from the side of the *Dawn*. Freed from the gravity generated by the *Dawn*, I activate the magnets on my boots and plant my feet on the deck, holding firm as we accelerate away. Shen turns to the other controls and traces a line across what appears to be a plain panel. Symbols light up as his fingers dance across the controls.

'It's why the ship got brought down so easily when we first encountered it.' He glances back at me for a second. 'One person can pilot it, but anything needing any skill needs two.'

'All right.' I bring the ship about and stare out into the darkness; it's like looking at the inside of my eyelids—only the afterimage of shapes remains. 'How fast does this thing go?'

Shen grins like a bandit, and I feel the acceleration through my boots as the ship surges forwards like an atmo-racer. I put my finger to my ear as the comms chime.

'Get clear!' Morgan's shout is distorted by the distance from the ship. 'We're coming in on your starboard. Make the run when we start firing. Better hope those cannons of yours still kick like one-oh-fives.'

'They will.' I try to grin as a tendril the size of a dreadnought whips through space, the *Dawn* slewing to the side to avoid it. 'Don't get too close.'

'Don't worry about us,' Morgan yells. 'Just g—'

The comms are cut off in a burst of static, and I see the *Dawn* trailing a river of molten energy behind it as a tendril brushes against her hull. I force myself to look back at the Beast, spotting a light beyond it in the darkness, and turn the wheel towards it. Lazy, thrashing tentacles whip into space all around us; there's no way to get clear.

We can't make it through there—we just need to stay alive till the drive kicks in.

'Everything we've got,' I shout behind me. 'Aim for that star.'

'Gonna do *what*?' Shen's disbelief is tangible and has the faint smell of his last meal.

'It can't hit us if we're too close,' I yell. 'When's the timedrive activating?'

'Within a minute,' he shouts back. 'We just need to stay out of the way. Turn around.'

'We move faster, or it hits us. We're not the size of the *Dawn*, and we can't get through that sea of tentacles,' I howl back. 'Give me everything we've got.'

The horizon blurs as Shen pushes the ship to full thrust. The light wavers as we hurtle towards it. As the tentacles close in on us, I realise that I'm not looking at the star, but at something else, and the Beast divines where we're going. The tentacles start to close around the light, but it's slow; it's spent countless years eating planets and not fearing anything. I bank the ship over, and draw up level with the light ahead of us. The cabin seems to grow colder as something focusses on us. My head buzzes as I sense something older than space looking down at us without understanding.

I sEE yOU...

Errin's voice echoes in my head, magnified like it's being howled through a loudspeaker, muffled as if the words were being shouted through water. The light shines in on us, and Shen screams, before collapsing to the floor in a quivering heap. It feels like there are spiders in my head, crawling around my brain, and it's all I can do to cling to the wheel and hold the course. My whole life flashes before me, and it's a half-second before I realise that it's not because I'm dying but because *it* is sifting *through* me. It recognises the possible threat, and my hand comes up to wipe the blood from my nose as it begins to crush my mind. I hold tight to the memories I have, scrabbling at my flight suit to take out the photo of my parents, clinging to that memory as the ship lances forwards. The engines behind me howl, and there's a lurching sensation as my vision blurs and the universe bends around me again. I fight the encroaching darkness, but it's too much for me.

Me

I wake to find myself swaying at the helm, my boots holding my feet to the deck, the rest of me drifting loose. I look around, every part of me aching as I flex my hands. It takes three tries before any of my brain's commands get through to my body but my thoughts thaw the numbness within my hands and I see my fingers moving. I look through the front screen as a faint light shines into the ship, and see the revolving core of the Beast haemorrhaging into space, blood spreading out like a cloak around it. It spins, uncontrolled, the timefield having torn it away, the body still trying to use parts that are no longer connected. The light shifts away from me, and I glance backwards at Shen, unconscious on the floor.

Got to get out of here before it recovers enough to catch us.

I pull the telegraph back one notch and the ship pushes away, the body of the Beast still turning without purpose in space.

dEAth sUffEr blEEd.

Errin's voice in my head again, though faint now, confused, no longer all powerful. I can't tell if it's a threat or just what it's feeling for the first time. The ship turns, and I push the telegraph forwards, the ship responds as it did before, and I keep my touch light, not trusting my hands yet.

Nothing we can do to it here.

Shen comes around after several minutes of gibbering. The ship is now far enough away that the Beast can't get to us, but close enough to still keep an eye on it. I wait for him to compose himself before turning to him.

'Made it.' I force a cheerful tone into my voice. 'Don't know where *it* is though...'

He staggers upright, his brain working on autopilot as he consults the charts on the ship, then looks out of the window. 'That *thing* can't get to us, can it?'

'It makes one move, and we're out of here.' I keep my eyes on it. 'Be good if I knew which way to go though...'

'All right.' He takes a deep breath and examines the charts again, tracing the lines with his finger. 'We're on the far side of the Stenlarian divide.'

'Where's that?'

'The other side of the galaxy from where we were. And, if this is right'—he points at the clock above the wheel—'twenty years before *when* we were there.'

'Just like that? How do we get back to when and where we just were?'

'We don't.' He shakes his head, tapping the time controls. 'I might be able to figure this out, given a month or so, but the next jumps are back to the time we came from, some thirty thousand years back, and then to a date several million years ahead of us. We make the choice to get off or go back where we came from, or there's no guarantee what is waiting for us.'

'What are you doing?' I already know the answer.

'I'm getting off at the next jump.' His smile is one of relief. 'We know this ship can do it, and we know we're safe to jump in it—next stop for me is home. I won't be setting out again.'

'Ever?' I raise an eyebrow.

'Enough excitement for this man for one lifetime. I'm never going to risk my family being left without me again.'

I wish I had that chance.

'Reckon you can steer this without me?'

'Been out here twenty years. Not much in the universe I can't pilot. Besides, all I've got to do is wait for it to jump and then get off.'

'All right, where's the nearest base from here?'

'Weeks travel on a normal ship. This thing could probably get there within the hour if we push it.'

'I think turning up faster than any ship in history would probably get us put away for a long time. I'm fine with travelling at a slower pace if you are.'

'I packed enough supplies for a few weeks.' Shen glances around the ship. 'Don't know what else we've got here though.'

'Let's get going first and then see what we have.' I point at the Beast. 'Show me the way out. We'll check our supplies when that's way behind us.'

'We're just going to leave it here? What happens if someone else finds it?'

'Someone else *will* find it. *That* out there is Errin, or whatever *transformed into* Errin. It will get back to where we just came from; it'll take it the next twenty years, but it'll get back there.'

'Seems wrong.' Shen stares out at the Beast. 'We should find a way to get rid of it before it does any more damage.'

'How long before the next jump?'

Shen glances back at the charts. 'Ten days.'

'Reckon we can build the *Dawn* in ten days?'

'No.' He sighs, and his shoulders sag. 'No, we couldn't.'

"Reckon we can convince someone else to come out here and shoot it up?"

"No," His sigh is deeper this time and he nods, accepting my truth.

'Then we're out of here,' I say. 'Show me the way.'

The ship doesn't have an autopilot, so Shen and I take turns at the wheel, heading towards what he believes is the nearest starbase. The ships we see on the way are far more like the *Starlight Eagle*, airtight boxes bristling with weapons.

Something must have happened in the years in between.

Searching through the ship, I find that someone has placed my personal effects in the hold, complete with the journal that Raley gave me when I first came on board the *Dawn*. I turn it over and open it. A folded piece of paper flutters out of it to the floor. I pick it up and unfold it. The note inside is in my handwriting, but it wasn't me who wrote it. It reads:

Catarina

We came out into the stars looking for adventure and seeing you now has shown me that what I thought might have been the case, truly is. I don't know what will happen to you in the time between now and when we will meet again, and I don't know what will happen to me after you go, but I've had twenty years of the best adventures I could ever have hoped for. I believe that they will now be yours to enjoy. The contents of the bag are for Shen. He'll find a quiet corner of the universe and live the life he promised his family. You do not need anything from in there. Live bold—the rewards are there for you to take, and trust your heart. Remember that you love bookstores.
One day, you will write this letter, but you won't be you anymore, I'm sure of it.

Till we meet again.
Morgan

I fold the note and close my eyes for a second. If Morgan is right, if I am her, then I have the greatest of adventures to look forward to and, somewhere along the way, Errin's going to get her revenge by turning me into a cannibalistic psycho.

I hope the future isn't as written as she thinks it is...

Planning For An Unclear future

I look into the box and take out the black bag within, tipping the contents into my hand. Twenty Invarian blood sapphires gleam from my palm, and I draw in a sharp breath, remembering Raley's words.

Just one could buy almost any ship I wanted, twenty...

I shake my head and turn to the back of the journal. My personal papers are attached there, along with the citizenship award from the Martian colleges, and my photos. I open the journal at the first page: blank, not a word upon it, but a metal pen with a pressurised cartridge waits in the book loop for a hand to bring it to the page.

'How many days to get where we need to go?' I ask.

'Three, maybe four.' Shen shrugs. 'Do we need to get there faster?'

'No. What's the date?'

'Sixth of the tenth.' He answers without looking up from the wheel, extending his left hand to point at the date on the ship's charts. 'The year, 4358. Why?'

'No reason.' I try to keep my voice light as I think of the date that the journal started, my handwriting two days from now. I control my breathing as my heart pounds, the realisation that she... that I...wasn't wrong. *We are the same person.* I sit in silence for a minute as I think of all that must have happened to her. The possibility that things could change, that I could change them, but then I smile, if she was me, then she had these same thoughts, and...

I open my eyes and look around the cabin, Shen still steering the ship without a care in the world, secure in the knowledge that he'll see his family again, the only part of his future that matters. The realisation that I'll never know if I took the same path as she did, and I'll go crazy if I spend my life second guessing what I dd before. Live today, worry about tomorrow if it ever arrives. I take the blood sapphires from the black bag, knowing that even one would be enough for a family to live well for their whole lives. I take my keepsake box and pull out an empty envelope, place all the sapphires in it, and write *Shen* on the envelope, before sealing it. 'I think we may have lucked out on the cargo though; there's an envelope here for you.'

Shen reaches back, takes the envelope, and rattles it next to his ear.

'Careful.' I put my hand on his. 'If it contains what mine did, you won't want to lose any of them.'

He glances at me and opens the envelope with care, his mouth falling open when he sees the contents. 'Are these real?'

'As far as I can tell.' I grin.

'Never have to work again.' He smiles. 'Nice place out beyond the belt where the politics don't reach; maybe some real grass under our feet. What are you going to do with yours?'

'Get a ship and a crew and go back out there.' I feel calmer than I ever have before, the choice of what to do with my life now clear. Morgan is right: I don't need the sapphires to make my own way in the world now.

'Seriously?' Shen looks at me like I've lost my mind. 'Isn't the reason we work out here so we can one day get away from it all?'

'Not me.' I grin at him. 'I came out here to see the whole ocean of stars one at a time.'

'All right then,' he says, and folds the envelope in an intricate way that will prevent any of them falling out. 'On to a new life then.'

*

Four days later, the gleaming outlines of the Stenlarian starbase can be sighted on the far horizon. Shen has spent the last few days studying the ways of this universe and taps at the display. The cameras zoom in on the starbase. It's a brutal monument to the designers' lack of imagination, every part of it functional, not a single piece beautiful.

'We don't have permit papers, and we don't have identification. So, while we could dock, it would take us weeks, possibly months to answer all the questions and, by then, this ship, and my way home, would be gone.'

'Not the best way forwards.' I sigh. 'What can we do?'

'*We?*' He makes a point of not looking me in the eye. 'Nothing. We dock and it's over.'

'I can't come with you, and you can't drop me off.' I look at the steady lane of ships passing in and out of the station. 'What about a distress signal?'

'They come screaming out looking for whoever is needing their help, then they'll go screaming after the ship that's dropping its passengers.' Shen taps the display, where three spike-shaped ships covered in red and blue lights are roving in a tight formation around the station.

'You telling me that this thing can't outrun anything else in the system?' I raise an eyebrow, and start to smile again. 'I've still got my breathertech. All I need is for you to launch me in the right direction with a signal, then get the hell out of here.'

'I'd be abandoning you. I—'

'I'm abandoning *you.*' I take his hand. 'If I wasn't being selfish and wanting to stay here, you'd take me with you, wouldn't you?'

'Of course.'

'Then you are not failing in your duty to a friend. It was you who got me here, and I've got the whole ocean to myself, but you can't come with me.'

He looks down, then back up at me with a tight smile, and nods once. 'All right. You're going to cause a stir when you arrive wearing no suit, though. Thought about what to do when they start asking you questions?'

I grin. 'Plead ignorance and ask for asylum.'

'Be careful who you talk to.' Shen's still conflicted about leaving me behind. 'The wrong word in the wrong place and you'll find yourself on a slave barge to the Tyrannous stars.'

'I'll be fine. Come on, while you can still let me go without dying of guilt.'

*

I stand in the airlock, having changed my outfit to the light armour Morgan left for me in among my gear, my regular clothing in my box. I flip my breathertech on and look at Shen in his full vac suit. I shoulder my keepsake box with the straps and raise my right hand, palm up in the traditional Martian farewell. *'Gaan veili.'* I place my left hand over my heart and then up to my head. *Go Safely.*

Shen smiles and shakes his head, reaching to take my hand, turning it sideways in the earther tradition of showing that we are equals and holding it firm as he shakes it. 'Safe travels, Martian.' He shrugs by way of apology. 'I have no idea what you just said.'

'No Earther ever does. What's the point when everyone speaks Terran.' I grin and draw him close to hug, pulling his seals into place. 'I'll see you again someday.'

'I hope so.' He steps back, putting his hand on the controls.

I step into the airlock again, and it cycles shut in front of me. I turn to face the door and nod backwards as I see the station come into view. I hear a click and the airlock opens, all sound ceasing as I shoot out, adrift in the ocean of stars.

If This is the Way It Was, This is the Way It Must Be

I may have miscalculated the arrival vector...

Not much of an epitaph...

What I thought was going to be a gentle cruise across a few miles of space turns into a charge towards the darkness of certain death. I try to move, to change my course as the station hurtles closer, realising with a shock that I'm going to overshoot and that the only thing the breathertech will accomplish is to keep me alive till I die cold and alone.

Can't end this way.

There's a flare from beneath me as I fly past the station, and I feel something fasten onto my leg. I look down to see a loop of grapple cable tighten around my ankle, the line pulling me down towards the platform below. A lone figure secures the line to the safety rail on the side of the station, then jets up to catch me as I plunge towards the side, my heart in my mouth as I consider the very real possibility of this particular adventure ending before it's begun.

The figure twists with a grace bordering on the sublime, catching my arm and pulling me close, before turning to land like a dancer on one foot. Their visor is sunshielded, making it impossible to tell who, or what, is behind it. But the grip is sure, and the suit is well-equipped, all the way down to a sword with a red silk handle bound to its side. The figure guides me to the airlock and cycles the air back in, waiting till the pressure equalises before opening the suit and stepping out, and turning back to face me.

It's a woman, with short dark hair and iridescent blue eyes.

Her face is thin and high-boned, with hollow cheeks leading to a narrow chin. She has thick strands of muscle all the way down her torso, the results of years of hard work. She looks me up and down and frowns. 'How is it you're still alive?' Her voice sounds younger than her manner. She rests her hand on her sword. 'You're not Ascended, are you?'

'I'm definitely not Ascended.' I raise my hands in surrender and shrug my keepsake box to the floor. 'I came here to make my fortune. You know this sector, don't you?'

'Well enough to know that no one comes here on purpose.' She keeps her distance, her hand not moving from the hilt. 'What did you hope to find here?'

'An ocean of stars, a ship to sail them on, and a person to sail them with.' I smile and step towards her. 'Would you like to help me find it? Would you like to come out into the stars?'

'I've got a steady job here. Why venture further?'

I look down at the marks on my hands where the Invarian sapphires had sat and smile, raising my gaze to look deep into Raley's eyes.

'Because it's a grand adventure.' I hold my hand out to her, "You come with me and we'll roam the universe, we'll fight gods and monsters and have crates of Invarian Sapphires to ourselves."

'Crates of Invarian Sapphires?' She frowns, my words must have sounded like an empty boast. 'Where are people like us going to get those?'

"I don't know, but I know we'll find them, you and me together."

"And where are we going to go to find them?" She leans forwards, more and more interested by the second.

'To the far side of the universe and back. What's your name?'

'Raley, Constance Raley.' She cocks her head to the side. In her eyes is the jewel of the woman I met twenty years from now. She takes my hand; her touch is like electricity on my skin, and she leans closer. 'And what do I have to do to earn my place?'

'Make sure I don't do anything stupid.'

'Why do I get the feeling I'm not going to be paid enough for that job...' Her smile gets broader. She doesn't let go of my hand, and I don't let go of hers.

'Don't worry, I'm not as dumb as I seem.' I smile and step close enough to feel the warmth of her breath on my face. 'Come with me?'

'I will.' Her voice is almost a whisper. 'What's your name?'

'Morgan.' I glance at the reflection in the sun visor behind her, seeing the woman I'll become staring back at me. 'Call me Morgan.'

PART TWO

Forgotten By Time

The Titan's Boneyard

The immense tentacle thrashes through space, far too close for comfort, the rudder still not responding as well as it once did.

How long is this thing going to take to die?

I bring the ship around and up, into the bright light shining from the Dragon. The sails draw from the energy, and the *Dawn* soars high out of the path of the tendril. I look up from the wheel to the mass of the Beast.

Still moving, though not coherent—has to be random impulses from after we tore the core out. No way it can still be alive.

Raley comes alongside me and looks at the tendril sweeping back towards us. 'I presume there's a reason why we're still hanging around a trillion tons of dead meat?'

'Just want to be sure it's dead. Glad there's no air out here—the smell would have killed us days ago.'

'Whereas tendrils larger than Renis station are just a small thing for us to worry about...' Her frown doesn't fade. 'What are we supposed to do with that?'

'Honestly? I don't know. At the moment, no one's going to risk coming back here because they think this thing is still alive, but when they find out its dead, it'll be open season.'

'So what? Worst that happens is that we have to watch out for Beast burgers in every fast-food place near here for the rest of eternity.' The glint in her eyes carries the same mischievous edge from when I first met her, back when I was Catarina, so many years ago, the faint quirk of her smile unhidden despite her best attempts.

'You just want to get out of here, don't you?' I turn the ship over again.

'Well, out of the Broken Hollows, for sure.' Her fingers are playful on my forearm. 'But I'd settle for getting you *off* the wheel for a few hours...'

'I'm not going anywhere,' I say with a smile. 'There's plenty of time.'

'You've been some*thing* else for a while.' Raley pulls closer. 'I've missed you.'

'I've missed you too.' I smile to cover my unease, dark memories still dancing behind my eyelids. 'I just want to make sure that it can't do to anyone else what it did to me, y'know?'

'I know.' Raley looks up as the tendril shudders and then drifts, immobile. 'But it's dead, and we need to get out of here before we're as dead as it is.'

'We will.' I squeeze her hand and hold it to my heart. 'Another day, and we're gone, my word on it.'

'All right.' She draws close and her lips brush against mine, the press of her against me a happy thought while surrounded by all this death. She smiles, but it's a shallow one, as she turns away.

She's afraid that I'm still not me, that something of the Beast remains within.

I close my eyes for a second, the weight of memories getting stronger.

It wasn't me; it wasn't me; I had no choice...

The thought doesn't make any of what I did while it was in control of me any easier. I know the crew don't blame me, that they know it wasn't me, but must be hard to go from being promised a king's ransom each to finding yourselves alone on the far side of The Dragon in the boneyard of a biogenetic titan. I turn the ship again as another tendril thrashes closer.

Raley's right; we need to get out of here before one of these scores a lucky hit.

I glance back as I hear hesitant footsteps on the stairs behind me. Clara steps up on deck and steadies herself as I roll the ship over.

'Clara. What is it?'

'I don't know.' She makes her way along the top rail, making sure each foot is planted firm before picking up the other. 'But I've picked up a signal a few hundred thousand kilometres from here.'

'In which direction?' *I suspect I know the answer from her expression.*

'Towards the centre of that thing.' Clara points off to the starboard side. 'It's a repeating signal, sent on Stenlarian frequencies, but the code isn't one I recognise.'

'Play it for me.'

She pulls her hair back from her face and adjusts the controls on the side of her ear, opening her mouth as she tunes into the frequency. There's a sound of static from her jawline, and she adjusts her ear again, the sound becoming three short beeps, followed by three long ones, and three shorter ones—the code repeated over and over again.

'Like I said, not a code I'm familiar with,' Clara says, turning down the volume but leaving it broadcasting.

'Imperial Navy distress beacon,' Raley says. 'Very rarely used. Stenlarians don't like to announce that they're in trouble, so there's got to be a good reason for them broadcasting that.'

I nod to Clara. 'Where's it coming from? Have you managed to get a good fix on the position?'

'I have. Its frigate sized, but it's in the middle of the debris field. We'd have to get a lot closer to get a good view of it.'

'It's definitely on Stenlarian frequencies?' I ask.

'It is.'

'And you,' I say, turning to Raley, 'you're sure about Stenlarians not liking to announce when they're in trouble.'

'They sure don't.' Raley shakes her head.

'Could it be a trap?'

'You'd have to know Stenlarian codes to respond to it.' Raley shrugs. 'So, the only people who'd respond to it would be Stenlarian.'

'Or curious, like me.' I grin.

'No one's curious like you.' Raley returns my grin. 'Are we going to take a look?'

'Plot a course.' I nod to Clara. 'Avoid the denser areas wherever we can; I want to be out of here within a few days if possible.'

I bank the *Dawn* over and turn the sails towards the light.

*

The shadow of the Beast is a constant thing now, blotting out all but the tiniest remnants of the remaining star, just enough to keep the ship cruising without digging into the battery reserves, not enough to keep us moving at the speed we need to be at. Raley and I take turns keeping the ship on course—time that could have, should have, been spent with her, if only to reassure her that I'm still me and not whatever she's had to deal with these last few months.

Always subject to the requirements of my ship...

My comms chimes, bringing me back to the here and now as Raley comes on the line, her voice quiet but urgent. 'Mor, you'd better come up here now.'

I head up to the deck as Raley rolls the ship over and brings her to a stop. Above us, something huge and metallic rotates in the darkness, the faint light illuminating the deep gouges on the other ship's plating, where something broke its spine.

'ISN *Sonskyn*.' Clara points upwards as the ship's identification marks come into view. 'It's Imperial Navy, but...' She frowns and sweeps her hand backwards to encompass the whole of the ship. 'The colours are from a time before the schism with the Chere faction.'

'How long has it been here then?' I ask.

'More than a thousand years.' Raley drops the gravity anchors. 'It must have been here since—'

'Since the Chaeni wars,' Clara interrupts, adjusting her eye to view the ship in more detail.

'Yeah.' Raley frowns, examining the entire length of the ship then looking at Clara. 'You know something you're not telling?'

'Everything they ever recorded on it.' Clara taps the side of her head. 'I don't believe what they recorded though.'

'Why not?' I turn to face her.

'The Stenlarians sent two ships against the Chaeni, both of

them holding a new weapon designed to nullify the threat they posed.' Clara adjusts her eye piece and looks down at the pale deck, her eye now projecting an image of two ships, both identical to the one floating above us. 'The ISN *Swartgat* deployed its weapon thirty light years from the Stenlarian border, resulting in the Chaeni Worlds becoming what they are now. The other ship, the ISN *Sonskyn*—she points upwards and her voice goes quiet—'was reported lost with all hands.'

'That's not a warship.' I glance back to see Michaels stood behind me. 'It hasn't got the weapons or the armour to hold out in a fight—they'd have been torn to pieces.'

'Looks like they *did* get torn to pieces,' Clara muses.

'What was on it?' Raley asks.

'Same payload as the *Swartgat*. Six hundred souls, and a payload referred to only as an *eterster*, to be deployed on the other side of the Stenlarian Borders.'

Eterster. *Eater of stars.*

'There's no way a weapon that could be carried on a ship managed to compress all the Chaeni Worlds,' Raley says. 'The power required would be more than everything the empire has ever produced, and ever *will* produce.'

'They knew that. They had to use another source of power, and they found a way,' says Clara. 'The weapon uses the energy of the stars caught up in its effect to keep the field stable.'

'What?' I ask.

'Can't pretend I understand the science behind it,' Clara taps the side of her head again. 'The files I've got are the only ones that have been released, and most of those are Imperial propaganda saying that they froze the Chaeni in time so they couldn't cause any more deaths.'

'Just like that...' Raley deadpans.

'Just like that.' Clara's eyes go distant as she accesses the other files. 'Gravity distorts time. If you have enough of it, time almost ceases. Anything caught in the field of effect wouldn't even know it had been trapped. It wouldn't know anything had happened until the effect ceased.'

'The ship feeds on the energy of the stars within the field?'

'The field that the ship generates doesn't protect it from the effect of the gravity; the crew knew it was a one-way trip—they were going to be trapped in there forever with their enemy.'

'How do you reverse the field?' Raley asks.

'You don't,' Clara sighs. 'Come on Raley, Stenlarians don't play for halves. They'd be happy they didn't have to put any more energy into it.'

'Explains why no one goes near the Chaeni Worlds,' Raley says. 'The gravity is so intense that no one can navigate around it.'

'And if it contains more *things* like this,' Michaels says, staring beyond the ship to the remains of the Beast around it. 'Who would want to?'

'But *could* it be reversed somehow, hypothetically?' I ask.

'Theoretically, I guess.' Clara's eyes go distant for a second. 'If you believe what's in the files, you could reverse the field generator in this ship and that *might* release the field around anything else that was caught in it.'

'I'm not saying that I'm *looking* to reverse it.' I put my hand on Clara's arm. 'But knowing what we're dealing with would be a good thing, and I'd rather the weapon doesn't go off when we might be caught up in the blast radius. Don't much fancy blinking and waking up a billion years later.'

'We're in agreement there. I'll take a look through the files.' Clara stares upwards, her eyes wide. She seems to be enjoying the question of something that the computer in her head doesn't have the answer to, a feeling she hasn't experienced in a very long time. 'With your permission, captain, I'd like to take a look at the ship and see if anything can be salvaged.'

'It's not going to be pretty in there. It looks like it's been boarded, and corpses don't decompose where there's no atmosphere.'

'They're just bodies.' Clara shrugs. 'Wouldn't be the first time I've seen one; of a certainty, it won't be the last.'

'All right. Ships yours. Take a boarding party and make sure there's nothing waiting in there for you before you start investigating properly. You've got a day to make sense of it, and a day after that to bring whatever you find back. After that, we're out of here.'

*

It takes the boarding party less than six hours to report back that the only contents of the ship are corpsicles, both humans and Chaeni. The party loads all the bodies into the *Sonskyn*'s hold, and Clara comes to see me on the main deck.

'It's got power.' She points to the front of the ship and traces a line down the wings to the stern. 'Rudimentary solar sail by our standards but, back then, it would have been bleeding edge technology. The batteries are still functioning, but it looks like most of the sails stopped working over time, no engineer to watch over them...'

'Can we get it out of here?'

'We could try, but the controls aren't wheel-and-sail, like we're using. They're something else, all buttons and dials.'

Solid bet I'll know how to fly it then...

I keep my thoughts private as Clara points up and down to the hard points where weapons would have been mounted on the ship. No weapons there, but no sign that there's any damage to them either. I look back at Clara.

'Nope, no weapons at all. It's got meteor cutters in case of any debris but, in all other ways, it's got nothing at all on it.'

'Doesn't make sense.' I frown, studying every inch as it continues to rotate. 'Most merchant ships carry at least enough weapons to get themselves out of small scrapes and, this far out, you'd have had to be an idiot to think you were going to get far without any problems.'

'Mysteries within mysteries,' Clara muses. 'What it does have is the biggest reactor I've ever seen on a ship, and a whole bunch of tech that I've never seen anything like.'

I nod, glancing over at Raley as she motions towards our quarters.

Spend time with the living or spend time among the dead...

'Right.' I shake my head to clear the cobwebs. 'Get on board, see what you can figure out. Come back to me when you've got some idea of what the ship is carrying.'

'On it.' Clara grins and heads below. 'Back before you know it.'

A Ship from the Past

Eight bells, and I curse in every language I know, as someone pounds hard enough on the door that they could be beating to quarters. Raley smiles and brushes her hand against my arm as she disengages herself, slinking through to the toilet.

At least she knows I'm still me now.

I throw my tunic on and open the door, stepping back out of the way as Clara bundles into the room holding a swathe of papers in her hands. She hops from foot to foot, her grin broader than I've ever seen as she offers me the papers.

'Spare me the details.' I yawn. 'Give me the highlights.'

'The entire history of everything we ever knew is wrong. I found the data recorders on the bridge and got them working. The records that ship contained of the universe as it was are so different to ours.'

'So? History is written by the victors; it's always been the way.'

'Yeah.' Clara's smile doesn't falter. 'But the information on this ship shows that the Chaeni Worlds weren't engaged in a war with the Stenlarian Empire. That's how the *Swartgat* got so far into their domain—they were flagged up as a trade ship, bringing a valuable shipment to the Chaeni core worlds.'

'Waiting for the part where it makes a difference here...' I raise an eyebrow.

'We don't know the Chaeni language, do we?' Clara taps the side of her head. 'It's always been a mystery, right?'

'All clicks and squeaks.'

'*En tog doen ons dit,*' Clara butchers the pronunciation, but the words are clear.

'And yet we do...?' I frown. 'That's not the Chaeni language.'

'Yet it is.' Clara adjusts the control on the side of her head and turns to face the wall. 'I found these transmissions in the ship's data logs.' A light gleams from inside her skull, and an image appears on the far wall, showing an old ship display, back from the days when viewscreens were common because all ships were boxes that couldn't afford the liability of windows.

Something moves into view on the screen: human, male, but with a lump of green-grey biomass pulsing over his shoulder, attached all the way along the trapezius and into the back of his skull. He looks straight ahead and speaks, the words slow and slurred, as if he were saying them at someone else's behest. '*Ons Is een, koop vir almal,*' His hand moves to a control off-screen, and a list of goods scrolls up on the right side of the screen.

'They were trading?' I frown. 'When was this taken?'

'This was the ship that proceeded to attack them a few minutes later. No quarter, no warning, just opened fire.'

'Why did they attack?'

'I haven't found that out yet, but I've only just started to go through the records. I'd need weeks to study it in detail.'

'We haven't got weeks. A handful of days at most. Get what you can, and we'll come back when we've got time and food.'

'All right.' Clara's expression tells me that it's anything but that, although she knows better than anyone how much food we've got on board and how much chance we've got of hunting anything out here.

Unless the Beast proves edible, and I'm not going to be the one who tries making a burger out of it...

Clara nods again and leaves without a backwards glance.

'So, the Stenlarians are bastards who trapped an entire race of peaceful traders?' Raley's voice drifts out of the toilet.

'Not buying it?' I ask.

'I just think that maybe Clara has outstanding issues with the Stenlarians.' Raley steps out. 'She might not be thinking too much beyond the fact that if the Stenlarians were wrong about the Chaeni, they might have been wrong about her.'

'There's a difference between retribution for a mistake made in war and imprisoning an entire species just because they're different.'

'Only if you're not one of the ones they wronged. I've seen enough of Stenlarian justice to know it's indiscriminate and brutal, and that's now, when there's not much to challenge them.'

'It's not like there's going to be anything we can do with the information,' I say. 'It happened a thousand years ago, and those they wronged have still been neutralised.'

'Maybe.' She doesn't look convinced. 'It could still be damaging for the Stenlarian Empire. It's a perspective thing; everyone knows you don't mess with us, but that doesn't mean there won't be anyone who tries to use the information to leverage what they're getting from us.'

'Then we keep it quiet. That's not what's really bugging you though, is it?'

She pauses for a second, taking a deep breath and glancing back towards the Dragon for another second.

'You're not Stenlarian like me. There are always two sides to the story, particularly if you're part of the empire. If Clara is right, and the information gets back to the empire...if there is technology here that we lost long ago, it'd be enough to restart the Tear Wars all over again.'

'Give the information to everyone—that way no one has to go to war for it?'

Raley laughs loud, and pulls me close. 'If the universe was as naïve as you, it'd be a happier place all over.' She pulls back for a second, shaking her head. 'It's not enough that you've got the information; you need to make sure that no one else has it, particularly if it's something that can cage a whole galaxy in one hit.'

'I hadn't thought about that.' I sigh. 'Okay, we'll hold till Clara has the information and then see where we are. If it's something like that, we destroy it and speak nothing more of it. Deal?'

Raley looks deep into my eyes, and I feel the tension drain from her arms. 'Deal.'

*

Up on deck, the *Sonskyn* is still rotating above us, but there are more lights on inside it and faint gusts of escaping air where the atmosphere generators are coming back online.

All that should have escaped centuries ago.

I tap my comms. 'Morgan to Clara.'

'Clara here.' There's an edge of weariness in her voice, and a whirring sound in the background.

'You're losing air from a number of places there.'

'Won't be for long.' A high-pitched shrill reverberates down the earpiece for a second and the venting air ceases. 'You've got to come over here; the tech on this thing could make you rich beyond imagination.'

What good are riches if you can never spend them?

'We're just pulling the logs, then we're out of here.' I keep my voice even.

'You *need* to come over here.' It's a plea, not a request.

'Fine.' I clip my sword to my hip and scramble up the torsion line to the hole in the side of the ship.

Up close, the damage on the *Sonskyn* is far worse. The huge gouges across the dorsal armour were what breached the ship, but the hull is covered with burns and scrapes where smaller creatures have swarmed all over it like locusts.

What must it have been like to be trapped in a ship covered in a million things whose every purpose was your death?

It's not a cheerful thought, and I drift down into the main entryway, moving in silence through the darkened hull. The insides of the ship are as broken as the outside, a silent memory of the hundreds that died in here, all the contents vented when the ship was breached; the things which followed the breach have left their marks everywhere. The airlocks are open wide, no damage on them—looks like the crew didn't get a chance to close them.

Death moves fast...

I scan the lines of the ship. Back in the academy, I saw a prototype for a Beyondlight drive system that would allow any ship using it to go so far beyond the normal light-speed of most other ships that they'd make them look like they were standing still. The drive allowed for frictionless travel, with no resistance. If the theory could be proven, it could achieve infinite velocities, but only in straight lines, though it would cause massive devastation to anything nearby when it engaged because it left holes in space where it had been. The mathematics of it back then had been pretty rudimentary, but the prototypes had looked a lot like what I'm seeing here.

And that's what this is, this ship must have been faster than anything ever built before or after, so why didn't they just jump away?

The bridge airlock cycles, and I step through. The room beyond is well lit. The atmosphere doesn't smell like the normal recycled air most ships emit; it's cleaner, thicker, almost like the Olympus Forest back on Mars.

But you'd need real trees for that...

Clara glances back from the console with a tired but wide grin, tilting her head backwards and exaggerating sniffing the air. 'Knew you'd notice that.'

'How?' I take another deep breath—it's like inhaling honey.

'The ship has a nanite repair system.' Clara runs her hands over the controls in front of her. 'They didn't have time to engage it when they went down, but the power's still up, and the nanites are working just fine.'

'You've limited them to structural repair only, yes?' I look around the bridge at the various glowing terminals, all of them seeming like they're working at peak efficiency.

'Just set them to repair. Figure they're not going to repair anything that doesn't need it.'

'Including the ship's on-board computer and programming?' I put my hand on hers.

'It was a merchant ship,' she says. 'The most dangerous thing they've got on here is the point defence, and that's got a range of no more than a few thousand metres.'

'Which would put the *Dawn* within range of it, wouldn't it?'

'Yeah.' She blushes, realising that her need to get the ship up and running has compromised her usual analytical thought process. 'Sorry, captain. I'll ensure the weapon systems stay offline.'

'Good. What else then?'

'Records.' Her hands dance over blocks of black obsidian,

the surfaces lighting only when her fingers touch them. I reach over and run my hands over the gleaming edges, though nothing lights up for me. 'Sorry, captain. It only responds to recognised personnel.'

'So how are you using it?' I raise a sceptical eyebrow.

'Well, er...' Her blush deepens. 'I may have...'

'Clara...' I use the kind of tone reserved for truculent juniors.

'One of the bodies on the bridge had rank insignia. I used their handprint to gain access to the ship's controls and gave myself access.'

'Me as well then.' I pull my glove off and place my hand on the console.

Clara's fingers fly across the controls, and the obsidian glows green beneath my fingers, trailing light as I lift my hand from the smooth surface. Clara grins and touches her fingers to the centre of the console, motioning for me to stand back from the display. 'Don't jump.'

She brings her hand up and spreads her fingers, the trailing light spreading into a wide, kaleidoscopic display as all the ship's systems come to life in a glowing rainbow arc around her.

This ship is decades ahead of where they were meant to be back then.

Clara turns, the light display moving with her, so that she's always got the display in front of her. She moves her fingers, and the lights dim in the room—same colours, just muted.

'Activate station two.' She tilts her head upwards as she speaks, and a second rainbow encompasses me. Something shines in my eyes for a split second, and then the display in front of me resolves into crystal-sharp lines.

The whole ship at your fingertips.

I examine the displays. The fuel levels are topped out, and there's enough remass in the short-range thrusters to get the ship back beyond The Dragon and out into Stenlarian space, but it doesn't have shields like the *Dawn*'s, so the trip would be cut short by the ship burning up in space.

Could go around, but it would take forever.

I take care not to move my hands too much, not wanting to activate anything by accident, but realise that everything my hands touch will be doing just that. 'Clara,' I call out, 'deactivate this please.'

'Deactivate station two.' Clara speaks without shifting her attention from what she's doing. 'It's all voice and touch, captain. One person could run this ship without any effort at all.'

'Can you download everything in the memory banks in a format that we could read?'

'Figured you'd ask.' She grins and makes an elegant motion with her hand which disengages it from the light controls, and points to the side of the captain's chair where a tablet rests. 'I've already put everything remaining on here into that tablet. Take a look; some fascinating stuff in there.'

'Thanks.' I pick up the pad and start to scroll through the contents: thousands of pages of material.

She wasn't joking about putting everything on there.

'You going to be all right here?' I glance over at Clara.

'I'm fine, captain.' She enunciates the words with care, taking her time to try and cover her fatigue.

'Uh huh.' I jerk my thumb back towards the airlock. 'I want you back on board within the hour. You have my word I'll give you enough time to study all of this, but you need to get some rest. I'll send Petra over here. She knows more about thrusters than anyone else on the ship, so she'll be able to help with this.'

'I'm fine. I don't need any help.' Clara doesn't shift her eyes from the screen she's modifying.

'Understood, but you're back on board within the hour, clear?'

Clara pauses and nods, looking at me with a weary smile. 'Understood.'

The Starborn Sisterhood

Raley has a frown on her face that hasn't been caused by frustration. 'I've been receiving intermittent power signals from all over the sector.' She motions to the holo-chart. 'Nothing large, nothing moving; just flares of power here and there.'

'Could it be the Beast?' I ask. 'Ships caught by it but now freed and charging up again?'

'Possibly. It's not the signals out there that concern me though.' She pauses and reaches out to touch one of the points on the chart as it flares and then disappears. 'See that? It came online long enough to be seen, then shut itself off.'

'Explosion?' I watch as another appears, followed by two more.

'An explosion would leave a lingering residue while the blast dissipated.' Raley taps the chart again, following the flares around the chart. 'These are very definitely on, then off.'

'Send one of the skiffs to take a look?'

'If they get stuck, we might not be able to pick them up again. This only shows the power signals, not the trillion tons of roadkill still floating out there.'

'Yeah.' I sigh. 'Who'd have thought a galaxy-sized creature would be so much trouble after it was dead... Anything else to report?'

'Not externally,' Raley says. 'On the ship, though...'

'What is it?'

'Crew are spooked. They'll never say it to you directly, but they're all just hoping to make it back in one piece. Those promises of riches which never materialised aren't helping the situation. And while they can all see it wasn't you who promised that, they just want to be out of here and back doing honest work, not dealing with monsters and relics, y'know?'

'They're not the only ones.' I flash her a grin, though Raley's known me too long to be convinced by that. 'We'll be out of here soon.'

'I know it. But it's not me you need to convince.'

'Yeah, I know. Ring the dinner bell. I'll speak to everyone.'

*

I make a detour to my cabin to pick up the bottle of fifty-year-old Metirian from my cabin. It was our first big score when we came out here: delivery of a thousand bottles across the D'Cla divide. The normal acceptable loss terms for a delivery like that are more than twenty percent—we didn't lose a single bottle. The client was so pleased that they gifted me five crates as a bonus, and I gave all but one to the crew. Most of them sold theirs and that cemented our path together—any captain who lands you a bonus of a thirty-grand bottle of rum is one you want to stay with. I had figured on saving mine for retirement, when I no longer wanted to be out among the stars.

But that's never going to happen; I'll never give up the ocean.

Five minutes later, and I'm facing what remains of the crew I started with. Of the thirty we had when we first set foot on the *Dawn*, nineteen left today and the memories of those who came and went. None of us are as young or as bold as we were back then, all of us carrying the wear of a decade's hard work. In all those years among the stars, I've never given them any reason to doubt my judgement.

But the thing that wore my body for a few months wasn't me, and it'll be hard to separate the two.

Jensca brings out the usual bottle we reserve for toasts, and I shake my head.

'Today,' I say, smiling and placing the rum on the table, 'I have something else.'

A murmur ripples across the gathering, and I reach down to pull the seal.

'Whoa there, cap'n.' Esme leans forwards, her voice still the rich contralto that lifted our spirits on the front line of the Trinity wars. 'I'm sure it hasn't been that good a day.'

'Nope, it really hasn't.' I smile as my tension lifts, more glad to be among them in that instant than ever. I pull the seal and allow the thick scent to drift out into the room. 'But sometimes you've got to remind yourself that the good days have come before, and they will again.'

I take the time to pour a measure into every tankard, setting one aside for Clara before setting the half-empty bottle down and lifting my tankard. 'Hell of a thing.' I glance up towards the deck. 'Of all the places I thought we'd end up after all these years, this wasn't among them.'

There's a ripple of muted laughter across the room, and I see all of them smiling at me, the years where we've all fought for each other now reminding us that our bonds cannot be broken by something as simple as a Beast that eats stars.

'We'll get out of here.' I take a sip. The aroma is like rich coffee, the taste more like battery acid, till it mellows on the tongue. 'It's not going to be easy, but we've been in worse spots than this. Anyone remember Beto IV?'

'I remember me being the one that got you all out.' Mirri grins, twirling her hair around her fingers.

'Yeah, well, we only asked you to take *one* for the team' Zulay snarks from behind her, 'not *ten*.'

'Didn't seem fair to leave them all with headaches and no jobs without providing them with *some* good memories of the whole thing.' Mirri's grin gets broader and, for a second, she's still a young girl wanting to live the pirate's life, rather than the best navigator in the air today. She glances back at Zulay. 'I still get letters from a lot of those guards, y'know.'

'I have no doubts.' Samara's grin is wider even than Mirri's. 'We thought someone was torturing cats while we were waiting for you to come back.'

'Well, you know, some people got to learn—'

'The hard way!' Half the crew finish her sentence for her, and the mood lifts high as I pull up one of the stools and lean in towards them.

'Clara will be done with the *Sonskyn* within the day,' I say, 'and once we've got that data, we turn for stars not surrounded by a trillion tons of roadkill, and we never look back this way. I can't promise that we're going to find riches at the end of it, but—'

'None of us signed on for riches,' Zulay says. 'We signed on for the adventure of a lifetime and, so far, you haven't let us down on that, even if the road's been bumpier than usual these last months.'

'We did think it was strange when the *other* you promised us all the wealth in the world to stay with her,' Samara says with a smile. 'You'd never have asked for that—you already knew what we were here for.'

'Thank you.' My sigh releases the tension I hadn't realised I was holding in. 'Thank you all.'

'Don't thank us,' Mirri says. 'This time it's you who's got to get us out of here.'

'I will.' I finish my rum in a single slug and raise the bottle again. 'Another?'

There's a general shaking of heads as most of them place their tankards back on the table and grimace.

'I think it's good for selling...' Jensca sniffs at hers as if it were a toilet, rather than a tankard. 'And for degreasing things if we ever run out of soap, but I'm not drinking it again. Don't think my arse needs bleaching that much.'

'All right,' I say, standing. 'To your stations. We're out of here as soon as Clara's finished.'

Mirri waits until everyone else has gone before approaching me. 'I didn't want to say anything with the others around.' She keeps her voice low, though her tone is urgent.

'What is it?'

'I'm doing what I can with the ship, but we've been several months without airdock and several more since we've done a proper overhaul. Since Catarina left on the other ship, we haven't had an engineer and, while we're still managing to keep moving, if we take many more hits, we'll run out of food before we manage to limp the *Dawn* into port. I don't think Clara's been keeping track of stores while she's been on the other ship, and without her here, rationing has been absent.'

'How bad is it?'

'Come below; I'll show you.'

*

It's been a long time since I came down here, back when I was Catarina, and even then, I didn't see most of the lower hall and racking. This bit is held together with loose welds and tight ropes.

'*Al Mi Booswigte,*' I utter, reverting back to low Martian for a second. 'How long have we been this bad?'

'Since the other you refused to stop and do repairs and, after Errin took to roasting anyone who complained, I figured I'd just try and keep it going in case I ended up riding something that wasn't any fun.'

'Can't say as I blame you on that one,' I reply, unlocking my harness and taking out my old tools from the locker on the wall. 'Come on, let's get her back to where she should be.'

*

It's more than twelve hours later when we finish. The welds are solid, the ropes are gone, and it's possible to move without bumping into the last repair we made. She's still not tip-top, but it's far better than she would have done a half day ago.

'I'll get back at it tomorrow.' Mirri's eyes are dull with lack of sleep as she yawns. 'Playing with a welding torch when I'm this tired is altogether more dangerous than leaving it as is, I think.'

'Yeah, know that feeling.' I smile, glad to have had the chance to do something constructive rather than having to command. 'Call me if you need me.'

'Will do.'

I drift upwards and head towards the deck, the sound of snoring following me all the way up to the deck. Raley is waiting for me above, her sword slung loose on her hips.

She only does that when she's off duty...

I realise as her hand closes on mine just how tired I am, and I lean in close to her.

'Come on,' she whispers. 'We all need to rest sometime.'

The Darkness of a Weaponised Past

I wake to find Raley already out of bed. Grabbing my breather, I step into the shower bag. Two minutes and the faint sensation of drowning later, I wait while the vacuum dryer tries to pull my hair out for a few seconds and then step out, scoured and stinging, but clean.

There's something to be said for the little luxuries.

I look in the mirror, seeing the same eyes that set out into space years ago, framed by a face with more lines than it had back then, and a smile that doesn't come as when called for as it once did.

There's a price for everything we do in life...

I leave my make-up on the side—too many memories of the lunatic that the Beast turned me into. There's something to be said for letting the world see you as you are, rather than hiding behind the image of what you think it wants you to look like. There's a faint gurgling from my stomach. I look down, and put my hand on it as I feel something turning. There's a moment's horror as, not for the first time, I consider what would happen if the Beast had left something of itself inside me.

Still growing there, waiting to turn me back into the monster again...

I close my eyes and breathe in slow, breathe out slower, patting my stomach as I walk back through into the cabin. I pick up the bread from the table and bite into it without care for my teeth. The crust gives way to thick dough, laced with dried cheese and a fine line of relish laid through the middle. There aren't many who get to eat the bread that Clara makes once a week—I've always been glad I'm one of them.

Clara...

I get dressed fast and wander up to the bridge, where Raley is still watching the power signatures blipping on the chart.

'Did Clara make it back last night?' I glance upwards at the *Sonskyn.* 'I didn't check.'

Raley pulls the sheet and checks the boarding log. 'Nope, you were the last one to come back over. By all accounts, she's still there.'

'Right.' I nod. 'I'm going over. Plot us a course out of here; we need to be concentrating on the living rather than the dead. We'll pull what Clara has and get gone while we still can.'

*

Up on the *Sonskyn,* the bridge airlock is closed. The seals have been replaced since I was here last, and the pressure stabiliser is showing green. I drift up to the entrance and press the intercom, moving close enough for my bubble tech to envelop the microphone.

'Yes?' Clara sounds weary.

'Me,' I say. 'Open up.'

'Be there soon.' She cuts the connection without waiting for me to speak again.

A minute later, I press the button again.

'Yes?' She sounds irritated now.

'Open. Up!' I enunciate the words with the tone of an irritated parent.

'Sorry, captain.' I hear her move away from whatever she's doing, and the pressure seal shows green as the secondary airlock engages.

She'd only closed one of the pressure doors—sloppy, very sloppy. Not like Clara.

I step into the airlock, and it cycles through, opening onto the bridge of the ship. Clara is stood by the controls as I pass through, and she cycles the door back up, making sure to close the second airlock this time. Her mechanical eye is set for close-range work, and she has the appearance of someone who hasn't slept since the last time I saw her. To the side, Petra is working through lines of code on a black screen; she looks just as tired.

'Come on, both of you.' I motion towards the door. 'We're out of here.'

'We can't leave.' Clara fixes on me with feverish intensity. 'I'm close to finding out what happened.'

'We *know* what happened,' I keep my voice low. 'Everyone died—the only thing here is ghosts.'

'But it's not.' She bustles over to the console and brings up the flight recorder. 'The Chaeni Worlds, everyone on them, they're all still alive.'

'How can that be? You couldn't compress things like that and leave them undamaged.'

'You know how gravity affects time?'

'I know the basics. The more gravity, the less time moves?'

'Something like that,' she says. 'So, infinite gravity equals no time. The weapon they used to lock the Chaeni Worlds together didn't destroy them; it brought them together and held them there, but the gravity is so intense that time is passing at a rate that we can't even measure.'

'They're unharmed?'

'I...I don't know. There are so many variables that I can't even begin to compute, but the weapon only draws things together. The energy field feeds from the stars in its area of effect, so it only wears off when all the energy in that field is drained.'

'When that happens, all the energy, everything, goes back to how it was?'

'Where they were in space. However, with no stars to keep the worlds they were on alive, they'll be just as dead as they would be if the stars had gone out. The only difference is that they'll never know they spent thousands, millions of years in stasis.'

'We're close to having this thing back online, captain.' Petra finishes the coding she was working on and turns to face me. 'With the drives on this operational, we'll be able to travel anywhere in the universe in a few days at most."

'That's great,' I say. 'But the pair of you haven't been back on ship for too long so, as of now, you're both coming back with me.'

'We can't leave right now.' Petra sounds desperate. 'We need to monitor the calculations and make sure the programming still works. If we stop now, we'll have to start all over again.'

'What's so important? There's something you're not telling me, isn't there?' I focus on Clara's mechanical eye as the images she's reviewing flash up in its lens.

'I think we can reverse the field of effect. This ship has the same weaponry the *Swartgat* had. It'd take us a few months to get the thing working, but we could bring everything back, and they'd never know that anything had happened. We could be the ones to put everything right.'

I look past her at the data streaming on the other screens. 'Are you sure?'

'Almost certain. If we trigger the field the way the *Swartgat* did, it'll cancel the field and return everything to the position it was before.'

'Minus a few stars?' I raise an eyebrow.

'Again, I don't understand the science behind it, but they kept the briefings simple in the files detailing how it works.' She lifts up a handful of data chips from the command desk. 'They built it in such a way that if the weapon went off too early and trapped several of *their* worlds, they would be able to reverse it.'

'That just leaves the matter of explaining how some of the stars went out while the rest of the universe advanced a thousand years in a heartbeat.' I move alongside her. 'I can't imagine that the Stenlarians would want to do that sort of explaining.'

'That's the other thing.' Clara raises her hand and draws down a screen of light from the ceiling, her fingers cycling over the data displayed there. 'The Chaeni aren't a different race at all.'

'What?'

Clara turns the screen to face me and points at the information on it. 'The Stenlarians use hard tech to deliver their punishments now, don't they?' She sweeps her hair back over the implant in her head. 'Before they started doing this, they didn't use hard technology; they used biotechnology.'

I examine the data scrolling up on the screen: images of biogenetic implants which could be controlled via nerve impulses, and provide a living connection between all those fitted with them.

'Except, as usual, they didn't think too far ahead,' Clara says. 'The head scientist on the project found a way to engineer the implants so that they could provide a sense of clarity, of purpose, to those who had them. Those fitted with them became joyous, fulfilled even, at being part of the greater whole, connected to every member of their new race, all in perfect harmony.'

'Why attack them then?' I ask.

'Because the Stenlarians think everyone behaves the way they do, so they couldn't chance a race with no internal divisions turning on them one day.' Clara cycles through the data again. 'It was decided that they needed to be brought to heel before it became a problem, so they brought in a specialist from the Metirians to ensure that the implants couldn't be turned against them.'

'A specialist?'

Clara sighs, and her fingers dance over the controls. The screen changes to display a single image. My eyes go wide as my breath catches in my throat.

Errin.

'Errinea Chaeni.' Clara gives a humourless snort. 'Within six months, she'd managed to convince the Stenlarians that all was well and, within a year, she'd managed to lobby for complete control of the programme, all to ensure the greater glory of Stenlar.'

'But she wasn't working towards the greater glory of Stenlar.'

'No, she wasn't.' Clara's fingers twitch in an elegant pattern and a map of the known universe appears, the areas shaded in the colours of the empire that they belong to. I see areas of red starting to spread out at the top and bottom of the map. 'She took those who had been implanted and sent them out to the far ends of the universe, where no one else wanted to work and, there, they started to take over other worlds.'

'Can't see why the Stenlarians would have had a problem with that.'

'They didn't. Not until Errinea declared her independence from Stenlar and, the Stenlarians found themselves facing their worst nightmare, an empire of beings acting with a single purpose, and all the supplies they'd been receiving from the edge of the universe now coming with a price tag.'

'And they weren't prepared to trade for goods they'd been getting for free before.'

'Stenlar tried to keep them down, show them that they should still be happy *servants* of Stenlar, but *Errinea* had other ideas, so the two empires started to face off.'

'Resulting in the Stenlarians trying to stop both Chaeni fleets before they could overrun their empire, and they decided that the best way of doing that was to lock them up forever,' I say.

'Using something that would remove the threat in a *humane* manner, because it's all about the optics.' Clara is glaring at me as if I'm the Stenlarians.

'We can't just release the Chaeni though, not without considering all the options.'

'There aren't any options to consider here.' Clara's tone has turned sharp. 'Come on, Morgan—a whole *race* imprisoned because they stood up to the Stenlarians, and we can put it right.'

'*Right* is a subjective term.' I keep my voice level as the internals of Clara's mechanical eye become visible. 'Something like this would have repercussions for the whole universe. How would you feel when you realised you'd spent a thousand years in a prison, and no one on your world had even noticed?'

'Exactly!' Clara drops the chips back on the table and steps close. 'Exactly! You agree! All of them deserve the chance to get back at those who did this to them.'

'And the universe will burn while they take their revenge.' I lower my voice to a whisper. 'Millions, billions would die in the wars that follow.'

'Billions will die when the weapon wears off. Billions who did nothing wrong, who only wanted to live out their lives in peace.' She's less than a handspan from my face now, her organic eye angry, the tension in her body so strong that her mechanical eye is adjusting its focus without her moving it. 'We have to do something; we can't let them die like this.'

'And we won't.' I take a half step back from her. 'We need to do this properly, though. We need to talk to people who know about these things; we need to make sure that the universe is prepared before we just go ahead and open the sixth seal, y'know?'

'Sixth seal?' She frowns.

Been here twenty years and still forgetting I'm not from around here...

'Armageddon.' I look her in the eye. 'The end of all things. A war that size won't just stop there; it'll burn the whole damn ocean of stars.'

'But the guilty would be punished for what they did.' Her voice rises to a level where I know rationality has left the argument.

'The ones who did this are long dead.' I step back and gesture to the bridge. 'The ones who did this have got nothing to do with what you want to do now.'

'They're still *doing it.*' She sweeps her hair back to show the plate in her head. 'They never stopped doing it. We could—'

'No.' I deliver the whisper like a jackhammer. 'We'll deliver this technology to the Metirians and let them make the call on what to do with it?'

'The Metirians?' Clara stares at me in disbelief. 'They've never been in a war; they don't know what this feels like.'

'Exactly,' I say. 'But their council has most of the elder statespeople from the last hundred years working with them, from the Stenlarians to the Tarlin to the Illenials, and they make the right choices as a result. If they think it would be a good idea to reverse the field, they're the only ones I'd trust to make that call.'

'We can't give this up.' Clara grips my arm hard. 'We have to use it; we have to—'

'No.' This time my tone brooks no dissent. 'Come on, we're out of here. We'll use the *Dawn* to tow this to the Metirians and then be on our way.'

Clara's lips close in mid-thought, and she looks down, waiting a few seconds before she nods, her voice all but a whisper. 'All right.'

A Chance to Make the Wrong Things Right

Back on the *Dawn*, Raley has the look of a woman who doesn't want to be here at all. She waits till Clara goes below then checks to make sure that there's no one in earshot.

'We've had a few more blips on the transponder,' she says. 'These ones didn't blink out; they're definitely ships this time.'

'What sort of ships?'

'The sort that don't have beacons and aren't broadcasting any identification.'

'Pirates then,' I say, with a sinking heart. 'How big are they?'

'Smaller than us. If their transponders are accurate, they're little more than atmo-hoppers.'

'That makes no sense. Even if they get what they came for, they'll have no way to get back without capital ship support.' The thought isn't a cheerful one—risk-taking isn't in the pirate code... unless it involves getting others to take the risks.

'Something brought them here, and for something that opportunists must have thought was worth their time and effort.'

'Get Clara on the frequencies. There must have been something going out that we missed. In the meantime, get the guns ready. If we do have to engage, I don't want us firing blanks.'

'Right.' Raley sighs and glances skywards to the *Sonskyn*. 'Got to hope all this is worth it in the end.'

'Time will tell; always does.'

It's two hours before the first of the ships comes into range. Raley is by my side as it rounds the top of the mile-wide tendril and turns to face us. I don't recognise the class of ship, but it's too small to be anything but a scout ship.

'No way a ship that size got out here without support. They'd have had to pass through a jump gate to get here, and then there'd be no hope that they'd make it back.'

'Something else...' Raley squints against the brightness of the remaining star behind the ship. 'That's an unmanned ship.'

'Drone? How did it get out here?'

'It didn't. The clan symbols on the side are the same as those on the *Sonskyn...*'

I look up at the Stenlarian ship and realise with a sense of mounting dread that it's stopped rotating and the lights are on along the whole length of it. 'Get Clara and Petra up here,' I snap, pulling the *Dawn* into attack position against the drone, as a second, then a third, soars over the tendril, all of them forming up in a perfect line. Raley leaps from the top deck and sprints away as I align the starboard gun ports. 'And get everyone up.'

The rapid staccato of drums echoes up from below when Raley hits the alarm on the way past the hold entrance; a light rumble passes through the whole ship as every person on the ship rises and runs for their stations. I look up as the *Dawn* turns like a dancer, the gun ports lining up with the drones above us, then drift us to starboard, increasing the distance to give us more time to fire.

What I wouldn't give for a bank of Lance cannons right now.

The drones don't move, and neither do I, the only tension showing in the faint tremble in my hands.

What are they waiting for?

We stay at that range for more than ten minutes, by which time, I'd pay money for them to just get on with it. There's a sound of a gloveboot on deck behind me, deliberate so that I'd hear it.

Raley, still making sure I don't get a fright when she arrives—just as well.

'Guns up, sails turned; we're good.' She keeps her voice low, looking at my knuckles wound white around the wheel.

'Where are they?'

Raley comes alongside, easing her hands under mine to take the wheel. 'They're not on the ship.'

'What?' My hands tighten on the wheel, and I turn to face

Raley. 'Where are they?'

'Quarters cleared, nothing remaining.' Raley glances upwards. 'If I were to take a guess, I'd say they've jumped ship.'

Cold like an unseen wave on a dark beach envelops me, and I see the *Sonskyn* beginning to move, slow, but with a precision that even machines would appreciate. 'She's going to set them free.' It's a half-second before I realise the words came from me. 'Bring us about, prepare to fire.'

'On Clara?' Raley pauses for a second. I can see in her eyes that her doubts about me are back.

'She's going to free the Chaeni Worlds.' I grab Raley by the arm and point upwards. 'That ship has the power to do it.'

Raley nods, keeping her eyes averted as she starts to turn the *Dawn*. I hear the crackle of the comms.

'Don't try and stop me, captain.' Clara's voice, distorted from within the *Sonskyn*. 'You know this has to be done.'

'We can find another way, a way that doesn't end up with everyone dead.'

'Look around you.' I can hear the weight of emotion in her voice, almost see the tears coming from her one good eye. 'Everyone is already dead. They killed them; they killed all of them. Someone needs to make them pay.'

The *Dawn* is almost in alignment with the *Sonskyn* now. A few more seconds, and we'll have it in our sights. 'They *will* pay,' I shout, leaning in to the comms. 'But don't make the rest of the universe pay for what they did, please!'

'The rest of the universe already paid.' Clara's voice becomes calm as lights grow bright along the length of the ship, power conduits transferring reserves it has been absorbing for more than a millennium. 'I'm just going to settle the account for them.'

On the far horizon, the drones break formation and come at us from two sides.

Clever—if we shoot at her, we'll be defenceless against the drones for a few minutes; more than enough time for them to cripple us.

'CLARA, DON'T DO THIS!' I howl, watching the *Sonskyn*'s fins shift to drive configuration. 'DON'T MAKE *ME* DO THIS...'

'It's your choice, captain.' Clara's voice is calm as I hear the computer spooling up behind her. 'Save the *Dawn* or kill all of us.'

Raley mutes the comms. 'Mor, she's right. We need to stop those drones; we can always catch up with her.'

Except we can't. The Dawn only gets just past lightspeed. If Clara has managed to get the Beyondlight drive working, she'll be on the other side of the universe before we've turned the Dawn around.

'Top battery,' I call. 'Target the power lines on the starboard wing of that ship. Single salvo only and reload with grapeshot.'

The dull thump of six cannons firing ripples through the air, and six glowing bolts arc like stars to embed themselves in the hull of the *Sonskyn*. A coruscating mass of electricity sparks from where the bolts hit, but the ship keeps turning, the main drive angling away from The Dragon. I watch as a panel opens and a figure climbs out onto the surface with such ease that it has to be Petra.

'STAND DOWN,' I yell into the comms. 'DAMMIT PETRA, DON'T DO THIS.'

'We need to do this.' Petra's voice is calm. 'We are one mind, one will.'

'INCOMING!' I hear Mirri's shout when the sails turn, the first drone shooting past while Raley cranks the wheel around as fast as she can. The ship shudders from a million tiny impacts as the *Dawn* rolls her hull into the face of the incoming fire. A loud, high-pitched whine fills the air, growing louder by the second as the *Sonskyn* rotates, ragged trails of energy now pooling out from its damaged wing. I realise with horror that Clara's going to engage the main drive.

If any of the drives on that engage, it'll suck all the air out of us, and she knows it.

'STARBOARD HARD,' I yell, turning back to Raley. 'GET US BELOW THE JUMP LINE.'

The *Dawn* shudders again, the rudder still not responding the way it should. The whining sound ceases, and the ship's field pulls away from the *Sonskyn*. I watch as an energy pulse spreads from the reactor down the ship, towards the engines. The bank of drones turns in the darkness below us and swarms back in a wide formation.

'All port batteries engage at will,' I snap; 'every target is righteous.'

There's a spray of light from the port batteries as the guns spit shards in a wide shower of molten destruction. Two drones detonate in a burst of flames as another pinwheels out of formation, trailing sparks. The others go wide, and I see the tiny cannons on the front lining up again.

'COVER.' I look down at the deck as Mirri pulls the rigging tight to keep the sails working. Samara maintains the tension on the line while she glances skywards at the fire from the drones peppering the ship from bow to stern. The drones break formation and scream past us, the sound of their engines audible for the split second that they're in our atmosphere; then they're gone.

'Turn us, TURN US,' I shout, trying to keep an eye on all directions. 'Reload all batteries.'

I lift my head to see Petra drifting back towards the panel in the *Sonskyn*, the shell that had damaged the drive now dislodged. She glances back towards us and must realise we'll be ready to fire before Clara can make the jump, because she stops and turns in the air, focussing on me as she spreads her arms wide. Any shot we take at the *Sonskyn* will hit her first.

And she knows I can't kill innocents.

'Petra, get out of the way,' I say. 'You know we can't let that ship leave.'

'Fly now.' Petra's voice is clear, unafraid. 'Fly free, before they can stop us.'

'Are you aboard?' Clara's voice answers.

'Fly now, fly free.' Petra's hands move in the same wavy gesture she made when I first met her. 'Make it right for everyone.'

Too many will die if that ship releases the Chaeni.

My hand drifts down to the comms as my resolve hardens.

The *Dawn* continues to turn in the darkness, the rudder all but hanging off as Raley struggles to bring us back to skywards. I look up, seeing the *Sonskyn* hanging in the darkness, the engines glowing as if they're housing a sun; bright, liquid energy is still spilling from the holes in the wing. The drones attach themselves to the underside, the panel seals with Petra still outside, and there's a blur in space as the main drives go online.

For a second the universe pauses...

Then the *Sonskyn* is gone.

No blurring, no shift, or the image of the *Sonskyn* stretching into infinity; just gone. The comms channel reverberates as Petra's open comms channel stretches with her into infinity, as the Beyondlight drive engages.

'Shit.' Raley struggles with the wheel as the gravity shifts, the universe protesting at its laws being broken, drawing everything into the hole which the drive has left behind. 'Any sign of those drones?'

'Forget about them.' I hang on the rail and clip Raley on before attaching myself, glancing over the side as the *Dawn* rolls out of control, passing altogether too close to the tendrils that have been drawn towards the hole. 'Get us back on the level; we'll worry about all that when we get clear.'

Counting the Cost of Survival

It's another five minutes before Raley manages to bring the ship level, during which time we haven't been attacked again. There's a faint keening noise from the deck, and I look over the side to see Mirri kneeling down beside a deep crimson stain spreading across the wood.

Raley engages the gravity anchors, and nods at me. 'Go. Get down there.'

I jump over the top and down to the lower deck, coming up behind Mirri, her shoulders shaking as she tries to stop her emotions running wild, the blood now everywhere. I look over Mirri's shoulder at the remains on the deck. There's nothing left of the head, and the body isn't recognisable as a body anymore, but the strips of dark green silk to the side aren't Mirri's.

Which means that this... this was Samara.

I crouch down next to Mirri, and she turns to me, her eyes red and rimmed with tears, trying to choke back her emotions. I pull her close, and she dissolves into a howl of pain, not words, just noise, primal, from a time when humanity didn't have words. I don't feel anything.

This red sludge isn't the woman who stood next to me on the Echan Plains, who outdrunk, outfought, and outwitted everyone who ever came after her; who—

The memories are enough to break the armour around my heart, and my tears fall alongside Mirri's. I close my eyes. I don't know how long I'm there for.

I don't care.

I open my eyes as Esme's voice starts the *Da'Sanim*, the prayer of Samara's people. Samara was never religious, but whatever gods count her as their own should know she's coming. The rest of the crew are gathered around. One more of us gone. One more we'll never see again.

And it was one of us who did it...

That thought burns in my mind, and I look up to see a faint sparkle of energy trailing towards the edge of The Dragon. Clara couldn't plot a course through The Dragon, so she'll have had to go around and, because that was a Beyondlight drive, she wouldn't have been able to get there in a single jump. Also, something like that would have to use a lot of power, so she couldn't make continuous jumps without having to recharge.

Or maybe she could, but I refuse to accept that we can't stop her before others pay the price.

I look down at the remains on the deck, then at the damage pattern: eight lines of tiny holes. Not enough to penetrate the inner hull, but enough to ruin the deck above, closing to a single stream of rounds just before they struck Samara.

'What happened?' Those shouldn't have hit her.'

'She saw—' Mirri chokes back another sob points down the ship at the parallel lines. 'They would have hit me, Jensca, then you and Raley as they went over the top deck. She...' Mirri can't finish the sentence, pointing to the main mast where the remains of Samara's equipment is stuck under a cluster of ball bearings.

'Diverted all the shot into the mast.' I nod, trying to keep my eyes from the blood still covering most of the rounds. 'She was still wearing her harness, wasn't she?'

Mirri nods. 'She hit the clamp, and then everything—'

'Hit her.' I take a deep breath. 'She chose to save us over herself.'

'Why did she do it?' Mirri looks angry now.

'She cared more for us than—'

'NO!' Mirri shouts. 'Not Samara. *Clara.* Why would she do this?'

'I don't know. When I saw her last, she was talking about a weapon that could reverse what happened to the Chaeni Worlds; something that could restore them to what they once were.'

'Restore?' Esme's usual serenity turns sharp, and she stares at me. 'Why in God's name would we want to restore them? It's just a thousand planets full of blood-drinking mutants.'

I pause to order my thoughts. Telling the crew everything won't help now, not while we still don't know the truth of it. 'We need to take care of our own and then stop Clara from doing whatever she's doing. Then we'll know why.'

'I'll...' Jensca steps forwards, looking down at Samara's remains. 'The rest of you need to get the ship going; I'll see to Samara. Let's make sure she's the last of us who dies out here.'

'All right.' Mirri crouches down and puts her finger in the pool of blood, bringing it up to draw a line down her right cheek. 'Your heart is carried with us, sister. Your blood goes on in us.'

It's a vow only a Tarlin would make, and I remain silent as Mirri begins the twelve prayers of vengeance, motioning for the rest of the crew to get on with repairing the ship.

Looking up at Esme, I say, 'Take inventory of what we have; we need to know how long we can follow her before we need to stop for supplies.'

*

Four hours later, Raley finds me looking between the dismaying lack of supplies we have left and the massive large list of repairs that we need to do to get up to full efficiency.

'How bad is it?' she asks.

'Well,' I sigh, putting both lists on my desk, 'to put us back on anywhere near good terms would take a month in airdock, and we've got enough food for a fortnight on half rations.'

'We've got a crate of Ledi powder that's missing from that food list. Isn't that edible?'

'Ever seen someone eat it?' I manage my first smile of the day.

'Nope, but you just add water, don't you?'

'Not just water: any moisture at all. A pinch of it is enough to feed a person for a day, so you need to make sure that you've managed to mix all the powder in with water—the rehydration is near instant, so there are often dry bits in whatever you've just mixed.'

'What's the problem with that? It's all food.'

'A single grain gets to the size of an apple in a half-second. Put it in your mouth, and it'll break your jaw or suffocate you. I've only seen Ledi eaten once, and that was an assassination.'

'Assassination?'

'Remember Rassda, back when we were working on Taka starbase while the *Dawn* was being built?'

'Big bastard.' Raley nods. 'Corrupt cop, wasn't he?'

'Yep, took payments every month from all the local businesses, till they found out his badge had been taken off him years ago. That's when the Vess syndicate made sure that the next meal he took had some added ingredients.' I mimic an explosion over my stomach. 'No one could prove what happened. He dropped while he was on his patrol and, by the time the medics got there, his insides were outside.'

'Oh yeah? So how do you know what happened?'

'I was working the kitchen on disposal. All the staff used to take home the leftovers but, that evening, the owners made a point of making sure the leftovers were disposed of. I dropped what I thought was rice in a puddle and all but shat myself when it turned into several pounds of meat.'

'Right.' Raley mimics being sick. 'We're avoiding that then; why have we even got it on board?'

'Also makes for excellent sealant when you're filling holes. You can drop a handful of that in any coolant leak, and it'll seal it over in seconds.'

'What are our options then?' she asks.

'Rebuild the rudder, get back through The Dragon and then stop to pick up supplies as soon as we get clear.'

'You want to fly The Dragon in a ship with a rebuilt rudder?' Raley raises an eyebrow.

'Nope, really don't, but we either take The Dragon, or we follow Clara's route and hope we all make it back before we turn cannibal, or get so desperate we consider eating Ledi—'

'All the choice in the world then.' Raley shrugs and kisses me on the forehead. 'Times like this, I'm glad I'm not captain.'

'Times like this, I wish I wasn't.' I smile and grab her hand, holding on for a second before letting her head back out onto the deck.

Got to figure out how to catch Clara.

I rest my head in my hands for a second, and my elbow slides on something on the top of the desk. I look down to see the tablet Clara set up for me and start flicking through the information there, checking the data from the drive on the *Sonskyn*. Not just one drive from it though—all three of the drives on the ship. I scrabble for a pen on my desk, and start to make notes as I go.

*

It's a few hours before I come back up on deck with my eyes hurting. 'Right.' I wave the handful of paper at Raley as she tests the wheel again, the rudder responding much faster now. 'I know how we can catch her.'

A Flight into Darkness

'The *Sonskyn*'s been absorbing energy since it was left to drift.' I spread the paperwork out on the deck, pointing to the notes on the secondary drive. 'And the Beyondlight drive can only travel in straight lines. They managed to crack the velocity, but not how to turn while travelling at those speeds.'

'All she's got to do is pause once in a while and turn the ship to a new heading,' Raley says. 'I don't see how that's much more of a bonus—can't take too long to turn that thing around.'

'No,' I reply, turning the sheets over. 'But the Beyondlight drive only works when you have a course plotted, and that course was plotted years ago, to a place that the crew knew to be empty at the time. The drive slots you into the space you're heading to, although, at the speed you're travelling, there's no way to avoid a collision if something else has arrived there in the time since then.'

'So, Clara could be a cloud of fragments right about now? Something tells me it's not that simple.'

'No. The drive won't engage if it doesn't see a clear way through, which is why they couldn't jump away. There were Chaeni ships all around, and the drive wouldn't engage.'

'However, it just did engage.' Raley points at the distant horizon beyond the flaming maelstrom of The Dragon. 'Gone in less than the blink of an eye.'

'The scanner that the drive uses only works for areas it's been before, or it has to spend the time required to scan the area it's planning on jumping into, which is why it could make the jump just now—it was on a retreat course.'

'Still not seeing the win here.'

I take out the tablet and bring up the navigation data. 'If she wants to travel back to where she started, then she has to follow the same route that the ship took in the first place. Any deviation from that, and she has to use the normal drive, which is slower than us.'

'But if the way is clear...' Raley says, frowning.

'It can't be. When it came this way, there wasn't anything there. The ship could just jump straight in and not worry about anything else. The only object it couldn't traverse was The Dragon, and that's why she jumped the other way. Now she has to wait till the ship scans ahead far enough to use the Beyondlight drive, or it continues on normal power. Given the amount of power the Beyondlight uses, we'd have caught up with her by then.'

'What if she doesn't go back that way?'

'She knows that we're faster than her. If she tries to make it back under normal drive, there's every chance we're going to catch up with her, and there are no weapons on that thing that can affect us. She won't take the chance.' I pick the papers up from the deck and look Raley in the eye. 'Trust me, Ral, we can do it.'

'One condition...'

'Name it.'

'You fly us back through The Dragon.'

I glance back at the deep glow at the far side of the system and draw in a deep breath.

When I flew that, my eyes were younger.

'Okay, I've got it.'

*

It takes another half day to rig the rudder so it's solid enough to take the pressures of The Dragon, but it's time well-spent.

Better we're late than tumbling in an endless burning hell.

I call everyone into the mess and raise a glass to Samara, looking over the same faces I led in another toast only a short time ago, knowing that things will never be the same for any of us.

'What do we do when we catch up with her?' Mirri's voice is

hard. 'She has to pay for what she did.'

'I need to tell you all something: that ship isn't just another ship; it's one of the ships that caused the Chaeni Worlds to be the way they are.'

'Trapped a billion blood-hungry bastards in a timeless prison?' Mirri shrugs. 'Not seeing the problem.'

'Except they're not blood-hungry bastards.' I sigh, putting the tablet on the table and punching up the transmission from the *Sonskyn*, waiting till it finishes before looking at each of them in turn.

'So, we started the war,' Esme growls, 'and Clara's just looking to make it right?'

'From her perspective,' I answer, 'maybe.'

'Don't care,' Mirri snaps. 'She could have just left; she didn't have to open fire on us.' She pauses for a second and draws a deep breath. 'She didn't have to kill us. She knew the code; we all know the code.' She exhales and looks me in the eye, tears brimming. 'We all know how things have to be.'

When you're out in the black, there's no room for shades of grey.

'Yeah, we do. However, we know the code also calls for the crew to make a call when someone carries out an act of betrayal. It's not just down to me; it's down to all of us.'

There's a murmur of agreement around the room, and everyone sits up straighter, the mood changing, crackling like static electricity in the air.

I set my sword on the right of the table and my sash on the left, signifying that I will not make a choice till the rest of the crew have. The code is clear: leave your sword for death, your sash for mercy.

When everyone has made their choice, it isn't even close— twenty-eight swords, two sashes.

There's no mercy when you've killed one of your own.

I nod without comment, picking up both my sword and sash and looking to each of them in turn, holding my hand out with palm upturned as I move away from the door, allowing them to pass.

The second chance. If you want me to hold your wish, leave your sword blade visible as you walk out. No one will know from the back if you had the sword unsheathed or if you were just leaving your hand on it, so while your vote shows how you feel, how you hold your sword determines your truth.

One at a time, they move past me to go back to the main deck. Two swords remain unsheathed; the rest are not. Two swords unsheathed to bring death, two sashes to give life.

It's one thing to show solidarity with your crew, but it's something else to put someone to death, but that means that the decision is mine now, mine alone, perhaps as it should have been all along.

I nod and head up to the deck, holding silent wishes for wisdom greater than I've ever known. Mirri is waiting for me as I clear the lower stairs.

'Through The Dragon?'

'Through The Dragon. Plot me a course that'll get us close to a station we've still got some credit with.'

'That we've *still* got credit with?' Mirri grins. 'Last I checked, we never had credit with them in the first place.'

'It's either that or piracy, and I could do without the complication of the Dark Stars chasing us for robbing rich bastards. All right.' I take the wheel and turn the *Dawn* towards The Dragon. 'We're out of here.'

Riding up The Dragon's Back

I keep everyone else below deck and Raley on the backup wheel in our cabin as we soar towards The Dragon. I feel my stomach flip-flopping when the thought occurs that we only made it through last time because I could remember what I'd seen when I was Catarina.

No safety net this time.

I bring all the sails up to full and focus the shields close to the ship in the hope that the smaller profile of it will cause us less shearing when the Dragon starts to get really rough.

'All hands ready,' I announce down the comms. 'Dragon in three, two...'

The ship slams sideways as we enter the outer range, the stars all around us merging into a single vortex of multi-coloured fire. I keep my eyes on the compass while we slip downwards, pulling us back into line as the pressure increases on all sides. There's a groan as the top mast is hit by a strong flare, and the *Dawn* tumbles in space for a second, the wheel coming back to true without my prompting it. I feel the vibration of the private comms in my ear, and a voice I haven't heard in a very long time comes through.

Pay attention, oh captain, my captain; it would not do for our story to end here because you can't fly me.

Dawn. I reach up to my ear with a smile as the ship's voice resonates. 'It's good to hear you again.'

It is good to have you back at the helm, but it seems that we are wandering into fiery pits of doom again. Did we not learn the first few times?

'We have no choice,' I whisper, knowing she can still hear me. 'We have to chase something that's faster than we are.'

Should have given me more sails.

'Then you'd have been a fat bugger, rather than the sleek hotness that you are.'

Sleek be damned. in one piece is what's needed.

'Thank you, for helping Catarina with Errin.'

She was you, and it was the map of her mind that passed into me. How could I have refused?

'I haven't heard you in a long time—where were you?'

As I have always been, watching over you and our people.

'But you used to talk to me all the time.'

When there were fewer on board, it was safe to do so. Don't forget that I'm illegal in most of the star states.

'I know, but I miss our conversations.'

I have always been here; I will always be here. Make time for me once in a while; I will know when you are alone.

'I will.' My heart soars.

But keep your mind upon the stars, and we will get through this...together.

'As we always have.' I pat the wheel and feel it vibrate under my hands—the ship's equivalent of patting me in return.

As ever, we shall. Now bring us high. the Keeper is playing in the blue star—I think she likes ships.

'Who wouldn't love you?' I hug the wheel for a second.

Galaxy-eating bastards and parasites from the dawn of time, but that's why we're fighting them.

I pull the wheel back, rolling us up into the higher levels of The Dragon, watching as the Keeper banks close, swimming in the wash of solar flares. It unfurls polychromatic wings ten times longer than the ship and wraps them around us, the temperature lowering all around as we speed up, the resistance from the stars around us lessened by the wings protecting us from the buffeting. I look up to see the Keeper's iridescent scales resting against the upper shields, the energy crackling against its stomach. I hear the click as its claws lock on to us, and we roll over, the Keeper soaring on the edges of each of the stars, using the gravity to pick up speed again and again till the fires in front of us are no more than a blur.

I think it likes being scratched.

I look up as the Keeper gathers against the shield again, its scales parting and the embers of dying stars falling from between them. The scales are moving more now as chunks drift away from our shields, falling from the stern of the ship.

'Think that's why she looks after ships?'

Everyone likes being fussed over.

I smile and lean close to the wheel. At the speed we're going, it'll be less than two hours before we get to the other side of The Dragon, and I intend to make the best of the time I've got with *Dawn*.

*

The Keeper releases us at the far side of The Dragon, looping up and trailing embers behind it as it soars back towards its fiery home. I hear a ragged cheer from the deck when the *Dawn* breaks the gravitic pull of The Dragon and we all feel the lurch forwards as a darkened star field lies ragged ahead of us. I hear the captain's door opening below me.

Call me when you need me.

'I will.' I hold the wheel tight as I feel *Dawn* going back into hiding.

Raley comes alongside me, and her hand closes on mine. She locks the wheel in place and draws me close, her strength bolstering my resolve while the rest of the crew crowd around, every one of them just thrilled to be alive.

And this was the easy part...

'All right.' I squeeze free. 'Let's find where we are and plot a course. We're all going to be on short rations till this is done. Where's Mirri? We need to find out where we are."

'She's been spending a lot of time with Michaels these last few days.' Raley doesn't meet my eyes. 'I, erm...' Her voice trails away.

'*Michaels?*' I ask. 'Why?'

'He's got a good pair of ears,' Raley says. 'And I'm given to understand that if he can't sort your head out by listening to you, he's got other skills.'

'Other...' I raise an eyebrow.

'Oh, come on, don't make me spell this out.' Raley grins. 'Our crew is all women; space gets cold when you don't have anyone to cuddle up to. Most of them had a shot at the married navigator who was more faithful than any man I've known, and now you leave a piece of beardy beefcake like that in the hold and *don't* expect them to have a go on him?'

I blink. Hadn't considered any of that, but then I've always had Raley with me. 'Okay, see if you can *rouse* Mirri and get her up here.'

*

Mirri's up on deck within twenty minutes. She looks well relaxed.

'Any idea where we are?' I ask.

'Do I have any idea? Please...' Mirri grins. 'We're in the Desolation of Tanis, grid 14'4.'

'How the hell do you know that?' Raley stares at her in wonder.

Mirri turns and points high in the sky to the blue-gold maelstrom off the starboard bow. 'You lot are still trying to navigate by the stars; you never think to just look for things that don't exist anywhere else. That's the Ritarin supernova... We've just come out of The Dragon...' She spreads her arms wide and pirouettes once. 'Desolation of Tanis, grid 14'4.'

'Which way to get back to the Stenlarian Empire?' I ask.

'I've got it.' She slides around the back of Raley and takes the wheel from her. 'After what you've just pulled, you need a rest.'

'Get us to a starport somewhere near, one that takes credits,' I say. 'We need to restock a few things at least, or we're going to be eating each other before we get to the far side.'

'I could go for that.' Mirri sticks her tongue out as Raley cuffs her on the back of the neck.

*

Back in my cabin, Raley looks concerned. The *Dawn*'s hull is still creaking from withstanding the pressures of The Dragon, and looking back out through the rear shields, I can see that the starshields are dripping with plasmatic discharge.

Or the Keeper's droppings...

'What do we do when we find her?' Raley pulls her attention from the creaking to me. 'It's not like we're going to be able to pull her over.'

'No, it's not. We need to get help from people who could stop that ship.'

'It's not going to be a question of stopping it; it's a question of how much we want to keep Clara alive.'

'The vote came out even. Everyone indicated that they wanted her dead as a mark of respect for Samara but, when the vote passed, it was even.'

'Surprised it even got as far as that. Clara doesn't have a malicious bone in her body, and everyone knows that.'

'Still, there is the question of who could help us stop her.'

'I still know a few people in the Imperial Navy,' Raley says. 'I could send word ahead and have a small force waiting when she gets there.'

'They'd take the choice out of our hands.' I sit at my desk and pull out the charts for between here and there. 'They'll not take the chance that she might make it past them, and just blow her out of the sky.'

'That might be just as well.' Raley crouches down next to me. 'She's on her way to release a whole race who've been trapped for hundreds of years—there's no way this ends without bloodshed. Hers, theirs...there's going to be blood in the skies before the end of this.'

'Other options?' I ask. 'Any way we *can* make it through this without violence?'

'Only way that happens is if Clara calls it off, and I can't see that coming to pass any time soon.'

'All right. Make the call. Send them the coordinates the Beyondlight drive will be using, and get them to put something in the way—that should be enough to keep the ship from blowing straight past them before they even know it's on the way.'

'I will.' She nods towards the bed. 'Get rested; there's going to be mayhem enough before long.'

*

I wake to find Raley lying beside me. Her breathing is deep and even, and she's wrapped one arm over the top of me.

Just so I know she's got me.

I lie there for a few minutes, thinking about how we got here, wondering if there was anything else I could have done with the situation. I think back to the academy, to the ethics classes every Red student had to take. I remember one of the professors, ancient at the time, I thought—must have been all of fifty years of age—and his lecture about not looking too far beyond what you can do. *If life was not the way it is, but it is, the lament of those who didn't act through the ages.*

I didn't understand it at the time because, then, if life wasn't how it should have been, you'd just change things, make a deal, change a course; you'd *make* things the way they should be. Then you got dealt things you couldn't change—the Tanahan incident; the Terran Tithes; Olympus, where Mum and Dad gave their lives for mine—and you start to see that you can't always change how things are going to be, so you have to manage with the things you can change.

I move Raley's arm without waking her and climb out of bed, looking again in the mirror. It's not that I don't see anything of who I was in my reflection, it's just that I don't see enough of the person I always thought I'd be. I was ready to be a good Martian, to do my part for the Red Nations, make sure I could help my people create the green-and-blue paradise we were promised, but it was an old-fashioned view, and one that the new colonies had lost faith in. Why bother trying to colonise an uninhabitable world when there were new easier colonies out there to be found? Mars was never an easy sell—not enough water—but it was close enough to Earth to get there without lightspeed and attempt to build something in the harsh environment. That was until they cracked intersystem travel, and most people chose ready-made worlds rather than the hard labour option their parents had died for. Who could blame them?

And here I am, hunting down a friend to keep millions enslaved...

Who am I now?

Raley stirs, opening a tired eye to look me over with a faint smile. 'Still beautiful,' she murmurs, pulling the sheets tight over herself. I take a clean set of clothes from the trunk and flex, shifting into the seventeen forms of readiness that Raley taught me all those years ago, knowing that she'll hear what I'm doing, knowing she'll be watching by the time I get to fourteen. I finish the thirteenth form, and there's a rustle of sheets.

'Get your ass pushed out.' She yawns. 'Shouldn't be a crease in your pants when you do that one.'

'You just want to watch.' I stick my tongue out while looking up at her from the floor.

'Every time.' She throws the pillow at me. 'Now get pushing!'

I abandon the forms and move over to the bed to lie next to her. 'Seriously, Ral, what are we going to do with Clara.'

'We're not going to do anything.' She pulls me close. 'I made the call to Stenlarian command, sent them the details of the ship's course and, when they asked what was so important that they needed to stop it, I told them the basics.'

'They're going to kill her then?'

'I'd be surprised if they don't just have a dreadnought waiting for her.'

'Where are they going to intercept her?'

'Evenside Station,' she replies. 'It's right in the path of the *Sonskyn*, and they can use the station's tugs to move it to a place where they can cut right in and pull Clara out.'

'All right.' I roll off the bed. 'We need to aim for Evenside and get Clara back. It should be us doing what needs to be done, not strangers.'

'Not sure they'll see it that way.' Raley rolls to the other side and shrugs into her clothing.

'She's not done anything so far.' I look back at her. 'The only thing they've got on her is bringing a Stenlarian ship back without authority.'

'You know Stenlarians. It's enough that you've *thought* about committing a crime. But taking a ship and bringing it this close to the Chaeni Worlds? A repeat offender who's already been data pumped? You might as well make her last meal out of Ledi—it'll be less painful than what they'll give her.'

'We'll see.' I strap my sword on and start the fourteenth form. 'Wouldn't want you to be disappointed.'

'Never.' She grins, and follows me down to the deck.

Evenside

It's three days' travel at the best speed the *Dawn* can manage before Mirri signals that we're receiving comms traffic from Evenside Station.

'Strange though'—She has her head cocked to the side as she listens in—'I'm not getting anything from any other ships; just the Evenside's automated nav-beacon.'

'Send word, we are on approach and will need to make repairs when we dock.' I look out to the prow. We're not close enough that I can make out the Moonpiercer lights on the top and bottom of the station, but it won't be long before they're visible.

Mirri goes back to signalling as Esme comes up on deck—she has her prayer band exposed, and her fingers are working an intricate pattern on them. She motions for me to move to the back of the ship, just out of earshot. I take a quick glance to the prow and then join her.

'Something is wrong.' She glances down at her band and then up at me, speaking faster than normal. 'Something has gone very wrong somewhere; it's interfered with the natural order of things.'

'Whoa there.' I hold up my hand. 'What's happened?'

'I no longer hear the prayers of my brothers and sisters.' She rubs the band again. 'I do not hear their comforting words; all their thoughts were cut off a short while ago.'

'Is it because we've been out here so long?' I know the prayer bands operate on a variable frequency and that the channel they use varies from sector to sector, but that's about it. 'Could you have lost the signal?'

'I lost it out beyond The Dragon. When we came back in, though, I could hear the voices of my clans—that's how I know something terrible has happened.'

'Right, head below, and make everyone ready for whatever we might find.' I walk back to the wheel where Mirri is still shaking her head. 'Nothing at all?'

'Like a hole in space. Even if there was nothing else going on, I should be able to pick up other ships in the vicinity.'

'Are our systems working?' I look down at the wheelboard: all power on, all functions enabled.

'I could get a straight line to Stenlarian command if you wanted one.' Mirri's frown deepens. 'I just can't hear anything from one star over.'

'Rig for silent. Kill our transponder and take us in dark.'

*

It's another three hours before Evenside Station's Moonpiercer lights are visible but the beam is intermittent, like an old earth lighthouse. Mirri sails us in at a wide angle, not pointing the ship straight towards the station, but drifting instead in the manner of a rogue asteroid. It's the sort of move that'll get you shot to pieces by a meteor cutter but makes you invisible when an active scanner is looking.

Except no one's looking.

Raley races up the stairs, and points high on the starboard side to where an Ascended Cathedral is floating in the black, its immense white walls dull, not a light on its hull, nor anything moving anywhere on the structure.

'Ascended couldn't have taken out the station,' I whisper. 'Not even a Cathedral.'

'You ever seen inactive Ascended?' Raley whispers back.

'No...' I hear Mirri's gasp and look to the prow.

Evenside Station is no longer even...

One of its sides is missing.

I stare in mute horror as the station continues to roll on its long axis, the movement of its torus rings continuing even as flares from exploding materials ripple across the superstructure. The space around it is littered with minute fragments of metal and endless bodies turning in the void; hundreds, if not thousands of them.

There's still power in some parts of the station—whatever hit them didn't get the reactor, but...

I take the wheel from Mirri while she stares at the devastation, offering no resistance as my hands slide under hers. 'Get me comms with someone on that station,' I say. 'Anyone at all. We need to find out what happened.'

Mirri nods, and heads down below as I bring the *Dawn* to a halt—no sense venturing into the debris field until we know where we're going. I turn us over, to get a better picture of what's happened to the station. The long spire leading up to the main station has been ruptured, air and fluids are pouring out at a rapid rate, and the main body of the station has a massive gouge down one side, like we saw in the Broken Hollows. Only, this gouge has removed most of the plating down the port side of the station, with no regard for all those needing that plating for survival. The high spire for controlling communications is still functioning, and there are a number of ships floating around it. All of them show signs of having vented their atmosphere from the points on the vessels where they would have been docked with the station.

'Anything?' I ask Mirri.

'Distress beacons everywhere.' Mirri checks the comms board. 'Not a ship out here that hasn't suffered some form of catastrophic damage. I'm receiving an SOS from the Evenside command deck.'

'Put it through here.' I tap on the wheel, waiting until I hear the familiar static on the line. 'This is the *Unbroken Dawn*, unaffiliated ship in the Evenside sector, responding to distress signal from Evenside Station. Do you read?'

'—t someone. WE GOT SOMEONE,' the man on the other end of the static shouts. 'THIS IS EVENSIDE COMMAND DECK. WE HAVE WOUNDED ON BOARD. CAN YOU ASSIST US?'

'We're a light merchant vessel,' I respond. 'How many are you?'

'Thirty command crew, with over seven hundred more holding

in the cargo bays that still have power. How many can you take?' His voice holds an edge of hysteria. I hear masses of people yelling in the near background.

I remember Esme's list of remaining supplies and do the maths to the next nearest station. 'We can hold maybe a hundred, but we have no supplies for feeding them—we were coming in to repair our ship and resupply. What happened here?'

'Prepare to receive our logs,' the man replies, as the sound of rending metal echoes over the line. 'I can bring supplies to the cargo bays if you're willing to take people with you, any of them, please.'

'Which bays have power?'

'Two and three. I'm rerouting the lighting so you can see where you're coming in.' The lights on the lower landing bays blink on, the high beams glowing in the darkness on that side.

'We see it, Evenside. Can you stabilise the station at all? Don't fancy trying to get in there while the station is still rotating.'

'Will do what we can, *Dawn*.' His voice is strained, with a faint trace of an Illenial accent. 'Never trained for half the station being torn off.'

'Understood, Evenside.' I turn the ship over, drifting her down towards the second bay. It's clear that the gravity is offline. The centrifuge must have failed when the station got hit; everything not bolted down is floating free, bodies, equipment, cargo, no way to get in without wrecking everything. 'Evenside, this is *Dawn*. We see bay two, but there are no holding mechanisms in place.'

'We have that, *Dawn*.' His voice goes quiet. 'We know none of us are making it out of here. The nearest support ships are more than two hours away, and something has damaged the main reactor. We're looking at a core breach in less than an hour.'

'We understand.' I look up at the command hub below the main spire. 'What's your plan?'

'We're going to vent bay two and use the docking tractors to move whatever we can over to you.'

'Whoa, Evenside, repeat please?' I pause as the enormity of his words hit. 'Sounded like you're going to vent bay two?'

'Confirmed, *Dawn*. Everyone in there is dead if we don't do anything. This way...' He sounds like a man who's accepted his own death and now just wants to save whoever he can, however he can. 'This way some of them make it; this way we don't lose everyone.'

'There's got to be another way. Extend your shield?'

'Shield variance is offline.' It's clear from his words that he's had this conversation with those around him. 'If I extend it, it'll pulp all of you. This is the only way, *Dawn*; I wish it wasn't.'

'Understood.' I bring the ship back to holding. 'Where do you want us?'

'Vertical, up a click.' The nav-laser realigns and cuts a path into the night. 'Where we're pointing now. When we open the bay, it's going to vent everything into space. The release of air will send Evenside into a spin that we're not going to recover from, but we've calculated how we'll spin, and we'll accommodate for that with the tractors.' He pauses. 'When the tractors cease operation, you need to get out of here, and fast—the reactor won't be far behind that failure.'

'We'll be ready.' I bring the ship upwards. 'Anything else you need?'

'A thousand more lifepods?' His voice holds the notion of a humourless smile.

'Understood, Evenside.'

'Tariq. It's Tariq.' His voice is much closer to the mic.

'Catarina,' I reply, gripping the wheel at the emotion in his voice.

'Tariq Al Shujae, ibn Alia Jalayer.' His voice is louder now, sounding much younger. 'Imperial Navy, rank of captain, first of my class to make it, tell Mum...' He pauses and his voice catches. 'Tell her she can be proud.'

'I will,' I reach up towards the command hub, as if I can take his hand and tell him everything will be all right. 'I will.'

'And I will not let you down, Catarina,' he shouts, as the station thrusters start to splutter, the station beginning a roll that it will not recover from. 'Catch who you can, and remember us to those who will listen.'

The shield on bay two flickers, and there's a venting of air

like a ram jet. Debris flies out in all directions as the station rolls
backwards, the air moving it on the lateral axis as I struggle to
keep the *Dawn* on point. The docking tractors come alive, each
one stabbing out with pinpoint accuracy as they bring everything
they can safe to us. Bodies and cargo rain down upon the deck,
some landing soft, some hard, no difference between people
and possessions. I look up as Evenside rolls back. The venting
ceases, and a tear opens in the dorsal reinforcements with fire
and electricity surging out of it before the lack of atmosphere
smothers them. The tractors blink and fail as the power goes
offline, and Evenside tumbles away into the darkness. I pull the
Dawn away, remembering Tariq's warning.

   The reactor won't be far behind.

Not Thinking Straight

We're less than ten thousand clicks away when Evenside's reactor gives up the fight. There's a bright pinprick of blue, followed by the absolute black of the implosion and an orange-green corona around the sphere. I turn the *Dawn* to face the black, angling the prow towards what I know is coming. There's a ripple of screams and shouts from the top deck as the living refugees' squall in fear and dismay, watching what would have been, for many of them, the only home they've known, consumed by plasmatic fire.

Like watching Mars from the colony ships when Olympus erupted.

I keep the *Dawn* steady while the shockwave ripples over us, the prow and shield riding out the worst of it without incident. The sails gleam with energy when I steer us up and over the wave. It's more than twenty minutes before the shockwaves subside, and twenty more before I'm happy to turn the ship around and continue towards our destination. I look down at what the Evenside's crew managed to get over to us.

Thirty refugees, twenty boxes of cargo.

From a station that held more than seventy thousand souls and turned over four million tons of trade.

My crew move among them, some reassuring them, some treating the wounded, others assessing what was brought on board.

First order of survival, make sure we can feed everyone.

Within the hour, Raley comes to me at the wheel with the details.

'Of those thirty,' she says, nodding down at the deck, 'four won't make it—internal injuries, burns, vacuum damage. They'd have had more of a chance if they'd been warned what was going to happen.'

'If they'd known what was going to happen, they'd have tried to take the station, and that would have killed all of them. What about the others?'

'Fourteen walking wounded.' Raley examines the list. 'Twelve with cuts and bruises. Miracle we got any of them unharmed; the Evenside had some damn good people on it.'

'Yeah.' I nod without further comment.

'As for the supplies...' Raley notes my silence and continues down the list. She's known me long enough to know I'm listening, even if I'm not talking. 'Again, good people—they knew what to send. We've got crates of liquid seal—three of them, high-grade stuff; the sort that seeks out the damage and patches it. We've got food, some fresh, some packaged, and they sent water, sufficient to keep all of us alive till we hit the nearest station. Damn good people.'

'Yeah.' I pull my attention from the refugees on the deck and focus on her. 'Did they send all their logs over?'

'They did.' She glances down towards our quarters. 'Figure they're the sort of thing that we don't want take a look at out here within earshot of everyone.'

'I hear you.' I pull her close for a second, needing to feel the warmth of a human body against me for a second. 'Send Mirri up to cover for me, and I'll come down to take a look at them.'

I spend more than an hour talking with the people on deck. Most of them are worried about being dumped on a privateer vessel and ending up being sold as slaves at the nearest port.

It's a reasonable worry—a less scrupulous captain would just say they perished along with the others on the Evenside and take the profit.

I get Esme to pull her vestments out of the trunk and hold a brief service for those lost in the catastrophe. I know it's not her calling anymore, but the sight of a Tarlinian low priestess among the crew helps provide the understanding that we have no intention of selling them as slaves.

It's just as well Esme never made it as far as high priestess; she cared too much for others.

I leave as she starts the service, heading to my cabin, where

Raley is waiting. She's already sifted through the logs for the relevant data. What's on the screen are Evenside's command screen visuals from a few hours ago. I turn up the volume.

*

'Evenside to unknown craft, please provide your identification and trade warrants.' Tariq's voice is clear and calm.

The picture shifts, and we see the ragged outline of the *Sonskyn* coming into view. It's travelling at far below sub-light speed— the sheer number of ships in the vicinity of Evenside making it impossible to go to Beyondlight.

'Evenside to unknown craft, please provide your identification and trade warrants.'

It changes to split-screen as the *Sonskyn* opens a channel to them, half now showing the bridge of the *Sonskyn*, the other half displaying visuals from outside of the station.

Clara...

It's apparent from the wiring protruding from her head that she's interfaced with the computers on the *Sonskyn*. There's a thick data cable attached to a suspension harness to prevent the weight of it pulling the attachment from her head. She looks up at the screen, her eyes fluctuating between focussed and not.

She must be taking on the piloting functions of the ship as well.

'Evenside.' Her voice is slow, almost slurred. 'This is the ISN *Sonskyn*, commercial merchant vessel operating from Stenlar Prime under the orders of the empire. We are just passing through, no refuel or trading required.'

'*Sonskyn*, this is Evenside.' Tariq hesitates. 'Your ship is unregistered. Please hold at outer perimeter while we verify your identity with Stenlarian High Command.'

'*They must not know we are coming.*' Clara's voice is full of venom. '*You will not warn them.*'

The *Sonskyn* surges forwards, no weapons evident, but the acceleration is far more than any station would allow in such close proximity.

'*Sonskyn*, this is Evenside.' Tariq's voice is urgent, but calm. 'You must cease your advance, or we will be forced to engage defensive protocols.'

'You must allow me to get my ship aligned.' Clara's voice is clearer now. 'I only need to line up for my next jump; I'll be out of your space in minutes.'

'*Sonskyn*, this is Evenside, we are deploying defensive drones. You must stand down till we can confirm your identity with Stenlarian command.'

'*You will not.*' Clara's voice is venomous again, as if the mere mention of the Stenlarians is all it takes to set her off. 'Stand down, Evenside. We remember when you were just being built. Much of your construction was carried out by our empire; you owe it to us to allow us to return to our empire.'

'*Sonskyn, STAND DOWN.*' Tariq is louder, but still composed. 'If you progress any further, we will open fire upon you. I have sixty-seven thousand souls on this station and two refugee transports fleeing from Stenlarian pirates—you must withdraw to a safe distance. I cannot allow you any closer till you are verified. Please, *stand down.*'

The *Sonskyn* accelerates again, the massive engines at the back flaring blue-gold.

'All defences, weapons free.' Tariq's voice is calm, the decision made. 'Target propulsion units only, scramble strike one through six immediate.'

The defence drones circle, spiralling down towards the *Sonskyn* in a cloud of metallic precision. The screen still has Clara on the other side, and I see her eyes shift into a thousand-yard stare as her machine-enhanced intellect calculates every possible way out of the situation she's in. There's the faintest trace of a smile when the solution presents itself, and the *Sonskyn* turns to port, the engines slowing as it drifts towards Evenside's dorsal spine.

The drones circle the rear of the *Sonskyn*, tiny flares erupting as their short-range flensing cannons open up. Designed for holding off enemies till the main fleet can be scrambled from the main hangars, the damage they inflict is negligible, just minor dents and scrapes along the hull. Nowhere near enough to cause serious damage but, as I watch, the *Sonskyn*'s engines splutter and die, leaving it drifting towards the station without purpose.

'*Sonskyn*, this is Evenside, your drives are disabled. Stand down and prepare to be boarded.' Tariq's voice remains composed. 'We will send an ambassador to meet you.'

There's a glint in Clara's eye that only one of us could have recognised. 'Understood, Evenside. We are standing down and preparing to be boarded.'

The *Sonskyn* continues to drift forwards, the drones thudding against the hull and pulsing in unison to bring it to a halt. The *Sonskyn* stops less than a hundred metres from Evenside, and the drones start to push it back towards open space as the strike craft swoop in, flanking on all sides, their weapons aimed at the cockpit.

Classic Outer Rim positioning—if you move, our guns are trained at your head.

'Evenside, this is *Sonskyn*. We are experiencing a fluctuation in our drive core.' Clara's mechanical eye widens to full aperture with the intensity of her calculations. 'We may need to offload our crew to you till we've managed to get to a safe distance.'

'Understood, *Sonskyn*.' Tariq's tone is guarded now. 'Moving drones to safe position. Strike one through six, move to close formation on Evenside.'

The *Sonskyn* drifts forwards again, the strike craft falling into flanking positions behind it, their guns still lined up on the engines, rather than the solid core of the Beyondlight drive. I see the tell-tale lights of the drive charging, looking for all the world like a fire spreading through the ship. The split screen shows Clara's mechanical eye refocuses as she calculates more and more permutations, discarding those that will not give her the result she wants, the nose of the *Sonskyn* shifting by fractions of degrees as she lines it up.

'Evenside, this is *Sonskyn*.' Clara's eyes clear, and she stares at the camera. 'Lock down all your bulkheads immediately.'

'*Sonskyn*, this is Evenside, confirm your last message please?'

'Evenside, go to lockdown protocols; we cannot be delayed any further, and we cannot allow you on board the ship.' Clara's expression is resolute. 'You have thirty seconds.'

'*Sonskyn*, you are ordered to stand down.' Tariq sounds concerned but remains steady. 'Strike one through six, move to holding protocols.'

The six craft move upwards, the ships now hovering around fifty metres from the *Sonskyn* with their active weapons trained at what they think is the bridge. The drones move in to secure the *Sonskyn*.

Clara sees this and moves her gaze down from the screen. 'Forgive us.' Her hand moves to the controls, and *Sonskyn* disappears from the screen. There's a moment where the universe resists, and then a ripple of gravity tears the strike craft into tiny shards. I look at Evenside's external feed.

The station *ripples*...

There's a cry of alarm as the Evenside's outer plating is torn free by gravitic forces stronger than anything the designers could have expected. Clara's request now understood as the warning it was as the comms chatter gives rise to a sea of screams and distress beacons. The two refugee ships above tear loose from their moorings as Evenside is torn out of its orbit, the cameras going dark one-by-one in quick succession, the gravity wave tearing them free with the casual ease of an angry universe.

*

I pause the recording, and sit down without care. 'She knew. She knew what it would do, but she did it anyway.'

'That's not our Clara anymore.' Raley taps the screen. 'None of us would have done that; none of us *could* have done that. What sort of a person chooses to cause that much damage, just because they're going to slow you down?'

'Thousands against billions.' I look at the screen, frozen at the point when those thousands understood that they weren't going to make it. 'If she makes it to the Chaeni Worlds, she can bring all of them back. When you reduce it to the maths, it's not even a sum.'

'She can't do maths. They took that from her, remember?'

'That computer the bloody Stenlarians put inside her head

does; damned them by their own machinations. A human resolution would have considered all angles. The machine just sees large and small numbers.' I turn to Raley; she's pale from what she has witnessed. 'She understood that engaging the drive in close quarters would cause catastrophic damage to Evenside, and she made that choice anyway. She was just stalling for time to line up the *Sonskyn* for the jump to Beyondlight.'

'We have to stop her.' Raley looks down at the screen. 'If necessary, we have to kill her.'

The Path Home

I stare at the images on the screen. 'Where was she pointing when she jumped?'

'It'll take me some time; I could do it faster if Mirri was helping. You should be up on deck anyway—those refugees need someone to reassure them beyond the religious.'

'Yeah, I know.' I kiss her, then leave the cabin.

*

Mirri still has the wheel, but she looks distracted, one eye on what's behind us as she stands side-on. She sees me and steps back in front of the wheel, looking a little embarrassed.

'Sorry, cap'n,' she murmurs. 'I can't help thinking about all those people.'

'They won't be the only ones if we don't beat Clara to the Chaeni Worlds.' I move alongside her and take the wheel, nodding back towards my cabin. 'Give Raley a hand—I need the best route to make sure we do just that.'

'All right. Esme's managed to calm most of them down, but there are a few who are demanding we go back and pick up everyone else.'

'Everyone else is gone. They know that.'

'Yeah, but knowing it and accepting it are two different things...' Mirri smile is sad as she heads to my cabin.

I peer over the deck. The survivors from the Evenside are below, though there are a few of them leaning over the side, staring back at where we've come from. It reminds me of watching Mars tear itself to pieces in the aftermath of the Olympus eruptions through the ship's rear ports. The countless millions who'd been left behind: friends, loved ones...

Parents.

The memory hits me hard: Mum swapping her flight patches with mine, Dad bundling me onto the shuttle, the sure and certain knowledge that they weren't going to make it, though through their sacrifice I would. I sigh and lean hard on the wheel as Esme joins me, still dressed in her vestments.

'Did what I could, cap'n,' she murmurs, her voice quiet enough that no one on deck can hear. 'Truth is most of them are still in shock. That's not going to last long; then they're going to be angry. Best we get most of them off our ship before that happens.'

'Thanks, Esme,' My voice is quiet.

'You okay?' She puts a hand on the wheel. 'Hell of a time the last few weeks have been.'

'I'm fine.' I know she can tell I'm lying.

'Yep... Here if you need me though.'

'Since we set off.' I smile and pull her close for a second. 'I know. Might want to keep those vestments handy for when the shock wears off.'

'Easy for you to say.' She smiles, putting her hands to her waist where the corsetry has her pulled in thinner than my thigh. 'You're not wearing one of these.'

'Surely you can get away without that out here?'

'Ever seen a fat Tarlinian priestess?' She raises an eyebrow.

'Nope.'

'Sure you have. But everything that was here'—she puts her hand over her stomach—'has been pushed up here.' Her other hand brushes her chest. 'There's an image to maintain, and I've been living out here among you heathens for a long time. So I'm not as waspish as a pious woman should be, and the only way you can pass for a still-active priestess...' She puts her hands on her hips. 'I'm just glad I can still get into it.'

'Sorry.' I blush. 'Didn't realise it was going to be so much trouble.'

'Of course you didn't. First time you met me I didn't need the corset.'

'Still sorry.' I let my hand drop down to her stomach. 'Enough pain out here without me causing any more.'

'It'll be fine,' she says. 'Just tell me the nearest station is close.'

'Got Mirri working on it,' I say. 'Think it'll be more than a day though.'

'No worries. I'll just head to my quarters and make like I'm being pious.' Her hand brushes mine as she turns to leave. 'Come and see me, if you need me.'

I nod, turning my attention back to the stars. There's no comms traffic out here; the whole area is quiet, like the Broken Hollows were. The thought occurs to me that the wake caused by the Beyondlight drive would have caused similar disruption all the way along its course.

Not just to the Evenside.

Two of the refugees are up on the deck now, both of them seeming afraid to approach me. I motion for them to join me alongside the wheel. It takes them more than ten minutes to get here—they take every step on the way to the top deck as if it will bite them. I take a closer look as they clear the top step: a man in his early twenties, wearing the dark orange of a deckhand with the tell-tale silver lines of someone once-Ascended running along his bare arms, and a woman in her late forties, with a D'Cla command insignia on her neck. Her uniform has seen better days, but she holds herself upright, straighter than the *Dawn*'s mast.

'Captain Morgan, *Unbroken Dawn*. What can I do for you?'

'Sasha Tiribova. D'Cla Void Shadow, requesting that you drop us at the next D'Cla certified station,' the woman says.

'We're in pursuit of the ship that caused all this.' I keep one eye on the bow of the ship. 'I can't afford any diversions from that mission.'

'Captain, what I saw that ship do... No one can catch that thing. Unless... you have some idea of where they are headed?'

'*Some* idea, yes. Also, that drive can't just take them straight to where they want; it has to avoid running into any obstacles in its path.'

'Which in turn relies on the notion that they can't find a way that has no obstacles... The better way to do this would be to ensure you've told everyone in its way that it's coming—we can't risk another Evenside.'

'Agreed,' I say. 'That's why we aren't stopping. This ship doesn't have comms that can reach across systems.'

'If you drop us at the nearest D'Cla station, I'll use my clearance to allow you to send a transmission using its main comms. We could get a signal out in no time at all; you might not even need to continue on.'

'There's one of ours on board. If only for her, we have to continue.'

'Great. Can she just stop the ship then?' Sasha asks.

'She's the one piloting it. She's carried a grudge against the Stenlarians ever since they removed part of her head.'

'It's heading to the Stenlarian Empire?' Sasha's hands clench for a second. 'Why?'

'You wouldn't believe me if I told you.'

'Try me. I've been out here more than thirty years; seen most things.'

'It's the key to freeing the Chaeni Worlds. There's something on the ship that can reverse the gravitic field which is trapping them.'

Sasha pauses for a second and stares at me. 'If you don't want to tell me, I get it.'

'If you don't believe what I'm telling you, I get it...' I meet her stare without flinching.

'The Chaeni Worlds freed? Bring back a race of merciless killers? In the name of the endless stars, why?'

'Because they weren't really killers... History is written by the victors, and the Stenlarians won. She's just trying to set that right.'

'If what you say is true, then I can see how she'd feel that. And while I *was* Stenlarian before I was ever D'Cla, I can't see why you'd want to stop her from doing that, if they were innocent, all you're doing is setting the wrong thing, right." She pauses to think. "But if you need to, then getting word to the Stenlarians would be the best way of stopping her. If the navy is mobilised, nothing would get past it.'

'Your word that we can use the station's comms to send the broadcast, no charges to us?' I fix my gaze on her. 'And you take all the other refugees with you, with a guarantee of safe passage.'

'I can't speak for them—' she starts.

'You're a Void Shadow,' I cut in. 'On your word, whole planets can be razed to the ground. Looking after a few displaced people is well within your grasp. Give me your word now.'

'Fine. My word is given.' She extends her hand. 'I'll give you the coordinates.'

I shake her hand and look around her to the man. 'And what about you?'

'Alexi, my bodyguard. Anyone who's been Ascended feels no pain or fear. You only beat them by dismembering them and, even then, the severed bits will still try to get you. Alexi here owes me his life; I freed him, and he chose to discharge that debt by ensuring nothing happens to me.'

'All right...' I say, shrugging. 'Let's have those coordinates.'

A Legacy of Hate

The nearest D'Cla station is four hours out of our way; a million tons of unreflective crystal floating in the void, just coming into view when Mirri moves alongside. 'You sure about this?' She keeps her voice low.

'Not sure about any of this,' I murmur, 'but the comms on there have enough range to get the word out to Stenlar Prime ahead of her arrival—it's a chance we need to take.'

'As long as the D'Cla don't have any plans to take us instead. There's no heart in the Void. You know that.'

'No heart means there's no chance of them getting emotional either. No reason to betray us; nothing in it for them.'

'No.' Mirri looks unconvinced. 'Then again, when have the Void ever needed a reason?'

'It's only me and Raley from our crew going on board.' I look at the Void station, the black crystal that makes up its walls seeming as sharp as knives, like a slow-turning, spiked animal. 'The rest of you stay here and wait for us.'

'You don't mind if I point us the other way, so we can make a quick exit?' Mirri looks even more concerned as the shadow of the station falls over us.

'Not at all.' I smile with more confidence than I feel. 'Be happier knowing that my escape route is already sorted.'

The aperture on the station which has been designed for ships smaller than the *Dawn* is lined with rough crystal edges that would snag and tear our sails to pieces. I find Sasha on deck and point up at them. 'We'll take the skiff in; there's no way the *Dawn* fits in there.'

'No need.' Sasha puts a hand to her chest and raises her other hand high.

The crystal exterior changes shape, its rough edges becoming smooth as they detach from the aperture and form a long bridge between the station and the ship. Sasha watches as it gets to within a metre of the ship and lowers her arm. She nods towards the structure and hops up on the side of the ship, straddling the gap between the two.

'Seriously?' I stare at the long crystal bridge, looking like it'd break if a child stood on it.

'It's more solid than the deck you're standing on. Come on, the comms array can be accessed from the main bay.'

Raley seems uncertain as I step up on the side of the ship and reach with care to test the flat crystal platform. There's doesn't seem to be any give to it though; no different to a station platform or even the surface of a planet. Sasha nods and hops off the ship, and walking with confidence towards the station, where another piece of crystal is forming into the shape of a door.

'You sure you want to do this?' Raley leans in close as she takes a step onto the bridge.

'Nope, but any message sent from them will get the word to the Stenlarians faster than anything we've got—and when their long range sensors pick up the *Sonskyn*, they'll know the Void were telling the truth.'

'No one knows the Void, but the Void.' Raley adjusts her sword to the ready position and follows me across the bridge.

*

Up close, the Void station is massive in the way mountains are, its outer surface smooth as glass, the faintest hint of what's going on inside its interior visible through the dark, opaque sides. Sasha stands at the doorway, keeping one hand on its frame, as if holding it open.

'Just in case the ship thinks you're an intruder.' She nods towards it. 'Better safe than sorry.'

'Yeah.' I step inside the station, Raley following a half step behind me.

Sasha waits for Alexi before joining us, the crystal door closing as she enters, leaving us standing in front of a smooth wall. I look back at her with a frown, and she smiles, putting her hand on her heart and pointing to the wall with her other hand. It transforms into a screen and keyboard, with what appears to be a microphone reaching down from the upper surface.

'Set the comms according to what you want it to do, and let me know when you're ready to send.'

'From here?' I ask. 'Isn't there a central communications bay?'

'Void station.' She looks around her as if that was all the answer I should need, then smiles at my expression. 'Every part of the ship can be whatever we need it to be; we just adjust our thoughts, and the ship reacts.'

'Every part of the ship can be whatever you need it to be?' Raley looks stunned. 'Every part of it could be an engine, or a gun?'

'Ever wonder why you've never seen a standard Void ship?' Sasha says. 'Each vessel is what the captain needs it to be; there's no such thing as a standard ship. And if you ever come up against one of us, be warned that we react faster than you do.'

'Good to know.' I turn to the keyboard and consider how best to phrase my message. Raley leans in and nudges me away from the keys.

'I got this.' She types for a few minutes, then glances at me to indicate for me to check what she's written. I read it:

Code 47-40 imminent threat to Stenlar Prime inbound using experimental technology. Do not allow it to approach the Chaeni Worlds. Ensure that a perimeter of ships blockades it at all times. Approaching ship is the ISN Sonskyn, *former Stenlarian Registry.*

'Reckon that'll do it?' I ask.

'47 is an interplanetary distress signal, used only to signify that a planetary body is under attack by overwhelming forces. 40 is the code to let them know that there's nothing they can do to improve things for us—we're already gone.'

'We're still going,' I say, frowning.

'You've still got the last transmissions from the Evenside,'

Raley says. 'Attach them to this.'

'Won't they be suspicious that the transmission isn't coming from the Evenside's location?' I ask.

'We can deal with that,' Sasha says. 'It's not hard to replicate your transmissions or their source of origin.'

The realisation of what she's just said sinks in. I turn to her and hold up my log. 'Let me upload the transmissions, then it's good to send.'

Sasha puts her hand on her heart, and an interface forms in the crystal, allowing me to plug the log in so it can cycle through the transmissions. I attach Evenside's last words and nod, turning back to Sasha.

'That's everything?' she asks.

'That's everything. Send it to Stenlar Prime, immediate priority. Leave the return transmission point as the *Dawn*. That way we can respond to any return messages from them.'

'All right.' Sasha steps forwards to put her hand on the crystal, and the message disappears. 'Sent.'

I hear a sound like breaking glass, and the wall to my left forms into a rough-cut crystalline figure, its features sharp, its eyes dark pits of opaque crystal. It turns to face Sasha as she drops to one knee. Alexi mirrors her.

'My Lord,' she says.

'A transmission sent.' The figure speaks, though it sounds more like someone trying to imitate vocalisations by way of whistling. 'A warning to the Stenlarians?'

'A warning to all of us, my Lord.' Sasha keeps her eyes averted. 'The Stenlarians were responsible for what happened to the Chaeni Worlds, but if the Chaeni are returned now, the loss of life will be colossal.'

'The loss of *Stenlarian* life will be colossal.' The figure turns to us. 'Name your price for rescinding the message with the appropriate codes, and leave the Stenlarians to their fate.'

'If the Stenlarians fall, the Chaeni won't stop there.' I try to meet its gaze, but its lack of eyeballs makes this difficult. 'If that ship reaches its destination, it'll ignite a war the likes of which no one has ever seen.'

'I have no issues with that.' The figure looks at me, then Raley. 'You are the one with the codes. Give them to us, now.'

Raley takes a step backwards, her hips shifting as she moves into an alert stance, her sword angled. 'They're not for taking,' Her words are quiet.

'You have mistaken an order for a request.' The figure mirrors her position, its fingers growing long and sharp, their tips thin like razors. 'The codes, now...'

'My Lord.' Sasha is still kneeling. 'These came here under protection of my word. To harm them would be to violate my trust.'

'Your word was given that you'd allow them to send their message.' The figure's fingers click together as it paces to the right. 'Your trust remains inviolate, but we must look to the future of the Void, and removing the Stenlarians' ability to resist us would be worth much to those who would assist us.'

'At the cost of millions of lives,' I adjust my own stance.

'Not *our* lives,' it replies with a tilt of its head. 'But we can see how it would trouble you.'

'We are the Void, my Lord.' Sasha moves along to the edge of the wall, placing herself between us and it. 'We are pledged to the greater good. Nothing good can come of so many deaths.'

'You have much to learn.' Its head follows her as she moves. 'Millions are inconsequential compared to the billions that will be allowed to live if that ship reaches where it should. The greater good will be served.'

'We can't know that they'll still be alive if that ship frees them,' Sasha says. I glance towards her—the set of her face shows that how unhappy she is with the decision she's being told to make. She glances towards the space where we entered through the wall. 'We must allow them to continue.'

'No.' The figure glides forwards, it's legs not moving as it slides without noise over the crystal floor.

'Captain,' Sasha says, her voice going quiet, but urgent, 'activate your bubbletech.'

The figure pauses as these words reach its ears, a hundred spikes emerging from its arms and shoulders, its arms splitting, and then splitting again, now an eight-armed monstrosity of dark crystal.

'Alexi.' Sasha nods towards it as she plants one hand on the wall and her other hand on her heart. The wall splits and opens wide, air rushing out of the gap, venting out into space. Alexi lunges at the figure, managing to uproot one of its feet as it recoils in surprise. The other foot clamps to the floor like a magnet as Raley grabs me and launches backwards, using the vacuum to assist her jump, and both of us sail out into the darkness. Sasha dives out after us, and Alexi sprints after her while the figure regains its balance.

Raley spins, firing her grapple downwards and hauling us toward the *Dawn*. I flip when we reach the edge of the ship's bubble, Raley's arm tight around my waist as she brings us down to the deck.

'GET US OUT OF HERE!' I roar at Mirri, seeing the D'Cla station shift again, the smooth walls forming into long, grasping claws.

The *Dawn*'s sails gleam like stars as Mirri pushes us to full power, and we surge ahead as the crystal claws arc down from above us. She rolls us over, and the claws tear into the topsail, sending shards of the mast spinning down towards us. The D'Cla station rolls again. It has the size advantage but, as anyone who's ever tried to catch a mouse knows, size isn't everything. The crystal station shifts again, forming not into a claw this time, but a long-barrelled cannon. I sprint to the top deck, watching in horror as it takes aim at us.

'Get ready to roll...' I put my hand on Mirri's shoulder.

'FLY STRAIGHT!' Sasha shouts to us from above as she enters the *Dawn*'s bubble, landing hard on the lower deck.

'It'll blow us out of the sky,' I yell.

'It fires lasers.' Sasha staggers upright. 'It's a living ship; the only thing it can fire other than energy is parts of itself, and the Prime loses control over the crystal as soon as it leaves the station.'

'You sure?' I stare down the barrel of the huge cannon, and see a glow building at the base of it.

'Trust me. There's a good reason the D'Cla don't engage out in open space these days.' The station begins extending long crystal shards again.

There's no hint of attempted deception in Sasha's manner; no sign that she's being anything but honest. I look up to see the longest arm become a mass of sharp edges.

'Oh shit...' Sasha goes pale and runs towards us. 'TAKE COVER. GET DOWN. DON'T LET THE SHARDS TOUCH YOU.'

The arm reaches for us. There's a bright flash, and the mass at the end of the arm detonates into a hail of splinters. I grab Mirri and dive over the top rail, swinging down against my cabin door. Sasha sprints towards us as the top of the ship is peppered by a thousand tiny pellets, Alexi close behind her. He dives forwards, shielding her, then goes prone, his hands locked over hers, his body jerking from the multiple impacts. Everything goes silent for a moment, and I glance upwards to see the arm growing more sharp edges.

'Get up there,' I say to Mirri, motioning to the top deck. 'Get us out of here.'

I move over to Sasha, keeping my eyes on the other shards. Alexi rolls off her and lies silent on the deck. The wounds aren't large, but it's all he can do to move his head to look at me.

'Fly straight...' She looks down at Alexi, then at me. 'Your sword please.'

'We'll get him down to the medbay.' I reach down towards her. 'Get those treated.'

'No...' She taps my sword. 'We need to kill him.'

'What?'

'Crage.' She glances down at a hole in Alexi's chest. 'Feeds on life, and will grow till he's dead. Then it'll come after us.'

'Best get it out now then.' I reach down again, take her hand and pull her up.

'Sasha,' Alexi gasps as he clutches at his chest, the sharp crystal edges embedded in him visible under his skin, spreading through him like a wave. 'My debt?'

'Was paid before you ever decided to serve me.' She turns back to him for the briefest of seconds, then to me, a single tear slipping down her cheek. 'Your sword, please.'

I draw it as Alexi convulses, the tiny spikes now breaking through the skin on his fingers, the bones beneath becoming long shards of smooth glass. I hand the sword to Sasha, and she stabs down into his heart, the sword penetrating not more than an inch before it meets crystal. Alexi's eyes close with a faint click, his body tensing as he starts to rise up. Sasha pulls the sword out and lays her hand on the side of Alexi's head, taking care not to stand on any of the shards embedded in the deck.

'Move back, captain.' She keeps her voice low. 'Get us out of here before they fire again.'

I step back as Alexi transforms into a crystal statue. Sasha puts her hand to her heart and looks towards the edge of the ship. She takes Alexi's hand and walks him over to the edge, maintaining contact as he climbs the rail and leans out into the void, until the only thing keeping him on board is her.

She lets go...

The statue goes berserk, slashing and flailing in all directions as it drifts out into infinity. Sasha turns to me as the D'Cla station retracts its arms, seeing that we're already out of range and moving faster than it. She motions for me to stay where I am as the station recedes into the distance.

A Matter of Paperwork

It's the best part of an hour before Sasha moves, striding across the deck and crushing the crystals under her feet as if they nothing more than normal glass. I wait by the wheel, and she comes up to join me. Mirri keeps herself in front of the wheel, afraid to move from where she's standing.

'The shards are no longer dangerous.' Sasha's voice is thick with emotion. 'But we would do well to sweep them from your deck while we have the chance. They only contain a small amount of power, but any D'Cla in the vicinity would be able to reactivate them.'

'I'm sorry about Alexi. Do you want us to drop you off at the nearest station?'

'Sasha Tiribova, former Imperial Navy, requesting a position upon your ship.' She stands upright. 'I'm skilled in close quarters and tactics, though I suspect my references may no longer be sterling.'

'You're D'Cla. Once D'Cla, always D'Cla.'

'I thought so too.' She doesn't relax her posture. 'But that's the view from the outside; the Glass Golems don't appreciate treachery. I just cost them the chance of crippling the Stenlarian war effort; they'll turn me into a wall ornament if I go back. If my misjudgment of the D'Cla is sufficient to warrant you not trusting me, then I understand, and I will leave at the next station.'

'You can stay, if that's what you want. You know more about these shards than any of us—are they safe to be brushed from the deck?'

'They should be inert for the most part.'

'Then your first job is to clear the decks of them.'

'At once. Where are your brushes?'

'Just like that? You don't want to know your wages or conditions?'

'Alexi did not owe me his life.' She pauses. 'I saved his life years ago when I extracted all the Ascended's wires from him. I asked no debt from him, but I see now why he did it.'

'There's no debt to me either.' I glance sideways at her.

'Not as far as you're concerned, no.' She makes a passable attempt at a smile. 'However, just as Alexi knew in his heart that he needed to repay me, so I must pay you back, even if you do not hold me to any debt. Besides, you're correct—I am the best person for clearing away those shards; I'll know if any of them are active.'

'Very well. See Raley for your weapons and equipment. For your quarters, see Cl—' The name sticks in my throat, and the realisation of how much I always relied on Clara hits hard. 'I'll sort out your quarters later,' I continue. 'You'll find Raley in the armoury, I have no doubt. Dinners around eight bells. Won't be much, but it'll be edible.'

She nods and heads downstairs.

I wait until she's gone before turning to Mirri. 'Remember when we used to just carry cargo and passengers?'

'Nope. Never been a time when this ship carried just anything.'

'I think we're going to start that when all this is over. I've had enough adventure for one lifetime.'

'Nah.' Mirri tries to disguise it with a smile, but it's obvious that she's shaken. 'Maybe take some time off though... Do you think saving the empire pays well?'

'Never seen a hero retire rich.' I lean on the wheel. 'Hell, never seen a hero retire.'

'That's because the cause is never won.' She leans alongside me, holding the course steady. 'A hero always finds something else to do. They're not in it for the riches—they're in it for the journey.'

So was I when all this started.

I watch as Sasha starts to sweep the shards from the deck, then focus on Mirri again. 'Are you still in it for the journey?'

'To the end.' Her smile is genuine this time. 'Wherever we go, however we get there.'

'How long till we reach Stenlarian space?'

'Edge of it, a few days. Where the Chaeni Worlds are located? More than a week. The bigger question here is, will the Stenlarians take the warning seriously?'

'Nothing we can do if they don't. Just get us there as quick as you can.'

*

It's three days on half rations before we reach the first Stenlarian inline colony. Two cargo ships and two mining cruisers are locked into place on the fuel convertor accompanying it. As we watch, a sun skimmer approaches from the far side and docks with the convertor, unloading fresh plasma to keep the reactor online. The colony has been modified several times, and it appears the fixings were made from the remains of other ships that passed this way, making the whole thing look like a child was designing a ship using the building blocks they had, not the blocks they wanted.

As we bring the *Dawn* around to what I presume is the front of the station, two drones detach from the front of the mining ships and square off against us. It's clear from the speed they're moving at that Stenlarian efficiency still holds sway here.

'This is the *Unbroken Dawn*,' I say through the comms, 'inbound with refugees from the Evenside Station. Request docking to allow for reloading and restocking.'

'*Dawn*, this is the *High Frontier*, you may dock at bay two. We'll take any refugees you have from Evenside, but we're short on supplies ourselves.'

Great...

Mirri brings the ship around, and we wait while the clamp is extended all the way out to us in the same way that the D'Cla ship's crystal bridge was.

Only this time, it's just good old mechanics and not those bastard crystals.

The station administrator walks along the clamp with the easy gait of a man who's done so a million times, and the manner of someone who doesn't use one word when thirty are available. Around his neck are the trappings of a Tarlin Initiate, glittering as if they've been polished within the last ten minutes.

'Administrator Prime Denisov.' He looks down at Raley as she secures the grav-clamp. 'Where do you hail from?'

'Broken Hollows,' I shout across the ship. 'Heading to Stenlar Prime to deliver a warning.'

'Would that be the same warning that was sent broadscale a while ago?'

'47-40?' I ask, coming down the stairs.

'That would be the one.' He starts to step on board, but checks himself. 'Permission to come aboard, captain?'

'Granted.' I nod as I close the distance. 'Captain Morgan, *Unbroken Dawn.*'

He steps onto the ship and takes a good long look around, then waits for me with his arms folded, holding his clipboard to his chest. 'How many refugees do you have on board?'

'Less than thirty.' I think about Alexi for a second. 'When's your next supply run due?'

'Three days. But the greater issue we're facing is the inevitable questions that will arise when we find ourselves with all these evacuees and no Stenlarian ports in the vicinity.'

'Interstellar Law applies—you accepted those who were fleeing from imminent disaster.' I wait for the inevitable show to follow.

'The paperwork alone will double my workload for more than a month. Unless, of course, you've already *done* the paperwork.'

'Emergency operations.' I stare at him with disdain. 'We work in places where stacks of forms aren't always to hand.'

'Everyone should be prepared for all eventualities.' He stands a little taller, puffs out what chest he's got and does his best attempt to look down his nose at me. 'I can see that a junker like this might not have the wherewithal to ensure that proper paperwork has been done, so I'll be sure examine the registry while I'm checking things. Of course, you'll have to wait till I've completed that paperwork before you're allowed to continue through Stenlarian space.'

'We're on an urgent run to the Chaeni Worlds. We can't afford to be held up by paperwork.'

'Every captain is on an urgent run.' He doesn't bother to keep the sneer from his lips. 'In my experience, a prepared captain is ready for these eventualities.'

'I'm sure we can make it worth your while.'

'*Me*? This isn't for *me*, madam...' He gives his clipboard a theatrical flip, bringing it up with his stylus at the ready. 'We'll see whether or not you've got something we can trade to make up the difference. Mining doesn't bring in enough for the luxuries and, out here, it's salvage, not interstellar law that applies.'

'Very well.' I turn to Raley. 'Let him look through the stores. Nothing we need. Anything else is fair game. Would five hundred be sufficient to cover hiring another person to help?'

'A thousand would be... *sufficient* to ease the transit to port for those poor refugees...' His expression tells me that he sympathises with their plight about as much as a Challan Tarmit sympathises with its next meal.

I nod and motion him downstairs. Raley turns and signs *One, Two*, then follows him down. I keep the smile off my face as I wave for Mirri to join me.

'We've got an *administrator* on board.' I point downstairs. 'Help Esme get suited up so she can have a word with him.'

'I could probably do better. You know how administrators like to take bribes, especially out here.'

'Nope, this one's a *pious* man.' I raise an eyebrow.

'One, Two?' Her right eyebrow mirrors mine.

'One, Two.'

She's down the hatch in a trice, and I wait on deck while the refugees start to filter up onto the deck, all of them looking like they'll be glad to get back onto a station. After ten minutes, they're all lined up and eager to go.

'INFIDEL.' The shout can be heard across the ship.

That'll be Two kicking in then...

Denisov is back on deck within a half-minute. Esme is a heartbeat behind him in full regalia, walking like Mirri was a little overzealous with fitting her corset. Raley follows behind.

'Call yourself an Initiate?' Esme punctuates each word by stabbing her finger into his chest. 'Twenty-eight souls in need of respite, that the captain took in without question or compromise, and you're here trying to profit from it?'

'Mistress,' he babbles, clutching his clipboard to his chest, 'I—'

The sharp crack of Esme's hand on his cheek echoes around the deck. 'REMEMBER YOUR VOWS.'

Denisov recoils from the slap and drops his head, his voice trembling. 'I need to do...'

Raley steps towards him, and he slumps to his knees, dropping the clipboard and placing his hands flat on the deck, making no further sound. Esme crouches beside him.

'Do you remember the covenants?' she asks, her voice soft and warm now.

'I do.' He doesn't look up.

Her voice lowers. 'What is the fourth?'

'Provide help to those who cannot help themselves—

'Without...?'

'Without thought for material gain or benefit.' The words trip over themselves in his haste to get them out. 'Forgive me. I have been out here so long.'

'Sometimes our faith is tested'—she reaches over to him and tilts his face up as a mother might her child—'in ways we cannot imagine. What matters is how we rise to those tests.'

He sets his face and shifts back into a kneeling position. 'Forgive me, Mistress, I have been weak.'

'It is not for me to grant forgiveness. It is for you to earn it and prove that you still deserve to wear the rank of Initiate.'

'Yes.' He closes his eyes and nods. Rising up in silence and putting the clipboard behind his back, he turns and looks at the refugees, gesturing to the clamps. 'Please, come on board. We will send word immediately to your people to let them know to come and collect you. Till then, you're our guests for as long as you need.'

Less than ten minutes later, the deck is clear. Denisov doesn't wait to be told; he hops up on the clamp and retreats to the station, before turning back and raising his hand in a Tarlinian penitent salute. Esme stands at the clamp and makes several motions with her hand in response. Denisov nods and averts his eyes, the clamp releasing the *Dawn*. Esme waits until he's gone before loosening her corset and glancing over at me with her cheeks flushed.

'One, Two never fails,' I say.

'Didn't even get as far as One. Just looking at the sanctimonious bastard was enough to piss me off; I didn't wait for Mirri to set up One.'

'Not like you to get so annoyed.'

'He wasn't looking for supplies for the colony; he was looking for things for himself.' She sighs and taps her corset. 'Look, I know I'm not a priestess anymore, but I still live by the covenants wherever I can. He wasn't even putting on a show of piety, just using his credentials to scam us.'

'Just trying to make a living?'

'Just trying to scam one.' Esme tries to smile, but I know the reason she left the church was because too many of them were just using their robes to extort a better life for themselves. 'It is the way it is...'

'Come on.' I give her a hug. 'Let's go make the universe better for all of us.'

A Soldier from Long Ago

It's another three days at full tilt past the edges of the Stenlarian Empire when we start to get comms traffic from civilian ships as well as colony ones. Nobody seems concerned about the *Sonskyn* or the threat it represents.

If I know the Stenlarians, they won't have told anyone about it.

I pause in the mess hall as Michaels comes through looking like he's running on empty. His beard isn't as well-groomed as it was before, and it takes him more than a few gulps of black coffee before he's aware enough to notice I'm in the room.

'Captain.' He raises his hand to his forehead in a half salute. 'I trust all is well?'

'As well as it can be. Are you okay?'

'Living the dream.' His tone suggests he's doing anything but that.

'Seriously?'

'It's been a long few nights. The crew is more than a little on edge and most of them have been coming to see me more than usual.'

'And it would be a poor officer who neglects his *duty*?' I ask.

'Oh, don't get me wrong,' he replies with a wry smile, 'the job has its *ups*, but it also has its downs and, when *I'm* feeling grim, there's no one for me to talk to. *Quis custodiet ipsos custodes.*'

'Who watches the watchmen? If you ever need someone to *talk* to, come and see me.'

'No offence, captain, but you've got a ship to run. You don't need to be worrying about me.'

'You're my crew,' I say. 'If I didn't care, you wouldn't be here. Besides...' My fingers move to my waistline as I sign in Airless, *I might understand more than you think.*

His eyes go wide, and he sets his coffee down.

'Captain to the bridge.' It's Mirri's voice on the Vox. 'Approaching Century barrier.'

'To be continued.' I nod, letting my fingers brush against his arm. 'But I meant what I said—come and see me if you need someone to talk to.'

*

Up on deck, I take the wheel from Mirri and draw the *Dawn* to a halt as we approach the barrier. Raley comes up on deck to stand next to me. To the low starboard, there's a Stenlarian dreadnought holding position, the main weaponry not pointed at us, but there isn't a single inch of space that doesn't have one or more of its secondary guns covering it. Given that they're firing shells larger than this ship, it's understandable why they're not concerned with us.

We move through on its port side, the deep yellow of the Stenlarian sun casting the ship's shadow over us. As we get closer, I realise that its weapons and armour are fitted to the immense sheath encircling the ship from bow to stern, rotating while the core of the ship remains still. The polymer plates of armour are larger than the *Dawn* and are interlaced to form a protective hull over the dreadnought's essential systems. It has a reactor that could power a planet, a crew numbering more than the number of people who used to man Evenside, and the cargo space to move most of a world's population in a single jump. The sheath continues to roll high on its flank, the ship's name growing visible just as the comms chime.

'ISN *Abandon All Hope*, to the ship broadcasting as the *Unbroken Dawn*.' It's a woman's voice, the vowels short and guttural, sounding like she's from Tharsis province. 'Move to secure communications immediately.'

I adjust the comms to tight beam. 'This is the *Unbroken Dawn*,'

I say. 'We are not trading; we are on a mission to warn Stenlarian High Command of an imminent threat.'

'Your warning was received.' The tension in her voice eases. 'This is Grand Admiral Elenya Vaskova. We need you to dock so you can transfer all the information you have on the vessel that you identified as the *Sonskyn*.'

Raley's hand on mine stays my response for a second. 'If they've sent Vaskova, they're not messing about. Vaskova the Damned, they call her; she takes zero shit.'

'Are we safe docking with them?'

'Safer than we are out here. Out here, they can just nuke the ship...'

'Great!' I flip the comms switch. 'This is Captain Morgan of the *Dawn*. Which bay are we docking at?'

The dreadnought's shield rotates and I watch in wonder as a bay five times the size of the *Dawn* opens up like the maw of the Beast, the lights inside so bright that I wouldn't be surprised if there was a star in there. The Dreadnought turns to keep the gravity going while the plates are stationary and I sail us in, coming to rest close to the loading platform. The main doors leading in to the bay open as the outer doors close and the atmosphere changes, the *Dawn*'s sensors registering that there's air beyond the shields a second before we smell air that's been through the recyclers enough times for it to be not just clean, but *Stenlarian* clean.

A rank of soldiers marches out dressed in the red of Imperial Praetorians. They line up on the deck, forming a cordon lining the way for the lone person dressed in command-blue to walk through. She reaches the edge of the deck and looks at us, extending her hand and signing something in a language I'm not familiar with.

'Information quarantined,' Raley says, reading the signing. 'She wants us to pass over the information by hand and ensure that there are no copies left on board.'

'Well, you know what to do then...'

'Wipe the ship's log and hide the backups. On it.'

I head down to the rail to get a good look at the woman. She has two duelling scars on her face, both of which look deep enough to be genuine rather than the fashion lines that most officers get to mimic the real thing. She's stood at ease, but her hands are poised over the guns at her hips.

'Captain Morgan,' I call over.

'Vaskova.' The single word is all the explanation she needs to give. 'Have you verified all that you've sent to us in your first transmission?'

'As much as we could. The tech on that ship is—'

'Not to be spoken of in open air,' she cuts me off. 'Permission to come aboard?'

'Do I have a choice?'

'Just say the word. Stenlarians do not trespass.'

'Permission granted.' I extend the plank.

She crosses without a word and hops down; her landing suggests that her knees don't thank her for the manoeuvre. She reaches down to her belt, and the air around us is filled with white noise.

'What do you know about what you found?' she asks.

'In what way?' I stall till I know Raleys done what she needs to.

'I studied the *Sonskyn* and the *Swartgat* when I was still in flight school.' She leans in closer than she needs to, the tightness of her mouth not just on account of the set of her lips—I recognise the invariable tension that results from rejuvenation treatments. 'Back then, they were just legends, but I knew there had to be some truth in it; the truth that gave rise to the legend.'

'What do you know about why they were built?'

'They were designed to end the threat from the Chaeni. One of them succeeded, while the other one was lost when it encountered a creature that was large enough to consume worlds. We had thought that the Chaeni were limited to small ships and the worlds they'd conquered. None of our data suggested something the size of the thing they found beyond The Dragon.'

I nod.

'Which means that you've seen the creature,' she continues. "No need to confirm. Tell me, what state of repair was the ship in when your crew took control of it?'

'Wrecked. Holed in more places than it was patched.'

'But the nanite repair system was still operational? Or you'd never have got the Beyondlight drive functioning again.'

'You know an awful lot about this ship. And you're out here, when you should be at a desk somewhere, co-ordinating the operation.'

'It's good to feel a deck beneath your feet once in a while.' She smiles, the stretch in her cheeks looking painful. 'Don't you think?'

'I think that you're here because you want to be.'

'Yes, yes I am.'

'And that the information we have is not something you want out there in the universe.'

'Much depends on what it is that you found.' Her manner is still guarded, her hand resting near her guns. 'Be truthful with me now; lies will not benefit either of us.'

Raley arrives back on deck. I take the data slate from her and pass it to Vaskova.

'We saw everything on that tablet,' I say. 'Including how the Chaeni Worlds weren't the threat they were made out to be.'

'They were every bit the threat they were made out to be.' Vaskova's tone is sharp as she flicks through the top level information and the transmission that Clara found. 'That you saw a single trading vessel means nothing; you didn't see the thousands of casualties left by their daily raiding runs, the worlds they were eating without mercy.'

'No. No, I didn't, but you don't develop technology like what's on that ship without a very good reason.'

'We had the best of reasons.' Vaskova takes the pad and plugs it into the implant on her finger. Her eyes vibrate as she skims through the content in seconds. 'And the Chaeni knew it. That's why the fleet that the *Sonskyn* was close to went berserk when the first weapon went off; they knew our fleet couldn't come through The Dragon at the time and neither could theirs. The *Sonskyn* and the Beyondlight drive were the only things that could penetrate The Dragon, so they settled for ripping the *Sonskyn* up. I can only presume that losing so many of their own number when the first weapon detonated was the reason they didn't strip the *Sonskyn* and take the Beyondlight technology for themselves.'

'That creature could never have made use of that drive.'

'The smaller ships of the Chaeni might have been able to. Then all they'd have had to do was what your crew did, and they could have freed everyone we'd imprisoned.'

'Are you so sure that there were smaller ships on the other side of The Dragon?' I ask. 'That creature looked like it would take a lot to feed it.'

'You have to see the Chaeni from another perspective. We have antibodies to help us against bacteria; the smaller ships would perform the same function for something that size.'

'Can't say as I'd blame them.'

'No. In the eleven hundred years I've served the empire, we've never had to make a decision like that before...or since.'

'Surely there was another way.'

'There wasn't anything else we could have done.' She turns away. 'We were losing planet after planet. Of the two hundred colonies we started with in the outer rings, we were down to less than thirty, and we knew that as soon as The Dragon burned out, the other fleet would be all over us. We had to show them that they had to stop their advances into our territories, or we'd be forced to defend ourselves.'

'There must have been something you could have done to stop them.'

'I saw the flesh vats.' Vaskova turns back to me. 'I saw them melting living creatures into protoplasm and the slurry of our people pumped into moulds to build ships and weapons. They only respected strength; we *needed* to show them our power.'

'And the only act of self-defence you could think of involved killing a galaxy's worth of people...?' The lack of belief is evident in my tone.

'The best defence is offence.' She unplugs the pad from her finger. 'You can never know the peace and security we bought for this universe, and the only cost was ending a race of vicious predators who were led by a single controlling mind.'

'A single mind? The creature we saw on the greeting to the *Sonskyn* was independent; it wasn't under anyone's control.'

'You believe that?' She shakes her head in dismay. 'I thought better of you, captain. When the Chaeni get their claws into you,

you don't come back. They get inside you and twist you and make you do a million things you don't want to do. Can you imagine what that feels like?'

I can do more than imagine ... The Beast was the mind behind the Chaeni?

'Yes, I can. But the creature that controlled them all is gone. They won't be a threat anymore.'

'Gone? You'd need the combined firepower of all the ships in the fleet to bring that... *Beast* down.'

'And yet'—I tap the pad—'that contains our logs. You can see what remains of it now.'

She plugs back in, and her eyes go distant while she scans the data, coming back to me a few seconds later. 'And your friend, the one who took the ship, did she seem in any way distant to you before she left?'

'She was never one for being affectionate. But she wasn't all that different.'

'Did she have implants of any sort?'

'A Stenlarian calculatrix implanted over her brain, because of a failure in her military career.'

'Had she downloaded the information from the ship to her brain?' Vaskova seems more concerned as her gaze shifts between Raley and me.

'Easiest way for her to work through it. She did that often, and the data was from Stenlarian computers, so she was best placed to study it.'

'Then we have a larger problem.' Vaskova raises one hand to signal behind her. 'That ship may be on its way to free the Chaeni Worlds but, once it's done that, it'll turn that weapon on our universe.'

'Clara wouldn't do that,' I say without hesitation. 'She'd never do anything to hurt innocents.'

'The Beast has been inside you, hasn't it?' She stares straight into my eyes.

'I got it out.'

'When the Beast was in you did you have any control over what you did?'

I begin to speak but stop myself, unable to voice the truth, and she goes on. 'Or did it *make* you do things...?' Her eyes are bright with fervour. 'Did it control you like a toy and make you bring suffering and pain to all those around you?'

'It's been in you as well.' Raley puts her hand on Vaskova's. 'Hasn't it?'

'I...' Vaskova looks at each of us in turn. The expression on her face is the same one I've seen many times when I look in the mirror. 'What's on that ship is no longer your friend. She will free the Chaeni beasts and, when she's done, she'll imprison all of us till the stars go out, and be gleeful as she does so.'

'But the Beast is dead. It can't hold sway over the others now.' Raley says.

'What is within your friend is only a shard of the Beast, enough to control her and her actions; enough to get the ship here, and enough to release the rest of the Chaeni Worlds from the effect of that weapon.'

'But, without the Beast controlling them, they'd be free to do whatever they want, right?'

'You're thinking from the perspective of someone who's never had no control over their actions before.' Vaskova's voice goes quiet. 'Try and imagine being a part of a greater whole, of never having to worry about any action you take, because it is all done with the approval of your god.'

'No fear of anything you do being wrong—that's the sort of thinking that the Ascended made a religion out of.'

'Except this one isn't delivered through a controlling wire in your spine; this comes from the living creature that's a part of you. Can you imagine that?'

'No.' Raley shakes her head. 'I can't.'

'Do you now see why the deactivation of that shield would be so catastrophic?'

'Wouldn't it just be like having no voice inside your head?'

'No, it'd be like waking up without eyes and ears. The Chaeni all hear the ongoing voice of the Beast, their reassurance that they belong.' Vaskova shakes her head and sighs. 'Those who had only recently been taken by the Chaeni would still have symbiotes external to themselves, so they'd be able to tell that the symbiote is no longer making the link; however, for many, the symbiote will have burrowed deep inside them and, as much as they may not have wanted it when it first got into them, they'll now be so used to that constant presence in their head that the removal of it would be like having half your senses go missing. Then you need to consider the time shift. For them, no time will have passed, and they'll go from a world where there was unity and purpose and strength in their united bond, to a place where they are what they were to begin with: just tiny creatures in the face of the void.'

Vaskova pauses. It's clear that whatever the Chaeni did has never left her.

As it has never left me...

Vaskova takes a deep breath. 'Then you have to think that many of them are not even whole anymore; they were hurt or broken when they were taken, and they were remade using parts of other creatures. The individual parts of those creatures will still remember who and what they were before the Chaeni got hold of them, and they're going to wake up, realising that they were torn asunder and turned into the servants of an interstellar empire. How long do you think sanity will prevail then?'

'Not long.' Raley's voice is low.

'For all that Stenlarian justice is harsh, at least when we change something, we make sure there's no possibility it'll turn on us.'

'And yet, here it is.' Raley puts her hand on Vaskova's again. 'All tyrants pay the price for their tyranny, no matter the empire they were in service of, it's just a matter of time.'

It Wasn't Me

I look out into the darkness as the *Abandon All Hope* slows to a halt and deploys its drone fleet into the void, hundreds of thousands of miniature ships, none of them good for anything but anti-fighter work.

But every one of them large enough to trigger the collision warning on the Beyondlight drive...

Vaskova comes alongside me and leans on the rail. 'All your stores have been replenished, your weapons reloaded, your ship repaired, and your crew given the best of quarters.' She sighs. 'It is all I can do for now. Your actions have gained us time to try and mount a defence. Whether or not it will be enough remains to be seen and, if it is not, all the repairs in the world will not help in what is to come.'

'Let us go out to meet her, try and talk her down.'

'Like I said before, it is not your friend on that ship. You do not see that yet, but you will. Our best chance here is to bring her down, cripple that ship before it can do its work, and *then* see what we can do to bring her back to you whole.'

'When did it get you?' I can't meet her eyes as I ask the question.

'Eleven hundred and twenty years ago.' She looks out into the void, and her gaze hardens. 'My ship was among the first that went into the deep void. We encountered them out beyond The Dragon and were annihilated. Our mistake was allowing them to take us alive.'

'We don't have to talk about it if you don't want to. I understand.'

'And how rare do you think it is for me to find someone who

understands? How many know what it's like to be under the thrall of that *thing*?'

'Not many, I hope.'

'It sent me back with my ship to gather information and relay it back, and I did just that for more than twenty years, no pause, no resistance, till I was discovered.' She unclips the top of her uniform. 'In the empire, there is no room for forgiveness, only penitence; I chose to serve my empire.'

'What did they do to you?'

'What I asked them to.' She smiles, her skin pulling taut over her cheeks, as she opens the top of her uniform to show the gleaming metal that covers her skin. 'They replaced all the parts of me that the Beast had touched; they left my face and some of my brain.'

'Is that why they call you the Damned?' I ask. 'Damned to serve?'

'Honoured to serve.' She stands straight and reseals her uniform. 'Damned, because it was me who led them to us. The least I could do was maintain a vigil to ensure that they would never again threaten my homeworld.'

'For eleven hundred years?'

'Forever, if that's what it takes, they can and have rebuilt me hundreds of times.' Vaskova smiles, reaching up to her eye for a second before shaking her head and dropping her hand down. 'I still feel like I can cry, even though there are no tear ducts. We're tracking the ship now; it's approaching at normal speed and will be with us within the hour.'

'Why not stop it where it is?'

'Your friend has *sought* the protection of pirates, promising them a share of the worlds that it will open up I have no doubt, not telling them the true nature of what she is leading them into.' Vaskova brings up the display on her personal screen. 'She didn't expect them to follow her as close as they did, so now she cannot speed away from them to get the jump on us. If we engage the pirates, she will have her chance to make the jump—you see our dilemma.'

'I just want my friend back. Nothing more than that.'

'If she stands down, there is every chance you will see her

again. I could find any number of clauses that would allow her to live a long life, far from the empire.'

'And if she doesn't stand down?'

'Then we will have just one chance when she comes into range.' She glances upwards at the cannon running the length of the ship. 'And we'll be taking it.'

'Is there any way you can open a channel that she could respond to? The *Dawn*'s communications won't reach that far.'

'No guarantee that she'll respond, but if she's still be on those old Stenlarian codes, you can try.'

The comms station is a relic, looking like it has seen better days, the baroque stylings reminiscent of the old Martian navy—when it wasn't enough to be good at something, you had to *look* good doing it as well.

'It is from the first ship I ever served on.' Vaskova reaches down to stroke the top of the station.

'Nothing wrong with being sentimental.' I grin, examining the controls which are of a kind I was taught to use countless years ago.

'It works a little different to normal comms.' Vaskova reaches down.

Without thinking, I stretch my hand out and tune the frequency, switching the circuits over and engaging the plasmatic coils. 'Yeah, but the classics are the best.' I grin as she studies me for a second, and I shrug. 'Student of history. This model has never been improved on, no matter how much money they spend on R&D.'

'Why I keep it around.' She rests her hands on the Vox, and there's a moment of contentment as both of us listen to the coils powering up. 'I'll be in the next room—I can't imagine that your friend will want to have a serving member of the navy listening in on your conversation.'

'I imagine not.' I wait till she departs before cycling up the comms.

The first call goes unanswered.

The second one eats static.

I change the frequency to that of the *Dawn* and try one last time. The transmission blinks for a few seconds before a humming can be heard in the background, and the screen blinks from unused to blanked.

'Clara? Clara, it's Morgan.'

'MOrgAn.' There's static on the line, but I can make out Clara's voice. 'WhAt Is It?'

'You need to stop, Clara. You need to stop; they're going to kill you.'

'ThEy cAnnOt stOp mE.' Her voice sounds angrier, the strange inflection reminding me of something else, something I heard in my former life.

'Clara, is that really you?'

The screen flickers, and the dark insides of the *Sonskyn*'s bridge appears. Clara moves to stare into the camera, and I struggle to keep the shock from my face.

The implant on the side of her head has now been pushed out. It's still attached, but in the manner of a tumour, like something that isn't part of her anymore. She looks at me through pale eyes, both of them organic.

'SUrprIsEd?' She tilts her head sideways. 'ThIs Is why thE StEnlArIAns fEAr thE chAEni; wE cAn rEpAIr thEIr pUnIshmEnts.'

'We? We, Clara?'

'WE...' She shakes her head, her pale eyes darkening to her normal brown. 'I-it's me, Morgan, I'm just getting UsEd to the use of my vOIcE again.'

'And that's why it sounds like there are two people in there? Come on Clar, the Beast's been in me as well—I know what it does.'

'That was before. It was united in purpose; the voice was a constant singularity. nOw thErE ArE A mIllIOn wOrds All spewing out.'

'You need to stop.' I lean in closer to the mic. 'Clar, they're not going to let you do this—they can't take the risk.'

'ThEy cAn try to stop mE.' Her face is twisted between anguish and anger. 'But they will fail; they don't know where I'm coming in from.'

'Clara.' I keep focussed on her—every time I say her name, her eyes darken to a deeper shade of brown, as if the reminder of her individuality brings her back to the fore for a brief moment. 'Clara, where are you approaching from.'

'I'm inbound on the w—' She shudders, the flesh around the implant pulsing. 'ClEvEr, cAptAIn, bUt wE ArE lEgIOn; shE cAn rEsIst Us nO mOrE thAn yOU cOUld.'

The words bite deep, and I feel a surge of anger rising within, knowing that I have seconds before the Chaeni cut the link between us. 'Clara, the Stenlarians say they're sorry.'

'SORRY?' Clara's eyes flare open in fury, now deepest brown. 'THOSE BASTARDS WILL GET WHAT'S COMING TO THEM WHEN I COME SCREAMING OUT OF THE WEST GYRE. SEE HOW SORRY THEY ARE THEN.'

I smile as Clara's rage cuts through whatever control the Chaeni are exerting, her eyes fluctuating between colours as she fights against the thing working inside her. I see the beginning of a tear in her right eye, before she regains her composure and stares without emotion at the screen.

She knows that what's happening is wrong. It's been the Chaeni all along...

The screen goes black as the connection is cut. I have no doubt now that none of this is Clara's fault; nothing which has happened has been anything that she herself did, or would have done in her right mind.

She wasn't the one who caused all those deaths.

The thought is cold comfort against the very real possibility that, if she manages to outmanoeuvre us, it won't matter who caused those deaths. I shut down the station and knock on the door to let Vaskova know that I'm done. She opens it and pauses for a second while I order my thoughts.

'You get where she's heading for?' she asks, with hope in her eyes.

'She's approaching from the West Gyre; I don't think she'll be alone.'

'Good. Now I know I can trust you.'

'Was there any doubt?'

'Stenlarians never trust anyone; not until we know we can.' She gives an elegant shrug. 'Generations of war and hate have left us few options.'

'And fewer still if you never trust anyone to begin with.'

'Centuries of disappointment with humans.' She taps the side of her head. 'I'll set the long-range scanners to see what's coming at us and when.'

*

Half an hour later, Vaskova comes to me as the station crane lowers the last pallet of supplies into the *Dawn*'s cargo bay. I look up from the manifest, and she signals for me to join her on the dock.

'What is it?' I ask.

She looks around before speaking. 'We picked up the *Sonskyn*.'

'And what else?'

She pauses and takes a deep breath. 'There are a lot of ships with it. Most of them have pirate transponders, but some...'

'What?' I reach out to her as she goes pale.

'Some of them have transponders from ships long-dead, and others have transponders from ships that were dead when I first went out into the dark.'

'How can that be?'

'Do you know much about the Chaeni?'

'Only from I've experienced of them internally.' I feel heat rising in my face. 'But that didn't leave me with anything real knowledge of them.'

'Chaeni ships are alive. If they get hold of a normal ship, they can take over running them. The ship has no more free-will than one of our drones, but it can still fight, and it won't care how many holes you put in it.'

'Best course of action?'

'We're taking the *Abandon All Hope* over to the West Gyre and setting up there. But the chances of us breaking through the escort is low. We need to distract her long enough to get a shot at the drive.'

'We're the only ones who have any chance of success with that. So why the hesitation?'

She pauses for a second, weighing up what she can tell me that will keep me as an ally.

'You're not going to attempt to bring her in alive, are you?' I phrase it as a question, even though it's not.

'No. You understand my position.'

'One life measured against countless billions. I understand where you're coming from, but can you give me any time at all to talk to her?'

'Just enough for you to get through to her and slow her down.' She stares at me with the calm gaze of someone who's been around long enough to see empires rise and fall. 'The second we have a clean shot, we will fire at the engines if we can, but—'

'But you're more likely to go for the reactor.'

'Will you help? If you can slow her down so we get a clear shot, we can knock the engines offline and have time to do what needs to be done. We can still bring it down even if you don't slow her down, but the only option then is to saturate the sky with explosives. At that point, it won't matter what's coming in— Chaeni, pirate, hapless innocent returning to Stenlarian space—all of them will be consumed in the firestorm.'

'And plenty more people will die in the meantime.' I sigh and place the manifest to one side. 'I'll try. I'm not going to make any promises though.'

A Fight for Yesterday, Today and Tomorrow

It's always the waiting that's the worst.

I glance up at the stars, feeling the looming presence of the *Abandon All Hope* to our rear, almost eclipsing the Imperious Moon, the closest Stenlarian starbase. It's more than a hundred thousand miles off, but still clear in view. I look at the rack of weaponry on the broadside of the dreadnought, some of the barrels larger than the whole of the *Dawn*.

If she opens up with everything, we'll be caught in the crossfire.

One of the lights far above moves, and breaks into a multitude of stardrive trails.

'*Hope* to *Dawn*.' Vaskova's voice is quiet in my ear. 'There must be more than a hundred of them; the *Sonskyn* is leading the charge.'

'Give us warning if you're going to fire.' I adjust the frequency on the transmitter that's been brought aboard the *Dawn*. 'Clara, Clara, this is Morgan.'

'mOrgAn.' The response is instant this time. 'WhAt cAn I dO fOr yOU?'

'I need to speak to Clara, not you. Clara, are you there?'

'MorgAn.' The voice is strained, as if struggling against something.

'Clara, come back to us. Talk to me.' I lower my voice, keeping calm.

Above us, the ship lights split into a wide formation as the smaller ships move ahead of the main ones.

'Morgan.' The resolve in her voice gets stronger as the larger ships break out into three formations.

'Clara?'

'Morgan...' A moment of silence.

'Clara?'

'We're cutting away.' Her voice is calm. 'I'll fly straight as long as I can. Aim high.'

I watch as the largest of the drive trails jinks to the right, heading straight towards the Chaeni Worlds. The other crafts don't follow, and I see the ship wobbling as Clara fights with the creature in her head.

'Vaskova.' I press the other comms. 'AIM HIGH. THE *SONSKYN* IS BREAKING FORMATION.'

'We have it.' Vaskova sounds calm. The *Hope* turns upwards as its drone fleet surges past us.

There's a sensation like a wave hitting the *Dawn* when the planet-breaker cannon on the *Hope* fires, the speed and size of the shell enough to cause a gravitic distortion around the front of the ship. I pull us back and to starboard, bringing all the sails up as we move at speed to flank the oncoming ships; there's nothing we can do in the main fight, but we might be able to pick up any crippled ships limping off to the side.

'Main batteries coming around to fire; all friendlies stay out of glide path.' Vaskova directs fire to the other incoming ships while the planet-breaker shell streaks towards the *Sonskyn*. I look at the shell and the *Sonskyn*, struck dumb for a second by the precision with which the shot was fired. They weren't aiming at the ship but rather where it was *going* to be.

'Load all guns, both batteries,' I announce to my crew. 'We're going to miss the party, but we'll be picking off stragglers.'

Raley comes alongside as the stars are obscured by the flak cannons on the *Hope*. A wall of fire to rival The Dragon erupts in space, hundreds of thousands of tons of explosives launched without targeting—anything emerging through that will have suffered a few holes at least, more than enough damage for the drone fleet to finish off anything that makes it. I push the *Dawn* faster, a mixture of emotions swelling in me as I see that the shell is faster than the *Sonskyn*; Vaskova's aim was true.

But that means Clara will be lost...

'Morgan, MORGAN.' Clara's voice, now panicked. 'DETONATE THE—'

'Clara? CLARA!'

'FoOlIsh crEAtUrEs.' Her voice is distorted again. 'WE knOw yOUr mInds.'

There's a gleam along the length of the *Sonskyn* as the Beyondlight drive comes online. I reach down to the other comms. 'VASKOVA, BLOW THE SHELL. BLOW IT NOW!'

Time stands still for a second. Then the bright blue flare like a star going supernova ripples outwards, forcing me to look away. I turn the *Dawn* into the advancing wave, refocussing the shields towards the flare, as fire and plasma ripple down the side of our hull for a second. I glance back to see the glowing afterimage of the *Sonskyn*, illuminated by all the fire that was sucked into the gap left by her passing.

'THEY MADE THE JUMP; THEY MADE THE JUMP,' I howl into the comms.

'Then we'll deal with them when they come back.' Vaskova sounds strained, and I turn back to see that the wall of explosives has dissipated. None of the smaller ships made it through, but the three main ones are converging on the *Hope*. 'Stay clear, *Dawn*. We can't cover you and defend ourselves. Recommend retiring to Stenlarian lines; we'll hold here.'

I pull the *Dawn* around as the *Hope* retrains her batteries towards the largest of the incoming ships, keeping us to starboard as we cruise past its firing solution. Raley looks to the stern as lasers slide off the starshields. Her voice is all but a whisper. 'What the f...?'

I glance back and see the space where the *Sonskyn* disappeared start to warp. The stars begin to change position, new stars emerging, along with new planets, and ships...

Not new...

They just haven't been here for a thousand years...

The Chaeni ship drops out of transit close to us. The hull appears to be rigid chitin in most places, but its rear is pulsing like a living thing. The metal plates display Stenlarian colours and a faint blue light emanates from its core, where the reactor is exposed.

The comms light up with a single communication request. I reach out and respond.

The pilot is young, as young as I was when I set out. Her head is shaved on one side to allow for the biomechanical cable to extend down into the bridge of her ship. She looks up at me with eyes which are yellow to begin with, but fade to brown as I watch. She brings a hand up to the side of her head, and she starts to tremble as she'd been dealt a mortal wound.

'The link...' Her voice starts off soft and low, before escalating into a scream. 'The LINK, THE LINK, THELINKTHELINKTHELINKTHELINK...'

The two tubes at the front of the ship bulge as something loads into them, and I bring the *Dawn* broadside, lining up with the ship as it starts to roll. The comms light up, with a thousand other signals all coming through on the same channel. The screen shuts off, unable to cope with the volume of incoming calls, but the screams are all the same.

When they went into stasis, the Beast was still there to provide them with instructions. Now all they've got is themselves.

The ship rolls again as it lines up with the *Hope*. The words from the comms are now a chorus, some a millisecond behind, some ahead, all speaking the same words.

'FOR THE QUEEN.'

The ship turns and lances towards the *Hope*. All around us, the other Chaeni vessels angle their thrusters and drive forwards, none of them firing, just rushing headlong towards the dreadnought. The pirate ships pull away. Seeing the vast Chaeni defence fleet return as if from nowhere had already shaken their confidence; seeing them attack is enough to break it.

'*Hope*, this is *Dawn*; inbound Chaeni fleet at your two.'

'We see them, *Dawn*.' Vaskova still sounds unhurried. 'It's been a while! Stay out of our firing solution, and we'll take care of this.'

The dreadnought turns faster than I would have reckoned possible for a ship of its size, and I pull the *Dawn* downwards and out of the line of fire as the broadside batteries open up again. The shells smash through the Chaeni ships like blades through paper as the un-coordinated attack blunts itself on the explosive rounds. I look back to see another two ships, capital class, blur into view, each of them shaped like the head of a spear, no guns evident anywhere as they lance forwards.

'Incoming capitals,' I shout over the comms.

'Understood.' Vaskova tries to bring the *Hope* around—the flak batteries won't have any effect on the main crafts; only the main gun will do. I raise the sails again and speed away from the battlefield.

No way we survive out here for more than a few minutes.

The dreadnought turns enough to get a shot at the first ship; not a planet-breaker round this time, but instead focussing the entire power of the reactor into the forward cannon. The beam burns brighter than the stars around it, cutting into the vessel the way a knife would into overcooked vegetables. The Chaeni ships speed up, as if the impact to the capital ship was felt by all of them.

The lead Chaeni ship shudders and turns in space, burning, the tissue in its semi-organic hull charring as the energy beam tears all the way through it in a matter of seconds. The other capital ship turns high and accelerates forwards, the long spike on its front growing longer. The dreadnought tries to turn and get another shot off, but it was designed for holding actions against entire fleets, not dogfights. The Chaeni craft's engines pulse, and it leaps forwards, the spike penetrating the *Hope*'s side armour. The drone fleet disengages from mopping up the pirates and swoops around the capital ship, lighting up its hull with a storm of small arms fire. It's much like a swarm of bees assaulting a honey thief—they might do some damage, but it'll be a long time before the thief recognises the threat they represent.

'Get to safe distance.' Vaskova's voice remains calm. 'We've been boarded, but the ship's systems are still functioning. Keep clear. We may have to deploy heavy munitions again.'

'Understood.' My heart is in my mouth hearing those words. I watch as the creatures swarm out of every door on the Chaeni ship, all of them making for the hole that's been torn into the dreadnought's side. 'Is there anything we can do?'

'Observe Stenlarian courage.' Vaskova's voice is full of glee, the switch in mood sudden. 'No longer will I face my enemy over a desk with smiles and tea ceremonies.'

'Right...' I pull the *Dawn* all the way back as a second rank of ships breaks from the attack and heads past the *Hope*, towards the Imperious Moon. 'Imperious, you have incoming. Three ranks of ships, all snub fighters.'

The dreadnought slews to the side, the thrusters on full as it tries to shake the ship that has buried itself deep inside. For a second, we're inside its atmosphere, and I hear the groaning of star-forged metal being rent asunder. I see bodies falling into the void—Stenlarian, Chaeni, no way to distinguish between them—many of them still fighting while they drift towards the edges of the atmosphere. I roll the *Dawn* underneath the ships, bringing us up on the far side as the sound of an explosion echoes through the atmo-field.

I move at full speed towards the Imperious Moon as several more of the snub fighters swoop past, moving far faster than us with their pulse drives. Lights flicker on the far side of the *Hope* as the fighting progresses through the decks. Some of the glass shatters, silent explosions in the void.

'*Abandon All Hope*, to all friendly units.' The sound of hammering against the bridge doors can be heard behind Vaskova's voice. 'Maintain distance from us; we have the matter under control.'

The nearby space ripples as several more Chaeni capital ships drop into the combat zone, two of them with spikes on their prows, and four with an array of huge cannons down their spines. Vaskova brings the dreadnought around and the forward cannon drills a hole through the core of one of the incoming crafts, but the others take a wide berth, each of them approaching on a different attack vector.

No way we can win this one.

A Chance not to Repeat History

The airwaves fill with chatter from the pirate vessels as the Chaeni engage everything in range. One signal comes through with more amplitude than the others.

'This is the Imperious Moon, Harmony Base to *Abandon All Hope*. Harmony Base to *Abandon All Hope*.'

'*Unbroken Dawn*, allied ship responding.' I glance back at Raley. 'See if you can isolate that signal from the others.'

'*Dawn*, this is Harmony Base, operator twenty-four. We're taking hits here.'

'They're only snub fighters,' I say. 'Shouldn't be able to get through your shields.'

'They're not fighters.' I can hear the sound of something thudding in the background. 'They're torpedoes, raining down on us. We're losing cabin pressure in some of the exterior modules. Our point defence isn't holding them off; we need assistance.'

'Signal Stenlar Prime to divert the rest of the fleet. *Hope* isn't in any position to assist.'

'This is a civilian base.' The noise in the background gets louder. 'The fleet is hours away at best; we need to get out of here now. How far are you from us?'

'Nine minutes to your perimeter.' I check the charts. 'But we're a light trader, not a warship.'

'You need to—' The voice is cut off by an explosion. Screams fill the air as the Chaeni burst into the command centre. 'THEY'RE INSIDE. HELP US, PLEASE HELP US—'

A bestial roar, and the voice breaks off, replaced by a faint, liquid gurgling on the comms.

'*Hope*, this is *Dawn*; we're headed to Harmony Base.'

'Understood, *Dawn*.' Vaskova sounds almost cheerful. 'We have an excellent fight to occupy us here while you're gone. Make sure our people are safe.'

I turn the *Dawn* and raise the sails again, moving into range of Harmony Base within minutes. The main colony dome is on fire. The atmo-shield is holding, but it's clear from the trail of fire and devastation that the Chaeni aren't taking any prisoners. Several more snub fighters scythe past us, not paying us any heed as they lance straight past Harmony Base towards the world beyond it.

'What world is that?' I glance back to where Raley is continuing to work the comms.

'Stenlar Three.' She looks up as a second salvo shoots past us, clearing the moon's gravity before engaging their main drives and disappearing from view. 'Shit, that's the Stenlarians' garden world, a quarter of a million miles in that direction. The speed those things are travelling at, it'll take them minutes.'

'Give me an open channel to all Stenlarian units, as far as we can broadcast.'

Raley flips a switch, then nods.

'*Unbroken Dawn* to all Stenlarian units in the vicinity of Stenlar Three. There are several salvos of Chaeni ships heading towards you.'

'Waystation thirteen responding; we have them on the lidar.'

'Do not allow them to close in on you. They are not fighter craft; they are torpedoes. Harmony Base is down; *Abandon All Hope* can't stop all of them getting through.'

'We have it.' He sounds almost bored, the consequence of a lifetime of unshakable faith in Stenlarian military might.

'Those are not normal torpedoes—they're Chaeni torpedoes. Do not allow them to get close.'

'We have it.' His voice doesn't change in pitch or timbre.

'Harmony Base to *Unbroken Dawn*, Harmony Base to *Unbroken Dawn*.' The comms clicks in again. It's a different person this time, unhurried, sounding like they're in a wide-open area. 'Please come in.'

'This is the *Dawn*.' I flip the channel. 'Who's there?'

'This Is operator twenty-four. wE have wOUnded here, plEAse send help.'

Raley cuts the comms. 'Could the Chaeni have them already?'

'I don't know.' I roll the ship and look down to see the Chaeni breach the living quarters and the atmosphere vent into space. The last remaining structure is a warehouse with armoured doors and a pad above for docking ships. 'We have to try. Get below; we'll bring them in on the lower deck.'

Raley runs down the stairs, and I bring the *Dawn* in low to the surface, trying to avoid drawing the attention of anyone running around in the lower courtyard.

No chance of that...

'Door open.' Raley signals upwards. 'I've got Esme with me. Give them the go code.'

'Harmony Base, this is *Dawn*. Ship on standby for you, above the landing pad on the warehouse.'

'Copy that, *Dawn*.' The voice is strained. 'On oUr way.'

'On their way, Raley. Watch when they come out.'

'On it.'

A shriek echoes up from Esme. I don't need comms to know what's emerging from the warehouse.

'CHAENI,' Raley howls. 'GET US OUT OF HERE.'

I haul the *Dawn* upwards, the ship responding as if she rolled out of the bay yesterday. The sails fill with energy, and we rise slow, the ship weighed down on the starboard side. I see the door close on the lower levels, but it's clear that we've got unwanted passengers. Raley runs back up, her sword out as she scans the starboard side, Esme following her, blood trailing down her left arm.

'GET US UP. CLOSE THE GUN PORTS,' Raley yells.

'Close all gun ports, all crew on deck.' I call into the comms. 'BASTARDS ON BOARD.'

The first creature claws its way on deck, Raley meeting it with a sword through what used to be its head. A second meets the same fate, then a third. Esme runs to the upper deck, turning at the top to draw her sword. She risks a glance at me as the rest of the crew rush up from below.

'Get us out of here.' She stands tall. 'I'll keep them off you.'

Within a minute, the deck is full of my crew and what were, minutes ago, other humans. I see now why the Stenlarians were so afraid of them. Zulay flinches when one of the creatures slashes her across the hand. She looks down at her arm in disbelief as the muscles within bulge and twist, the infection spiralling up inside her body. She looks over at Raley, her eyes going wide as her mouth opens in shock. Raley spins and slices upwards, pulling Zulay away from the severed arm, pushing her towards Esme as the rest of the crew are forced backwards.

No way we make it out of this...

'Morgan.' It's Vaskova, sounding resigned but not afraid. 'Withdraw behind the Imperious Moon, now.'

'What's happened?' I keep one hand on the wheel while trying to see what's behind us.

'Too many, too fast.' There's a snort of humourless laughter. 'All my life waiting to stop these bastards, and they run at us fifty to one; we only have one option left.'

'We can't hold without you.' There are explosions all the way along the dreadnought as it starts to lose stabilising thrusters.

'We no longer have the luxury of pretending that we'll make a difference here.' Vaskova sounds almost cheerful. 'At least, this way, we take a few million with us.'

'You can't; there has to be—'

'*Run*, Morgan.' Vaskova's resolve is clear in her voice. 'The blast will wipe out everything this side of the moon.'

I turn the ship again, engaging full sail to the dark side of the moon. Every instinct in me wants to leave the wheel and join my crew, but I know that, if we don't get clear, nothing we do will make any difference. A wave of energy lances through the space behind us, a shower of rock and debris following in its wake as the sunwards side of the Imperious Moon spreads across the stars.

'Clara. CLARA,' I howl down the comms. 'This is Morgan. Come in, please come in.'

The viewscreen changes to show Clara standing in silence at her console. The mechanical implants from her head are now sitting in front of her. She looks up at me through two organic eyes, one brown, one yellow, the side of her head that had been metal now covered in thick chitin.

'M-Morgan?' She looks at the screen, her shoulder twitching as the Chaeni's influence continues to flow through her.

'Clara, they're everywhere. We're dying here. Please, you have to help us.'

'The Chaeni Worlds are freed?' She enunciates every word with care, her head bobbing up and down as if to emphasise my agreement.

'They...' I pause as her brown eye looks straight at me, the yellow one still unfocussed. 'They're free; they're roaming free again.'

'You see?' She turns her head to look at something off-screen. 'As I promised, you're all free.'

I don't answer, but Clara nods and looks back at me.

'The...Stenlarians, paying for their crimes?'

'In their thousands. Clara, I—'

Her right hand twitches to forestall what I was about to say, her fingers signing *tell them what they want to hear*. She looks off-screen and then back at me.

'The Chaeni are victorious?'

'They will be.' I glance down the stairs to see the crew spreading out around me. Raley is still fighting a desperate holding action as the creatures start to swarm upwards. 'We're all going to die...'

'You promised that you would show mercy.' Clara's conversation isn't with me. 'You promised you would be all that you should have been.'

Clara glances back at the screen, then at something behind it. A tear from her brown eye rolls down her cheek, and she shudders, her yellow eye closing as the force of her anger overwhelms the controlling influence inside her.

'Forgive me, Morgan.' She stares at the screen. 'I thought to bring justice upon a race of vicious killers. I didn't realise I was unleashing another. I hope, in history, I am remembered better than I truly was.'

'There won't be any history of you at all if we don't make it out of here. Clara, please...'

She nods, and her yellow eye opens again, staring at the screen with all the hate of a starborn thing.

'Vae Victis.' Clara smiles, her brown eye glances sideways as she listens to the voice only she can hear. 'Oh no, not them.' Her hand moves on the controls. 'Y—'

Her words go unfinished, and the screen freezes as the connection is lost. A half smile beneath Clara's brown eye, the other half of her face wide eyed in shock, the mouth filled with sharp teeth open as if to shout, but whatever words were going to come have been stretched out into infinity. The *Dawn* spins, rolling on all axis as the *Sonskyn*'s payload detonates and the universe protests as the Swarm worlds are compressed back into stasis. All around, the Chaeni cease their assault, every one of them holding what passes for a hand to their heads, each of them babbling as their link is cut.

My crew show as much mercy as the Chaeni creatures were willing to show us.

In less than a minute, the *Dawn* is clear of all the invaders, and Esme is tending to Zulay, who is laid on the deck holding the bandaged remains of her arm.

'Is it over?' Raley glances around as she pushes the last of the Chaeni over the side of the ship. 'What happened?'

'Clara.' I turn the ship back towards the sun. 'Clara happened.'

The Thanks of a Grateful Empire

On the other side of the moon, the shattered superstructure of the *Abandon All Hope* floats in low orbit, the charred hulks of the Chaeni capital ships burning alongside. Nothing else is left. The blast from the reactor core going nova has wiped out everything this side without exception. We sail through dead space for a few hours, making sure there are no life pods, then we turn to look towards the Chaeni Worlds, once again frozen in gravitic stasis. The view blurs from the intensity of the surrounding gravity.

'Clara's in the middle of that?' Raley comes alongside me. 'Do you think she felt anything?'

'In the end, we're only here *because* she felt something.'

'What happens now?'

'In a billion years or so, the weapon burns its way through all the stars trapped in there, and the field releases again.'

'And then what?'

'Will we be here to care?' I look at her, weary beyond reckoning as the events of the past few weeks rest like the burden of Atlas on my shoulders.

'No, guess not.' Raley leans on the wheel next to me. 'Incoming comms from Stenlarian command.'

'I think we can let them wait for a second.' I draw her close and nuzzle into her shoulder, longing for something other than war and death for just a moment. 'How's Zulay doing?'

'Okay.' I sense her blush. 'There wasn't anything else I could have done—another minute, and it would've been in her brain.'

'It's all right.' I hug her tighter and run my fingers through her hair. 'We're in Stenlarian space—if there's anywhere we can find a new arm for her, it'll be here.'

'Let's not plan on staying too long, yeah?' Raley leans back a little. 'Only a matter of time before some Stenlarian general tries to claim that he could have done better than Vaskova and that we only got in the way.'

'Stenlar Prime to any ship still in the vicinity of the Imperious Moon...' The comms picks up the transmission as it goes wideband.

I know that voice...

Raley feels the sudden tension in my shoulders and frowns at the comms. 'What is it?'

'It can't be.' I stare at the comms, disengaging from Raley and bringing up the viewscreen. It fills with the image of a man.

No...

'This is Charles Godstorm, calling from Stenlarian High Command.' He straightens up, presenting a chest full of medals. 'We are seeking confirmation that the Chaeni fleet has been removed by our brave soldiers.'

'This is Captain Morgan of the *Unbroken Dawn*,' I reply. 'The Chaeni fleet is down.'

'Ah, Captain Morgan.' He stares at me for a second longer than is proper as he recognises me, all thought of the fleet gone. 'It's been a few months since last we met—glad to see you're on the right side of things now.'

A few months?

For him maybe, and the Morgan he met wasn't me...

My pause for thought is mistaken for reverent silence as he leans closer to the screen pickup and smiles. He nods and transmits coordinates to the ship, waiting till Raley acknowledges receipt, before speaking again.

'There will, of course, be recompense for your efforts in the war. Meet me at these coordinates, and we'll arrange for your rewards to be delivered.'

'We'll be there.'

And then we'll see what you're up to...

PART THREE

The Storm of Gods

New Mars, Same Tyrants

With the *Dawn* anchored off the Atomas docks on Stenlar Prime, I stand on solid ground for the first time in a very long time. The *Dawn* is a sturdy ship, and the field generators are still working as well as they should, but the 0.75g generated by the ship is no substitute for the 1g planetside. Every step feels like I'm wearing lead boots, and there's a dull pressure around the base of my spine as my own body weighs heavy on me.

Sooner we get this done, the better.

I've never been on Stenlar Prime. The surface is covered with huge buildings, each of them built to withstand the sharp storms that the Stenlarian weather cycle can bring, shutters on every window, and glass that can deflect bullets. The walkways are covered in a light dusting of red sand, and I look up the side of the mountain, my eye following the path all the way up to the capital at the top. The angle isn't much, but the distance must be more than ten miles.

'Why build a starport so far away from the capital?' I ask Raley.

'It's a reminder that all things worth having are worth working for. The further out you go, the more likely you are to encounter menial workers and habitats. They have to walk up the mountain every day to remind themselves what their *betters'*—the word sticks in her throat—'have had to do to live up there.'

'Not the truth?'

'Every person on the top of that mountain was born to it.' Raley glares at it, not even trying to conceal her anger. 'It's why I left and never looked back.'

'Why build it on a mountain though? There must have been easier places to do it.'

'There were. Stenlar Three is a flat garden world with huge lakes and food growing everywhere, but the founders wanted something that reminded them of the place they came from.'

'Which was...?'

'Mharrz. The people were known as the Milhion. It was a red world with a mountain that reached up into the heavens, whose inhabitants were so fierce that the rest of the universe feared them and strove to drive them away.'

'Mharrz? Milhion? Really?'

'If you believe the legends, their enemies destroyed the Mharrz mountain and sent the Milhion on ships into deep space. They have been plotting to return and reclaim their birthright ever since.'

I was on those ships when Olympus detonated, but it wasn't enemy action that did it—we drilled too deep, our hunger for ore and gems too strong to be satiated, even though the warning signs were clear to everyone.

I think back to the government of the time, fierce and warlike, unwilling to consider actions that weren't military, and devoid of any compassion. The reason the other planets feared us was because of what we *could* do, not because of what we did.

And here we are, a legacy of hate written by the tyranny of the idiots in power...

'Don't suppose there's any chance of us getting a lift up there?' I say, with a sigh.

'None at all. Even heroes have to work for their rewards. Come on.'

*

It's a weary three hours later when we reach the gates at the top. I'd have traded the profits of the last three years to have avoided that walk, and I resolve to find a sled while I'm up here so I can slide all the way back down. The guards who have been watching us for more than an hour look disinterested as we reach the top, one of them stepping forwards with his rifle slung, while the other is paying more attention to his phone than us.

'Papers?' The first guard asks.

'We were sent for, by the Stenlarian Council,' I reply. 'We've just come down from close orbit and don't have paperwork—we were told to present ourselves at the front gates.'

'Papers!' The first guard is on autopilot.

'We don't have papers. If you'll—'

'No papers, no pass.' The guard turns away and marches back to his post without a backwards glance.

'If we hadn't just walked up a hill for three hours, I'd say bugger it, we're out of here. But I'm damned if we've gone through all this to be turned back by an officious knobber with a superiority complex,' I say to Raley.

'You do know,' she says, a sly smile playing across her face, 'that the city beyond that gate is *populated* by officious knobbers with superiority complexes...'

'As I suspected.' I'm too tired to smile. 'But I need to find out what Godstorm is up to.'

'How much trouble could he be? I mean, he's been here, what, six months?'

'I don't know, but back where I come from, he was trouble all over—had no problem with killing the whole world to save himself. Whatever he's doing here, it can't be good.'

'All right.' She's looking over my shoulder at what's happening behind me. 'I think something's happening.'

I turn back towards the gate. The guards are both stood ramrod straight while a squad of Imperial Praetorians clear the gates and march towards us, their long, red cloaks billowing behind them even though there's no breeze, their heads and shoulders so still and level that it looks like they're gliding. As they draw closer, I realise that even the smallest of them is a metre taller than me and twice as broad.

'Captain Morgan.' The lead Praetorian pauses in front of me, then goes to his knees so that his face is level with mine. His skin has the rough edge of someone who's been out in the sharp sand too often, his eyes so blue they seem to be glowing.

'That's me.'

'We know. Forgive us the delay and the confusion at the gates. I am Four Odyssey Fifty-Two, you may call me Odyssey. Governor Godstorm is waiting for you.'

'*Governor* Godstorm?' I say.

'Yes.' He stands. 'Appointed by the Council High. Come with us.'

The others flow around us like water, forming a cordon leading to the person in front of us. I glance at Raley with a raised eyebrow.

'This is a protective formation,' Raley whispers. 'It indicates that they've pledged their lives to us; they'll die before they let anything happen to us.'

'What's with his name?'

'Odyssey is the name of the suit he's wearing. Four means that he's the fourth person to wear it, and fifty-two is the number of people he's killed in the execution of his duty.'

'Good to know.' I try and examine the landscape beyond the other eight in the squad—no joy. All I can see are the buildings towering above them. The Praetorian move as if welded together, no deviation in speed or direction, and no sound from their footsteps. 'We just stay in the middle then?'

'Praetorian protection is absolute. Any one of these will die for us.'

'Gleefully, and with the enemies' throats in our hands.' Odyssey glances back over his shoulder while continuing to glide forwards. 'To die in service is the greatest honour.'

'Good to know.' I look over at Raley. 'At least Godstorm doesn't seem to be bearing a grudge.'

'Why would he?' She cocks her head to the side. 'All he did was give up his whole crew, from what you told me. I doubt it was the first time he made that bargain.'

'No....' I stare upwards at the massive white marble structure of the state building that's now looming over us. We enter it through doors made of real wood, the floor carved by a million hands, from what was once the Martian Empire. I only visited the state building on Mars once when I was young, but walking through this building now, it's clear that those who constructed it had had every intention of preserving their heritage.

Odyssey halts and moves out of our way with an ornate spin

that becomes a bow. My focus turns to the room ahead. There's a long table, with thirteen people seated around it, and an empty seat at the far end, its occupant having risen and moved towards us. He's thinner than he was the last time I saw him, the maniac gleam in his eyes muted somewhat, but still there, lurking.

Godstorm.

'Captain.' He marches forwards, his arms wide as if he thinks I might hug him, but changing to an offered hand when he gets close and realises there's no way that's going to happen. 'It's an honour to meet the saviour of our planets, face to face...'

There's a flurry of clicks and flashes, and I realise that my attention had been so focussed on him that I hadn't seen the entire press corps sat to the side, waiting to capture this historic moment.

'Governor.' I keep my voice level. 'We're pleased to be here—'

'Of course.' His grin broadens as he keeps hold of my hand and turns to face the cameras, his other arm around my back.

Like a python trying to secure breakfast...

I weather the flashes and clicks for a few minutes, until the press are ushered out, and I turn to face the Council High.

'Captain Morgan.' I recognise the woman from propaganda posters: President Wagner, a woman as hard as the Martian fleet and twice the size of it, the first mine born person to ever rise above the castes. She regards me with dark eyes that seem sunk into her angular face, broad, as all miners are, the telltale signs of genetic enhancement. 'Our session was just finishing; would you join me and Governor Godstorm please?'

'My second, Constance Raley.' I look back at Raley as she eyes Godstorm with undisguised malice.

'You are both welcome.' President Wagner stands, the chair creaking as she relieves the pressure on it, the movement enough to indicate to the council that they are dismissed.

The rest of the Council file out in short order and the door closes behind them. Wagner waits a half-minute until she knows the room is clear and then steps over to us, her stern visage splitting into a smile she intended to be welcoming. The longer than average incisors giving her the appearance of a predator seeking lunch. She leans down to me, the movement causing her shoulders to rise, giving her the appearance of not having a neck. She offers her massive hand, the palm not so dark as the rest of her skin. 'My genuine pleasure to meet you both.'

'And ours.' I take her hand, wincing as the power of her grip renders my hand limp.

'Forgive me.' She glances down at my hand and releases it. 'I forgot you were many months out in space. I am just pleased to see that our world will not have a billion invaders descending upon it.'

'It was Vaskova and the *Abandon All Hope* who really blunted that attack. We were just there to help where we could.'

'And that is what we must speak of.' Wagner gestures to the seats next to hers and waits for us to sit down. 'Could I offer you food, drink?'

Raley cuts in: 'Whatever you're having, would be our honour to share with you.'

'Then so it shall be.' Wagner beams and presses the comms button on her desk, her tone switching from warm and welcoming to the sharp bark of someone in complete control of those around her. 'Our guests are hungry; nourish them.'

She sits down in the chair opposite us, her bulk making it creak again as she leans forwards, her trapezius muscles looming huge through her official robes, veins visible in her neck with blood pumping at high pressure underneath. Her smile without the teeth is radiant.

'My family, they were *Einigkeit*.' She rests her left arm on the table, the ridges of muscle thick down her forearm. 'Indentured workers, enhanced to be stronger, more durable—a legacy of times long-since passed. You've heard of them?'

I grew up in the time when the notion was just being floated, when they were criminals, not engineered slaves...

'I have. I've just never—'

'Met someone broader than you are tall.' She grins with genuine mirth. 'But my family, they educated me, taught me that working with my hands would put me in an early grave, that working with my mind would give me a chance to live beyond my thirtieth birthday.'

'It worked well then.' Her smile is infectious to the point that I find myself smiling with her.

'Not yet. My thirtieth birthday is later this year, so we will see.'

There's a knock at the chamber door, and she taps once on the table in response. The door opens, and servants, with their eyes downcast, bring in sufficient food to feed twenty, laying it on the table before us before bowing low and leaving the room, never once raising their eyes from the floor.

'Please...' Wagner gestures to the food. 'It would not do for me to eat before my guests have begun.'

Raley doesn't need a second invitation. She cuts off a steak from the side of beef, the middle still running thick with juices. I cut a smaller piece and lean back to wait for Wagner and Godstorm. Wagner stands without effort, her extra bulk not impeding her at all. She cuts a slice four times the size of the one Raley did and then surrounds her meat with all the different vegetables from the platters. She sits and waits until Raley has taken a bite before digging into the mountain on her plate.

We eat in companionable silence for twenty minutes before Raley pushes her plate away and washes the meat down with thick fruit cider. Wagner finishes her plate and leans back, having just eaten more food in one serving than I've had in the whole of the last week.

'Enhanced metabolism requires enhanced eating, but the mines never had food like this.' She takes a sip of her drink and leans forwards again. 'Now, a meal is not the level of reward that you were promised, so how do I thank those who risked their lives without care for themselves to save the empire?'

'Repairs and resupply would be enough. We didn't do it for the reward.'

'No, you didn't. But if the people do not see that great heroism provides great rewards, many of them will not be inclined to such acts.'

'Heroism isn't a paying job.' I stare at her.

'I agree, which is why there are so few heroes.' Wagner meets my gaze with her own calm eyes. 'And the world could do with many more who would go over-and-above without expecting to be paid to do it. You are the first of my generation to save countless lives without any thought for pay. If I did not make a show of rewarding your diligence and bravery, the empire would think I did not value it.'

She turns in her seat and presses a button on a control console to her right. The wall she's now facing starts to retract, showing the massive glass dome of the state building just beyond it. The floor we're on moves into the glass dome, allowing us to see over the entire cityscape below.

'There are a hundred million people in this city alone, the resources of a whole planet, and there is nothing I can entice you with?'

'We've got a few people who need to heal, and we could do with some repairs.'

'Couple of million credits in non-sequential, low denomination bills.' I can hear the grin in Raley's voice.

'Ah, but money is no true reminder of a hero's worth.' Wagner paces out onto the glass, hands on hips, and looks down to the city below. 'The freedom of the city for all of your crew perhaps? A house in the high peaks for each of them to enjoy? Or would that cause too many desertions for you to be able to fly again?'

'Most of my crew have spent twenty years in the sky on prayers and the promise of a payday someday. It's nice to have somewhere to go, but we're space monkeys—we belong among the stars.'

'Oh, to live a life so uncomplicated and filled with purpose.' Wagner smiles as she turns back to me, her wide eyes showing me that the young girl who wanted to make a difference is still in there, even if the woman she became has had to grow, both in body and spirit.

'Only way to be.' I stand from the table and wait to be dismissed.

'Is there nothing we can do for you?' she asks again.

'Cover our resupply and medical needs and promise us that you'll keep watch for idiots planning anything similar again.' I say. 'And there may be a time when I'll need to ask you for something else.'

'Deal.' She offers her hand and shakes mine, careful this time not to crush every bone in it.

'If I could have a word with the captain.' Godstorm sidles forwards. He'd remained quiet until now, giving the impression of a loyal and faithful servant, every part of him radiating sincerity.

Much like a commercial I saw in a previous life.

'If you're agreeable?' Wagner says to me.

'Anything for the *Federation.*' I make a point of emphasising the last word.

'Very well.' Wagner nods to Raley and claps her hands once, tapping on the table where two cards are now flat on the surface. 'You call if you need me for anything. This number reaches me, and me alone—no one else will answer.'

'Thank you.'

'I do not forget those who come to our aid when we needed them. Whenever you think of what else you might need from me, just call, and I will be there. When you go back to your ship, go via the requisitions office; there's a small token from the empire's private reserves for your crew to toast with.'

She leaves without another word, and I wait while Godstorm walks out into the glass dome. We hear the door click behind Wagner, and Godstorm turns to face us.

'I remember you.' His tone is calm, conversational. 'From when I first arrived here. Our talk was brief and to the point and, just as you had a deal for me then, so I have a deal for you now.'

'We already have the president on speed dial.' I take both cards off the table and pass one to Raley.

'I can offer you things that she can't.' He has a smug look on his face. 'The things I can offer you, the things I can *give* you, are far beyond what an elected official could.'

I say nothing, waiting for him to continue.

'I have something to show you.' He gestures towards the door.

*

A half mile of marbled corridors and forgettable conversation later, we arrive at the second dome, and a series of checkpoints manned by Imperial Praetorians. Godstorm pauses only long enough to secure us passes to the area and then continues on, still droning.

'This is the Imperial Science Division,' Raley whispers to me. 'Experimental section. This is where every innovation that's ever been out in the empire began. This is where the *Sonskyn* and the *Swartgat* came from. No one gets to come down here except the Council High—the stuff they're working on is bleeding edge. All the great scientists—Chups, T'sall, Viran—they all worked here.'

Godstorm leads us down a long corridor with inch-thick glass windows on both sides that allow us to look down from the walkway into the various labs. He pauses before the third window and points at the wide-open bay there.

'Recognise that?' he asks.

I stare down, my breath catching in my throat.

I do recognise that...

A Life of Leisure?

The ship in the bay below is almost constructed; several different scientists are gathered around it, following the direction of the one on the high catwalk. It's a small ship, sufficient for two or three passengers in comfort. Its shell has huge brass-coloured plates all the way around it, what looks like valves on the wings, and an airlock with a cycling mechanism on the outside. Across the lab are the internals; the controls have no buttons—it's all levers and dials, handles and gauges, every part of it rendered in brass and silver. There are no plastics used, no polymers. It's all metal and wiring, like something that was made a thousand years ago. The panels are hand-finished, more care taken in the building of this ship than any ten I could name.

The timeship...

'I see you recognise it.' Godstorm's voice comes from the side of me. 'That, or at least something very similar to it, was what brought me here to this place.'

'Is this...your...project?' I ask.

'This? No, this was going on when I first arrived here.' Godstorm waves his hands to encompass the entire lab. 'As the governor, I'm permitted to view the ongoing projects and check on their progress. This one intrigued me most, as I'm sure you can understand.'

'What intrigues me,' Raley says, 'is how you managed to get elected to a post that most people take decades of hard work to reach, within the space of a few months.'

'The empire needed funds. Funds that I had from investing with wisdom, in firms that knew not to cross me; funds that I collected when I came here then passed on for the *good* of the empire...in return for suitable *societal* improvements to my standing.'

'He who has the money makes the rules?' I say.

'As it has always been, as it shall ever be, but this leads me to the part where you can help shape the future for the benefit of the empire.'

I'm about to turn and leave when Raley leans in. 'I'm listening.'

He points down at the lab. 'We both know that this ship will work but, in a short while, something will happen, and I need you to be there for me to get away from it.'

'And what do we receive in return?' Raley asks.

'Anything you desire. When that ship is complete, there is no place we will not be able to go, nothing we will not be able to defeat. There will be a united empire for the first time any of us have known.'

'Let us think about it,' I say. 'Can we reach you here, without having to walk ten miles up a hill again?'

'Of course, an oversight on my administrative staff's part.' The casual way in which he shrugs the matter off tells me that his administrative staff had nothing to do with it. 'Call me, and I'll ensure that you're brought to me direct.'

'Alright,' I reply. 'Give us the day, and we'll get back to you.'

'My car will return you to your ship, unless you'd rather have quarters within the city for the night—our hospitality is quite something to behold.'

As are your listening devices, I'm sure...

I smile. 'No, the crew are on the ship, so we'll do all our discussions there.'

'Surely the crew have no meaningful discourse to add to the captain's decision?'

They never did when you were in command anyway.

'Just how we roll. We'll be in touch.'

*

Back at the *Dawn*, the rest of the crew are looking more relaxed than I've seen them since before the Beast got its tendrils into me.

Zulay flexes her new metal arm towards me as we enter the mess hall.

'Bit shiny,' I quip, grinning as she touches her thumb to each of her fingers.

'Best on the free markets.' She rotates the arm, testing every angle available, including several her original arm couldn't manage. 'How much is this going to set me back?'

'Compliments of the empire. The president was very happy with our work out there.' I glance at Jensca, who is bringing down the case that President Wagner left for us at requisitions. 'And we've got to decide what to do next.'

'Is there an alternative?' Esme looks over at me as she lounges against the back wall. 'Can we resupply and get back out there.'

'We got that for free, but I'd be willing to bet that the president's gratitude extends as far as the freedom of the city and a house each for us all to live out our lives if we so desire it. Suitable reward for the heroes who saved the empire.'

A murmur ripples around the room, going quiet when Jensca draws the first bottle out of the case.

Metirian rum—first pouring, over three hundred years old...
Priceless.

'Whoa now.' Mirri examines the bottle. 'If it's all right with you all, I'll take a bottle of something fresh from behind the bar.'

'Yeah, me too.' Esme starts over to the bar. 'I don't think my arse has recovered from the fifty-year-old stuff. We should sell that and buy our own tavern instead.'

'One possible option,' I reply. 'And I remember my arse from the fifty-year-old stuff too, which is why Jensca's spent all day restocking the *Dawn* at the empire's expense.'

'Thank God.' Zulay sits at the far table, her metal hand clinking on the surface. 'Drinks, and you can tell us all about why you want us to stay in the air.'

'That transparent?' I snag a bottle from the fresh crate.

'More than a decade in your company. We know when you're being shifty.'

Two rounds and a good meal later, I tap my tankard on the table and the room quietens.

'All right.' I stand and look around. 'We've been offered all the money we need, and a good place to stay, but we've also been offered another commission to help someone I'm pretty sure we can't trust.'

'What makes that any different to any other job we've pulled?' Raley says.

'Will the offer of a place to stay remain open?' Esme glances up from her beer.

'For as long as President Wagner is still president, I expect so.' I take another draw on my cider. 'But I've seen more than fourteen different presidents in the last decade, so I've got no illusions about the potential longevity of that offer.'

'So, if we want it, we should take it now?' Mirri asks.

'If you want it.'

'What's the other option?' Zulay is still flexing her hand around the tankard.

'Remember some months back when that ship came out of nowhere: the captain dropped all his crew so he could keep his ship and goods, and then made a run for it?' I look around at each of them in turn. 'Turns out he's now one of the governors on the Council.'

'And how did he manage that?' Esme seems suspicious. 'Takes years of kissing ass to even get a junior spot on the Council.'

'Don't know, but I do know that he can be counted on to act in his own best interests. He doesn't like sharing, though he'll do whatever he needs to in order to get what he wants, and that may involve paying us at some point. Look, you all know which way I'm going to vote, but both offers are on the table, and none of you owe me anything. This could be the only chance we're going to get to take a win and rest without having to think about where our next payday is coming from.'

'Can't we take the reward and still go out for a leisurely cruise among the stars once in a while?' Mirri says, raising an eyebrow. 'I mean, best of both worlds and all that.'

'I'm not much for taking a place if I'm not going to use it; the *Dawn* has been my home since we built her.'

'Yeah...' Mirri looks wistful for a second. 'All right, I've heard enough.' She bangs her tankard on the table. 'I'm for going back out.'

'Yep.' Esme thumps her tankard down in agreement. 'With that.'

'Yes.' Zulay takes her turn to crash her tankard down, using her new arm. The impact leaves a ring embedded in the top of the table, and she glances up with wide-eyed delight. 'But not till after we all arm-wrestle.' She grins.

The vote goes around the room in five minutes. No one spends more than a few seconds thinking and, at the end of it, the crew of the *Dawn* have voted to remain with the ship that's been their home for so long. I let out the breath I hadn't realised I'd been holding in and raise my tankard.

'To the *Dawn*...'

Memories of Another Time

It's the middle of the morning when I wake with a headache that tells me I would have been better staying asleep. I glance down at Raley, who's still sleeping, and sneak out of my quarters, going down into the canteen and admiring the rest of the crew sprawled over the tables. I'm interrupted by Michaels pouring himself some coffee. He still looks like he's had less sleep than anyone.

'Still liking your job of First Studmuffin for the crew?' I grin.

'Oh, it's a good job.' He sips his coffee, grimacing when the flavour doesn't compare with the scent of it. 'But, like I said, I've been more of a ship's counsellor than a studmuffin.'

'Ever regret staying with us?' I pour myself a cup and lean back against the bar.

'There are worse places to be than on a ship crewed by bold souls out to make a difference.' His smile is weary but genuine. 'But that isn't what you wanted to talk to me about, is it?'

'Who says I want to talk about anything?'

'You only ever drink coffee when you're concerned about something, and almost everything that troubles you can be sorted between you and Constance.'

'*Constance*? First name terms, are you?'

'Only when she comes to talk to me, which isn't that often and, even then, it's only when she hasn't managed to resolve things herself.'

'What sort of things?'

He taps his nose and shakes his head. 'What good would I be if I shared what was told to me in confidence? Even with you, captain. Now, what can I do for you?'

'On deck.' I glance upwards.

The morning sun here matches the rising sun over Olympus I remember from back when I was young. Whoever chose this planet as the capital recognised the symbolism it would hold for all those who revered Mars. Michaels paces towards the rail and takes another long sip of coffee.

'Like the sunrise over Olympus on a calm morning.' Michaels says, as if reading my mind. He breathes deep and his smile drops for a second. 'Forgive me—memories of a place I used to love to visit.'

'You visited Mars?' The words are out before I can stop them.

He pauses mid-sip and lowers his cup, turning to face me. 'I did. I used to love the warm breeze that rolled over the Amazonis Planitia before it rose up the hill and turned cold on the far side.'

I smile. I never got to stand on the Amazonis side—that was for those with money; we only ever experienced the cold air coming down the other side.

Michaels looks at me and leans back against the rail. 'Also, the fact that you called it Mars, asked if I'd been there when it's been gone for so many years, and didn't even blink when I described the breeze from Amazonis...the fact that you can sign in *Airless*... means you know a few things that a native of this time wouldn't.'

I take another sip of my coffee and nod. It's not often that I miss the place I grew up, not after spending so long out here; but every once in a while...

'Catarina Solovias,' I say, 'pleased to meet you again.'

'Cat?' He coughs a mouthful of coffee back into his mug and stares at me.

'You stayed, while I went back and took the long route to get here. Shen stayed in the timeship and travelled back to the time we came from, and I don't know what happened after that.'

'Why tell me now?' he asks.

'Because at the top of that hill is Charles Godstorm and the shell of the ship that will one day bring us all here.' I glance up to the top of the mountain. 'And I don't know how that could be.'

'Time doesn't change.' Michaels shrugs. 'My personal theory—

if this is how it is, then it is what must be. If that ship up there is the reason we were brought here, then it will still be the reason someday, no matter what else happens in the meantime.'

'If he gets hold of a *timeship*, if he gets hold of the power to change things however he wants—'

'Then he will try to change things to only benefit himself. He'll place wagers to increase his fortune, and he'll keep doing that till he dies rich.'

'Remember the Olympus detonations?'

'All too well, my brother lived on Olympus.' He pauses for a second, taking a deep breath, "I used to enjoy breakfast with him once a month, but I was late that day. When I heard the first detonation, I knew I would never see him again."

'Remember those three investment firms that flourished from betting on Olympus exploding and wiping out Mars? Remember how their directors were brought in and questioned about it, and how each of them said they'd had a tip from a man they'd come to know as being accurate with his predictions, though they never named him.'

'He doesn't think that far ahead.' Michaels shakes his head.

'How did he get that rich? How has he given up his crew every time, never doubting that he'd be okay?'

'He couldn't have known about everything. The number of times we ended up beating odds that the gods themselves wouldn't have even bet on us for... At the start, I enjoyed the unpredictability, the adventure. Then I realised that he wasn't planning any of it; he'd just upset someone and they were coming after him, so he had to get out of there before it all went bad.'

'And yet, he always made it...'

'I see what you're saying, but I signed on with Godstorm five years ago—his hair was still black, and he hadn't lost a kidney to someone stabbing him in an alleyway. Even if *this* Godstorm goes back, what's he going to do? Tell his younger counterpart not to be so stupid?'

'Doesn't matter *what* he does; all that matters is that that bastard will have access to something that could allow him to change the past, the future, everything...'

'What do you suggest we do?' Michaels looks up the hill to the palace. 'He's governor of Stenlar Prime. The only person with more security than him is the president.'

'We've got to find a way. How about we pretend to work for him and then do the deed when he trusts us enough to let us get close.'

'Do the deed? Even if you did kill him, you'd have a half-second to savour the victory before the Praetorians ripped your atoms apart.'

'We can't do nothing.'

'Oh, I agree. I just don't know what we can do.'

'I'm going back up there today to find out what he's up to. Then we can think about what we can do to stop him.'

'You think he's figured out who you are?'

'You didn't,' I take another sip with a wry smile. 'What chance has that egomaniac got of remembering one of his crew who had only been on his ship a few weeks?'

'You were the one who handed them, well, you, his ship. He doesn't remember anything important, but he does remember everyone who ever wronged him...'

'Well, I'm twenty years older than the last time he saw me, so let's hope he doesn't make the connection.'

'You're right though: if I didn't make the connection, solid bet he won't,' Michaels says. 'I meant that, at some point in time, when you weren't *you*, you took his entire crew off him. That'll be what he remembers about you...nothing else.'

The Machinations of an Interstellar Tyrant

The journey back to the city is much easier in a car. Good exercise is no substitute for the ability to travel ten miles in as many minutes. The car avoids the main palace and travels out to the governor's residence, a wide dome filled with thick greenery. The sand-covered highway gives way to a rough-cut stone cobbled path. I climb out as it comes to a halt, and walk through the trees to the front of the house, which has been constructed using massive stones and looking like it could hold a hundred people, rather than just the one.

It's meant to show everyone else that you have more space than them.

Godstorm is stood outside, wearing his full regalia.

'Captain Morgan, good of you to come.' He gestures to the house, standing back from the path to allow me to pass. 'Please, we have much to talk about.'

Still feels wrong turning my back on him.

He follows me into the house and snags two glasses from a cabinet, before picking up a crystal decanter of deep brown liquid.

'Benefits of rank.' He pours more than a double measure into both glasses and hands me one. 'You understand this, captain to captain—it does well for the underlings not to be involved in important matters like these.'

'What can I do for you?' I take the glass but don't drink.

'I must first ask where your allegiance lies. Are you for the empire, or not?'

I recite the first line of the privateers' code. 'I'm bound to the stars. I roam for the money when I need it, for the cargo when it comes, and for—'

'The cause, when it pays the most,' he finishes the line for me. 'Excellent. So, you will serve when I call for you?'

'Depends. What are you needing?'

'I want to go home. That ship is my chance to do that.'

'Where's home?' I ask.

He turns to face me and, for the first time, there's the hint of a genuine smile on his lips. 'If I told you that, you'd think me insane.'

'I just ended a war in which a single ship imprisoned an entire empire. Try me.'

He gestures to the chairs by the window, sitting down in one of them and pointing to the other. I sit and put my glass on the table beside me.

'It's not a case of where.' He puts his glass down and leans forwards, his hands clasped in front of him. 'It is a case of when...'

'When?' I frown. 'What do you mean?'

'I come from another time—not this one, and not the one that ship brought me from either. When I was young, I dreamed of being a captain, of sailing the stars, but in the time I come from, social standing determined if you went out into the stars or if you stayed forever on the ground to break rocks and be paid a pittance for it, dying young and unloved under the banner of universal freedom.'

I say nothing.

'A long time ago... well, a long time ago in my life, but a time far in the future from now, a scientist got hold of research that had long-since been outlawed, and she built a ship which, in theory, could make use of that research. She'd heard a lot of what life was like in the time she was planning on travelling to, and she wanted to make sure that she would make it back, so she hired me to guard her on the trip.'

His eyes go distant.

'The ship worked or, at least, it worked to the extent that it took us into the past, but that's where it failed, and she couldn't repair it using the technology that was available in the time period we had travelled back to, so she did what any good scientist would do and found a quiet corner to wait out her time.'

'But you didn't.'

'In the time I was from, I had a wife, a son.' A tear rolls from his left eye. 'I only took the job to provide for them, and I would have done anything to be back with them again, so I signed up on another ship and, before long, I had enough wealth to buy my own ship. That's when I started searching for something to get me home.'

'How long ago was that?'

'Thirty-six years.' He shakes his head. 'I was barely a man when I took that job; I'm nearing retirement age now, but I promised them I'd come back, and I've never wavered from that quest.'

'What does this have to do with me?'

He pauses and looks around the room as if making sure no one is listening.

'Two days from now,' he lowers his voice, 'the president will be killed in an act of sabotage by a Stenlarian conscript when she goes out to visit the labour mines. She goes there to free them all from their servitude, and the uproar following her death sparks a civil war on Stenlar Prime. The conscripts rise up against their oppressors, even though they would not have had to, had they let her deliver her message.

'The war will envelop the entire city and, in the midst of it, the science division will be burned to the ground. A probe is launched with as much of the data as they could cram into it, but it's lost in the gravitic chaos around the Chaeni Worlds. The scientist I worked for is the one who finds it, more than ten thousand years later.'

'If this already happens, what do you need from me?'

'When the science division burns down, all the tech within it is lost, no survivors. Within a month, all these cities are gone, and barbarism rules for a hundred years before the Tarlin come in to stop the slaughter.'

'I'm still waiting for the part where you tell me what it is you need me for.'

'That ship—the one that we know works—I intend to take it and return home.' He looks at me with feverish intensity. 'I will see my wife and son again.'

'They won't know you.' I gesture at him. 'You've been gone too long.'

'But they *will* know me.' He leaves his chair and starts pacing. 'I may have grown old, but I can still fulfil my promise to them. I can still give them the good life they should always have had.'

'And what do we get out of it? If the city's burning, and everything ends in fire and death, there's not much to recommend staying here.'

'It's only here and, after the Chaeni incident, after the universe saw what the Stenlarians were capable of, they saw it as fitting punishment for all the atrocities they had committed over the course of the empire. Everywhere else, there are good places to be, where nothing bad happens. You could retire to the Metirian retreat and live there in peace forever.'

'That would take more money than I've got...it would take more money than God has to get in there.'

'God doesn't invest the way I do.' Godstorm stops and reaches down behind the chair, drawing out the same bag that he bargained my life for when he took the *Eagle* back. He reaches in and pulls out his journal, opening it and sitting on the table in front of me, pointing to the entries there. 'This records where all my wealth is kept, the passwords and details for each of the accounts, and the amounts therein. This stays with you when I leave; there's no need for money where I'm going.'

And yet you say you took the job to provide for your family—if money wasn't needed where you came from, you wouldn't have needed to take that job in the first place... The trouble with lies is you have to keep track of them all...

'All right. What do you need from us?'

'The riots will start a few days after the president's death. On the third day, there'll be an explosion in the merchant quarter, and the fighting will start. All the official channels will be locked down—I need you to get me across to the science division. I give you the journal, and you drop me on the roof. I'll take it from there.'

'That's it?'

'I also suggest that you break atmo and get out of there as soon as you've dropped me off. There's going to be nothing happening on Stenlar except the war for a very long time.'

'Show of faith then.' I nod towards the journal. 'Prove to me that the journal contains what you say it does.'

'Of course.' He smiles and passes it to me. 'Take any page as down-payment for our agreement.'

I open the book and rip one of the pages out, folding it and placing it in my pack.

'Do we have an accord?' he asks, offering his hand.

I shake his hand once only. 'We have an accord.'

'Excellent. Then I will be in touch the day after the president's death.

To Save a Civilisation's Hope

The car drops me back at the *Dawn*. I climb up to the deck, the chill down my spine nothing to do with the cold breeze blowing in from the south. Michaels is still there, with Raley close by. They stop talking as I clear the rail.

'So how is the mad bastard?' Michaels asks.

'I don't know.' I motion towards my cabin. 'But I'm not talking about it out here.'

*

'He told you what?' Raley stares at me in disbelief.

'President dies in two days, the world goes to hell, and he just wants to go home... I don't believe any of it, but that ship is almost finished, and I know he's not above murder to get what he wants.'

'No way he can get to the president. No way the Praetorians would allow anyone to get close enough to do something like that.'

'They can only stop what they know about,' I say. 'If she's out visiting the mines, a falling carrier would do the job just as well as a bullet, and the Praetorians couldn't stop that.'

'We could try.' Raley starts to pace the room. 'She's the first ray of hope the Stenlarians have had in more than a decade; the first one not to be born into old money and hatred.'

'We've got a way to contact her but, if he's right, and we save her, we'll alter history.'

'Not history.' Michaels shakes his head. '*His story*, and if saving the world from a hundred years of war is all we achieve, I consider that a win. You have to bear in mind that that man would tell anyone anything in order to get what he wants. Spend enough time in his company and you'll catch him in a lie.'

'You figure?' I try to keep the sarcasm out of my voice.

'I know.' Michaels gives a wry smile. "If his mouth is open and he's saying something that sounds good or right for anyone but him, you can be sure it's a lie.'

'So, no trusting him—I can live with that. How do we get in there though? No one in the establishment is going to want her to be around any longer than they have to put up with her; they're not going to allow anyone to help her, not if it messes with their plans.' Raley's pacing is getting more agitated. 'And no one unofficial will be able to get anywhere near her as a result.'

'Maybe we can though.' I tap the comms. 'We've got her ear, and she owes us a favour.'

'What do you have in mind?' Michaels asks.

'I think having the heroes who saved the planet accompanying her wouldn't be a bad thing. It would help her ratings, and it would keep us in easy reach of her.'

'Godstorm will see us out there with her though,' he counters. 'Wouldn't that change his plans?'

'What if he *wants* you out there with her?' Raley says. 'What if he already *knows* how she gets killed, and that you're caught in the crossfire?'

'Why bother making a deal with someone you know is going to die? If he's seen all of this in some future we know nothing about, he might know everything and just be playing the part he needs to.'

'Or he doesn't remember it well enough,' Michaels says. 'When I met him, he said he was hired muscle; muscle doesn't tend to have a history degree. He might remember some of it, but it's been years and, where comes from, there might not be any books relating to what happened in the future.'

'Either way, if we prevent her death, that's a success, isn't it?' Raley pauses. 'Do you think she'll go for it?'

'Only one way to find out.' I activate the comms and take out the card that Wagner gave me.

She answers on the second ring.

'Morgan.' She sounds like she's out of breath. 'Good to hear from you. Have you considered how I might pay you back yet?'

'Is now a good time? You sound like you're—'

'Working out.' She takes a deep breath and holds it, calming her voice. 'The gods of iron are cruel. If you do not pray to them every day, they take what they have given you and give it to someone else.'

'President Wagner—' I begin.

'Aaltje,' she cuts in. 'To you, I am Aaltje.'

The force of her personality transmits through the comms. 'Aaltje, I gave it some thought and decided that I wanted to help with the unification process. I'd like to come out with you on your official engagements, show that we're supporting you.'

'Excellent. I have a few appointments in the coming days—are you free?'

'I am.'

'Come to the palace tomorrow. We'll outfit you for the day after, then we'll take a trip out to the sand mines at Larack. I'll travel on your ship—show them that heroes travel with presidents when they do their part for our world.' Her breathing slows as she gets herself back under control. 'If you'll excuse me now...I have a second set to go for.'

'Knock yourself out.'

'Not since I started. I will see you tomorrow, Morgan.'

The line goes quiet. A few seconds later, there's another click as her intelligence service cuts the line.

Just hope Godstorm doesn't get access to her calls...

I look back across to Raley and Michaels. 'Right, get your best clothing out—we've got ourselves a presidential visit...'

*

The following day, a car is waiting for me when I wake. Mirri is already on deck and points to it. 'It's been there since sun-up. Driver said I wasn't to disturb you, but to mention the car was there when you got up. Is that the president's insignia on the side of it?'

'Yep.' I wish I could go back to sleep. I'm only just beginning to repay the toll from the events of the last few days. 'Keep an eye on the ship; I'll be back soon.'

I climb down to find Odyssey waiting for me. 'Four Odyssey Fifty-Two,' I say in greeting as I reach the bottom of the ladder.

'Four Odyssey Seventy-Five now.' He seems almost bashful about it. 'Yesterday was a busy day.'

'I'm sure. Are you all right?'

He looks at me as if I had asked the question in a language he doesn't understand.

'Are you all right?' I repeat, laying a hand on his arm.

'I... Yes, I'm fine. Forgive me. I'm unused to people asking that—part of a Praetorian's job is to deal with anything that is thrown at him, without thought for the consequences of those actions.'

'But you're still human under there, aren't you?'

'Almost, though I'm not allowed to let that side show too often.'

'Well, you are allowed when you're with me.'

'I shall not abuse the privilege, captain.' He bows lower than is proper, a sign of great respect, before opening the door and stepping back. 'Please...'

Odyssey follows me into the rear of the car, perching on the seat in front of me, looking like he might fall off it at any second.

'Is something wrong?' I ask.

'There have been rumours of unrest in the mines recently.' He glances out of the window. 'There's a possibility that those who have to work out there may be deciding their lot is unjust and that they should do something about it.'

'Not a problem here, though?'

'If the miners rebelled, the Praetorian would be hard-pressed to keep a lid on it.' He glances out of the other window. 'There is only so much force you can apply to a situation before something breaks.'

'If they've already rebelled, surely it's already broken?'

'The situation, to be sure, but not the rebellion.' He looks at me, his blue eyes burning bright again. 'I was once of the slave caste. It's why I applied to the Praetorian when President Wagner began her ascent from the mines. I saw in her someone I would die for.'

'Not much of a retirement plan. Never understood why anyone would want to take a bullet for someone else.'

'It's not that I would take a bullet for *her.*' He puts his hand to his chest. 'I would take a bullet for what she represents, who she could one day become. To those of us who worked in the mines, she is everything. She represents the chance that, one day, we too could stand in the cool air of the city, rather than in the boiling steam of the mines.'

'You made it out.'

'I made it out because of the sacrifice of others, like she did. There's not a person who has worked the mines who ever got out by themselves.'

'Do you know much about her? Honestly?' I ask.

'Everyone does. She is the dawn of a new future for our people.' He leans back and smiles, taking ten years off his appearance. 'She's older than me by a decade and, for as long as I remember, I've pledged my strength to her.'

'A decade...' I look at the bulging musculature of Odyssey, and his face, lined and hard. 'That makes you a teenager?'

'Two years to my second decade.' He nods, looking up at me with a wry smile. 'Years in the mines are like dog years: each one counts for five.'

'You're not kidding.' I look him up and down. 'How?'

'We're on stimulants from a very early age. We can lift more than most full-grown adults by the age of five. Most of us don't make it beyond the age of twenty, and it's not like any of us are having kids, is it now?'

'No? I'd have thought that all the extra hormones would have led to a lot of kids.'

'No.' He rests his hands on his knees and sighs. 'A little testosterone is a good thing, but the amount most of us are on prevents natural conception.' He pauses for a second and smiles. 'Not saying there isn't a lot of screwing going on, though that's just a good distraction from the situation we're in.'

'Sounds a bit crap.'

'It is, but you learn to love what you have and live while you can.'

'Can you think of anyone out at the mines who'd want to kill the president?'

'Loads of people, but none of those who actually work *in* the mines. Why?'

'I've volunteered to go out there with her. I like to know the odds I'm up against when I walk into a situation.'

He looks out of the window and adjusts the weapons at his belt. 'We're arriving. When you're at the mines, there'll be me and four others like me guarding her...and you,' he says, giving me a smile. 'It's not the workers you have to watch out for; they'd all give their lives for her. It's the Slavers who have something to lose if she stays in power...'

I nod.

All civilisations are built on the pain of their lowest castes. Nothing changes.

A Woman's Work

The car stops outside the Red House, official residence of the president. Odyssey is out in a half-second, making sure the area is clear even though there's more than a hundred guards in the vicinity. He nods and beckons for me to join him. The air is clean, like breathing in a forest, not the dry acidic scent of the desert outside. He motions to the door with a swift hand gesture and moves aside so I can go in without him blocking the way. I head past him, Odyssey not making any move to follow me.

Inside, there are no staff. I hear a recognisable steady clanking of heavy metal from one of the side rooms: I've been in enough gyms to know what free weights sound like. I approach, and wait by the door until President Wagner finishes her set. The plates on the bar weigh ten times what I could lift. She sets them back on the bench with the same ease that I might move my coffee cup, then glances over towards me.

'Morning, Morgan.' She takes a long swig from a flask next to the bench. 'Didn't get you up too early, did I?'

'Not at all. I didn't interrupt you, did I?'

'Oh, this is an easy morning.' She shrugs, the movement like tectonic plates shifting across her shoulders. 'Only been working out three hours so far.'

'Every day?' I stare at the massive plates of metal on the bar.

'I did say the gods of iron were merciless. Want a go?'

'I'm good, but I know where to come if I need a power loader.'

'That you do.' She rises from the bench, peeling the suit off her shoulders to reveal a back still carrying the scars of a mineworker.

'Do those hurt?' The question is out before I consider its wisdom.

'They serve as a reminder.' Her bronzed skin ripples as she puts her hands on her hips and leans all the way forwards, causing her back to pop and click as she stretches everything. 'You see the two lines at the top of my back?'

I lean closer. 'They're not lines...'

'That's right. Have a good look at them.'

There are a series of letters and numbers stretching from one shoulder to the other.

'What are they?' I ask.

'All miners are imprinted with a code when they leave the growth chambers at age five.' She slips out of the rest of the suit, showing the tattoos all the way down her back and thighs, before grabbing a dressing gown the size of a double mattress from the rail. 'They mark your birthday each year by cutting the code into your back again.'

'Why?'

She shrugs into the gown and does it up at the front. 'Because we heal. That's what we do—we survive, and we heal. The owners of the mines are only interested in keeping us as their property.'

'You've got tattoos. They're permanent.'

'That's the point.' She grimaces and sits back on the bench. 'They need to show us that they can hurt us when and how they want, and that the only thing we're owed from them, even on the anniversary of our arrival into the world, is pain.'

'What are the other tattoos?'

'They're how we communicate in the mines.' She opens her gown a little and runs her finger down the colourful line from her deltoids to her collarbone. 'This tells everyone that I'm not to be used in the harsh environments.' She tilts her head back and points to just underneath her wide chin and then down to the top of her trapezius. 'These show that I'm not to be left alone with the mine owners ever.'

'I don't understand.'

'There's a real fear among the mine owners that the miners will rise up one day, and all the workers will go and work for someone else—that they'll get a life while the owners lose theirs.' She extends her right arm, tracing the words written in tiny script across her forearm. 'These are the workers who died, so that I wouldn't have to.'

I say nothing.

'When the owners get the idea that one of their workers is getting popular, accidents occur—everything from poisoned rations to cave-ins, just to kill off *any* hope.'

'They *died* for you?'

She turns her hand over and points at each name in turn. 'Alijae swapped rations with me after the first time I got noticed; her heart burst before she got out of the mess hall. Tsara took my shift the day after and was impaled by a crane and pulled apart. Jamal slept in my bunk that night, and was stabbed a hundred times.' She pauses and runs her fingers down the lists, more than a hundred names in all. 'All so that hope wouldn't be extinguished.'

'Couldn't they just have killed you, regardless?'

'People don't know for certain that an accident isn't an accident, that a mistake isn't a mistake, but they *do* know when something is deliberate. If they had made it obvious, there'd have been a riot that the gods couldn't have stopped, so they did everything they could to remove the problem without taking direct action.'

'How did you get out? Didn't they know what you'd do?'

'They didn't believe.' She draws the gown closed. 'Always the same when people are considered inferior, especially when it's an entire race of people who have been underestimated. We paid a lot of money to get me lost in transit between the mines and, from there, I started the Peoples' Party. I lost some of the muscle, showed them that miners had minds. I made a joke of it at first, like I was aiming above my station in life, but we were counting on them not believing I could threaten the status quo.'

'They could have killed you at any time outside of the mines. Why didn't they?'

'Because, for people like them, you can't show any fear of something that is inferior, so they let me form a political party, and run for election. Then they shit a brick when they realised that's what we'd been waiting for.'

'What?'

'Miners are still citizens, and they outnumber all other types of citizens fifteen to one.' She spreads her arms wide. 'All the miners on the planet took the day off to vote, and one landslide victory later'—She pats the bench—'here I am, working out on presidential weights.'

'Surely, they haven't stopped trying to kill you, just because you're president. I know Stenlarian politics.'

'Well, as you say, some things don't change.' She gestures to the next room, where a table has been set with a hundred different meats and fruits. 'Breakfast?'

'As long as it's not going to burst my heart.'

'Only if you try to keep up with me.' She grins.

As before, she eats five times what I do without pause, seeming like she could take on another five without much trouble. The cooks keep the food coming, and I look down at the remains of the single omelette I've managed so far.

'You're not a miner—I don't expect you to lift like one or, God forbid, eat like one.'

'Just as well.' I take the last bite.

'Well then, tell me the truth of why you want to come with me to the mines.'

'Maybe I just want to be a part of history.'

'Sure. However, if that were the case, you'd have taken the win I offered when first we met. You saved all of Stenlarian space, and that was how I would have written it in the records.' She smiles, her eyes wide and bright. 'Come on, Morgan, I thought we had enough of an understanding to at least be truthful with each other.'

'Governor Godstorm mentioned that he'd heard about a plot to remove you from office. I wanted to stay close, to see if I could prevent it.'

'You think you can do a better job than my Praetorian? Just you and your crew?'

'No, but if I let the future die without trying to save it, I could never rest again.'

'Interesting.' She rises from her seat. 'Remember what I said about politics? Come with me—there's something I have to show you.'

She walks up the stairs, her footsteps light despite her mass, every movement controlled, precise. The ten rooms for the ten councillors of the first Martian Council are just as they were when I visited the original Red House as a child; the symbols the same, with the names of the first Council carved by hand in intricate script on the doors to their rooms.

Someone really wanted the empire to remember Mars.

President Wagner walks over to the Olympus room balcony, stopping at the stone railing at its edge. I stand next to her, then flinch as something clips the edge of the railing, the whine of a bullet ricochet unmistakable. I throw myself against the president to try shove her out of harm's way. I might as well be trying to move the Red House itself.

'Every morning, I come out here, to this balcony, where Heinrich the Second was shot down, to give the rich and discontented their chance to voice their displeasure.'

'By letting them shoot at you?' I scan the distant horizon, trying to pinpoint where the shooter was firing from.

'There's a shield around this balcony that would require heavy artillery to pierce it.' She taps the inside of the rail. 'I like to know where my enemies are.'

'No sense in taking unnecessary risks though.' I scan outwards, but it's impossible to see anything with the bright morning sun in my eyes. 'Presi—'

'Aaltje. To you, I am Aaltje, remember. Please, Morgan, I have fought my whole life to get to the highest rank so I can prove it should be no barrier.'

I look down from the balcony to the car, where Odyssey is still stood. 'Aaltje, do you see there, by the car?'

She follows my gaze. 'Siegfried?'

'No, Odyssey.'

'Who is actually Siegfried, son of Joanna, who was the daughter of Hannah. I know him well. I looked after him when he was first born, before either of us tasted the air of the mines.'

'Well, he would die for you, and I suspect he is not alone in that; but he told me, as you have just now, that there are others who would die to ensure that you do.'

'It is the risk any president runs when they step out in the morning.' She looks unconcerned when a second bullet clips against the stone. 'The politics of Stenlar are not averse to the machinations of force.'

'But you're the first president from the mines.' I follow her back into the Olympus room. When she sits at the table of the Crimson Lords, I take a seat next to her. 'You're the first one to offer your people hope. The fact that there are people merrily taking shots at you when you're out for a glance at the morning sun should be enough to tell you that the hope of your people is a more dangerous adversary than anything they have ever faced... and something they will do anything to keep down.'

'What would you have me do? A president has to be seen to be respected; she has to be seen for the person she is, not the craven they would seek to paint her as.'

'Perhaps not though, when she holds the promise of a future for so many who have lived without hope.'

'I see your reasoning but, in two days, I travel to the Mines of Tharsis to sign an order freeing all my people from the bonds that have held them there since before either of us was born.'

Not since before I was born, but that's a story for another time...

'Then let me travel with you. Your Praetorian are better warriors than me or my crew, but we represent something that none of them do.'

'And what's that?'

'The possibility of unity with those who were not born of the same caste as you.'

'There is that.' She leans in close to me. 'What caste were you born to?'

'Arbeit,' I say, without hesitation. 'My mother and father were both born to nothing and worked hard their whole lives to give me the chance to study engineering.'

'Then they will not see you as anything different from them; they grew with the same struggles that you did.'

'And, like you, I overcame those struggles with the help of those who loved and cared for me. *Unlike* you, I am not one of them in body, and they cannot tell my caste from my face. Let them see that there are those of us who do not hate them because they were born different.'

'When they get out, they will soon discover that most *will* hate them simply because they were born different.'

'True.' I look at the map of Mars, remembering a time when I walked upon those sands. 'Every journey begins with a single step, though.'

'It does.' She is silent for a minute. 'So, we need to get you an outfit to wear for your appearance before the masses.'

'I have one. Been wearing these clothes for a good long while.'

'And they have that very appearance.' Her grin is still infectious. 'First lesson of politics, Morgan, is that, if you don't win them over before you start to talk, you won't get to talk. Heroes must look the part; presidents must, unfortunately, look presidential.'

She stands and flexes arms wider than my waist. 'Do you think I like wearing suits that were designed for people who have no muscles?' Or that skirts are a good choice for a woman with thighs that can lift a car? If I had a choice, I'd wear what I'm wearing now all the livelong day and, on days when I needed to work, I'd wear the onesie that all mineworkers are given, designed to keep you cool when you need it to, able to withstand any amount of pressure.'

'Isn't that the point?' I ask. 'You're going to these people as one of them, to free them from their chains—should they not remember that you were once one of them? Should they not glory in that?'

'You're just trying to avoid having to get changed.'

'I am...but I'm not wrong.'

'We'll see...'

*

I endure four hours of trying on outfits, ranging from foot-high shoulder pads to military overcoats with so much starch in them that I can't bend in the middle. I find myself longing for my other clothes, left folded in the changing rooms. Aaltje grins from ear-to-ear as I enter wearing the latest outfit, which is every bit like several bandages placed in strategic locations. I open my arms wide and look down at the absurd lack of coverage.

'Heroes should be seen.' I twirl. 'But maybe not this much.'

'What do you think then?' Aaltje leans back against the wall, dressed in the mining suit she talked of earlier, with a hundred pockets across its surface, enough to carry every tool a miner would ever need. 'Give me your truth.'

'I think you need to be their past and their future.' I take a towel from the rack beside me and wrap it around myself. 'I mean, look at you—you're perfectly happy with what you're wearing.'

'Doesn't look presidential though.'

'Isn't that the point? You're making a new world—perhaps you should start with a new beginning? One where you don't have to be what society demands?'

'You're definitely just trying to avoid getting changed,' It's clear that while she's trying to make a joke of it, the thought is now circling in her head.

'Do you remember Miyata Chan?'

'Ancient history, back in the days of the first empire.'

'Yeah, she was the first to break tradition and decide that a woman should not have to wear the official garb that was designed for men, remember?'

'It was a bold move.'

Inspired hundreds of us to refuse the traditions of the time.

'It was. And, from her came us.'

'Agreed. Your point?'

'If we came from her, then who will come from you, and what lesson will they learn from what you do?'

She nods, her smile growing wide. 'I have an idea: I'll have your usual rags cleaned up, and you can wear them as you wish. I'll have something made for me that will allow me to make the point I want. I'll meet you tomorrow at your ship. The mines are on the other side of the Deimos Shadow, so I'll be with you before ten in the morning.'

To Kill the Future

True to her word, it is just past nine when she arrives by truck. She disembarks from the back, wearing a long cloak that conceals her entire body. Alongside her are the four Praetorian who make up the Imperial Cordon, Odyssey being the last to step off the truck.

'I don't fit in a regular limo,' she calls up to me, as I look over the rail.

'I don't think you'd fit on a regular ladder either,' I shout back, motioning for Mirri to bring the ship down and lower the cargo ramp.

'Well, I wouldn't be president if I did everything the same way you lot did.' Her voice is brimming with mirth, and she pauses as the ramp locks into place. 'Come on down then. I don't fancy getting lost on the way over.'

I swing over the side and slide down the ladder, the Praetorians shifting into position so that there isn't a clear path to the president.

'Good to see you, Morgan,' Aaltje says. 'Allow me to introduce the Imperial Cordon. Odyssey you know, but this is One Titan Nine Hundred Twenty-six, Seven Tower Seven Hundred Fifty, and Three Oracle Two Hundred Twenty. Each of them has served the last four presidents with honour. If you're wondering what to call them, their second name is their callsign.'

'Captain Morgan.' Titan bows her head to her chest, making her only two feet taller than me rather than three. 'A pleasure to meet you.'

'Captain,' Tower drops to her knees. Oracle does the same without a word.

'You are welcome on my ship.'

'Excellent.' Aaltje smiles, walking up the steps, her cloak swirling around her ankles.

'Tell me you've got something on under that,' I say, with a grin.

'Oh, there's something special going on under here. Come on—the sun sets faster on the far side. I don't want it to be dark by the time we get there.'

The trip out to Deimos' Shadow takes half a day. The landscape beneath us has been crafted with care by a million hands to resemble a homeworld that no one from this time would ever remember, and very few would care about.

But, for me, it's a reminder of a home long-since gone, where mistakes made by the rich destroyed the world for everyone.

Aaltje moves alongside me as I stare over the ship's rail, caught up in my own thoughts.

'Never been out here?' she asks.

'Not here.' I try to smile. 'It just reminds me of somewhere I knew a long time ago.'

'Truly?' She leans back against the rail. 'Where?'

'Oh, nowhere you'd have seen.'

'I don't doubt that—especially seeing as you don't exist, as far as anywhere in the universe is concerned.'

'Been checking up on me?' I turn to face her, leaning on the rail with as much calm as I can muster.

'No, but my staff have. Standard protocol for the Imperial Intelligence Corps is to check up on every person I'm going to be spending any time with and find out if there are any dark secrets in their past.'

'And they didn't find any of mine?'

'Morgan, captain of the *Unbroken Dawn*, a ship that she had built to her own specifications. Been out on the solar waves for the best part of two decades. Doesn't spend more than a week in any port, and emerges from nowhere to save the universe... I regret to say that my intelligence service was baffled by much about you, in particular your name.'

'Morgan?' I ask. 'What about it?'

'First name, second name, family name?' she asks. 'They

couldn't even find that.'

'Just Morgan. Never had the need for anything else. The only time you need titles is when you think you're important, and the only time people use more than their first name is when they're trying to prove a point.'

'And you're not?'

'No. I went out into the universe to sail on the ocean of stars. I never wanted anything else. Never asked to save the universe. Never wanted to.'

'"Fate does not always make of us what we wish",' Aaltje quotes from the words of the Red founders.

'"But we must answer when it calls".' I recite the second line without pause.

'I am curious though: you must tell me about yourself someday.'

'We survive today, and I'll tell you all about me.' I nod towards the immense rock archway over the Phobos crater now looming into view. 'Right now, you need to get ready.'

*

The miners are still filtering through when we arrive. From the look of most of them, they've run to get here. The mine is larger than anything I've ever seen: more than fifty miles from one side to the other, the ridges lined with massive people, all wearing regulation black mining jumpsuits with glowing reflective strips along the arms, legs, and chest. The huge loading cruisers move away from the loaders and Mirri brings the *Dawn* in close, lining her up to hover above the central platform. I join Aaltje down below as the Imperial Cordon surrounds her.

'No.' Aaltje murmurs, loud enough to carry to all of us. 'I walk out there with Morgan. You four will follow in close formation, but behind me, not around me.'

'Miss President.' Titan drops to one knee in front of her. 'We cannot stop a round if we are not in position for it; I ask you to reconsider.'

'I appreciate your request. However, this is the start of something new—we have to begin as we mean to go on.'

'I cannot be the one who fails our people at this time.' Titan looks up, her bright blue eyes imploring. 'I need to keep you safe, for all of us.'

'We talked this over,' Aaltje says. 'You know what to do if anything happens.'

'I do, but that is a duty I would rather not perform.'

'Then let us put our faith in this world's better nature.' Aaltje reaches down and draws Titan up, the way a mother would a small child. 'Behind me, so our people know that we do not fear them.' She turns and nods to me.

I flip the controls on the cargo doors and blink against the blinding sunlight that fills the whole of the cargo bay.

'With me, Morgan.' Aaltje's hand brushes against mine, and I move with her.

The air outside is acrid, the scent of burned metal and sand heavy in the hot air. I walk behind Aaltje, one step back and to the right, my hand at my side but not far from my sword. The wall of noise that greets us is tangible: hundreds of thousands of voices raised as one—a single word, repeated many times.

'EINIGKEIT. EINIGKEIT. EINIGKEIT.'

Unity—not just the caste they were born to, but the creed they've forever lived by.

Aaltje walks to the edge of the platform and raises her hands, leaning towards the microphone. The mineworkers hush, the sense of anticipation so thick you could cut through it.

'My people.' Aaltje's voice is soft, but it carries all around the mine. There's an intake of breath from all of the mineworkers as their hands come up to mirror hers, as if the planet itself has sucked the air in to fill the void created by the silence of a million hands being raised without words. 'There is not one of us who has not given their blood, their sweat, their pain, to bring Stenlar what it needs. There is not one of us who has not known hard work.'

She shrugs out of her cloak, the sun catching on the reflective stripes across her arms, legs, and torso, making them glow against the black of the work-suit she's wearing. The roar of approval reverberates around the mine like a wave; not a word, just a sound—a sound of hope, of a dream from a thousand years ago, when I was a child, and never realised until this moment. Aaltje raises her hands, and the din quietens to a low murmur.

'It isn't enough,' Aaltje says. 'It's not enough that we work and die for Stenlar. It's not enough that we provide for the needs of the empire—it will never be enough, for the empire will never stop growing.' She pauses. 'There will never be a time when we can stop working because, without us, the empire can no longer grow, and then what?'

The silence has become uneasy. She has their attention, but now they're thinking...

'Why is that your problem?' Aaltje asks, her voice low and urgent. 'We were told, from the moment we were born, that the empire would fall without us, that service and death in service to Stenlar was the highest honour we could achieve in our lives.' She reaches to the top of her cloak and unclasps the buckle there. 'And I agree. Death in service to Stenlar is the greatest honour we can achieve, but who says that we have to die here, breaking rocks and bending metal? How many of you have ever seen beyond these ridges, have looked over the top of the mine? How can you imagine a brighter world if you've never seen what it looks like?'

The murmur grows louder as Aaltje steps forwards.

'How many of you know what you are without this?' She pounds her fist against her chest. 'These are designed to live with us till the day we die—you all know this. This is the promise we made to the world, and the promise it made to us. For us to be better, though, for our people to achieve more than we were made for, we have to be brave; we have to take a step we've never considered.'

She moves around the rail so the whole of the mine can see her, reaching up with her right hand to unclip the buckle that keeps her suit pressurised. The suit hisses as the seal releases, and there's an intake of breath as all those below witness someone daring to do what has been forbidden since before the mines were opened.

'What are you beneath your chains?' She glances around the mine and grabs hold of the suit, pulling hard with her right hand, the material resisting but not able to withstand her strength. The sound of it tearing ripples over the arena, and she leans forwards, ripping the left sleeve from the suit to reveal her bare arm, the skin still showing the stretch scars from where the muscles grew too fast, too large, when she was young.

'I need every one of you to see what you are, beneath the chains we were born under.' She reaches with her left hand and tears the right arm off the suit. 'I need for you to be brave enough to come with me now and build a new world, one where we can live to know grandchildren, where we will one day be able to stop working, not because we can no longer work but because we will have done enough to secure a future that will in turn be able to look after us.'

She pauses as the sound of tearing suits ripples across the mine. She glances back at me with a radiant smile on her face. Turning back, she raises her bare arms high.

'THESE ARE THE ARMS THAT BUILT OLD STENLAR; I NEED YOUR ARMS TO BUILD NEW STENLAR, ARE YOU WITH ME?' There's a slight distortion to the words at the volume of her voice, but the miners hear her all the same. A wave of noise builds from deep within the mine, not words, emotion, raw and unfettered, it's impossible to hear anything else. Aaltje surveys her people, arms held high, she brings them together, her left fist clenched in her right hand.

A million hands held...

The crowd falls silent as each of them brings their hands up to match. My own arms go up, and a tear rolls down my cheek as the dream of a united people manifests. I scan the upper levels of the mine, and the glint of something bright and shiny from one of the radio towers distracts me for a second. I peer closer, a cold chill running down my spine as I realise that there shouldn't be anyone up there. I turn to shout to Aaltje...

A Division of Empire

Tower is moving before the words form on my lips, pulling Aaltje to one side with such speed that I can't follow the movement. She staggers as the round meant for the president strikes her chest. Aaltje falls to the side, and Tower turns to face the assassin.

There's a strange, muted thump, and the entire platform is sprayed red as Tower explodes, bits of her armour lacerating my face as the round detonates.

'MOVE, MOVE, MOVE!' Titan hauls Aaltje off the floor, while Odyssey and Oracle form up between the president and the sniper.

Aaltje is just staggering to her feet as the roar of the crowd below surges upwards like a storm. Rage, Fear, a people seeing their hope being taken from them.

'PINPOINT THE SHOOTER!' I shout, trying to help Aaltje back onto the ship.

Oracle straightens up as he spots a tell-tale glint again, spreading his arms and backing up in front of the president, making it impossible for the shooter to target her. There is no hint of regret on his face, and the roaring drowns out any last words he might have. Odyssey points upwards as Oracle staggers and then dives, leaping off the platform into the open air.

I run down to the microphone as Odyssey points to the second tower, flinching as Oracle explodes in mid-air, his blood and equipment showering the crowd below.

'ON THE TOWER; THE TOWER. THE SNIPER IS ON THE TOWER,' I shout into the microphone, the speakers blasting my voice across the mine.

The miners react as a single organism, a lifetime together in the mines giving them the presence of mind to work as one. All four radio towers tremble, and the next shot goes wide, striking the *Dawn*'s hull. Hundreds of miners dismantle the towers like children pulling apart building blocks. The sniper fires downwards, and several of the miners are torn apart by the rounds raining down on them.

'KEEP THEM ALIVE,' I shout. 'WE NEED THEM ALIVE.'

I turn back from the microphone to see Odyssey stood with his hands up, blocking my view of the president.

'Why?' Odyssey is asking, his voice calm.

'We follow the orders of the empire, not the orders of the president.' Titan's voice is even, not a hint of emotion in it. 'The empire decided that she is no longer of use.'

I peer past Odyssey's cloak. Aaltje is on her knees in front of Titan. Titan's pistol is pointed at Odyssey.

'You're one of us.' Aaltje's voice is close to breaking.

'I *was* one of you,' Titan snarls. 'I didn't have any help climbing out of there; I got out by myself—that's the test we have to pass to be worthy.'

'That's what they'd have us believe.' She tries to rise, only to be met with a sharp slap.

'That's how it *is*. Without struggle, we are nothing. You would have us forget all that we are.'

'I would have us *live*.' Aaltje tries to rise again, only to be sent sprawling by Titan's boot.

'We do live. It's the life of struggle that gives us the strength to prevail.'

'Words.' Aaltje moves to a crouch. 'Words of the founders. Words from the world that made us slaves, from the time that taught us we have nothing to offer this world but our lives.'

Titan shakes her head and then looks past Odyssey to me, her eyes narrowing as I draw my sword.

'Ah, the captain.' Titan's voice is full of scorn. 'Do you think I cannot see you, Morgan? Surely, you can understand this is my duty.'

I flip my personal comms on, tuning it to Raley. 'I understand they've got to be paying you a lot less than they'd have to pay me to betray my president.'

'You understand duty, captain.' Titan draws the sword at her belt, pointing it at Aaltje. 'My duty is to bring her back alive, if I can, but cored down the middle if not: an example of what happens to those guilty of incitement to rebel.'

'The president is the will of the people,' I say. 'She can't rebel against herself.' I flick the microphone speaker on behind me.

'The people have decided against her.' Her voice ripples around the mine, and she stares at Odyssey with a frown. Titan pulls back the hammer on her pistol. 'The decision was made in closed session by the Council this morning; I received the orders a moment ago.'

Behind us, the mine has gone silent as every ear below burns with the sound of betrayal.

'As did I.' Odyssey steps to the side. 'But I chose to ignore them.'

'Orders are what made the empire.' Titan lowers her voice, but the sound is still loud enough to carry to the microphone and ripple around the mine.

'That was then.' Odyssey braces himself, preparing to leap forwards. 'We miss this chance now, and all of us will be in chains for the rest of our days.'

'You are too young to understand.' Titan shakes her head. 'In time, I would have been able to teach you, but now...'

I glance up without moving my head, and see Raley and the others clustered around the stern of the ship, all of them looking down at the tableau below them. Raley nods, and I lunge forwards.

Titan's eyes narrow as she sees my movement. Odyssey springs into action a split second later. Titan's pistol roars as she empties the clip into Odyssey, before lunging at Aaltje, while the crew of the *Dawn* swing down towards her. Aaltje rolls backwards, howling in pain when the blade impales her left arm and pins her to the deck. Titan drops the clip out of the pistol and is slamming another one in when Raley lands on her, stabbing down. Titan lets go of her sword and brings her hand up to deflect the blade, sparks flying from the edges of her glove as Raley puts her entire weight behind her sword strike. Titan shifts her weight, burying her fist with a sharp crack against Raley's side, knocking her towards me. I leap over Aaltje and slice downwards, just as Raley taught me.

Like she's every bastard machine I've ever hated.

Titan rolls forwards, carrying her inside the arc of my attack as she spins in mid-roll. I realise when I hear the click of the clip sliding into her gun that there's no way I can beat her to the hit. I spin, trying to swing my sword back and at least land a meaningful blow with my last action.

This can't be how it ends...

A massive hand opens behind Titan's head and closes over the back of her helmet. There's a loud crack, and the helmet crumples, Titan's arms going limp as her skull shatters. Aaltje slumps backwards, her arm still pinned to the platform by the sword. She looks at me, her hand still clenching the helmet, face pale through the pain, before shifting her gaze over to the edge of the platform. I nod and move over to it, peering over the side at the remains of the four radio towers. The entire mine is silent, every one of them with eyes raised up towards the platform. I move away and flick the microphone off, before hunkering down next to Aaltje. Raley has pulled her shirt open and is nursing her side, where a dark bruise is spreading.

'Are you okay?' I ask.

'Fine,' Aaltje and Raley answer in unison. Raley puts her hand on Aaltje's uninjured shoulder and smiles through the pain.

'We need to show them that you're alive,' I say, to Aaltje, 'or this will turn ugly fast.'

'Get this thing out of my shoulder,' she replies.

Michaels takes hold of the blade, keeping it steady while the rest of the crew descend from the ship to support Aaltje and lie her flat on her back. Esme wraps the end of the blade in bandages, offering Aaltje a piece of wood to bite down on.

Aaltje bites down hard and then nods to me. Michaels doesn't wait for her to finish, and yanks the sword with all his strength. It comes free, the blade sliding clear without snapping. Aaltje groans, and Michaels casts the weapon aside, offering her his hands to help her up. He bows under her weight as the others help with the lifting. Esme binds the wound to stem the bleeding, running out of bandage as she wraps it around Aaltje's bulk.

The president stands, swaying as if a faint breeze might knock her over, glancing at the bodies of her Praetorian lying dead on the ground.

'Even the ones I held closest to me.' She sighs, pacing over to Odyssey's body and kneeling beside him. 'He wanted nothing more, all his life, than for his people to be free from the mines. I remember when I took office, he came to me and begged for the chance to serve me. He vowed on his life that he would never let anything bad happen to me.'

'And he lived up to that vow,' Raley is heavy on my shoulder, keeping her wounded ribs clear on the other side. 'He gave his life for yours, knowing that he had bought us the chance to keep you alive.'

'He did.' Aaltje looks back up to us, tears streaming down her face. 'What do we do now? You heard Titan—the empire voted against me; I can't go back there.'

'Did they know what you were coming here to do?' I ask.

'They did. But only after the morning briefing. As president, I'm allowed—I was allowed—to pass laws without their veto, but I knew this one would cause a backlash.' She reaches down and closes Odyssey's wide, staring eyes, her own eyes closing at the same time. 'I didn't think it would cause *this*.'

'And yet, now, you must follow through.' Esme kneels beside Aaltje. 'For him, and all those waiting for you beyond that platform.'

'But the bloodshed that will follow—' She places one massive hand over Odyssey's heart.

'That will never stop.' Raley tries to crouch beside Aaltje, but she groans and has to straighten again. 'If they were willing to kill you, they will be willing to kill everyone here.

'Yes.' Aaltje stands and turns to me. 'I need you to go back with your crew. Report that I was killed by a sniper, and my Praetorian were taken out by the rampaging miners.'

'They'll come here and execute hundreds as an example of the consequences of disloyalty for the mining class. They'll have all the reason they need to put a ban on workers being allowed to leave the mines...ever.' I say. 'And that's if they don't just drop enough bombs on this place to wipe it from the face of the planet. Or they could send the entire Praetorian corps to put down the insurrection.'

'The Praetorians are...at least I thought they were...loyal to me. Most of them are from the mines.'

'Why did Titan betray you then?'

'Oldest of the Praetorians; defended more than twenty presidents. Maybe she just saw that no one rules for long, while the empire always prevails...'

'What will you do?'

'I'll lead them into the desert, and we'll return through the stone tunnels of Malakar. The arguments among the Council will last several days and, until they choose my successor, they won't be able to remove the title of President from my name. The ruling rights dictate that the empire cannot be without a ruler, even if that ruler is dead. Their own ambitions should give us the time to put what we need to in motion.'

'What of your people?' Michaels says.

'Shall we see?' she asks.

Aaltje lumbers over to the side of the platform. As her head comes into view for those below, a roar rises up that could be heard half a planet away. She stands in silence for half a minute while the roars coalesce.

EINIGKEIT. EINIGKEIT. EINIGKEIT...

Aaltje reaches down to the microphone and clears her throat. Below, the noise ceases.

'They tried to stop us,' she says, her voice quivering with the pain. 'They thought that a dream could be stopped with bullets and the force that has ever held us down.' She pauses and takes a deep breath, her voice filled with emotion. 'But they forget that we are the strength of Stenlar. They forget that it was us who built their palaces, and carried the stone of the city. They forgot us.'

She pauses again. Taking her hand off the rail, she raises it high. Beneath her, a million hands rise in unison. When she speaks again, her voice is quiet, the anger threatening to spill out.

'It is past time they remembered...'

Time and Time Again

The sniper who was pulled from the tower does not hold on to his secrets for long and, in the end, three words from him are all that count.

'Sumner. Enas. Jain.'

Aaltje nods and turns away, her hands clenching hard enough for all the joints to pop. She looks at me, then over at the head of the miners, Jora, before nodding once. I turn away as the sniper is silenced forever.

Aaltje starts to pace the hall.

'Sumner,' she growls. 'Head of the mining guilds. Enas: head of the construction guilds—those I understand. Jain... Jain is the minister for cultural guidance. Why would she want to...?'

'Does it matter?' Michaels asks. 'If a person wants me dead, I ask those kinds of questions after I stop them getting what they want, not before.'

'None of them are in line to take over the presidency. Whoever steps into my place will still have power over them.'

'Not if they steer the choosing to a candidate they can control,' Raley offers, as Esme finishes patching up her ribs. 'Someone unlike you...'

'Are you ready to go?' Aaltje faces Raley, then me.

'Are you ready to stay?'

'I was born here. These are my people, and now I must lead them away, before the Council make a show of force against those who have killed their *beloved* president...'

'How will you get back to the capital?' I ask.

'Better you don't know. There are those within the guilds who can do things that mere mortals cannot in order to extract information. That which you do not know, you cannot tell.'

I nod without true understanding, accepting that telling me more would upset whatever she has planned. 'Then we're gone.'

'Fly swift, fly true.' She turns and offers me her hand on her uninjured side. 'When the wave meets the wall, do not bet that the wall will survive the challenge.'

*

There's no talking on the way back. Whatever happens when we get there, the blood of thousands is going to be spilled in the next few days.

What if Godstorm was right about the war, but just wrong about how it started?

Raley motions for me to join her in our cabin, holding the door open until I enter.

'You okay?' she asks, her voice still strained from the pain in her ribs.

'You're asking *me*?' I draw her close, afraid to hold her tight.

'You're the one who's going to be telling those bastards the story that never happened.' She pulls me close despite the discomfort it must be causing her. 'What if they decide to hold you so that you can't speak to anyone else?'

'Then you'll have to get me out. Remember that there's a certain spacefaring bastard who wants our help when the rebellion starts.'

'I don't trust him.'

'I don't trust *him* either, but I trust him to do what's best *for* him.'

'You think he'll go for it?'

'I think he'll do anything to get what he wants. And what he wants is that ship—this may be the only chance he gets to snatch it.'

'If he'd do anything...that includes killing all of us.'

'I know. The first time I met him, he was in the process of shooting the second officer.'

She blinks. 'Hell of an introduction. Why did you stay with him after that?'

'That was just before I found myself here, on the *Dawn*. If we'd managed to find a port in the meantime, I'd have jumped off there.'

'And then he gave you all up in return for his ship and his goods... You think he managed to buy his way into this position with what he had on the ship?'

'Who knows. If he is who and *what* he says he is, then he'd have enough knowledge from the future to make a stupid amount of money in a short time, without even having to do anything that elaborate.'

'That would change the future though, wouldn't it?'

'Only if he tried to alter the outcome of events. When I first met you, I had already met you; when you first came across me, you had known me for near on twenty years, though neither of us knew the truth of that. I knew I liked you back when I was Catarina; maybe I reminded you of a young woman you'd met all that time ago. Lord knows, I should have done.'

'And yet, here we are, nothing having changed...'

'If this is what is, then this is what will be... Any way we want to look at it, a day, maybe two from now, Aaltje's going to arrive back in the capital, and those who want her power are going to fight back. Whoever wins, there's going to be bloodshed on a scale not seen for more than a hundred years.'

'And we're going to be in the middle of it.'

'No, we're going to be *part* of it and, whatever we do, it may have already happened as far as Godstorm is concerned.'

'So, what *do* we do?'

I smile. 'What anyone should; like we always have—we do what we must and let history record that we did it.'

'That's my girl.'

'Forever.' I draw her close.

*

Twenty minutes later, the cabin lights up as if we're travelling too close to the sun, and there's a scream from on deck. I scramble out of bed as Raley rolls out the other side, her hand pressed to her side. Outside, Mirri is stood at the wheel, but she's facing backwards, rather than forwards. I sprint up to the high deck and stand slack-jawed for a second at the sight.

The towering mushroom cloud of a nuclear detonation is spreading high into the air, with a wall of sand racing towards us. I flip the comms to ship-wide.

'ALL HANDS, GET INSIDE AND BRACE FOR IMPACT.' I wrestle the wheel from Mirri and pull us upwards as the cloud hurtles at us. Moving to full sail in atmo isn't an option, so I retract them to prevent them being damaged. I turn as we arc up away from the tidal wave of dust. The rumbling of the detonation ripples over us and above it, a low whine, like the world is protesting at the injury dealt to it. I flip the canopy on the upper deck as Raley vanishes back into our cabin, and pull Mirri close, clasping her hands against the wheel, engaging the lock on top.

'We need to hold this course,' I say to her. 'Whatever happens, we need to keep moving upwards.'

The rumbling fills our ears, followed by the wave. The *Dawn* becomes no more than a leaf on the wind for a few seconds as the gyro spins wild, Mirri and I bracing against the force being applied to the rudder as we wrestle for control. The shockwave passes in seconds, and we coast downwards in its backdraft as the wave rolls onwards, the rocks below scoured clean of all sand they once held upon them.

'Do you think they got out?' Mirri whispers.

'It will have taken more threat than rebelling miners to launch a nuke,' I say. 'Even if they know trouble was on its way, that wasn't a standard military response.'

'How do you know?'

'Because the Star Force would have used Ortillery, not nukes.' I look back at the spreading mushroom. 'That blast was too slow and too large to be a regular nuke; a nuke's blast would have hit us before I even got out of the cabin.'

'Detonated the mine reactors?'

'I reckon so.' I check the sensors to ensure that there's no second shockwave coming and then retract the canopy. 'Good way to cover your tracks.'

'They didn't need to cover their tracks though. No one apart from us knows what really happened.'

'Not the Council. Probably Aaltje blowing the mines to cover what she and the mineworkers are up to.'

As we come in low over the red plains, it's clear that the city's state of alert has changed. The turrets on the walls are now active and scanning in sweeping patterns. All the lights are on, rather than just the ones for lighting essential roadways. We draw close, and the comms crackle on a direct line to us.

'*Unbroken Dawn*, this is Stenlar Heavy 120. State your purpose.'

'Stenlar Heavy 120, this is *Dawn*, returning from mine 159 with a report for the Council High.'

A pause on the comms, and I signal for Mirri to hold us out of range of the guns, just in case. It's more than a few minutes more before the response.

'*Unbroken Dawn*, this is Stenlar Heavy 120. Access granted. You are to proceed to pad three beside the War College, where the Council's representative will be waiting for you.'

'Understood 120. Proceeding...'

The streets of the city are deserted. There aren't even guard patrols present; just drones making circular passes over the same area again and again, too fast for anyone to make it across the street, much less move between buildings. The massive advertising boards are now filled with instructions indicating lockdown for all citizens, pending the Council investigating reports about the assassination of the president and the destruction of the mines. We come in low and hover over pad three, where six Praetorians are stood waiting. I turn back as most of the crew emerge onto the deck, all of them ready to come down with me.

'I'm going alone.'

'Like hell.' Raley takes my hand and holds tight.

'I have to. If this goes the way I expect it to, then I'm not leaving there today.'

Raley's hand tightens around mine. 'All the more reason you're not going.'

'Look around. We take off from here, and the guns will bring us down before we get above the Council building. I need to go and give the report that Aaltje wanted me to. I need to lull them into thinking that the danger has passed, that they can get on with planning for their new empire.'

'And what happens when they decide you're too much of a liability to keep around?' Raley's hand now grips mine hard enough to hurt.

'You can trust opportunists to make use of useful people.' I remove my weapons from my belt and hand them to Raley. 'We prove that, and the incoming government will find a use for us. You don't discard tools that are still fit for purpose.'

The crew doesn't look convinced.

'Besides, when they lock me up, I need you bleeders out here so you can come and get me out.'

Council High, Morals Low

The Praetorian form up on me as I descend the ladder. The smallest among them, still a head above me and twice as broad, bows low as my feet touch the ground.

'Seven Ganymede Forty-Three,' she says. 'I'm here to take you to the Council.'

'How have they taken it?' I ask. 'The death of the president?'

'This is Stenlarian politics. There will come a day when people no longer feel they have to kill each other to advance in rank and, on that day, we will be a healthier nation than we are now.'

'Did any of them seem happy about what's happened?'

'Not for me to judge. I knew Odyssey well; he and I worked the same mines from the start.' Ganymede retracts the lower part of her facemask, and I see her lips move without sound. *Say only what they want to hear in there.*

I nod, and she nods in return, her lips pressed together in a humourless smile, her facemask moving back into place.

'This way, captain.' She moves aside and gestures towards the door, taking up position one step behind me and to the right.

The halls are silent, like the city outside, the only sound the synchronised marching of the Praetorian, muted by the thick walls. We go down four lifts and through two transit walkways, the Praetorian stopping in the middle of a stone corridor with no doors in it. The Praetorian stand to the side as Ganymede steps up beside me and puts her hand on the stone next to us. There's a click, and a line forms down the middle of the stone to my left, the wall moving inwards and then rolling to the side to reveal two doors made of old wood. Ganymede stands to the side and looks at me, her facemask retracting again as her lips move in silence.

Only what they want to hear.

She nods and steps back, gesturing for me to go forwards. I step towards the door, and it hisses open, revealing a long stone corridor leading to another door. I walk forwards, and it hisses closed behind me, followed by the unmistakable clack of bolts racking into place and the grating of the stone wall moving back along its track. The doors at the far end open as I approach, and the faint smell of fresh flowers drifts to me from the chamber beyond. I enter and the door closes behind me, the bolts locking in place again.

The room is cut from crystal that glows with a pale blue light. The oblong table in the middle of the room is made of black stone, the chairs lined with leather that was old before this planet was colonised. Sitting at the table are eleven people, each of them dressed in formal council attire, their ranks and accolades displayed on their chests. The last seat is wider than the others, and empty. The only one I recognise near the top is Godstorm. He rises from his chair and gestures for me to approach the foot of the table.

'Captain,' he says, his voice low and urgent, 'a pleasure to see you again. So sorry it has to be under these circumstances. Please...'

I step to the foot of the table and stand to attention, waiting for someone to speak while Godstorm sits back down again. There's a minute of uncomfortable silence before a large woman stands and turns to face me with a pained expression. She's almost the size of Aaltje, but without any of the mine-born muscles, and it's clear that the excess of her lifestyle is now costing her.

'The Council recognises Senator Enas,' Godstorm announces to the chamber.

'In your own words, captain,' Enas voice is quiet, a lifetime of knowing that people have to listen to her, not her to them, 'what happened out there?'

'A sniper was waiting for President Wagner. She had just begun speaking before they took their shot, and she was killed.'

'Is that all? Because we were of the understanding that there was more to it than that.'

I stare at her for a second, her face showing the signs of too much rejuvenation therapy, and clothes that must have cost more than the *Dawn*, adjusted to seem like they're well worn. Her eyes are without any empathy.

She knows what happened. If I don't tell the truth, I won't make it out of here.

'The sniper missed.' I say. 'Her loyal Praetorian took the first and second shots, then she was stabbed and killed by a Praetorian loyal to the empire and not to her.'

Enas nods, and her face relaxes a little. 'As was ordered then. How did you get away from the mines?'

'The miners started rioting when the president was attacked. We hauled back into the ship and got out of there at top speed.'

A man built like a miner but with smooth skin and hands that have never seen manual labour rises, his eyebrows furrowing in a continuous line of hair across his forehead.

'The Council recognises Minister Sumner.' Godstorm sounds bored now.

'And the explosion that followed a few hours afterwards?' Sumner asks. 'We have a record of the mine's automated systems still functioning till the blast.'

'I don't know.' I spread my hands wide. 'The mood there was murderous when we left. They believed she was the start of a new tomorrow for them. When she died, so too did that hope.'

'We would have allowed them to keep their jobs; their lives would have gone on.'

'But without the hope that she had given them.' I examine his face—there's not the slightest hint of remorse there.

He smiles without empathy or care. 'A life in service to Stenlar is the greatest honour that any Stenlarian could be offered.'

'But a life of hope, in the service of Stenlar...' I stop as the expressions around the table switch to bland smiles. *I'm wasting my words here.* 'Is there anything else I can do for the empire?'

Godstorm rises from his seat. 'The empire thanks you for your service. We would ask for you to remain with us a day or so, in order to fill in the requisite paperwork on the president's last hours.' He looks around the table. 'Unless anyone else has any queries for the captain?'

None do.

'The Praetorian outside will show you to the guest chambers.' Godstorm gestures to the door. 'I will be along in a while to ensure everything is in order.'

I bet you will...

'Of course.' I turn and go back through the doors.

Ganymede is waiting for me in the corridor; there's no sign of the others.

'I'm to take you to the *guest* quarters.' Her inflection on the word leaves me in no doubt as to what she thinks of the notion. 'You convinced the Council, it seems.'

'How can you be so sure?'

'Because my standing orders to kill you when you came out were revoked just before you emerged.' She turns to me as I stop in the corridor. 'This comes as a surprise? If they're willing to kill a president, you think you even register on their radar.'

'Who rescinded the order?' I ask.

'Godstorm. The only person who could have challenged it is no longer with us, so you can breathe easy for a bit.'

'Only until he no longer needs me.' I start off down the corridor again.

'Isn't that the way of life in general?' Ganymede glances around and taps her helmet. 'Would you mind if I removed this?'

'Feel free.'

The helmet retracts, folding down into her shoulder armour. Underneath, her face is broad, her hair cut military-short, with allegiance tattoos on the back of her neck and campaign studs embedded in her forehead. She looks a lot older than I imagined.

'I thought you knew Odyssey from the mines?'

'I did.'

'But you're a lot older than he was.'

'Ha. I was Imperial Navy long before I was a miner. You know how the Stenlarians like to make the punishment fit the crime.'

Is there no one this empire hasn't tried to break?

'I'm...very familiar with Stenlarian justice. Several of my crew were former Imperial Navy; many of them still carry the markings of it.'

'And yet we keep signing up, for the propaganda machine keeps on rolling. You can be an officer in the corps, but you'll never get to enjoy what you worked for.'

'What did you do? What did they get you for?'

'I served well and with honour for more than twenty years. That was my crime.'

'You served well? That's not a crime.'

'Not *dying* in the service of Stenlar, and living to retirement age when you don't belong to one of the noble houses is a crime. Daring to apply to draw your pension is a crime.' She lowers her voice. 'Those crimes are called "dereliction of duty"; the punishment for that takes the form of being engineered for the mines and sent there to work. That's where I met Odyssey. When they put in for the latest round of Praetorians from the mines, I put my name forwards.'

'How come your record didn't flag you as a threat?' I ask.

'Because Stenlar records only what it wants to, and miners don't have names; they only have numbers to track what they've mined and what they've consumed. That way, when someone is sent to them, that person can never be found again. The perfect place to send people who you want forgotten about. The danger comes when those people manage to survive the mines and make their way out again...'

I step into the lift with her, and she pauses, tapping her finger at the side of the controls.

'To get to the guest quarters this lift goes down,' she says. 'The landing pad is above us...'

I say nothing.

'If I take you to the guest quarters, then you will be under their control. If they decide that you are not a useful asset, they'll either pump you full of steroids and drop you down the mines like they did with me, or kill you and leave your body in the recycling plant.'

'If I run now, I will never stop running, and neither will my crew.'

'How is that any different to your last decade out there in the stars?'

I nod with a wry smile. 'I have something that I have to see through; that means that I have to stay here till the end of it.'

'Very well.' She sighs, and I get the feeling that she's heard others use the same words before. 'I will keep an eye out where I can, but Praetorians are bound by duty and tracked, so I might not be able to help you once you get down there.'

'There may come a time when your duty can no longer be counted upon by the Council High.'

'You know something I don't?' Ganymede activates the lift, and we start downwards.

'No, I don't *know* it, but I *hope*...'

'I remember hope. May you never be disappointed.'

The guest quarters are far beneath the surface, well outfitted with everything I could need, the walls covered in large screens that alternate between an idyllic view of the perfect Stenlar and the news channels. Ganymede shows me around the apartment and then offers me her hand.

'Thank you for being there with Odyssey at the end,' she says.

I take her hand, feeling the strength there. 'It was my honour.'

She nods and leaves without another word. I close my hand around the small chip that she left in my palm, keeping the smile off my face.

*

I wake early the following morning with the entire room shaking, a low rumble reverberating through every surface. The screens blink out for a second and then come back with all the news channels showing the centre of the city. The headline at the bottom of the screen is a single line repeating.

RAIL SERVICES DOWN FOLLOWING TRAIN CRASH AT CENTRAL.

On screen, I see two massive people wearing black jumpsuits lined with neon green charge out of the central hub. A few seconds pass and another group of massive people follows them. The live feeds cut a few seconds later to switch back to the newscast.

The train arrived all right; just wasn't the one they were expecting...

The door chimes, and the screen shows Godstorm standing outside. I walk over and tap on the comms.

He looks cheerful.

'Ah, captain, it looks like the moment is upon us.'

'All right,' I say, 'get me out of here, and we'll get you over there.'

His smile turns vicious. 'Well, as it happens, being part of the Council means I can go anywhere I want, whenever I want, so I just have to travel over there myself and take the ship, and no one will stop me.'

'What did you need me for then?'

'You?' He shakes his head and taps the screen. 'I thought I would pay you back for the way you treated me when we first met. I thought a spell in the mines would do you some good.'

'You won't get away with this.'

'Really? How little you know, three-one-seven-nine-one-nine-five.'

'What?'

'I'll come back and see you in thirty years, and you'll answer to that number when I call it. Enjoy your reward, captain.'

He cuts the transmission without another word, and the lights in the apartment dim, the screens cutting out one by one until I'm alone in the darkness.

A Rebellion in Progress

I don't know how long I've been down here; time has no meaning without light and stimulus. The rumbling from above continues, punctuated by louder percussion every so often. I wait in the darkness as the screens spark and flicker, information coming through in split-second transmissions, enough to see that the world is going to hell without any idea of how fast. The door chimes, and I move around to the side of it. It opens, and light gleams in from outside.

They're not taking me without a fight.

The person in the corridor moves into the room, and I lunge, blinded by the glare from the corridor. There's a whisper of movement, and I find myself on the floor with a heavy boot on my chest.

'Good move.' Ganymede's voice is patient. 'But you should always know where you're going before you set off.'

I groan, trying to lift her foot off my chest. 'Thanks. Are you here to take me to the mines?'

'If I was, I'd have stood on your head.' She lifts her foot and offers me her hand. 'Come on, time to get out of here before the miners' army rolls over us.'

'Have you seen the president down there?' I take her hand, and she pulls me up as if I weigh nothing.

'You kidding? The Praetorian comms went down a half-minute before the train hit; the wall defences were shut down an hour before that for "routine" maintenance. I've never seen an incursion planned this well. Anyone with that kind of experience knows you don't put your generals on the front line, no matter what the films show you.'

'We need to get out of here. I need to stop Godstorm.'

'Godstorm? He's no threat. All the ministers are on the way to their safehouses.'

'He's not. Come on, show me the way back to my ship. I need to get over to the science division.'

*

The centre of the city is on fire. The miners have spread through the lower levels; they're not starting any fights, but they're finishing them. The city militia have been rounded up and are circled by more than a hundred of the largest miners. No one looks very hurt, but there's going to be a lot of people with headaches come the morning. I look down at the *Dawn*, now hovering high above the platform. The guns are out, but the sails are down, and I can see Raley directing the crew from the wheel.

'I need to get word to them. They can get us where we need to go.'

'The science division is just over there.' Ganymede points over the skywalk. 'We don't need the ship to get there.'

I turn to look, my eyes going wide when I see Godstorm emerging from one of the side entrances on the far side of the skywalk with his personal guard around him.

'GODSTORM,' I yell.

He turns to look, then points at me, and barks an order. His team moves around him and forms up on the skywalk, weapons trained towards me. He reaches out to the belt of one of the team, then rushes away down the corridor. The team turn to watch him run, and the one whose belt he touched glances down. There's an inarticulate shout, and the grenade on their belt explodes, the skywalk erupting in flames before plummeting to the road far below.

'Shit,' says Ganymede. There's a gap, more than five-metres wide where the walkway used to be. No way we can get across. 'Now we *do* need to get you to the ship.'

Just as Godstorm predicted—he would have needed our help to get across to the science lab as there's no other way in there. Except, he's already in there... If he'd been a time traveller, he'd have known that; he wouldn't have needed me...

'The communications centre is at the top of the Council building.' Ganymede looks up at the spire that reaches another thirty floors up.

'We don't have time. We can get there through the front door— it's less than half a mile.'

'Half a mile through streets full of angry miners... There's got to be a better way.'

'Short-range comms?' I ask. 'Anything in the building that could get a signal a short distance?'

'The reception out front.' She looks downwards. 'But that'll be full of miners as well.'

'Anywhere we go will be. Come on, if we get word to the *Dawn*, she can be here in minutes, then we can fly the rest of the way.'

She nods and takes off at a jog. Three flights of stairs down, we arrive at the edge of the main hall, and are met by the sounds of chaos within. Ganymede cracks the door open a touch and peeks in.

'They're everywhere,' she pulls the door closed. 'The comms unit is behind the desk. You need to reach there and send the signal—don't come back for me.'

'Don't what?' I ask, but she's already out the door and running, both her guns firing. The miners duck, not used to facing armed and capable people, only perils like falling rocks and crushing weight. Years of being oppressed causes certain reflexes to become ingrained; hitting the deck when someone opens fire is one that doesn't disappear inside of a day.

That'll only last so long...

I sprint towards the reception desk. The screams from outside grow louder as I get closer to the main doors, and it's hotter than it should be; something burning in the streets below. I reach the reception desk and duck under, snatching the comms off the top and dialling in the *Dawn*'s code.

'Anyone listening, this is Morgan.' I know the chance of being overheard by anyone isn't high, but I don't want to take the chance, so I keep my voice low.

'Morgan, it's Esme. Where are you?'

'Reception of the Council High building. I need you over here as soon as you can. Pick me up by the remains of the skywalk.' I glance back towards the main hall, where Ganymede is now fighting a running battle with the miners, all of them chasing her up the stairs as she flees.

I drop the comms and run back through the hall, then up the stairs again, heading for the remains of the skywalk as the *Dawn* comes down low. The main mast is up and charging, but the rest of the ship is running on minimal.

Can't put a ship on full sail when you're in atmo.

A line drops into the gap between the two sections of skywalk as the ship hovers twenty metres above. I hear a shout from behind me, and turn to see several miners emerging onto the walkway.

Nothing for it now...

I sprint for the rope, my pursuants pounding along behind. They're much slower than me, but I can't take the risk of them getting anywhere near—we may be allies, but by the time they've confirmed that, Godstorm will have escaped. I've almost reached the rope when I glance back; the miners are just a few metres behind, and I realise that, if I try to scramble up the line, the backswing will bring me into their hands.

And then it would all be over...

'GET OUT OF HERE,' I shout, as I leap for the rope and use it to swing across the gap. 'GET OUT OF HERE NOW.'

I release my grasp on the rope when I've swung over to the other side, glimpsing back as I keep running, knowing that my crew can see me, and hoping they'll get the idea. I head through deserted corridors to the labs far below. The observation deck is clear, the only light coming from one of the bays below. I stop to catch my breath, trying to hear over the pounding of my heart for any sounds of pursuit, but there are none.

Just hope none of them got on board the Dawn.

I crawl past the lit-up bay, staying out of sight, glancing over the railing to see the technicians working according to Godstorm's directions. The ship is finished but, thanks to the power cut, they've had to hook the main doors up to dynamos to get them open.

They would have already got the doors open if he'd helped them, but he'd never stoop to that.

I continue crawling across the observation deck and run down the stairs. All the doors have been opened—I could have my pick of all the Stenlarian special projects. I see his reasoning—anyone coming down here would stop to investigate what's on the other side of all the doors before they reached the hangar at the end. I slip into the hangar. The main doors are halfway open: he could fly out of here already, if he was careful. I look around the hangar; there's nothing that could be used as a weapon, and all of mine are on the *Dawn*.

Being sneaky it is then...

I move around to the side as the hangar doors crawl open, the technicians working the dynamo generators as fast as they can. But they're heavy dynamos, and it's taking everything they've got to move them at all. Godstorm is standing on the wing of the ship looking down at them, still wearing his robes of office. I scan my eyes over the rest of his equipment.

No weapons...

I look around the lab for comms of any sort, something I can use to signal the *Dawn*. If I can get word to them, they'll be able to block the exit. None that I can see, though there are several banks of computers, some of which have entry ports of various sizes. I take the chip that Ganymede gave to me and check the computers, finding a port I can slot it into. The screen blinks into life, and I see that the LED on the back of the chip is pulsing, but it doesn't appear to be doing anything else. I move to the back of the bay, to the rear of the ship. All the connections are detached, and the ship is ready to go. The monitors show green across the board.

What's he waiting for?

I glance at the techs on the far side of the room. Two of them are sat by the side of the dynamos, looking exhausted, their chests heaving as they try to draw in more air. Godstorm moves out of the way as the lead scientist steps out of the ship. She nods while marking off things on a checklist, before handing it to Godstorm.

He doesn't even look at it; just adjusts his helmet and looks at her.

'It's ready? Can it fly?' he asks.

'We haven't carried out all the proper checks.' She sounds weary, like someone who's heard the same stupid questions from a thousand stupid people who don't understand the science and can't even be bothered listening to her answers. 'The ship is sealed, the atmosphere is stable, thrusters are working—'

'The main drive? Does the main drive work?'

'It's scheduled for its test in a few minutes. That's why we're trying to get the doors open. We need to get it outside.'

'Morgan, Morgan, can you hear me?' I hear Ganymede's voice loud from my comms, she sounds like she's in the middle of a firefight. 'Where are you, Morgan?'

I mouth a silent curse as the sound of gunfire ripples into the air, shutting off the incoming line as fast as I can. Then I hear another more familiar voice from the direction of the ship.

'Yes, *Morgan*. Where *are* you?'

Today, Tomorrow, Yesterday

'Where I've always been,' I call from under the ship; 'getting in the way.'

'Well, not for much longer,' replies Godstorm. 'You got out of the mines faster than I thought you might, I must say. Full points for resourcefulness.'

'Helps when you have to work for a living.' I glance down to see my comms still blinking and flick them over to transmit so that everyone can find me. 'Besides, I owe you for the first time you dumped me somewhere I didn't want to be.'

'The first time? I only met you a few months ago, and it was *you* who left *me* in a position I didn't want to be in.'

'Do you remember Catarina Solovias?' I ask.

His voice turns sour. 'Snot-nosed academy dropout? She's the one who brought me to this time. When I catch up with her again, she's definitely going in the mines.'

'Oh, you've tried that already. And here I am, all caught up again.'

'You? You're not her.'

'Took me about twenty years to get from where you left me to here,' I call, moving around under the ship. 'But I never forgot you.'

'Really?' He sounds amused now. 'I never paid you a second thought.'

'Oh, I know.' I motion for the technicians to move away from the doors, coming into the faint glow of daylight shining in through the open hangar doors. 'And that's how I knew you'd be here, looking out for yourself again.'

'Then you know that this ship works and will one day make it to where we found it.' He stares down at me and smiles like a Venusian paddlefang. 'You know there's nothing you can do to stop me taking it.'

'I know that it wasn't you in the ship when it arrived at where we were.' I spread my arms. 'So, somewhere along the line, someone else gets this ship off you. I just don't know what happens between now and then, and I can't take the risk of a bastard like you being able to mess around with time; no one would be safe.'

'And how are you going to stop me? No weapons, no backup, and all it's going to take for me to leave here is to get on board and start it up.'

I hear the faint sound of a familiar engine outside, and grin.

'No backup, you say?'

'THIS IS THE *UNBROKEN DAWN* TO THE OCCUPANT OF HANGAR BAY THREE, FEEL FREE TO ATTEMPT TAKE-OFF BUT, IF YOU DO, WE'RE GOING TO SET THE RESEARCH DIVISION BACK A FEW YEARS.'

Godstorm sighs, looking more irritated than defeated. 'How small your minds are,' he says, turning to look at the scientist next to him. 'You say we're good to go?'

'We are. The main drive will engage in a few minutes. But, if you're testing it in open space, you'll need a pressure suit on—we haven't signed off full operational tests on it yet.'

Godstorm smiles. 'Excellent. Then it's time to take it out for a spin.'

'By all means. We just need to get that other ship out of the way.'

'Thanks for the warning.' He pushes her off the wing. She falls hard to the ground, and he looks at me with the same smile he had that first day on the bridge. 'Your younger self will never see me coming, Catarina, I want you to know that.' He steps into the ship, and the airlock cycles closed behind him.

'Is she okay?' I ask the technicians who are clustered around her.

'I'm fine.' She picks herself up from the floor. 'What's going on here?'

'Your experiment is a success.' I glimpse up at the vessel. 'This ship can travel through time and space.'

'I'm glad to hear it. But why is the governor trying to take it?'

'I'll tell you when we get him out of there.'

There's a faint whine from the rear of the ship, and the power levels on the monitors start to rise.

'Is that the main drive?' I ask.

'It is. He's going to take the contents of this bay and all of us with him,' she shouts over the increasing noise.

'He doesn't care about us or this bay. How do we get out of here?'

She goes pale and motions towards the exit. 'This way. We have to move fast. The field has a radius of more than two hundred metres when it engages.'

'We need to stop him before he can activate the drive.'

'It already has coordinates set. Five minutes from now, we'll all end up a few thousand years ago.'

'Out through the hangar door.' I point to the open bay. 'When we get clear, the *Dawn* can blow this place to bits—'

'But all the research,' she protests, clutching at my jacket. 'We can't lose all the research stored in here; it'll take us forever to get it back. We'd be set back years, decades maybe.'

'If we stay here, we'll be going back more than decades, come on.' I pull her towards the exit. 'We can worry about saving all this after we save ourselves.'

I run out of the bay, signalling up at the ship to move back as we clear the doors. The *Dawn* drifts backwards, the same guns I modified all that time ago remaining lined up on the time-ship, but they can't fire until we're out of the blast radius. The scientist falls as she scrambles over the edge of the bay. I haul her up, dragging her with me as the high-pitched whine builds in the building behind us.

'Can't run,' she gasps, hobbling along with me.

'If you don't, it's going to be a cold day in space a few thousand years ago,' I shout, feeling the air charge with static electricity, the hairs on my head standing up as the field intensifies. I signal for the *Dawn* to open fire as soon as we're clear. The woman glances behind and puts her hand on my back, pushing me hard, even as she falls. I stagger forwards as the whining reaches a crescendo and then is gone.

A sudden breeze picks up and the *Dawn* rocks in the air.

The ship is gone.

On the Ocean of Stars

A perfect sphere has been carved from the bay and the ground around it—everything within it has vanished, as if someone tore a hole in the world. I look down at the edge of the sphere, turning away when I see what's left of the scientist; she was still half inside the field when it engaged.

Another one he's killed; we're never going to catch him now.

One of the other technicians draws close, avoiding looking down at the remains.

'What the fuck is going on?'

'How long would it take to build another of those ships?' I ask.

'Years. If ever...'

'Why?'

'Propulsion and structure,' he replies, pointing to himself. 'Systems.' He gestures to the other technician and then waves his hand in the general direction of the scientist. 'Obik was the one who knew everything about the other drives. She came up with the theory and the knowledge that went into that.'

'What about the research archives?'

He points to the cloud of smoke rising from the opposite side of the building, and then to the hole in the science building. 'All the research was held in there. Standard Stenlar practice for top-secret research: make sure no one else can get to it.'

I nod as my heart sinks in my chest.

He got away with it again.

I look at the technician as he pulls his lab overalls off. The suit underneath has a deep blue weave over it, orange lines down the arms and legs, and a logo with a stylised phoenix engulfed by red flames over the right chest. I reach out, placing my hand on the phoenix.

'Where did you get this suit?' I ask.

'Standard research division pressure suit.' He glances down at it. 'They all come in this colour.'

'Were there any on the ship?'

'We always held a spare in the ship in case there was a problem with the pressure tests and the one we were wearing gave out.'

'So, there was a suit in there he could have used?'

'Yeah... yeah, he could have used that one. That would have kept him alive till he got to another station.'

I feel a sense of hope for the first time in a long time. 'Do you remember when the ship was set to jump to?'

'Some time in the second millennium: 2210, I think. She said that everything interesting happened then.'

Not everything...

'Do you remember the exact date?' I press him.

'It was something special to Obik. She loved science history; always said that, if she could go back in time, she'd go back to the day the Martians signed the order to move the seat of their parliament to what would one day become Stenlar Prime. Second day, eighth month... I don't know what they called the dates back then.'

'The second of August.' A wave of relief washes over me as I think back over the years.

We discovered this ship surrounded by rock, computers, and a single body. The occupant was dead when I got in there, killed thanks to the greed of one Charles Godstorm... I only hope he had time to recognise himself before he died.

The tech mistakes my laughter for sobbing and puts an arm around my shoulders. 'It's all right,' he says. 'We'll find a way to get him. We'll make it right.'

'No.' I look up, grinning. 'No, *he'll* make it right.'

The tech looks puzzled. The ladder drops down from the *Dawn*. I motion for the two techs to climb up, as the sound of a million miners shouting for their leader echoes around the city.

*

Mirri takes us up high, and we take a slow flight to the centre of the city, where Aaltje is standing on the steps to the Council High building, the city all around her filled with her followers. She looks up as the *Dawn* clears the science division and raises her hand aloft to us. A million hands rise with hers, and I feel a spike of joy strong enough to bring tears to my eyes as I look down at the promise of Mars fulfilled for the people who had only ever dreamed it before.

Raley comes alongside me, her good arm winding around my waist as we stand at the rail, the rest of the crew joining us and looking down at the scene below.

'Do you want to go down there?' Mirri calls from the wheel.

'No,' I call back. 'This is their day, their time. We'll come back when everything has calmed down, and she's got things set up how they should be.'

'Where to then?' Mirri calls.

I turn to face the crew. 'I don't know about all of you, but I've spent too much time groundside; too long dealing with galaxy-eating monsters and time-travelling bastards. I want somewhere where it's just us. Take us back to the ocean.'

I look up to the heavens.

'Take us home.'

Godstorm

Godstorm blinked as the drives disengaged. Staring out of the ship's wide front window, he could see no trace of the science building, only the fragments that the ship had dragged with it. Obik's severed body was floating frozen in space. He moved to the controls.

He'd made it, now there was nothing that could stop him.

Ahead, something banked high in front of the ship, bringing its weapons to bear. Godstorm squinted as the ship drew closer, recognising the lines of the *Starlight Eagle* as he saw the weapons begin to charge. His mouth went dry when he realised with certainty where he was, *when* he was. He scanned over the controls, looking for the comms, for the engines, anything that would prevent history from repeating itself. He looked up as the *Eagle* lined up with the timeship, both cannons now incandescent and, for the first time in his life, he felt regret for something he'd done.

Not the murders in the Olympus slums as a child, nor the theft of the Starlight Eagle, *or even abandoning all the crews he'd ever known. No regret for anything except this one thing—just this random act of piracy...against himself.*

Resigned to his fate now, Godstorm looked up at the bridge of the *Eagle*, and his own face staring back at him, watching his lips move, not hearing, but remembering the words he'd spoken: the words that would ensure the death of the timeship's occupant for no reason other than that he wanted the ship for himself.

What a thing! Killed by my own greed.

Godstorm closed his eyes.

Acknowledgements

I often wonder if only other writers read the acknowledgements in books, as only they are likely to be aware of just how many other people it takes to get a book out of a writer's head and on to the page, and there are dozens of people who've made small changes to this book over the years. But if I were to thank everyone, it'd look like an Oscar speech, and I'm saving that speech (and the outfit that goes with it) for another time.

To Jude, for being ever enthused over me writing, particularly when I wasn't.

To Mark, who I started writing for more than a quarter of a century ago when he asked me to tell him stories at bedtime.

Lee Swift, Maverick to my Goose, my constant companion in all things writing. Living proof that enthusiasm paired with patience will win every time.

Francesca T Barbini, *Ocean of Stars* wasn't an easy book to bring into the world, from the first conversations in 2019 and Francesca's leap, both of faith in me, and of vision in what *Ocean* could be, is what got us to where we are now, with a book literally centuries from where it started.

My Excellent Editors, Kat Harvey and Rob Malan. Any writer who doesn't tell the truth about how much of their book would be mush without their editors doesn't deserve to have it published. Without these two, *Ocean*, Would, Have, Been, Shatneresque, In, Comma's, and, Rogue Capitals.

Mum and Dad, how I wish they could be here to read this now, as they never doubted, not for any part of my life. The Dawn remains Unbroken because they showed me how to navigate my life.

Abs, Elaine, Marie, Megan, Mira, Rae, Ray, Sonya, Snoop, Sue, Sylvia, Tracey, I have always been able to count on the support of wonderful women through the years, but you were the ones who formed the crew of the Dawn over all the time spent writing the journeys.

Ed Wilson and John Jarrold, nothing boosts an author's confidence more than an agent telling them that they like their writing and, while *Ocean* isn't the book that I came to you with, your encouragement kept me going.

Finally, Andrew, my brother, who's read my stories since I've been writing them, and never fails to see something in them that I can't, often seeing the truth of the thing I've written, long before I realise it myself.

Thank You All
John
Dreaming the Impossible Dream
(and yes, there is a soundtrack to this book)

Lightning Source UK Ltd.
Milton Keynes UK
UKHW041702070222
398311UK00002B/98